Island Queen

Island Queen

A NOVEL

Vanessa Riley

wm

WILLIAM MORROW

An Imprint of HarperCollins*Publishers*

ISLAND QUEEN. Copyright © 2021 by Vanessa Riley. All rights reserved. Printed in the United States of America. No part of this book may be used or reproduced in any manner whatsoever without written permission except in the case of brief quotations embodied in critical articles and reviews. For information, address HarperCollins Publishers, 195 Broadway, New York, NY 10007.

HarperCollins books may be purchased for educational, business, or sales promotional use. For information, please email the Special Markets Department at SPsales@harpercollins.com.

FIRST EDITION

Designed by Bonni Leon-Berman

Illustration on page 563 from Rambler's Magazine 6 (April 1788), 104. *Created by James Gillray. Piece called* Wouski. © *The Trustees of the British Museum.*

Library of Congress Cataloging-in-Publication Data has been applied for.

ISBN 978-0-06-300284-5 (hardcover)
ISBN 978-0-06-311503-3 (international edition)

21 22 23 24 25   LSC   10 9 8 7 6 5 4 3 2 1

To every little Black girl who was told no,
that you can never be more.
Breathe.
Don't believe the lies.
Keep dreaming. Tell your story.

San Juan

PUERTO
RICO

VIRGIN
IS.

ANGUILLA
ST. MARTINS
ST. BARTHOLOMEW
BARBUDA

Christiansted

Basseterre
ST. KITTS
NEVIS

St. John's
ANTIGUA

MONTSERRAT

GUADELOUPE

Basse-terre

DOMINICA

Caribbean Sea

Roseau

MARTINIQUE

Fort-de-France

Castries

SAINT LUCIA

ST. VINCENT

Kingstown

GRENADINES

BARBADOS

Bridgetown

MT. QUA QUA

St. George's

GRENADA

*Atlantic
Ocean*

0   50   100
Miles

TOBAGO

MARGARITA

Port-of-Spain

Cumaná

TRINIDAD

Barcelona

CARACAS

Real Corona

Orinoco

Caroni

SOUTH AMERICA

Cuyuni

Georgetown

DEMERARA

Essequibo

Demerari

Island Queen

LONDON 1824: KENSINGTON HOUSE

Never knew a moment made better standing still.

Never knew an hour made perfect by silence.

It's been a long time since I'd had peace—moments of dance, hours in hymns. It disappeared when the Demerara Council forced its tax.

Fidgeting, I sit in the front parlor of Kensington House switching my gaze from the sheers draping the window to the finishing school's headmistress. Miss Smith, she's across from me in a Chippendale chair sipping her chamomile tea. Her fingers tremble on the china handle.

"Mrs. Thomas," she says with eyes wide, bulging like an iguana's. "Your visit is unexpected, but I'm pleased you've taken my offer to stay at Kensington to review our school. You'll see it's a worthy investment."

"I was always fond of the name Kensington."

My voice trails off as I think of walks, of choices, then my aptly named plantation. Kensington is a set of squiggled letters chiseled in a cornerstone back home.

The headmistress chatters on, and I nod. The white egret feather on my bonnet jiggles and covers my brow. I bat it away like the memories I want gone, but you never get to choose what comes to mind.

"Thank you for your hospitality, Miss Smith."

She dips her pointy chin.

The loud clink of her teapot on my cup's rim gives us both away— her nerves, mine.

"Sorry, ma'am. I don't know what's come over me."

She sets the pot on the mahogany table that lies between us.

"This silver service you've given to the school is always treated with respect."

Respect.

If I rest my lids, that word said in different voices from the past—friends and enemies—haunts me.

So, I don't move, not even a blink.

I forgive the headmistress's babbles. She's a good fund raiser, and I have a soft spot for females that know figures. "My late arrival must've upset you. I apologize."

Didn't think it possible for her eyes to spread wider. She mustn't be used to someone taking responsibility for causing trouble. I own mine, every bit.

"It's nothing," she says with a limp smile. "A benefactor is always welcome."

The demure lady with her sleek jet coif bobbling waves a tray of shortbread treats. "Biscuit?"

"No. The tea's enough."

"Oh, yes." Her head lowers. The poor thing looks deflated again, like a sloop's drooping sail the wind has abandoned.

Looking away to the empty street—no carriage, no visitor, I let a frown overtake my lips. A glimpse at the fretting Miss Smith forces me to wipe it away.

Arrayed in beige silk with shots of Mechlin lace along her sleeves, she's shifting, rocking back and forth. I don't know how to help her, not when I have to help me.

I've lived a long time.

I'd hate to reinvent myself now.

The Demerara Council can't steal my life. Those men can have none of what I built.

The curtains flutter.

The gauzy sheer, like fine *Laghetto* bark spun into a veil, frames the empty street. My restless, anxious heart begins to spin.

The headmistress's nervous tapping reminds me I alone am not at risk. All colored women are.

"More tea, ma'am? I was wondering if you wanted more tea, Mrs. . . . Mrs. Thomas. That's all."

Mrsss. Thomassss. She says my name like I like it, with all the important *s*'s in place.

"Out with it. Miss Smith, tell me what's the matter."

My voice sounds stern, and the poor woman sports a full-face blush, from chin to brow. She might fade into the parlor's pink-papered walls. She'd definitely pass undetected in the big houses of Demerara or Dominica or Montserrat. Grenada, too. The fair-skinned coloreds often did.

"Your granddaughter loves Kensington House, ma'am."

"I won't be moving Emma Garraway to the prestigious Marylebone school like I did her cousin, Henrietta. I prefer her to study here." Where she'll be watched and kept far from scandal or worse, a marriage that was beneath her.

I won't voice the last part.

The disappointment in my children's and grands' choices keeps company with my own regrets.

Miss Smith's lips ease into a smile. "We love Emma. She's most promising, but Henrietta Simon, now Mrs. Sala, was a brilliant student, too."

"Yes . . . she married her Marylebone music teacher." My Henrietta. My Henny. I had such hopes for my granddaughter.

"Did you come for her wedding? I heard she was a vision in silver."

"No. It was the wet stormy season in Demerara. I was unable to cross the sea then." I sent Henny my best wishes and a dowry. The latter might be more important to the couple.

"Your knees, ma'am. They're knocking. Are you cold? Do I need to stoke the coals or send for a blanket? Visiting from the tropics, it can take some time to adjust to London's chilly weather."

"No. No fussing right now."

The headmistress shifts in her chair as if I'd barked.

I smooth my pale plantain-yellow-colored skirt, heavy in lace, heavy in trim. These straight-shifted gowns do little to hide my tension. How will I prove my points to the secretary in his grand office if my knees betray me in a finishing school?

When trying my hardest to hide, something whispers my truth.

"Ma'am?"

Miss Smith is waving, drawing me back from the shadows. "We've done a great deal to the school. You'll be happy with your . . . all the investments we've made."

Her tone is fast as if she's racing in a dray, wheels spinning, horses hoofing. The woman should be confident in her work.

I sigh, my breath mixing with the steam of the lemony chamomile. She should know I see her. What she's created matters. I plink the cup like a clarion's bell. "Miss Smith, I'm pleased. The school is good."

Even as my eyes drift to the window, to the empty street, I catch the headmistress signaling again.

"Oh, I had Emma take up embroidery. That's new. We've added a live-in seamstress since your last visit. This is your third trip to England?"

"I've been to Europe many times since eighty-nine."

"Eighty-nine? That early . . . I-I-I hope you'll enjoy this one." Her words have peaks and valleys and a funny sense of surprise between her stutters.

"What's wrong, Miss Smith?"

"Nothing much, ma'am, but the new pianoforte teacher we hired, Miss Lucy Van Den Velden, she said you'd been here then. I thought she was confused."

Miss Van Den Velden is a meddlesome soul from Demerara. She tips her thin nose into others' business. Her father serves on the council under awful Lieutenant Governor Murray. Those men are happy to make laws threatening colored women. One would think the mulatto miss would voice concern, maybe change her father's mind. Then this burden wouldn't be mine.

"Miss Van Den Velden's quite anxious to see you. When I let her know you were coming, she told me she couldn't wait. She has news clippings to share."

Not news clippings, but a clipping.

A single image.

One solitary sketch printed in *Rambler's Magazine* to shame a young sailor and me. The memories. My pulse stutters. My cheeks burn. The truth lights matches to my skin.

If the scandal reaches the secretary of state for war and the colonies, the man who rules England's territories around the world, he won't take my meeting. He'll dismiss me, a woman who's worn shackles and the labels of whore, concubine, and cheat.

But no one knows my story, the shame and the glory.

Smoothing the crinkles from my shawl, I wrap it tighter about my limbs and force myself to remember I'm not that girl anymore, the one who ran from trouble or barreled toward it.

The survivor in me leans forward. "You make sure Miss Van Den Velden spends time with me. I'll end her confusion."

"Yes, ma'am." Miss Smith sips her tea and ignores the scythes scraping in my words. "The gardens. I haven't told you of them. Would you like to see the flowerbeds, now? What about a tart? They are freshly made." Miss Smith sweeps the tray closer as if my sight has dimmed.

It hasn't. It's still selective, seeing what I want. "No, Miss Sm—"

"Mrs. Thomas, I can't take any more." The headmistress's cheeks are fiery red, redder than the flesh of a cashew cherry. She flings herself out of the chair. "You're displeased. I'm sorry, but please reconsider. Don't end your funding of Kensington House."

"What?"

"Our girls need the education. We're the best place. We readily accept our young women from the West Indies. We make sure colored girls have the best beginnings."

On her knees, she clasped her hands high. "I try hard to prepare a good environment."

Setting down my cup, I grasp the woman's small palms, her light ones in my dark, dark fingers. Sharing my power, I help her up. We stand together. "Be at ease. I'm not unhappy with you or the school."

Can she see beyond my wrinkles to the pride bubbling? I've helped this woman build her dream, something good, something lasting.

Relief sweeps across her face. A small smile buds, then blooms with teeth. "Thank you, ma'am. Since your arrival, I've been fearful."

Then her lips shrivel, like her leprechaun's pot of coins has become lead. "Then why do you look as if you have bad news."

"I must meet with Lord Bathurst, the secretary of state for war and the colonies. He's the overseer of Demerara and all the Leeward Islands—my Dominica, Montserrat, and Grenada."

She glares at me. "But he's a high official. Ma'am, why Bathurst? A meeting, I mean?"

"The secretary can fix what Demerara's governing council has done. They've put a tax on colored women, just us. We're forced to pay the damages wrought by slave rebellions."

"Not all citizens? That's not fair."

"This is how legal terror begins. What will stop these men from making laws that cancel our leases, bills of sales, even manumission records? They'll enslave us again."

Miss Smith's face turns gray. "Then Godspeed to you, ma'am. You have to convince him."

"I know."

One chance, one meeting, that's all I'll get to persuade Bathurst. *Wham.*

The door of the parlor flings wide. It's my Mary, one of the youngest of my line.

"Look, look, GaMa."

Mary Fullarton struts across the room with a book on her braided crown. My grandbaby twirls. Her white silk gown floats about her as she moves from the hearth to the window. "Cousin Emma showed me what to do. She let me borrow ya book."

My book?

Mary probably saw hundreds shelved in my parlor. The child must think I own them all, everywhere. I smile, not correcting a thing.

Little girls need to dream and think they can own everything.

"Mary, sit with me." Miss Smith gathers the small child onto her lap. "I'll help you read. When you're older, you, too, can be a student here if your grandmother likes."

It's a fetching picture to see the two flipping pages, fingering words.

The injustice of what governing men can do to our women boils my veins. My hot blood is Demeraran sugar thickening to caramel, turning char black. I want every threat gone, burned to nothing.

I seize a breath, steadying myself in the soft cushions of the chair.

My friend, my *damfo*, is working to secure a meeting. It's been five days since I sent a note. Maybe promises said along the shore have grown brittle and broken with age. Time does that, breaks things.

I sit with eyes closed, listening to Miss Smith and Mary sound out words.

My gut says I'll win for her, for them. But my heart knows to get Lord Bathurst to rescind the tax, I'll have to smile and hold my tongue.

Being silent on matters of justice—that's something I've never done.

PART ONE

The lessons

My father never said
I should be nothin'.

MONTSERRAT 1761: A REBELLION

We were going to die tonight.

I knew it.

Huddled in my mother's hut, I circled the knot in the oak floor-board with my toe. The planks were long and worn. By my cracked window, I shivered in a blanket woven of cast-off threads, waiting for the rebellion to end.

We'd seen war off in the sea. Big British ships with silver cannons heading toward Martinique. My pa claimed they want to control the island and to return their enemies to France.

Those ships could come to Montserrat next. The French controlled here, too, and most folks served their Catholic god. The British hated that the most.

I wished they'd take over if it meant we'd finally have peace. In huts like this with shutters made of cottonwood and roofs of coco palms and thatch, we feared nothing but the overseers' whips. Nothing British could be worse.

"Dorothy, stay away from the window. All will be well."

My ma's voice found me in the dark; her tone, warm and brave and confident, wrapped me like a hug.

Guns belched and drove that feeling from my arms.

More screams, not the planters' smooth tongues, but our men's. The captives' cries.

Part of me wanted to light the firepit to see into the night. My ma, Mamaí, thought smoke puffing out of the roof hole would attract the fight.

I didn't think killers needed an invitation.

Hot air rising might signal a prickly iguana, one of those spiny big-eyed lizards, not men.

More drum-drum-drumming.

I capped my mouth before the fear in my gut dribbled out in sobs. I told Mamaí that I would be brave, but I'd be slaughtered in my fifth year.

Not fair, never fair.

This place wasn't to be for war. An Emerald Isle Pa called Montserrat. It was meant for Irish jigs and songs between chores.

"Dorothy? You stayin' away from that window?"

I bit my lip and peeked through the shutters I'd opened. I shouldn't have; I had to squint at the sooty sky. Stars might be out. Seeing the distant shimmers would let me know all was well.

"Dorothy? I called to you."

That wasn't Mamaí's angry voice.

I had a little more time to collect myself, and I rubbed my stinging eyes. That feeling of being cheated ripped at my lungs. Five small years wasn't enough living. None of the dreams in my skull had been born. *Please.* I couldn't die with dreams trapped in my head.

Water leaked down my fat mammee apple cheeks. Not fair to die tonight. Not fair at all.

"Dorothy?"

I couldn't answer now. The tears would tell her I was weak. She'd be sad. I vowed to never rob her of any more joy. Mamaí didn't laugh enough. Her smile was flat, almost a frown.

I swore I'd be brave when Pa was gone.

Don't know how to do that anymore. How to be strong with the smell of death surrounding the hut.

"Dorothy, come here, girl. Now!"

My ma stood at my door with baby Kitty asleep on her hip. "Knew you were being too quiet, my chatty girl." She pointed to the open red shutters. "Couldn't help yourself. That sky is talkin' to you. Readying you to fly away."

Mamaí's steady voice calmed the restless bits in my chest, but I couldn't move from the window. I had to see the rebels coming and the smoke rising from the town.

Bare feet slapped against the creaking floor. My ma came and yanked me up.

Wincing for a strike, I caught love, a strong hug, pulling me close.

I stopped shaking as she hummed in my ear. She offered me the tune that she saved for my sister to get her to nap. I loved it. It made good dreams.

Deciding I could be five and not brave, I cried against my mother's leg.

Her song had no words, at least none I knew, but Mamaí's arms were soft. I nestled my cheek again against her hip. The new allotment of osnaburg cloth she used to make clothes was stiff and scratchy, but I cared not. I held her tighter and marveled at the orange and yellow leaves she'd stained for the print.

"You'll be all right, Dorothy. The planters will put down the rebellion. The Irish and French always do. Poor Cudjoe. The fool will get everyone killed."

The old man who begs in the square with a hat that covers his eyes, he was responsible for the fields burning? That feeble fellow convinced folks to take up their scythes and shovels to kill the overseers?

No. That couldn't be.

"Pa should be here, Mamaí. He should be here to protect us. He always has when he's here."

She pulled away like I'd uttered something bad. The shadows in her eyes said I mouthed something very wrong.

Turning from me, she smoothed Kitty's rumpled pink tunic. "Massa Kirwan is away. That pa of yours has his overseers stocked with guns. Guns are more powerful than anything the poor rebels have."

My lungs stung. I looked up at her beautiful brown face and shook my fists. "Who do you want to win?"

"Numbers win, not right or wrong, numbers, Dorothy."

I gawked at her blank look, one my mother often wore, like she'd disappeared inside herself.

I didn't want to be sucked into that nothingness, where nothing mattered.

Couldn't we have the fear gone?

Couldn't we be on the side of good?

Couldn't we have both?

Backing up, I looked out and hunted my stars. "I'm better, Mamaí. Call me Dolly. That's what Pa says. I'm his little doll."

"Your name is Dorothy." The pitch of her hummingbird voice rose. "Dorothy."

"Dolly." My voice became harsh like a crow's call. "I feel special with Dolly. Pa picked it. He's always right."

She put Kitty on my blanket and swaddled her. "You have a cockle-stuffed toy I sewed you, nothing of the fancy formed paper Kirwan describes."

That was true.

Pa never brought me one from his travels, but that didn't matter. It sounded nice and pretty, being his doll and different from what the women at the cistern whispered. They said my skin was dirty like tar. They put lies in the air that I wasn't Pa's.

Being Dolly, his Dolly, proved it. I was pretty and black, black like a black diamond. "Pa says I have doll eyes, too. Light like the sun, like a star. I like Dolly."

"It's important what they call you. You were named Dorothy. It means gift. You're a gift of God."

"I want Dolly. Dolly. Dolly. Dolly. Pa calls me Dolly. You are always mean to him." My pout was louder than I wanted, but the guns had grown stronger, too. The fight was near our hut.

"Just turned five, and you talkin' back like you're big. You're not grown, Dorothy."

Mamaí's face held the deepest frown, then Kitty started crying.

"Too much nonsense, girl. Come back from the window. You'll sleep with me on my bedroll."

She waved at me, but I was stubborn and searched the sky a little longer, looking for the brightest one. I pinched my fingers together as if I could measure distances in the shifting fog.

I gasped as an outline of a beast dragging limbs came toward us.

"Mamaí? Something's out there."

She closed up the window and put her hands to my shoulder. She shook me; the sleeves of my berry-red shift loosened and tightened as I tried to wiggle free. "You saw nothin'."

A yelp blasted.

"Nothin' made a noise, Mamaí."

A strangled cry, the hurt clawing through my skin, made me knock open the shutters.

The fog parted. A man carrying a body staggered toward us.

"Help me!"

A woman's voice yelping in pain—I knew it. "Mamaí, that's Mrs. Ben. She needs us. They're calling."

My mother's face was stone. She'd gone away again to that faraway place, but I needed her here. I needed her to tell me how to help.

"Please, Mamaí. What do I do?"

"Nothin'. You saw nothin'. It's not safe outside these walls."

But I did see Mrs. Ben, a woman in need. "She's been good to me."

Five-year-old me could help even if I was scared.

"Waaahhh!" Kitty awakened with a loud screech.

It was enough noise that Mamaí's topaz gaze left me.

In that moment, my heart decided.

I crawled out and didn't look back, didn't listen to Mamaí's yells.

I ran a hundred paces, straight toward the man holding up my *damfo*, my special friend.

"Mrs. Ben, is she much hurt?"

The lanky man drew a gun on me. The smell, the gunpowder slapped my face.

He'd fired that weapon tonight.

He'd fire it again.

"Who are you?"

His hoarse voice sounded like a ghost's.

He drew the barrel closer to my nose. "Who?"

"Not gonna say if you're gonna shoot."

He moved the gun back an inch, but the thing still stunk, still taunted of death.

"Who are you, girl? I'm only asking this once."

"Dolly. Bring Mrs. Ben this way." I drew myself up like I saw no gun. "Come to Mamaí's hut. She works in the sick house. She knows the old ways, the herbs that heal."

The fellow put the barrel into his white breeches. "Lead us."

I started toward the hut.

With my back to him, I prayed each step, to whom I wasn't sure. One of my ma's gods—the saints or the Obeah spirits—had to keep me from being shot like a coward, like I'd run away. The overseers joked about those killings.

The man followed. His gangly arms wrapped about Mrs. Ben, not his weapon.

His slow steps seemed as if he'd walked miles. His waistcoat had rips and patches of blood. I wondered what his fog-gray eyes had seen this night.

"Not much farther to Mamaí, Mrs. Ben."

I led them toward the front door and hoped my ma would let us in.

She stood there waving a pitchfork. The sharp tines reflected bits of moonlight that had punched through the fog.

"Mamaí, it's Mrs. Ben. The nice woman who fed me ginger preserves that time Pa took me to the Cells's plantation."

"Please, ma'am," the man said. "This woman is mighty hurt. Everyone knows Kirwan's Betty knows healing."

His tone was easy, and his eyes were large in the low light.

My mother nodded and put down her pitchfork. "Bring her in. Dorothy, go get a blanket and my box of ointments."

I jumped over the bar meant to keep *pickney dem*, the little children like Kitty, from crawling out of the hut. In her room, I scooped up a blanket from the chest near Mamaí's bedroll. Then I snatched the anis for stomach ailments, the agrippa for swelling, and a dozen other things my ma stored in bottles. Her rosary beads shone on her mat. Red-painted balls for good prayers and gold ones for long life, Mamaí had taken Ashanti beads and used them to talk to her Catholic god.

Touching what I wasn't supposed to wouldn't help. Arms full, I ran back to the main room. "Here, Mamaí." I shoved the medicines into her hand, then spread the blanket by the coal pot.

She'd lit the chars. We used the pot for heat on nights with a chill. I guessed she didn't care anymore about smoke puffing through the roof hole.

The fellow laid Mrs. Ben down, then planted his palms on his dirty breeches and long embroidered waistcoat. "No harm for anyone."

Who would hurt him? He had a gun.

Maybe men were like boys, needing to say something that sounded like they had all the power. My half brother Nicholas did that, particularly when he was scared.

Mamaí took strips of cloth from her allotment, cloth she would have used to make new tunics for Kitty and me, and put them to the wounds on Mrs. Ben's arm and her gut.

"They burned my hut, Betty." The old woman winced as my mother put pressure to the places that leaked.

But none stopped.

This woman would die on our floor.

Mrs. Ben looked up at the man who leaned against our mud plaster walls. "Coseveldt, you're going back to the fight?"

The man maybe age twenty, maybe less, nodded. He came forward, bent, and captured the old woman's waving hand. "Yes, Merr . . . Ben. The rebels have scorched everything. My land, the Cells's house, is in danger. I won't lose it. I won't fail my father."

The gnashing of teeth sounded in his voice, but he didn't know this battle was won for him. His side, those one-godders, they had the important numbers, more guns.

Mamaí's candle lit his face. Dark loose hair, thin nose, cleft in his chin, and horrible bushy eyebrows shading eyes that now looked hazel. "Thank you, ma'am, Miss Betty—"

"And me, Dolly. I helped."

"You are a doll. And brave. Mrs. Ben is with friends, because of you."

Mamaí pointed to the big calabash of water. "Get that, Dolly. Bring it. Let's give her something to drink."

She used the name I liked. I sprinted, for I wanted to obey.

When I lifted the fat gourd and brought it to Mamaí, she'd stopped trying to hold cloth to Mrs. Ben's wounds.

She put her hands to the woman's face as if to shield her eyes from the candle.

I stood near watching my mother's face change from angry, to something, to nothing.

"You a Cells, Kirwan's neighbor, one his *pickney dem*?"

"Yes," he said with no hesitation—he understood Mamaí's Irish Creole—"one of Cells's children, his only living one."

She sat back on her knees. "Don't go. Your business is not done. This woman needs to be on Cells land. Mr. Ben must know."

"Mr. Ben died tonight. A neighbor said he knew the rebel leader's name. They shot the poor man when he didn't answer."

"No." My eyes became wet again. "He was nice, too."

"Dolly, give Cells the water, then go into your room, be with Kitty. Make sure she's safe. Stay there this time."

Tall Mr. Cells hunched over Mrs. Ben, pushing on her cheeks.

Mamaí gripped his hands. "Stop, boy. The mask's set. Go, Dolly."

I obeyed. I wanted to be away from this. I'd used up all my bravery climbing out that window. It was wasted. The sadness on Mr. Cells's face, on Mamaí's, said so.

At the entrance of my room, I turned for a last glance. The stillness of Mrs. Ben's eyes, the red tears—I'd never forget.

"Let me pray for her." Cells's lashes shut; I hoped he pictured Mrs. Ben smiling like she was a week ago when I snuck out and visited her.

"Sorry. Sorry, Mamaí."

No one heard my low plea or even looked up. They wept.

I hurried into my room and held my sister tight, her snores warbling like a swallow. I wept long enough for my stars to disappear. Like a butterfly or moth, I'd invited death into our hut to stretch its wings. I wasn't sure how to get it to leave.

MONTSERRAT 1761: A RUINING

A week had crawled by like one-legger bugs, slow and painful. Every man left on the plantation buried their dead or plowed the burnt fields. In Mamaí's trampled garden, I rooted for vegetables and used a pitchfork to turn over the rich black dirt to hunt yams.

Did the neighbors, like the Cellses, fare any better?

The lanky man by the name of Coseveldt, I didn't see him after that night.

Whoop. Whoop. One of Pa's overseers, Mr. Teller, blew a conch again. "We'll finish up tomorrow, lads."

The cheeky man with fire red hair brandished a pistol on his hip. "Go on back to your provision grounds and work on your own huts. We'll start again in the morn."

But Pa's house wasn't done.

I hit the hut's wall, my fingers stinging against the rough mud plaster. They needed to nail up the missing roof sections. Pa's house, the great owl house—large window eyes, shutter feathers sitting on spindly stilt legs to keep above the floodwater—looked abandoned, as if it'd been hit by another hurricane.

Why would Pa come back to this?

Mr. Teller watched the men leave, his fingers wrapping his pistol. He muttered, "Absentee planter."

That was an insult to my pa.

Anger wound all about my hungry belly. I wanted to go to my bedroll, but sleep stitched Mrs. Ben's face to my dropped lids. My gut growled. I'd only found two yams.

Two.

Folks ran off with the food Mamaí had grown. *Thwack.* I stabbed the ground with the pitchfork. Let it be an omen.

Entering the hut, I bent my head and went past Mamaí to my room. Lying down I stared out my window at the owl house, hoping to see shiny stars.

My baby sister coughed. It sounded scratchy and dry.

Should I get her water? There was only enough for morning. I didn't think Mamaí wanted me away from the hut even to fill the calabashes at the cistern.

My thin braids fell about me. I tried to right them, hide them beneath my favorite scarf, a red linen handkerchief.

Red wasn't the color of repentance.

Time to make amends. Sadder than a lone oriole's whistle, I moved to the main room. Mamaí, singing to Kitty, sat on the floor, very near the spot where Mrs. Ben . . .

The blood in my veins pounded. In my head, I heard the guns again, saw her red tears. "Sorry, Mamaí. Forgive me for bringing death here?"

Nothing.

No words.

No nodding of my ma's chin.

Nothing.

Kitty snorted, the noise like a tiny reed flute. Did my own sister think I wasn't sorry?

"*Pickney no hear wah marmi say drink peppa warta lime an sarl.*" Mamaí's Creole was about little ones suffering, drinking fire and bitter salty lime water. "Suffering is for you, Dolly, if you keep on. I don't want that."

My ma knew many languages, the old ones from Twi and Kikongo to French bits from Grenada, and chunks of Pa's Irish. The mix of them people called Creole. She'd vary her words depending upon whose ear she had, but she didn't talk enough.

"Forgive me, Mamaí."

She lowered Kitty into a pile of blankets and fingered the corset strings of her yellow tunic. Her beautiful brown hands glistened with the sweet-smelling coconut pomade she'd concocted. "You're too bold, Dolly. Your father calls it *misneach*, or pluck. I call you *minseach*, his Irish for billy goat. I fear the goat strength in you."

"Isn't it good to be strong? Cudjoe, the leader you've sung about, was he not bold? Was he not strong?"

"The true Cudjoe was strong. The Maroon leader bested them all and freed many. The false Cudjoes die horrible deaths."

Mamaí seemed tired, very weary though no women had yet returned to work. They were to stay safe on the right side of the plantation, in the huts and provision grounds.

"Dolly, Cudjoe was a man. They didn't want him strong. These men won't let you be strong."

I was small but I'd be more. "I want to grow big. I want to protect you until Pa returns. I want everything for us. The dreams I have are good, of houses, big ones. Fine clothes and boots, too."

"Dolly, they won't let you. They'll find a way to hurt you, to take all you have until you are grateful for no more pain."

Mamaí rubbed her elbows with the pomade she kept in the green calabash. Her skin shone in the candlelight. "No pain for you or Kitty. You must accept what we have. Suffer the bitterness in silence. It is the way."

She waved me forward. I came as if she'd lowered a scepter.

"I died so that you can live. Don't make my suffering in vain."

What was she talking about? Mamaí was alive, sitting before me, talking, breathing.

I rushed and buried myself in her arms, clinging to her. I couldn't. I wouldn't let her go. My heart panicked, the rhythm in my chest raged like a drunk fool at celebration. "Don't leave me, Mamaí. I'm sorry. I'll be good. Anything."

She brushed my slick curls, looping my poorly done braids in her hand. "I'm not saying this right. When you're older, you'll understand. All our women understand."

"Don't leave us, Mamaí. Don't go to sleep like Mrs. Ben. Don't. No. Mamaí."

"Your pa won't let me leave, and he won't sell my daughters, not like my own pa. So no one is going." She sat me on her lap and started loosening my hair. "The outside world keeps calling you. I will press Massa Kirwan to free you. If you girls are free, then I'll live again, too . . . even if I have to stay as Kirwan's chattel."

Her words felt heavy, smothering. Mamaí's voice was as wet as the rains of the hurricane. I grasped her neck like I was drowning.

"Mamaí, tell Pa you miss him. Maybe that will make him stay?"

Her eyes went wide. In the center, they held fire among the pretty tan rings and ash.

"There's much you don't understand. Dolly, you made a story in your head of how things are. I wish it were true. It's not."

I touched her face, the face that had my nose and the same shape of my deep-set eyes, but not my mouth or feather-thin hair. I got those from Pa. "Pa treats us good, better than the rest. You have the biggest hut. It's nearest his owl house. I don't understand."

"Dolly, you'll learn how small the world is for us. I hurt for you."

I held my mother and let her sob all down my shift, but it was the closest I'd felt to her soul. Mamaí had shown me that secret place in which she hid. Now I knew when her face went blank, she'd fallen into a well of pain.

A song rose in my throat. The melody I heard her hum to me and to Kitty.

It took forever, but the joy of that wordless hymn ministered to me, to us. Her sobs stopped.

I wanted to be big someday. I prayed that I could take Mamaí and Kitty and show them Pa's world. We'd follow the stars across the sea. I had to prove that we could have a piece of this big world. "I will get us my good dreams."

Mamaí's lips pressed tight. The fullness of them, pink and brown, were drawn to a dot like the bud of the Trinitaria.

"Sɛ wowɔ ahotɔ a, nna woyɛ ahotɔ ni. Only if you're free . . . then you can be." She said this, over and over.

The words drummed into my heart. I'd remember them and use their fire to go beyond our hut, beyond our provision ground, beyond Pa's plantation.

Bam. Bam. Bam.

The door to the hut vibrated. Something angry wanted in.

"No. No." No more violence. No more rebellion. "Go!"

"Shhh, Dolly. Shhh."

We were unprotected. Promises and prayers did nothing. I'd left Mamaí's pitchfork outside, lording over the empty garden. We were exposed. I wrapped myself about my mother and sister. I'd be their shield and die in their stead.

MONTSERRAT 1761: A RETURN

The door to the hut flung open.

Pa stood there.

Tall, thick arms bulging beneath his coat, his long black hair. "Betty, you and the girls are safe?"

Mamaí stared, uttered no words.

"Well, I can see you are," he said. "I was mighty fearful the rebels hurt you."

The twang in his Irish brogue sounded happy. I was. Pa was here. My soul rejoiced. On those stars I watched from my window, I'd wished him home.

My body relaxed.

The death grip of my fingers eased from Mamaí's shoulders.

But her silent eyes told me not to move or breathe.

"Betty? You've been crying. Are you well? Dolly?" He waved at me as if that could unglue me from Mamaí's lap. "You all must be in shock. Terrorized by the savages. I'll fix that."

With a kick, he knocked the pickney bar, strode inside, then slammed the door. He set a long-barreled gun against the wall and dropped his ebony jacket to the floor.

The man came forward with his hands above his knees, heaving air as if he'd run from the shore. The smell of salty sea clung to him. Maybe rum, too.

"Jumped off the boat. I had to see for myself the state of Kirwan Plantation. Had to see that you were untouched. Betty, I don't know what I'd do—"

"Mrs. Ben's dead. Her husband, too. Could've been the rebels. Could've been the overseers or one of your fellow planters shooting down an old couple."

Pa's lips thinned. He went behind us and took my sister up from the cradle. "Such a pretty baby. You are my Kitty."

Cradling her in his arms, he mumbled a jig or more of the Irish he'd been teaching me. These words, he said too fast to catch.

He set my sister down and turned to me. "My Dolly, my beautiful smart Dolly. You're going to act scared around me, too?"

Mamaí hadn't moved, but her iron fingers relented, her hold loosened. "Go on, Dolly. Greet your pa."

Caught between the father I loved and the woman who sacrificed for me daily, I sat not moving, holding my breath.

Pa pulled up his gray pantaloons and then got on his knees and crawled to me. "What's the matter? Dolly still frightened from the shooting?"

Mamaí stood, slipping between us. The hem of her bright skirt flapped near the unlit coal pot. The sharp scent of peppermint she'd used to rid the ants drawn to the blood—the spot Mrs. Ben died— swirled. It'd choke me if I kept still. My ma knew how to clean good from her work in the horrible sick house.

"You drunk, Massa Kirwan?"

"No." Pa reared back. "Not really. And you know I'd never hurt Dolly or Kitty. Or you. You're my Betty, my one and only."

His head whipped to me. There was something strong and stinging on his breath. "You're my Dolly. Such a pretty doll. The only black doll I've ever seen."

He stood, almost tipping over, but then danced about Mamaí before pulling her into his arms. "And you, Betty. I missed you, woman."

This sounded like Pa of old, how kind he was before he left, but that was months and months ago. Why was he always going away?

Whipping off his tricorn hat exposed more of his wild hair. "Betty, you and the girls—no one touched you? You stayed safe through the rebellion?"

"Through three since you've been gone. Three." She stepped from him and picked up Kitty. "She's grown bigger since you left. Dolly, too. Why are you just getting back?"

Rolling the brim of his hat in his fingers, he seemed sad or unsure. "The long English War with France—the British set blockades. They aren't letting all the boats through. When they do, if they find one thing wrong with our papers, they confiscate the goods. That happened with my first shipment."

With a flick of his wrist, he tossed me his hat, then he put his hands on Mamaí's hips and leaned over her shoulder to peek at Kitty. "I came back as soon as I could. I'd have been here to put down . . . a rebellion, too."

"You'd want to shoot at men and women who want freedom?" Mamaí's voice was shrill, not sweet and low like a hummingbird. She was no dove of peace, not tonight.

Pa lit the oil lamp he'd given Mamaí, one she rarely used. "Betty, if the governor ruling Montserrat demands the planters be part of a militia, what choice do I have? The British planters are taking more control. They hate us Irish, and they're winning the war against France."

He rubbed at his hair. "Looks like they'll finally take Martinique. The British are constantly marching. They win, I could lose all."

"Always a choice, Massa Kirwan. Always."

I clenched Pa's hat in my palms, my finger smoothing the brown pelt. It held the citrus smell of limes and salt.

Was this the *peppa* for *pickney dem*, a bad child like me caught between my pa and ma? Then I realized Mamaí's side was built on hurt.

"Pa, say sorry. Tell Mamaí how you care for us, how much you missed us."

"I did. I do. You know that, Betty."

"Kirwan, why don't you head up to your house? Come visit another day."

"Nonsense." He bent and lifted me in the air, swinging me about. His hat went sailing to the floor and he put me down.

Fingering the buttons of his shirt, Pa stared at my mother. "Betty, we need to talk. There's much I need to say."

With a pat to my head, he spun me like a top toward my room, then he took Mamaí's hand, lacing their palms. "I missed you."

Mamaí's expression was stone. Her eyes and lips had settled to nothingness. She'd fallen inside herself, back to that place that held secrets.

I tugged his coat. "Tell her you'll stay and make it better."

My father nodded and kissed Ma's knuckles. "This trip selling goods was hard. Many barrels of salt pork gone, many hogsheads of sugar—gone. Then I come back to Montserrat to insurrection. They burned a good part of Kirwan Manor."

Mamaí's eyes sharpened. Her gaze wasn't distant. It held flames. "The enslaved want to be free, Massa Kirwan, like you want to be free of the British. Like our girls should be."

He put his arms about my mother's waist again. "Betty, I promise on my mamaí's grave, I'll take care of the girls. I'll free them in time, but first I'll fix the birth records. The Tuites have a priest coming. They've used their money and connections to bring a Catholic priest. Might have service in the woods, but the records will be done before the British force all to be Anglican."

The Tuites were rich neighbors, probably better off than the Cells.

Kitty cried, whooping. My ma moved to her, away from Pa.

"Betty, the girls' births will have papers blessed by the pope. You said that's what you wanted. I listened. Everyone will know Dolly and Kitty are mine. They are Kirwans. They are my blood."

Mamaí blinked several times, then she extended her hand to him. "You're going to do that?"

"Yes, our girls." He clasped her fingers and put them to his chest. "Now come on, lass. I missed you."

He kissed her neck. "I always miss you."

She stepped away, scooped up Kitty, and led me to my room. She settled my sister into my bedroll. "Take care of your sister."

Mamaí closed the door.

Then I heard her sandals leading Pa's boots to her room.

I plopped down beside my sister. She stirred and put her little palm in mine. Her warm face pressed into my knee.

Her snores became a whisper, but the rhythm wasn't loud enough to smother my thoughts. I flopped down and counted the times Mamaí never said she loved Pa. The times Pa didn't say it either.

What did fixing the birth records do?

I was Pa's. Did paper change that?

Maybe it would stop my brother Nicholas's teases. He wasn't very kind to me the last time he came to Montserrat.

If we all could get along, if Mamaí and Pa could be sweet to each other, maybe we could go live in Pa's owl house.

When I get big, I wouldn't go to bed hungry. The right and left fields on my plantation would make enough food for all.

Pa's owl house sat below the brightest stars. I'd have enough money to repair it for him, then he wouldn't have to go away.

Closing my eyes, I tried hard to see nothing, but Mrs. Ben was waiting. She had no sweet preserved ginger for me, just that awful look that nothing could ever fix.

MONTSERRAT 1763: A REALIZATION

Only looking to the right, the side of Pa's plantation with huts and provision grounds, I held on to the sidewall of his dray for my dear life. Pa's rickety wagon walls felt rough against my palms, but I dug my nails deeper into the wood.

I wouldn't shame him by falling and giving my half brother another thing to crow about. He'd teased me so bad this morning. He didn't want me coming with him and our father.

Reins tight in his hands, Pa looked over his shoulder at me. A smile settled on his face, a wide one cresting under his hook nose, which I blessedly didn't get. Thanks, Mamaí.

"We're almost through town, Dolly, Nicholas. Then we ride to the top of Kirwan land. You both must see this."

The wagon pressed forward, shaking and shimmying as it crossed another gully in the dirt road. My bones shook.

"A *tarn loch*," Pa said with a mumble. Fancy Irish for a lake. Boy, I wanted to be taught more of the language of his ancestors, mine through him. I tried to talk like him and sound proper and I wanted to understand what the Irish planters said when the men in red uniforms were near.

"Hold on, little d . . . girl."

My head snapped to Nicholas.

On the other side of the dray, he grinned. He hadn't whispered the word *tarn*. Nor the harder word, *darn*, that rhymed. No, he said the clipped version of the priest's *damnation* in a voice heated with hell fires. If I'd done it, my ma would take a branch to me.

But his ma was dead. She'd never visited Montserrat. I felt bad for him, but that feeling went away when he teased.

Ten years older than my seven years, he sat stewing in a dusty brown jacket with a big straw hat covering his reddish-brown hair. The wide brim offered shade to his gray-green eyes and Pa's awful hooked nose.

I wished Nicholas liked me.

He didn't.

He proved it a little more every day. He'd say awful things when Pa couldn't hear, low jokes about the darkness of my skin as if I'd been burnt to a crisp in the sun. Tar and feathers and me, he'd say with a grin.

But that wasn't the worst.

The lie on Nicholas's pale lips that Pa wasn't my pa—that stabbed through my gut straight to my soul.

My brother wanted me to have no part of our pa's love.

It was hard not to hate Nicholas. The priest that righted the birth records, recording me and Kitty as mulattoes, as Pa's daughters, preached about forgiveness and peace.

How come Nicholas couldn't stop his hate? He went to see the priest. He stood in the woods like the rest.

"You going to fall, Dolly?" Nicholas's mouth pursed like he wanted to spit. "Your mother knows about falling low. Whores always know."

Could I get one punch in and not get in trouble? His pale white skin would hold a bruise that would tattle on me and send me straight to the stocks. Coloreds couldn't strike at whites, no matter whose blood you were.

"Nicholas, what are you telling Dolly back there?"

"That she shouldn't be here," he said in a growling tone. "Pa, she should be back with your whore, Betty."

"Nicholas. Don't talk like that. You're not too old for me to take a whip to you."

"My mother hasn't been dead long enough for you—"

"Nicholas!"

Pa pulled the dray to the side of the road and stood on the seat. The big man's shadow fell upon both of us. "Nicholas, I don't want you talking such. Betty is special. Betty—"

"Is property, Father. You bought her from a slaveholder in Grenada."

Pa was rarely angry, but now the veins on the side of his neck bulged. "Nicholas, she's my business. You hold your tongue."

"Yes, sir." My brother withered and put his head down.

"Good," Pa said and dropped into his seat. The dray started moving.

I looked away from my brother, holding a little gloat in my throat. Nicholas didn't like Mamaí. Many didn't. There were snickers at her from the women at the cistern.

My ma couldn't help being Pa's favorite person. He had to love her dearly. He gave her more cloth this morning, and she had the best provision ground on the plantation. Hearing Nicholas's hurt over the loss of his own ma when I had one, I could understand his hate a little better.

The wind, the one that always blew from the sea, cooled my hot, sticky skin. The sun was high in the sky. Only when we headed back up into the hills would the breeze overtake the heat.

Nicholas sneered and hit sand from his jacket.

Why did he and I have to be the sun and wind, always battling?

With a few more jarring bumps, the dray crossed into town. Men gathered around the Marketplace. This evil square in the middle of town held their attention.

But I looked back toward the hills, loving the roofs dotting here and there. Straw brown thatch on some, reddish clay tiles or palms on others. It was better to look at anywhere but the Marketplace.

"Don't you want to go and dance a jig on the stage, Dolly? Make it an Irish jig. The soldiers hate the Irish Catholics as much as the pickaninny coloreds."

Nicholas's tease was a whisper, but his laugh was loud.

"Son," Pa said, "what are you saying back there? I love a good joke."

My brother looked at me with sheepish eyes that begged me not to tell.

Before my charity fled, I turned to the stone steps of the government building.

"Nothing, Nicholas? I thought so." Pa's easy smile faded.

A soldier in a red uniform ran from the steps straight to the stage, waving a piece of parchment. He centered himself and cupped a hand to his lips. "The war is over. Seven years of fighting with France is done. The British have won."

People threw up their arms and cheered. "The French have lost. Praise King George!"

Pa clapped, maybe even pumped a fist in solidarity, but he didn't seem happy. I'd seen him filled with joy as he swung me around. That was happy.

This meekly raised fist was Pa pretending.

Wasn't the end of a war good?

All smiles, Pa tugged at the reins, making his horse move faster. "I think we'll do our business at the docks tomorrow. I'll let the town celebrate."

None of anything made sense. Things that should be awful were good. Things good were awful.

"Who do you think is Cudjoe, Dolly?" Nicholas asked. "I think it's Gustavus Vassa, the shipboy who works for Pa's friend, the captain of the *Charming Sally*. Vassa is black like you. Blacker. He's spouting off his opinions, thinking he's better. He's not. You're not, . . . girl."

He didn't just call me girl. He used another word, the hateful *N-word*. I'd learned to ignore it 'cause it was tossed around so often. Like it was rain on my face, sweat on my palms, I wiped it away.

And who cried at rain?

"N'girl." His voice cracked when he repeated it. His tone mirrored the hate of the overseers, the soldiers, the auction men hollering at Black and brown souls sold at the Marketplace.

N'girl was to put the coloreds low. When some yelled back blancas, whites, white planters, it was to accept that those pale faces were above us, that their power could never be had by me, or those like me, 'cause our skin was warm and dark.

I wouldn't accept this.

I'd never give Nicholas that hold. Nobody at all.

My dreams were big, and no one would stop me.

He growled again and repeated *N'girl* like I hadn't heard him. The fool ground his teeth on the *girl* part, too, like it was a cuss. The boy had no respect for girls, white or Black.

"You heard me?"

Mamaí's words about it mattering what they called you welled up in my chest. I cast Nicholas a slow smile. "Stupid boy, I heard. And why do you care about Vassa? Does he have power over you?"

Nicholas winced like I'd slapped him. "Nothing Black and worthless has power. You need to know that."

That's when I smiled at my brother. His hate came from fear, fear of me, fear of me having what was his.

I just had to figure out how to prove him right.

MONTSERRAT 1766: A RANSOM

Trudging past the owl house, I wanted to kick down the spindly stilt legs under the porch, to smash the wide window of Pa's study like I had a cyclone's breath. He'd left again and hadn't paid the money for our ransoms. Neither Kitty nor I nor Mamaí could be freed without those manumission fees paid, forty pounds for each of us. That was *fhortún*, a fortune of a hundred and twenty pounds.

The past few years, I was permitted to sit in Pa's study on Saturdays, and he'd teach me words in Irish like *misneach*, courage, or *ragaireacht*, for wanderers of the night. I liked that one. It sounded mysterious.

He taught me numbers, too, and buying and selling, the tools for the free to gain wealth. It sounded as if he wanted me to help run the plantation. How could I do this if I was enslaved?

Why wasn't Pa's word good? Did he not have the *misneach* to do it, to make us true family in the eyes of the law?

Pa read me letters from his business friends and from Nicholas. My brother usually sent a sole cut of foolscap that asked for pocket money, asked to come to Montserrat, and asked not to be left adrift.

I gloated.

Then my heart whimpered for the hope of a big brother who could teach me reading and about the world. Pa didn't have the patience to help me see the words. The letters flipped sometimes. The other children, the white ones and some lucky Blacks, could read, but I couldn't, not easily, no matter how hard I stared at the page.

But Nicholas would never share his book learning. Guess it didn't matter if Pa never meant to better my lot.

Heart pumping fast, I ran through the good side of the plantation, all the huts and fruitful provision grounds. The air smelled of sweet mangoes. My ears perked at the snap of the large leathery leaves of cracker bushes, some larger than my head and shoulders combined. The leaves were harvested by women to feed pigs, to wrap mango dishes, or to provide shade for garden chores.

The good side of the plantation always eased my pulse and cooled my temper. I slowed my steps as I made it to the redbrick cistern.

My sister Kitty, bright laughing Kitty, poured water into her calabash from the pump, then poured it into the base.

She looked at peace, playing.

Something in my spirit rose. I needed to save Kitty. She wasn't in danger of tipping over and drowning in the cistern, but I needed to be the kind of sister to cover her, to feed her, and give her more than me.

Moving close, I straightened her scarf, blue and white checks that wrapped her wonderful brown braids. Her olive face lifted and she grinned. Her heart showed in her smile.

"I'll always protect you, Kitty. I always will." That was my vow. I'd keep this promise in my pocket like a shiny pebble.

Three women came toward us. Two had pots on their heads to draw water. The middle woman wore a hat, a beautiful straw hat, not scarves, like me and Kitty.

The wide brim had bright orange banding. I'd only seen such on a planter's wife, never a colored woman's head.

I couldn't stop staring.

Kitty's topaz eyes widened and she pointed. "See, Dolly. Nice pots."

Painted blue and red, the clay vessels shone with a glaze. "They're lovely," I said. "They'll fetch a fair penny in town."

The three smiled at us, even the ones who'd talked bad about Mamaí last week when I gathered water.

"Dolly, you like my hat? I'm a freewoman. I get to wear a fancy hat."

The older woman sat, plopping down on a stone bench. "Girl, don't brag. Your lover has done what he needed to do."

The hat woman's face twisted with a smirk. "Guess your Betty doesn't know what she needs to do, Dolly. *De lard gib beard a dem who na hab chi fe wear i!* That is, Massa's favorite has all the advantages but can't make him stay." She laughed, haughty and loud.

This hat-wearing lady knew my name. I didn't know hers, but I recognized a mamba snake and a mean spirit. "Nothing for you to ever have worries about," she said. "Creole lover don't love no tar. White man, he'll never take you this far."

The third thin young woman giggled and repeated the awful rhyme. She was new to the plantation. Pa had bought her last month for fifty pounds. That was money he could have used to free Mamaí.

Slipping to Kitty's side, I opened the cistern's brass tap, splashing water onto my hand, forcing my mother's empty smile to show.

The mean hat woman hummed again, but I'd have to forget her awful song. I couldn't hear it, couldn't think on it, and forced my gaze to my pretty reflection in the water puddling near my feet.

Yet the hat was something to crave—something to add to my dreams. The desire to earn forty pounds times three seeped into my empty chest.

This feeling had to fill me before gossip and doubt took root.

A week of aching was done. I couldn't sit in the hut any longer. I started to town. The gray black dirt of the road looked good.

I had items to sell in my sack. Too many British planters were coming. As they squeezed out the Irish settlers, these newcomers needed things like Mamaí's blankets to decorate their confiscated homes.

My sandals kicked up clouds, but I didn't care. I was glad to be up, done with the uncleanness of my menses. My ma gave me teas to make it better, but not much helped. The changes in my body were unbearable. She called me a woman now.

Me. An eleven-year-old misfit, a misfit on a mission—a woman?

"Dolly, wait!"

I set down my sack, easy. The fine pot inside couldn't break. I paid a woman two shillings for it. I intended to sell it for six.

Kitty's spindly little legs pumped up and down as she skidded into me.

I wrapped my arms about her shoulders and kept her from slipping. "You're supposed to be working Mamaí's garden. If we grow more yams, we'll have enough to eat and sell in town."

"Always town. Always sneaking off and selling. Dolly, you used to play with me. It's Sunday. We don't have much chores."

"Kitty, I have made a little more than twenty pounds in a year. I need to make more. When Pa comes back, I can give him money for our ransom."

Her chubby face looked like it would burst. She couldn't understand what I had to do, what I'd appointed myself to do.

"Dolly, play."

"I have to huckster, Kitty, buy for pennies and sell for much more."

"You work too hard. Doesn't Pa provide?"

I tugged the corded strings that corseted my sunny yellow tunic. The bright color would attract attention from shoppers.

But that wasn't a problem anymore, attracting attention. Hiding from men was.

Kitty yanked on my skirt. "Dolly? What's wrong."

It was like staring at five-year-old me.

How do I destroy Kitty's innocence? Pa didn't provide enough for us when he was here, definitely not when he was gone.

I couldn't. I ran my finger over her lips until they bubbled, then spun my sister 'round and 'round. When she was dizzy, dizzy like a drunk, we laughed. "Walk with me to town, sis, then we'll play."

She nodded her chin fast, faster than hens clucking.

Kitty skipped around me. "My sister's going to play."

I slung my sack over my shoulder and took her arm.

Looking only to the right, the good right, we passed the Cellses' land. The field looked freshly plowed and ready to hold ruts, the horizontal pieces of sugarcane the planters buried to sprout green shoots. In a few months, the cane plants would grow big like bamboo, their wispy leaves whipping the air.

Were they back? The Cells family traveled as much as Pa. Some said they were with relatives in Barbados or a Dutch colony or even in a land across the sea.

"Kitty, this place may not spoil this year. The Cells—"

"Mr. Cells came back a few days ago. He was on the boat with Nicholas."

My hands became slick. My pulse throbbed in my ears. "He's back, too?"

"Yes. When you were sick, I saw them walking to the cistern."

Forcing myself to breathe in steady gasps, I pretended nothing was wrong. That I didn't fear our brother stopping me from buying our freedom.

After swiping my palm along my tunic, I clasped Kitty's arm.

"You're right—no work today. Katherine Kirwan, let's go play in the safe hills."

She smiled and moved with me.

Back on Pa's land, the good side, people had gathered at the cistern. One of the colored drivers brought out his flute. The tall fellow, whose sable skin shone with perspiration, blew fast notes.

Another man came with his *banio* as Mamaí called it. The planters called it a banjo or fiddle. He plucked the strings and made the harmony, stirring and smooth. Drummers joined the fray, offering a rhythm worthy of sweat and losing all your breath.

Women ran from their huts, dancing with their hands waving, skirts twirling. Like frigate flags the colors of French red, British blue, Spanish yellow, and Portuguese green, their colorful tunics flitted in the afternoon sun. Their osnaburg floated like the planters' daughters' silk.

A call went out: "Sɛ wowɔ ahotɔ a, nna woyɛ ahotɔ ni."

Then in the deepest tones the response came. "Only if you're free . . . then you can be."

Swaying and singing, the men and women looked happy. They'd transformed the gossipy cistern to worship. People praised with their bodies, whirling work-drenched limbs in a dance of joy.

Lies.

They knew the truth. They sang the truth, just like Mamaí.

This worship would disappear with one blow of the overseer's conch.

Dance was a miracle, but it would never fill a soul's empty well. This rhythm would leave them parched in the sun, damp in sweat, itching in the cheap osnaburg that clung to their skin.

Part of me wanted me to forget, to leap and spin, letting the beat drill through me. It needed to dig deep, deep into my spirit to make me sleep.

I couldn't let it.

The seductive rhythm was meant to deceive, to make me passive. I could never be content here, living without my dreams in this small life.

"Sɛ wowɔ ahotɔ a, nna woyɛ ahotɔ ni."

I turned my back to them and focused on town. "Let's work, Kitty. Then play."

She stopped clapping and followed.

We're running out of time. Unless being away had changed Nicholas, he'd do everything in his power to stop me. I could never let him win.

Rain fell as if the sky had scooped up all the water in the sea and dumped every ounce onto Montserrat. I stood on the porch, hoping the storm didn't worsen.

The ghauts opened up and flooded the fields.

Mamaí's hut was fine for now, but Pa had us come up to the owl house. The stilt legs that lifted the structure six feet from the ground would keep us dry if the high waters came.

Thunder crackled.

My heart shook against my ribs. I wasn't alone.

"Why are you out here, Dolly?"

I didn't turn. Nicholas's sullen voice made me not want to.

I held on to the column. "It's . . . it's too crowded inside."

"Oh, I thought you'd run out of places to avoid me."

For two months, I had. "I know my presence always bothers you. I don't want to ruin your time in Montserrat."

"Very kind of you, Dolly."

I heard his footfalls, his squeaky low slippers coming closer. Those things were meant for a social dance, not a rainy day. That's what Pa said.

My brother stood behind me, his shadow standing on mine.

Readying to run, I turned. "I should go see if Mamaí needs help kneading the bread. The cassava meal takes a lot of work to shape and then we have to let it dry before firing."

He touched my shoulder. "It's just a bad storm. You don't have to be afraid."

His eyes were like Pa's, just greener but with no hints of kind crinkles of wrinkles. He'd begun to sprout a mustache. Was that to look older? Wiser?

I wanted to ask him why, why he hated me. Was having a little of Pa too much?

"I need . . . May I pass, Nicholas?"

He pointed and allowed me back into the house, but I had to brush his side.

He was too close.

"Dolly, bring tea to Father's office. Perhaps as you serve me you can tell me what you do when you disappear."

With a nod, I tried to slip past him and held my breath to be as small as possible. But the back of my hand felt the smooth linen of his sleeve. Nothing coarse, not nankeen or osnaburg, but rich and smooth. That was the fabric that came from across the sea.

Never had I ever envied my brother, but a feel of the weave was my undoing. He had the world, I barely had a bedroll.

"Tea. I'll have it readied, Nicholas."

"Thank you."

His voice was curt, sort of nice. It didn't match his eyes, didn't take away the unease settling in my chest.

Inside, I did run, dashing down the whitewashed hall to the crowded olive-green kitchen. My sister and five other women were at the large table in the center of the room, peeling and dicing, working bread dough. The savory scent of roasted meat filled the air. Goat water stew.

Forgetting my newfound hunger, I had the new girl take tea to Pa's study. She always tried to smile at Pa. She welcomed the opportunity.

I refused to be near Nicholas and reignite our feud, and I didn't want to see Pa either. He'd returned with more excuses of why he didn't have money to free us.

"Mamaí, I'll get the long stick fork to help with turning the loaf."

"Take your time. It's too wet outside for the bread to dry properly."

It was her rare smile, like she'd given me permission to flee. And I did. I scooted out of the rear and kept running.

Trees bowed and stretched in the wind. Sections of thatched roofs of some huts flapped, but nothing danced like it did in a hurricane.

My stride quickened, and I made it to the cottonwood tree at the Cellses' fence. Fingering the gnarled white bark of the haunted tree, I searched its thick roots and heavy branches for an Obeah ghost.

One could be there, like Mrs. Ben, since the tree stretched over her old hut. The plaster walls of her home had a fresh coat of white-wash. All traces of the rebellion fires of sixty-one were gone. The Cellses must be readying the plantation for sale.

The wind lifted my orange skirt and spun the fabric about my knees like the ruffled feathers of a skittish oriole.

The rain fell hard again.

The Bens' hut looked safe and dry, so I ran to it and scooted inside.

It was empty.

No coals for a fire. No bedrolls, no signs of the happy life that once lived here.

Yet, were they happy, the Bens? Or had my younger eyes lied, seeing joy where there wasn't?

A splash, a splosh sounded outside.

Had Nicholas followed?

Would he tell Pa I tried to run? That would be stupid, being a foot or two off Kirwan's property.

The noise became clearer, harsher. Boot heels, not slippers.

The door slung open.

Tall, blocking the gray day's light, a man stood in the threshold.

Drenched worse than me, grumbling, stumbling, he marched inside and slammed the door. Coseveldt Cells lurched toward me with a gun pointed at my head.

MONTSERRAT 1767: A REMEMBRANCE

Shiny barrel, ebony handle, the gun had no smell of gunpowder. Coseveldt Cells lowered his weapon.

"What are you . . . Dolly?"

I didn't answer. I needed to be an orange-bellied oriole that could flit around this man and leave before he again lifted his gun.

"It is you, Dolly." The man put his gun into the pocket of his long dark coat that had pleats and flared from his waist to his knees. That was too fancy for everyday Montserrat. Didn't look like Montserrat at all.

The crisp daylight and the years had aged him from the picture I had in my head. No longer lanky but filled out with muscles. The face that was smooth now bore a hint of stubble for a beard. The cleft in his chin, had it always been there?

"There's nothing to steal. It's picked through, even the sewing needles and the bone thimble Mrs. Ben loved."

An image of the woman stitching in the corner talking about making ginger preserves filled my eyes, almost covering her death mask.

The memory of her dying hadn't left. It haunted me whenever I saw smoke in the night or heard restless drums.

"Not here for anything, sir. Just waiting for the rain to slow."

He rubbed at his face. His cheeks changed from pink to peach to white. "Your hut hasn't flooded? Is that why you're here?"

"No. Too many people in Pa's owl . . . in Pa's house. The rain slowed and I went for a walk."

He pounded closer, his boots making the floorboards tremble. "Oh. Not smart, Dolly. This weather is unpredictable. Kirwan's big house is sturdy."

Mamaí told me about men and to avoid 'em. Yet I couldn't cower or slink away, not with his hazel eyes judging me lacking. "Could ask the same of you? You're out here when you have a perfectly good house fifty feet away."

A half smirk formed. "I grew up running back and forth from here to the main house. I always did my best thinking then. Some habits are hard to stop."

He was winsome and shifted his stance like he hunted for something long gone. "There should be a pot for coals and wood. A fire will take the chill away."

"I left to be alone. Hard to do that with two."

"Dolly. A sense of humor to go with your boldness. Nice."

The man sat and put his hands to his knees. I had a sense he showed me his easy manner to calm me.

Yet those eyes with the tight crinkles in the corner said he wasn't easy at all.

As slow as a one-legger worm, I inched to the door. "I'll be going."

"Dolly, I never thanked you. That night, I was pretty turned around. I wanted to help Merr Ben, but you helped me."

Merr wasn't Irish, at least I didn't think so. "I didn't do much."

"You did more than most. It was brave. Thank you."

The back of his head was to me with nothing but an indigo ribbon cinched about his thick black hair. The sorrow in his voice guided me. He wouldn't hurt me.

"We still lost her, sir."

"Yes. Yes, we did."

The friendship I had with the old woman, Coseveldt Cells must've had one too.

"I've watched you sometimes from my study. Pretty little Negress walking past my plantation heading to town. It doesn't frighten you, walking alone?"

"Frightens me you been watching."

"Please come back. I won't hurt you."

I eased from the door and kept my eye on this man who talked to me like he saw me as human. "Most know I'm Kirwan's. I'm not bothered. You're not going to say I can't come near your property?"

"That wouldn't be neighborly."

"No, it wouldn't."

"So, Dolly Kirwan, what do you do sneaking to town?"

"I huckster . . . I do mercantilism."

He fell back laughing. Sprawled on the floor, he looked more handsome and even young, chuckling like a fool. Sitting up he slapped at the shaft of his boot. "A business-minded lass. How exciting."

"I have big dreams. I'm not meant to be living in a hut all my days. I want to earn enough to have a plantation of my own."

"That is a big dream." He leaned over and snatched up my wet scarf, making my hair fall. "This thing is sopping wet. You can catch cold."

Before I uttered a complaint, he'd wrung out my gray-checked scarf. Near his boots sat puddles like the osnaburg had cried.

Fancy silks and fine needlepoint with a tricorn hat on his hip, I felt small next to his splendor, but I wouldn't be cowed. I'd have fancy clothes, too, when I was free.

"What is it you want, Cells? Have you seen the pots or the blankets? Do you wish to buy? I see you fixing up things."

More humor covered his face, shifting his lips, changing the way the light hit his dimples and the dent in his chin.

"Dolly, I'm trying to decide if I should make a go here. My father, he'd want me to."

"But you don't? Trying not to let him down."

"Something like that. But I'm pushing uphill. The land's not as good or stable. My manager Polk says it's *no good. No good.*"

His tone flattened.

Cells was rich, one of those good praying Catholics. He shouldn't have worries, but not succeeding here seemed to hurt.

"Ya pa would understand. He wouldn't want you wasting money. Then there'd be nothing left in it for you."

"Something in it for me. You're a smart little girl."

"Yes. That's what my pa says. If you've done your best, no one can talk against you."

"Someone always will." He sighed and shifted his legs. "You save me the best blanket, but don't give me a discount. A friend should expect to pay full price."

Friend?

I didn't have any besides Kitty. Not sure if a sister counted if I could order her around. "Yes, full price."

My gaze met his and I accepted his attention fully. I had nothing to be ashamed of. I was a businesswoman after all. Watching Pa all these years meant I could charge a fair price.

Yet, after an eternity of Cells staring and me looking back, I lowered my eyes to the floorboard and fixed my dripping braids. "Say what's on your mind. I can't read your thoughts."

"I suppose you read some, though. Merr Ben could."

He said my *damfo*'s name again with such affection. I imagined Cells coming to her as I did to ask advice, to eat a treat of hot sugared ginger.

"It's better to ask and save my mind for important stuff, like charging goods. We haven't settled on what colors you want."

He craned his neck to the freshly thatched roof. "Do people ever question if you're mulatto, that Kirwan is indeed your pa?"

Sitting, I yanked at my braid, thin and fine, straight as the day is long and of the deepest ebony, just like Pa's. "Mamai said I got this purely from the Kirwans. Her own pa's Creole hair wasn't this straight. I wish mine was thicker like hers."

And if Cells had seen Pa's face when Mamai told him about Overseer Teller trying to visit, he'd know my pa wasn't letting anyone near her. "Why do you ask?"

"Most children of such a union have light skin."

I grasped my hands, folded them like I was about to shuck beans. I was darker than Mamai or Kitty, but I never fretted about my coloring. "I'm luckier, I guess. My black is beautiful."

His gaze remained steady. He even smiled though I doubted he believed the same. The planters believed that black was good for working the fields, nothing else.

I rose like Mamaí, slow, stately. "The rain has eased, Mr. Cells. I'll be heading back."

He popped up and went to the door and held it open. "You make sure I get one of those blankets. The finest one for me. I like blue."

Taking my scarf from his fingers, I put it in my pocket. "Just have your coins ready. We still haven't settled on a price. Blue may be trouble to get."

"I'll have a few waiting for you, Miss Kirwan. I will."

His chuckles followed me, but I didn't mind. I'd made a sale and maybe a friend.

MONTSERRAT 1768: A RUSH

I adjusted my shawl about me as I walked past the cistern. My sack was heavy with things to sell in town. Pa needed to return. He was gone again several months now. I'd earned sixty pounds mostly through selling things at the Saturday market and the rest to Mr. Cells. He'd become a steady customer, and I cleaned his house while he was away, keeping mildew, the green dust, from his treasures.

I walked past the old cottonwood and Cells's fence. I missed haggling with him and the humorous way his growing mustache twitched when he examined my bowls. His laugh when he told stories of his travels to Europe was so merry.

A carriage drove up from town. The hoofbeats sounded louder.

I ducked past the fence and hid behind the big cottonwood silk tree. Its shadow fell on the Bens' hut.

"Dolly?"

Had I wished him back? "Mr. Cells?"

He tipped his rounded hat of beaver pelt. His face was tanned, and he looked smart in his long emerald jacket and flowing white pantaloons. That coat had deep blue embroidery from top to bottom. Very fancy. Too pretty for Montserrat.

"As you can see. Made it all the way to London then down to Demerara."

I covered my eyes from the strong sun and stepped toward his horse. "Demerara? Where's that?"

"Beyond Trinidad. It's a boon. I'm building a plantation there. Hopefully one that sticks."

"That means you're leaving Montserrat again?"

"Expanding for now. Showed Kirwan. He thinks it quite fine."

"You've seen my pa? Is he back?"

"No. He had more trading to do in Grenada, I think." Cells's head tipped to the side. "You must be on your way to town. Still working on your fortune? Can you buy me out and the whole of Montserrat?"

Boy, he made my dreams sound silly. "Making fun? I knew I shouldn't have told you."

"No. Well, a little. But you and I actually want the same. Lots of money."

"And the world to know our names."

He bit his lip a moment, pressing down until the pink turned red. "You are perceptive, girl. What are you selling?"

I shook my sack made of strong scraps of osnaburg fabric. "Mamaí has made another fine blanket. It should fetch a lot of shillings."

"Have to admire a business-minded woman." He patted the bench. "Can I give you a ride to town?"

It would be safer, but what would people think of me in Cells's dray. I tugged on the light scarf on my shoulders. "I don't know. You haven't any room in the back."

"I'm your neighbor, Dolly. You've nothing to fear from me."

"You just came from town. It's wasteful to go right back."

He jumped down off his cart and helped me up. "No trouble."

"Well, since you jumped down and all. Thank you."

He hurried back to the other side and climbed into the seat. He whipped the reins. "Good, you're not stubborn. Young Kirwan says—"

"Stop the dray. Let me out."

"We're not to town yet, Dolly."

"I'll not be anywhere with you if I have to talk about Nicholas."

Cells lowered his hand on my arm, and I almost jumped.

"I take it you two don't get along. Odd. He's seems to talk about you a great deal. He's always asking when I last spoke to you."

I felt my eyes pop wide. "Don't ever tell him that we talk. He'll be mean to you."

Cells adjusted his gloves and tugged on the reins. "He won't hurt me. He doesn't know how."

"A baby viper can still strike."

"Has he bitten you, Dolly?"

My head dropped and I looked away.

"I guess he has." Cells's voice was low, drowning in the rhythm of the horse's hooves.

Mamaí didn't like how Nicholas looked at me. She told me to stay out of sight, but to be easy with him if he teased me. With Pa not here to keep him from bossing me, I hid all the time.

"Just take me to town. I have business."

He nodded. "If you ever want to talk, come over, cross that fence. Meet me at the Bens'. I'll be there. I'll pray for you, Dorothy, that you find peace with your family."

"What's a prayer to do to stop evil? Aren't you running from it?"

His eyes grew wide, the hazel dot drifting. "What are you talking about?"

"I hear things at the market. You're leaving 'cause the British set laws against the Catholics. They took your churches. You now pray to your god in the woods. You must be afraid of them taking more."

"These are dangerous times for Catholics. Our liberty and land are at stake. If Tuite pulls out, no Irish man has a chance. British are Anglicans. They hate us. It will only get worse."

"Why do Anglicans hate Catholics? Is their god the same or is it like the Obeah spirits and you have many?"

"That's a long conversation about the holy sacraments, but the hate is more about the heads of the faith. For Catholics, it's Pope Clement XIV. For Anglicans, it's King George. British don't trust our allegiance, not as long as we are Catholic."

He seemed agitated, like his voice had to thread through Mrs. Ben's needle.

"Will they keep bothering Catholics?"

"They'll do whatever they please, whenever they please."

"So you don't want overseers, but you force them on us? Seems like a bad circle, Cells."

He bit his lip then leaned in close. "Dolly, don't go to town next week. Keep your mother and sister in your hut."

"I have customers. St. Patrick's Day should be a big selling day. Everyone is happy and spending money. I'll make a fortune. A mighty *fhortún*."

He shook his head something furious. "I'll buy up everything you have, just don't. You won't be safe if you go."

His eyes held a warning, something dire.

Running my hand over the bright fabric, made soft by Mamaí beating it on the rocks, I didn't know what to do, but I believed him. "Hurry to town, Mr. Cells. I need to make enough to tide me over until you return."

"I should ask your father about you coming to Demerara. You and your family. It may be safer for all of you in the new colony. I want to help."

Something scared Cells, but I wasn't looking for a new owner. I knew Mamaí wasn't either.

"I leave by sloop, the *Dolus*, at week's end. I'm going to write to your father and ask. He has to see it's not safe here."

I didn't know what to react to, the unknown threat or the vague offer to buy me and Kitty and Mamaí. I lowered my face to my sack. "There are customers waiting. Please hurry."

MONTSERRAT 1768: A RECKONING

The smell of char seeped into my closed window. St. Patrick's Day, the Irish holiday to celebrate the saint and his miracles in Ireland, was made hell in Montserrat. This wasn't a simple uprising.

This was slaughter.

So many planters' guns, all their numbers, overwhelmed the enslaved's shovels and scythes.

The overseers boasted the troublemakers would die today.

The killing lasted hours. The blasts never stopped, nor the jeers. From my treasured window, I saw death on this side of Pa's plantation. It was never supposed to be here.

Wished my pa or Cells would come.

Arms folded, I shuffled out of my room and sat with Kitty on the floor.

Mamaí was on her bench stitching another blanket, this one of an oriole with its wings stretched wide. If we lived, maybe I'd be able to sell it in town.

"Dolly, play with me?"

My sister rolled the metal banding from a barrel between her palms. Her teeth chattered. She knew death was outside.

"Stupid Cudjoe," Mamaí said, "he's gone and gotten everyone killed. All our men, anyone strong, they'll kill tonight."

Anyone strong?

I looked at Mamaí and realized she'd said this to me like I was older, like I was an adult.

My sister tugged on my flowery skirt of orange and red. I'd worn it to make the day seem normal. Should've found mudcloth black.

"Can we go outside tomorrow, Dolly?" Kitty asked. Her eyes stayed locked on her hoop. "Will it be over then?"

Who knew? I shrugged my shoulders. "Let me do your hair."

"Again, Dolly?"

She pouted, but I'd tried and failed three times to finish plaiting her hair. Her fat braids were crooked. "I'll take care of us. I always will."

"You think Nicholas is safe, Dolly?"

Didn't care if he was or wasn't; I didn't want him near Mamaí's hut, not with the sweat of killing on him.

He had to know about the uprising as early as Mr. Cells but said nothing.

My friend had more care for us than my own brother. Since my neighbor wasn't here, he couldn't be hurt. So I chose a side. I wanted the rebels to win.

The door to the hut crashed open.

Two women came inside, one with a baby crying.

Mamaí welcomed them. "There's stew if you're hungry," she said, pointing to the bowl over the fire bucket. The big pot of vegetables from her garden and salt fish I'd brought home from the market.

I recognized one woman—one of the gossips at the cistern. I wanted to turn them away, but Mamaí kept showing them kindness.

Hugging her baby to her big bosom, the gossip wiped at her eyes. "Thank you, Betty."

That taught me something about Mamaí. Something new. Her heart was bigger than mine. Her forgiveness was much bigger too.

"Is the rebellion over?" my voice echoed.

"'Twas no rebellion," the second woman said. "Planters shot men in the sick house. They're killing all the Black men. They killed my husband. They did it because he complained to an agent of the council for putting me in stocks when I was so close to birth."

The poor woman sobbed.

Her friend held her by the shoulders.

The shooting sounded louder. Were these two followed?

"They're coming for my baby. They murdered—"

Mamaí clapped her hands. "Hush. You need something of your lover to survive? You have his son. That's all you get tonight."

Her words hung in the air, cold and true.

Cells had warned me. If only . . . If he had told me the whole of it, I could've gotten Mamaí and Kitty to his boat. I wouldn't be afraid now. Maybe he'd let me work every day to earn the money to be free, not just after chores or Saturdays.

"They're not done," Kitty said. Her whisper, shaky and low, reached my ear. "Maybe they want us all to be Cudjoe, the girls, too."

The door flung open.

My lungs stuttered then stopped.

It wasn't Pa. Nicholas stumbled inside. Brandishing Pa's long gun, he aimed at my heart.

LONDON 1824: KENSINGTON HOUSE

I stand in the gardens of Kensington House. The students, I'm told, often come outside and sit on the stone benches. Some study the flora. Others disturb the natural surroundings to make arrangements for vases and whatnots.

There should be a cistern right here. Something sturdy and bold like a Grecian or Egyptian work of art.

I chuckle at the notion but it's a distraction. I'm alone, tiring of two days of chatter and pleasantries. Still no word of a meeting, but my *damfo* is faithful and resourceful. I'm convinced that whatever problems there have been, they will be overcome. Godspeed to finding new ways.

The air is light. It's not fresh or washed in the sea's salt. The chill gives me shivers. Miss Smith showed me the purple saxifrage petals creeping at the edges of the emerald hedgerow and the yellow bulbs of the gorse to impress me. These vibrant colors do, and they make me think of home.

My eyes gaze again at the sowed beds. I'm searching for the yellow and red flowers of the peacock plants. The cure for a woman's ills if she's been abused.

I didn't understand much when I was young.

"GaMa?"

Mary has followed me outside. I school my face, hiding my tears. "Yes, dear."

"Why are you sad? I never see you sad. You are light, GaMa."

"Light?" I smooth my long skirts. It's been many years since I've been skin and bones. "I have a great deal on my mind, angel."

She dimples and clasps my hand.

We twirl arm in arm. Mary was born free, but I keep her papers with me when we travel. You never know when one will need to prove their rights.

"Are you enjoying your visit, Mary?"

"Oh, yes, GaMa. You take us in carriages with the softest seats. You rent fine houses in London, but I like it here, too."

Yes, we stay in comfort with servants trained in all the ways to treat elegant guests. I ensure all my grands dine on superb food, the best fish and beefsteak.

I can't let the world I'm showing Mary disappear. Not when this beautiful five-year-old girl needs to be a child for as long as she can. She must remember these moments when she's older. She'll know her worth.

We spin faster and faster.

"Cyclone Game." The words fling out of her all breathy and with a squeal.

Her legs lift from the ground.

She's a swallow taking flight. Her pristine white gown billows better than a ship's sail.

"Ma'am."

The headmistress stands at the garden's entrance. Her face is half shadowed by Kensington House's roofline.

Letting my swallow ease to the ground, I catch my breath. My eyes search Miss Smith's hands for a note.

Empty.

No word has come. No meeting with Lord Bathurst, yet.

I haven't found the way to win.

The woman jitters, her gray skirts flutter like butterfly wings. Seems she remains on edge, expecting airs from me.

Perhaps I should expend a little.

"Miss Smith. I need a scribe. I feel like dictating a letter. Can you send one of your girls to take notes?"

A young woman of good height and nimble limbs, someone who'd be sought after at the mulatto balls, steps into the garden and stands beside the headmistress. "I can take the correspondence for Miss Kirwan."

"It's Mrs. Thomas, Miss Van Den Velden." Miss Smith looks like she wants to swat the girl. Instead, she stoops to Mary. "It's time for lessons. Come along, little Miss Fullarton. You'll make a great student for Kensington House someday."

Mary pokes out her lips but scoots to the headmistress when my lips offer a scold. My frowns, I've been told, can freeze the air. Cold was something I didn't quite understand until my first boat trip to England.

The headmistress offers another polite scowl. "Miss Van Den Velden, I expect you to show the true Kensington spirit to our wonderful benefactor."

The young woman nods. "I will, ma'am."

I stretch my arms and prepare for this battle. "Miss Van Den Velden, shouldn't you get some paper and a pen?"

"My memory is quite good. I'm sure that I can do an adequate service."

"It seems you don't want to take direction. I suspect you wish to give it." I sit on the stone bench close to the tea roses. "Why don't I get comfortable? Then tell me all you wish to say."

Her eyes widen. My frankness has caught her off guard. I want to chuckle, but she needs to choose her path, to be a friend or a nuisance.

"My father says you are here to cause trouble."

Ah, she chose nuisance, like one of the chigger bugs of Grenada or the ruinous ants of Barbados. A lot of cattle were killed by those ants.

But a lot of ants died too.

"Your father?" I say. "Are you sure you know who he is?"

Her eyes blink rapidly. I can see her wondering if I know something of her birth records. She huffs. "You know my father. He's on the colony council of Demerara."

"Yes, one of Lieutenant Governor Murray's henchmen, I know him well. I hosted a reception for him and the governor of Barbados. He found my chef's gelatin molds delightful."

Her mouth drops open, wide enough for those ants to hop in, but then she says, "I look forward to having my own private chef, too, when my fortune comes in. My father will make it happen sooner if I can make you stop this folly and go home."

The refined, almost delicate, girl clasps her elbows. Her long, lithe fingers bear no scars or roughness, nothing to show a life of working in the fields or hardship or survival.

In her smirk, I see my past, dancing in the hotels, smiling pretty for the soldiers wearing their best regimentals, touching the gold dripping from the braiding at their shoulders. They sneered, too, thinking the singers and dancers were pawns in the games they played for entertainment.

I remember myself, a girl who had to relearn her worth when everything was made bad. Then made worse.

"What are you thinking, Miss—"

"Mrs. Thomas."

"Miss Doll Kirwan. My father calls you Dolly. He says that's the name you used when you were a prostitute, when you seduced your own brother and had his baby."

The white man wants to blame his sins on colored women. His depravity is our fault. If we take the abuse just to live another day, they say we are the seducers. They write the history.

"It's Thomas, *you fool*. Mrs. Dorothy Thomas. In Demerara, they know my name. You haven't lived long enough to know better."

Miss Van Den Velden sputters. Spittle froths at her mouth. "I was just trying—"

"Yes, you're trying."

"My father told me who you are! He knows all about you. He's written me quite a lot, since he found out you were coming to London. I know about the old days, about you. That's the message I'm here to deliver. Stop your noise and pay the taxes. Your ruckus is just as bad as another slave rebellion."

The girl knew nothing of the pain of rebellions or the power of men to humble a woman. Can't she see that submission makes it easier for men to make new demands? Submit once and they'll only invent worse laws to keep us under their thumb?

With poise, Lucy struts to the door. "Go back to where you come from."

"Next time you see me, have paper and a pen. And keep those pouty lips shut tight."

"I'm speaking the truth. You're a harlot ball girl. An old Black woman who's let a little money go to her head. Even if you did dance with a prince, you're tired and used up now."

"If you cross my path tomorrow, call me Mrs. Thomas. Unlike you, my money has already come. I've paid for my respect. You shall show it."

I stare her down as I had the empty street behind Kensington House and all those who brought hate into my life. "I fight for my grands, for me, even you, you fool."

Lucy stops at the threshold. "I don't need you."

"Yes, you do. Women need women willing to fight for all our rights."

I ease back onto the bench, flattening my bottom on the cold stone. "Remember, it's *Mrsss. Thomassss.* And next time bring paper."

Shaking her head, Lucy goes inside, muttering she'll show me.

The door closes with a shake. Then it hushes.

I look over the fence like it's a window to count stars. I'm still hoping, but I'm not sure my patience will win.

MONTSERRAT 1770: FORGING AHEAD

My little squiggle lay in her cradle. Little Lizzy, my daughter, a year old this month.

She was pretty and healthy and weaned. She'd started crawling. She might start walking any day.

If I could bear to leave her, I'd return to huckstering in town. Just cleaning Cells's house, keeping his books free of the green dust wasn't enough to free four.

Kitty leaned on me and looked over my shoulder. "She's small, Dolly. Like a doll."

"But she's getting bigger. I'll need you to watch her while I go clean for Mr. Cells."

Kitty's eyes popped wide like they might burst. "Lizzy might cry. What am I going to do if she cries?"

"Lizzy will cry, but you are capable of handling this."

Fear fled her eyes, and a toothy smile bloomed in its place. "You believe in me, Dolly?"

"Always."

I kissed her cheek and then touched Lizzy's brow. My daughter had my fine hair, but brown eyes with bits of green—the slightest bits of Nicholas.

This baby I loved with my whole heart. I didn't think I could. Not after what Nicholas did to me. But maybe the Holy Father had a plan for my life that I couldn't see?

All while I'd carried her in my gut, I spent time in the woods listening to the priest, looking for answers.

Still hadn't found them.

With another kiss to Lizzy's cheek, I lifted from my knees and started to the door.

"Dolly, you be careful. I don't want you sad anymore."

My sister and I walked arm in arm into the main room. I spun her fast until she dropped to the floor, dizzy and laughing.

Extending my arm, I helped her up. Then I handed her the scythe. "You go finish up in the garden like Mamaí asked. She'll be back from doing the wash soon. Lizzy should be asleep for an hour, but listen for her."

Kitty clasped the tool in her palms and twirled it when she popped out the door.

"Be careful. The toe of the blade is sharp."

"Hurry back, Dolly."

I walked into the warm air and glanced at Mamaí coming from the owl house. What was she doing?

My mother lifted her basket onto her head and hurried to me.

It took everything in me to school my face to not show betrayal.

"Dolly, we need to talk."

My forehead sprouted with moisture. "What have you done?"

She put down her woven basket filled with clean clothes. "I went to see Nicholas. He needs to have Lizzy's birth records righted. He needs to put his name to it."

My chest sputtered. I wasn't sure I wanted him to claim any part of Lizzy. Wasn't that the same as me claiming him?

"Aren't I enough for Lizzy? He hasn't even come to see her. It's been a year. The owl house is close, and he never thought to see about her."

"His name has to be on her records. It's the only way to ensure that your pa frees her, too. You're working hard to earn our ransoms. You don't want that baby to grow up left on this plantation."

I didn't, but I wanted nothing from Nicholas.

"Dolly, he says he will do it if you ask him."

It was a trap.

My brother was ready to begin his terror all over again. "No. No!"

Before she could catch me, I ran. I needed to be as far away from everyone as possible.

When would things work the way I wanted?

Being enslaved to my brother's lust wasn't going to happen. I wouldn't submit to stop his bruises and kicks. This time I'd kill him before he tried.

Heaving, I stood at the cottonwood tree at Cells's fence. Every time I passed it, I remembered the horrible St. Patrick's Day rebellion and Cudjoe's body dangling from a branch. It was Nicholas's idea to put him here, just so he could show me the depths of his evil.

Dusty naked toes swung back and forth.

The rope about Cudjoe's neck made him look like one of Pa's strung-up boars that he'd hung in the smokehouse to cure.

With his tongue half ripped from his mouth, I knew the man had suffered. His dark face contrasted with the white bark of the tree like Nicholas's pale fingers wrapping about mine.

I don't know how much time passed as we stood hand in hand looking at the tree, the feet, Cudjoe's death mask, but it wasn't enough to numb me for the terror to come.

Never did I want to think of it, that night and every time after.

My nightmare wasn't over. Nicholas would start on me again.

Wanting to scream, to flee, to cry, I eased from the tree.

Cells's dray, I saw it in the drive.

He was back. A hundred thoughts flooded me, but I centered on one. He said he owed me. Now was his time to pay.

No servant came to his door. I pulled the bronze key he'd given me from my pocket and clicked it into the lock. I pushed inside; how beautiful this grand house was, the moldings, the crystal sconces.

Yet the house was almost empty. Cells had taken more furnishings. He'd be gone soon. This time for good. He needed to take us with him, like he'd offered once before.

Something shuffled and made the floorboards creak. Was he in his study?

I wiped my face on my sleeve, then smoothed the blue checks of the fabric. Lifting my head, I walked down the hall into his study.

My heart lifted. He was here, sitting at his desk with his feet up.

"Dolly. You're a diligent creature. My house is dust free."

"Your house is almost empty, Mr. Cells."

"Yes. The Hermitage is ready."

"The Hermitage?"

"Well, I'm a bit of a hermit except for a few servants and you of course. Doesn't it sound weighty, the Hermitage?"

"Don't know about that." I took a rag from my pocket and started dusting the books on the low shelf. "I rather like the Cells's Plantation. Or Dolly's Plantation. That's what I call this house when you aren't here."

"Truly?"

"Yes. Then I pretend it's all mine."

He started to chuckle. "Do you put your feet up on my desk?"

"No, then I'll have to dust it again." My throat clogged. This easy banter felt wrong with Nicholas's terror looming.

My tears fell.

"Dolly?" He leapt out of his chair. His boots clacked with every step. And Cells was Cells, white breeches, black waistcoat, blue coat with buttons and pleats. "Dolly, what has happened?"

"My brother."

Cells clasped on my shoulders. "Did he hurt you? I talked to your father. He was supposed to warn him. He's coming back soon."

"He's not here. His version of soon will have me bearing that bastard another babe. I can't do it. I can't."

Cells put my head to his chest. His heart drummed. I liked the rhythm, it sounded safe and respectful and tender. "Dolly, he's not going to hurt you, again."

How would he know this? How could my friend look so confident and be so wrong. "Nicholas will. If he doesn't hurt me, he'll hurt the people I care about."

"You're giving the fool too much credit. He's not that smart."

"And you're not listening. He wants to humble me. And now there's Lizzy. She's a beautiful baby, another toy for him to twist me up until I break."

Cells took my hand in his, light and dark again, strong and weak. I craved his strength.

"Does she look like you?"

"She looks like Lizzy. She's beautiful."

"But a dark beauty or a white one? One light enough that she'll be called a quadroon or mustee?"

I squinted at him, not believing he'd voice such a question. "She's white as a ghost. Does that suit your curiosity, knowing her coloring?" I moved to the looming bookshelves. "Shouldn't you care if she's fed and healthy?"

"I do, Dolly." He pushed at his hair and retied the ribbon holding his jet locks. "I'm working on some projects with the governing council about damming a section of the Demerari River. The negotiations have my thoughts scattered."

"Your la-di-da work is important." My voice sounded bitter, but I didn't see the friend who cared. Cells was a man focused on his dreams.

His didn't include mine.

He leaned on the shelf near the one I polished. "I was hoping you'd bring Lizzy here."

"That'd be convenient for you, to bring an enslaved baby across the property line." I beat my fists on the shelf. A book toppled over.

"Dolly, I didn't—"

"Nicholas will take her. He'll punish me a thousand different ways. And I'll do anything just to get to see her. That's no life, Cells, not for me."

"What are you saying, Dolly?" He clasped my elbows and shook me. "You'll not do something stupid."

"What's stupid about wanting to end my waiting for the worst?"

"No. Dolly. That's fear talking. I chatted with Nicholas. He was apologetic. He says he was drunk. That he didn't mean to hurt you. He swore to me that he'd never hurt you again."

"And you believed him? He's taken me several times and only stopped when my stomach grew. He's threatened me even when I was with his child. He'll always hurt me. He won't stop until one of us is dead."

"I'll speak to him again."

Speak to him? That was all? Then I saw the ugly truth, hidden in his darting hazel eyes.

"You wanted to believe Nicholas. How could you? The liar raped me. He'll do anything."

Cells thumbed his lips, but he didn't argue with me.

"If you think he's telling the truth, then you've sealed my fate. You believe my pa 'cause he says he'll be back. Pa has been gone for over a year. All you planters are the same. You never intend to do anything to protect us."

"I did try for Mrs. Ben. I failed."

"No, I failed! I believed you were different."

"Watch your tongue, Dolly."

I threw the key at his head. "Give me my due. Then go to hell."

He stomped back to his desk and pulled out his purse. He fished out two pounds and set them on the desk.

When I came close, he knocked those shiny gold coins onto the floor.

I watched them roll round and round on their edges. One made a figure eight at my feet.

It wasn't worth stooping to get them.

My pockets were desperate, but not my pride. My soul wouldn't cede any more of me.

With my head high, I turned and walked out the door.

His footfalls sounded behind me. "Dolly, wait. I'm sorry."

No more lies. I ran.

"Wait, Dolly! Wait!"

His boots sounded louder, but I was fast. I slid down the hall and was at the front door in a blink.

Wham. I flung it open.

Then I froze.

Mamaí was there. Lizzy was in her arms. Both were crying.

"What happened?"

My mother looked pale, like she'd faint. "They took her."

I pried Lizzy from her. "They took who, Mamaí?"

"They took Kitty. She stabbed Nicholas with the scythe. He had her taken to town, to be whipped. She'll be sold off in the morning."

My heart . . . "No!"

"I'll go to town." Cells closed his eyes for a moment. "I'll see what can be done."

His words echoed in my ear, but I couldn't look at him, couldn't trust him anymore.

There was one man, one evil man, who was in control, and it wasn't the wavering Cells.

MONTSERRAT 1770: FALSE HOPE

Smoke twisted like a rope, dark and lanky curling about an escaping cloud. The chimney of the owl house spewed ash like a volcano's cone. This signal was meant for me.

It was the hottest part of the year, growing season. I stood in one of Pa's fields, on the left, the evil side. The young cane rose up to my thighs.

Nicholas wanted me to know where he was. He wanted me to come and surrender.

Rebel me wanted to rage and fight, but how?

I had left Cells in town. He talked to the officials. He got them to stop whipping Kitty, but not before the lashes had torn her tunic.

The bright green fabric of palm fronds was shredded, dotted in blood. The cat-o'-nine-tails left huge scars.

Kitty didn't look up, but I saw one eye was blackened. She was half naked with her head and hands in the stocks.

The agents of the governing body, even the ones who were supposed to investigate abuses against chattel, let no one, especially no one of color, come to her or cover her.

I couldn't hug my little swallow, tell her I loved her or that tonight I'd kill for her.

She cut Nicholas good, three inches down his cheek, Cells said.

I wish she'd stabbed him dead.

But Kitty's feet would have been made to float, hanged for striking a white man.

They could do anything.

We couldn't protect ourselves. *Holy Father, look away tonight as you have all my life.*

This was my fault and mine to fix.

If I'd just gone to Nicholas and submitted, I'd be the only one to suffer. Instead, I ran to Cells, and now my sister would be sold.

I glanced over the ridge toward Cells's plantation. I hated him, too. He made me believe he was different. He was just a nice landowner, a nice man who enslaved people, one who overlooked suffering just like God and all the planters.

Up the steps of the owl house, I moved my cold feet. I paused at the porch, knowing when I went through it, there'd be no going back.

I whirled inside. The house servants had gone to their provision grounds. This meeting would be me and Nicholas.

Stirring. The creaking of a chair.

He had to be in Pa's study.

I walked down the short hall and slipped into the room. "Nicholas."

"Afternoon, Doll . . . Dolly."

The Irish twang of my name meant the fool had been drinking. Maybe that meant he'd be easy, and I could talk the drunk out of selling Kitty.

"Nicholas. Came to see how bad our sister cut you. The folks in town said the wee girl got you good."

He chuckled. "She did all right. She's not as clever as you. Much easier to bait."

If I acted as if I were frightened, he'd be out of Pa's chair.

But I was scared.

The last time he beat me until I stopped squirming. I felt the punches looking at him, and he hadn't moved.

"You haven't come around much, Dolly."

"Been busy with the baby you saddled me with."

He guzzled more of his drink, something amber in color poured into one of Pa's fancy goblets. "Come closer. Let me see if you have your waist back."

Couldn't, wouldn't move.

"I came to beg for my sister." My voice cracked. "Mamaí has a tincture for cuts. It's at the hut."

"Betty's been witch doctoring."

"Suit yourself. She said you might get infected by the manure she uses in the garden."

He touched the long scar on his cheek. It was red and bulbous.

"Manure? Glad they flogged Kitty."

The smile on his face curled into a sneer. "A tincture is what she'll do for me, but what about you?"

He pounded closer. There was a wobble to his prideful stride. His white shirttails were half in, half out of his black breeches— all the signs of being good and drunk from celebrating what he'd done.

He fingered my tunic. "What about you?"

A tremble appeared in my elbow and spread to my whole arm.

Misneach! I said to myself trying to rally my courage. "You know why I came."

He took a swig from his glass, then turned and pitched it into the flames. The fire roared and spit ash. "You've come to be mine? Maybe I don't want you."

"Fine. I'll leave."

Before I could get to the door, he moved to me and lifted my chin with his bent index finger. "No, don't go, Dolly. Pretty little Dolly. Barely five foot, but all solid woman."

"I'm fourteen and your sister, your blood sister. Why can't you be decent?"

He traced my jaw. The stench of brandy oozed from his skin.

"If I let you . . . will you save Kitty?"

With his palm, he gripped my neck. "Angle your face and give me a kiss."

The fool had shaved off his stupid mustache. Maybe it wouldn't be as horrible as I remembered. Closing my eyes, I reached up and put my mouth to his. He bit my lip.

"Just because you want to play nice means nothing to me."

His laugh cut through me. I wish I had a rock. Something to smite him between the eyes.

Yet, with his hands on me, I disappeared inside, sinking into the bottomless hole in my chest. "May I leave?"

"No. It's been a year since you've spent time with me. Can I say I missed you?"

"Why lie?"

"I told your friend I was drunk. The St. Patrick's Day celebration overcame me." Nicholas released me, went to the sideboard, and drank from the bottle. His throat muscles tightened as liquor pumped down his long gullet.

Laughing, he set the bottle on the desk, then returned. "'Course. I might be drunk now."

It wasn't one time.

He hunted and had me over and over, until Mamaí's peacock seeds, her killing medicine, wouldn't bring my menses, till my belly showed. "I'm leaving."

Yawning, he gripped my shoulders, ripping at my sleeve.

"Let me go, Nicholas. You're hurting me. Be decent. Save Kitty. Fix the baptismal record. Lizzy's name needs to be right. She needs your name."

He tossed me aside and went back to the brandy. The angles of bottle captured the light. "What does that do?"

"It gives her a chance to be free. She needs to be acknowledged as a mulatto, as yours. Then Pa will have to free her, too. He's said his will frees us if he can't return."

"Wishing for Father's death, too?" He laughed and swayed. "That's a big thing to claim a bastard."

Nicholas's elbow hit the bottle. It fell and shattered into a thousand bits.

"I'll go get a bucket."

"No. Don't move." His voice was firm. "You might take a shard and cut me like Kitty. You might be more deadly than her."

I would be if I could. Just once, I wanted him to fear me.

He strode to me and put his hands on my waist.

His hold was too strong, too hurtful as his nails dug into my sides.

"Maybe I should sell you, too? Seeing you all greased and naked on the stage would give me such a laugh." He grabbed my face and shook it. "How high will you hold this chin then?"

"As high as I can. I'm still better than you."

He slammed me against the wall.

I'd come to give myself to him to save Kitty, but there was no surrendering to a fool. He needed to die.

The broken glass. It sparkled like the stars.

"What are you looking at?"

"How stupid you are. Small stupid man. You think Pa will forgive you for selling Kitty and me? *Adharcáilí*, you lustful man, you're a fool. Pa will hate you . . . maybe more than he does now."

"You take that back, Dolly."

"Castoff. Why do you think he kept sending you away or why he keeps leaving? It's not 'cause of me."

Nicholas shook me hard. "Stop it."

"Give Pa reasons to take your inheritance portion and offer it to his cousins, the successful Kirwans of St. Kitts. Or maybe, he'd even give it to me to make up for your evil."

The pressure of his hands became tight. I thought he'd rip off my arms.

Nicholas's eyes were half-open, drunken slits. I grabbed his chin and slapped it. "Why would Pa keep you? He'll know once and for all you're not worthy to be his son. He loves nothing your mother gave him."

Wham.

He struck me, and I crumbled again.

"You talk too much, like always."

I wiped the blood smeared on my lips. No more submitting. "Castoff."

I saw him wince from my words, but that was no solace for he tossed me over his shoulder. "I own you. I'll do with you as I plea'

Wriggling did nothing. He wobbled, but his band of iro'
had me.

Then he dropped me headfirst by the fireplace.

Pain dimmed my eyesight; I wished the impact had stolen my senses. I didn't want to remember the weight of Nicholas on top of me again.

I wouldn't yell or beg. No one would stop him. I was his chattel—a sow to be used.

Boots sailed over me.

Then breeches.

His heavy legs, the weight of Nicholas's knees, split my thighs.

He pushed my skirt up to my breasts. "Yes, Dolly. No crying, eyes alert and pretty for me. You remember."

I turned my head and caught sight of two curved chunks of the shattered bottle.

Four feet away—the sparkling pieces were out of reach. I couldn't stretch and seize them. I failed.

Yet I kept staring, kept dreaming, kept hiding my hopes deeper and deeper inside so Nicholas couldn't touch them.

"Look at me, Dolly."

I didn't.

The bits of glass had me, for they were broken and shiny and free.

I vowed to find my *misneach*—to heal, to find my power. One day, somehow, men like Nicholas would fear broken pieces.

MONTSERRAT 1770: FLEEING TIME

The morning light came and found me on the floor of Pa's study.

Everything ached.

Everything was raw.

Nicholas lay beside me, snoring, with an empty wine bottle by his mouth.

I eased from him. My anger whirled inside, echoing in my chest. I wanted my brother dead, but I needed a head start. My sister's life came before revenge. I could save her if Nicholas didn't rouse. I put his breeches and good boots in the fireplace.

It wasn't enough. I took the wine bottle from his hand and smashed it against his ugly skull.

He didn't move but kept breathing.

If I didn't have to get to Kitty, I'd burn down the owl house and stay to watch.

Outside, the strong sun set fire to my eyes. I fought it, running to Mamaí's to get my money.

She wasn't asleep. She was sitting on her bench waiting.

I looked at her, then little Lizzy in her arms. "I'm going to save Kitty."

Her gaze was on my torn bloody skirt.

"He'll kill you next time, Dolly. Take Kitty. Don't come back."

Her voice sounded dull, like she'd rehearsed the words. "Your money and clothes are on the bed. I added a sack of the peacock seeds. You don't want no more of Nicholas's children, no more of his hold on you."

My breasts were raw and sore. I wanted them to fill with milk for my child, to give her something of me before I left.

They were empty.

I was empty.

"Mamaí, how can I leave Lizzy, you?"

"If you buy Kitty, you can't bring her back here. You can't hide here. Nicholas will kill you. He'll kill all your dreams."

"But Lizzy."

"Kitty is all alone. Be her mother now. I'll be one to Lizzy."

"How can I leave my flesh?"

"Staying doesn't mean you get to keep her. You have an older sister, Dolly. They took her from me."

"What?"

"Yes, a sister, Ella. My father sold her off before he sold me to the Kirwans."

I put my brow to Mamaí's. "I'll make this right, somehow."

"You make things right by living. By keeping my Kitty alive."

Late at seeing my mother's strength, I was a fool. Now I had to survive without her. "Mamaí—"

"Kitty is my heart, but you are my soul. You have the strength of warrior women in you." My ma took my hand and led me to my room. She put Lizzy in the cradle and then washed my face with water from her calabash.

Then she prayed with her rosary, the one with the red and gold beads, and tucked it into my pocket.

Sobbing, I said good-bye to this room, to the window that framed my stars. Then I held my daughter, my Lizzy, who sucked her gums like a tooth rooted.

"Bye-bye, little one." Then I set her down.

With my purse of money and my sack, I ran.

The stench of Nicholas stayed on me. The blood on my clothes was what I needed to show the one man who could buy Kitty for me.

When I reached the property line, I saw Cells's dray was out front. He was readying to leave again.

Bursting into his house I called to him again and again. "Please. Cells. I need you."

He came from the long hall, in a dressing gown, bare feet. "Dolly, I'm glad . . . you're . . . Nicholas."

"Yes." Dropping my sack, I shoved my purse at him. "I need you to buy Kitty for me. You're a planter. They'll let you."

"I don't know—"

"You can keep all my money if you fail, just try. That's all I have in the world. I need help."

He stared at me. It felt like hours. Was he assessing the risks, weighing if there was enough good in it for him?

"Please. You know this is right. You said you owed me. Help."

His hand closed about mine. He took my coins and put them in his pocket. "Let's go."

For once I liked that he didn't ask questions. When he returned dressed in his white breeches, I knew things would be all right.

He offered me a blanket, one of Mamaí's that he'd bought. He draped it over my torn tunic. It hurt to climb into that dray, to sit on that hard seat, but I needed Cells to drive fast and wild.

In a blink, we were in town.

Crowds buzzed, milling in the Marketplace. With the big boat in the harbor sailing England's red-blue-and-white flag, I knew more people would be sold today. It was bittersweet that a slave ship would be the reason we had more time.

Cells parked in a field off the main road and tossed the reins into my damp fingers. "Stay here. If things get rough, you head to my land."

"I'm not leaving here without you or Kitty."

A look, then a mumbled prayer or curse crossed his lips. "Then stay put."

He pushed back his black hat, a tricorn with high sides and at the front a cockade of leather ribbons forming a knot. The fancy man straightened his tan pleated coat and walked across the graveled road to join the men and women in the square.

Cells disappeared among the planters and gawkers who came to laugh and lust at the chattel.

The breeze smelled of mushrooms. That was the horrid palm oil they slathered on the captives. Beautiful black and brown and tan bodies stood glistening in the sun waiting their turn on the stone platform. Oiled up and shining, these stars, the bits of glass were brought up one by one and sold.

After twenty, I lost count. The jeers from the crowd stuck in my chest, falling deeper into the pit of pain, that hole in my soul. I couldn't breathe.

Ducking my head into my lap, I sobbed onto my bruised hands. I only stopped crying, stopped remembering last night, when it was my sister's turn.

She looked small. They turned her, prodding her forward like livestock.

Everything in me hurt anew.

"Twenty." That voice sounded like Cells.

More bids came. He wasn't the top bidder anymore.

Had he given up?

In my heart, I tried to hold on to hope. I pulled Mamaí's rosary from my pocket. I begged that Cells for once would be a man I could trust.

MONTSERRAT 1770: FINDING FAVOR

The breeze, the steady afternoon breeze, swept over the Marketplace. I sat with my heart in my throat watching my sister be sold off.

"Fifty pounds!"

That voice was Cells's. He hadn't given up.

But then another bid fifty-five.

The numbers dueled. It finally stopped with Cells calling out seventy-six pounds.

That was all my money plus more. Sixteen pounds I did not have, that was the difference in keeping my sister.

Cells had won, and he led Kitty by her tied ropes from the Marketplace. When they crossed the road and stood by the carriage, he put his coat on her, then lifted my sister to me.

My friend climbed into the driver's seat. I put my hand on his arm. I stared into his gentle pale eyes.

He put my palm to the seat. "It's not safe."

The man snapped his reins and made the beast move.

I untied my sister and hummed to her.

She didn't sing back. I stopped too.

It was a long silent drive before we made it to Cells's house. Kitty jumped when he tried to help her down.

"I have you, Kitty. It's me, Dolly. I'll protect you."

She looked at me with soulless eyes.

"Inside, Dorothy. It's not safe. I need to hear the rest of your plan."

Muscles aching, maybe ripping, I struggled but carried my swallow into his house.

"Take her to the small bedroom down the hall. Get her cleaned up. You clean up too. I can't stand to see you like this."

He walked away.

Part of me felt horrible for making him choose. Part of me hoped this might help him stay out of the lukewarm spittle the priest preached about.

Hobbling all the way, I fetched water from the pump room and gathered towels.

I took away Cells's stained jacket and mopped at the rope burns on her wrists. "I'm here, Kitty."

When I cleaned her cuts, I noticed a discharge near her thighs.

Kitty's terror had been complete. She'd suffered so. Mamaí had put the valerian tincture in my sack. I wondered about giving Kitty some of that root to sleep, but I wouldn't trap her in a nightmare. I might take some, once I knew we were safe. I was used to the terror that filled my lids.

"Dorothy," Cells called from the hall.

I kissed Kitty's brow. "You're safe now, sister. You're safe. I'm in the hall."

She sobbed. "I want to be safe. I want . . . Never safe again."

Kitty's death grip on my hand churned up those tears I thought I'd spent. I pried her fingers free. "Just be a minute."

My sister pulled her head into the blanket, and I walked away with my heart under my feet, trampled under my sandals.

"Yes." I leaned back against the door.

Cells put his hand on his hips. "Dolly, as long as Nicholas is alive, he'll hunt you. You did leave him alive?"

My body started trembling. "Yes. I hit Nicholas, burnt up his things. Once his head's not thick, he'll figure things out. Oh, goodness. He'll be here. Where else would I go?"

Cells's lips opened, then pressed closed.

"I'll be in the stocks and sold. I don't have any more money to give you to buy me. I owe you sixteen pounds for Kitty."

"You owe me nothing. I just repaid that favor long ago with interest."

Cells clasped my shoulder right on a bruise. I yelped and clasped my mouth.

"That bastard."

"I don't care about him. I have to get Kitty away from here."

Cells did care. He looked like I felt inside, how I wanted to set Pa's owl house ablaze just to watch Nicholas die.

"He always wins. Cells, you've done enough. I should go to Mamaí, tell her my sister is safe, and wait to be hauled away."

He blocked my path. "No. You just freed your sister. And you own Kitty. You just gave me the money like a buyer's agent."

The thoughtful look in Cells's eyes gave him away. He had a plan. I wondered if it were the same as mine. Who would be brave enough to say it?

He thumbed his lips and left the begging to me.

"Take us to Demerara. Cells, take us, Kitty and me, now."

"You want me to help you run? Runaway slaves could be killed if they are caught. I could lose a lot, too."

"I'll be killed if I stay. Nicholas has already put a gun to my head. And last night he showed me again how he'll treat his chattel."

I lifted my blouse and exposed my bruised stomach, the cuts to my breasts. "Nicholas did this."

Cells closed his eyes. "Put your clothes back on. Go clean yourself."

"The brute will kill me. Or I'll kill him. That God you keep praying to wouldn't want me to murder."

"You can't be selective about faith, Dolly."

"And you can't be selective about right and wrong. Take us to Demerara. I'll work for you twice as hard to pay you back."

He started to his study. "I'm crafting a bill of sale to account for the money you gave me for Kitty."

"Who's going to award the purchase of an enslaved person to another one?" I clasped my fingers like a prayer. "Please. Nicholas will find a way to punish you if he figures out you bought Kitty for me."

Something crept across Cells's face that didn't quite look like guilt. Maybe it was a realization that Nicholas would make things difficult for him.

"Help us or take me back to Nicholas. Watch him beat me until I submit. Watch him press his knees—"

Cells clamped my mouth. "Stop. I beg of you, stop."

"What is your God telling you to do? To walk away or take me and Kitty to safety? Nicholas knows where to find me. The only man I trust is here."

Cells paced. "He knows I see your pa in passing, that I've done deals with Kirwan. Maybe I can tell him that his father and I agreed on your sale to me. But what about leaving your mother and your baby?"

"Mamaí will keep Lizzy until everything is safe."

"I have some thinking to do. Please go wash. I don't want that stench of Kirwan in my house."

He pushed past me and went into the hall.

I went back to Kitty. I washed my bruises, scrubbed everything Nicholas touched.

I didn't know if I'd ever remove his scent. From my sack, I put on a fresh tunic, then crawled onto the bed.

When I put my arms about Kitty, she cried. I hummed to her until she slept.

Closing my eyes, I hoped the next face I saw was Cells's, standing in the doorway telling me he'd do what was right and take us to Demerara.

PART TWO

My living

Learning to love me was hard.

DEMERARA 1771: NEW ROLE

The windows of the Hermitage were fantastic, the ones in Cells's study more so. I put my cloth to the louvered shutter, dusting it as part of my housekeeping routine. The slats moved as I brushed them, allowing more light, more views of the distant river. The Demerari River stirred brown and white, allowing flat-bottomed boats to transport goods to the mainland of the colony. Some of those *goods* looked like me, black and scared, just no pregnant belly.

Tapping down the Demerara shutters, I closed the sash window, then swiped at the glasses, twelve rectangular pieces separating me from the outside. Never touched such, was never close enough to put my fingers to them. Pa's owl house just had shutters. Mamaí's hut . . . I'd have to call what we had a hole in a mud plaster wall. Our shutters were just worn boards that shielded us from the rain.

Putting my forehead against a pane, I felt the strength of it, cold and distant from the streaks of the lawn exposed by the louvers. The land—trimmed with white hibiscus and thin wisps of fever grass—looked like I'd fallen into one of those books Pa read. In my dreaming head, I imagined this. Here at the Hermitage, Cells's Hermitage, I could go outside and smell the sweet honey of the flowers and hear the hummingbird's song as he nipped at diamond petals.

Mamaí would love to grow plants here.

Tears streamed. My insides wept, too, for my mother, my Lizzy. How could I enjoy being safe and protected in Demerara when they were trapped on Pa's plantation?

"Dolly?"

I startled and hit the glass a little.

Black tricorn hat in hand, a new low one with short sides, Cells stood at the door. He had on his beige sporting coat and dark pantaloons. That was his dress for exploring the colony, all the untamed land of this new world. Not sure how he'd succeed in the stifling heat all covered up.

"Dolly, are you all right?"

Moving from the window, I shifted my swollen belly. "Did you need something, sir?"

"We haven't been talking much. Very little since you and Kitty came to the Hermitage."

"Just moving a little slow. I think I slept wrong."

He came inside, his eyes squinting, looking gray like the day. "Didn't know there was a right or wrong way to sleep."

Not ready to hear another lecture or to pretend the tension between us wasn't my fault, I turned to the window and adjusted the velvet curtains.

"Lots of clouds, sir. It's going to rain. Make sure you keep that hat on tight. I know how you love your hats."

He moved behind me to his polished walnut desk and swiped the surface. "No dust, even when you are at the uncomfortable stage of your confinement."

"Of course. I don't want you to find me lacking. More lacking."

"I don't, Dolly. We've spoken of sordid things in the past. We needn't say more."

There was judgment in his tone, and it stoked my temper. I had been reckless when Kitty and I first came to the colony. The moment I knew I had another of Nicholas's babes in me, I went a little crazed. I spent days working hard at Cells's plantation, then danced nightly at the mulatto balls with sailors. At the brothels by the shore, I sold my worthless body.

It wasn't smart.

It earned money, which I needed for manumission. But truthfully, it was a punishment to my spirit. I didn't see me as good. Cells would never see me that way either.

Sighing, forcing guilt out of my lungs, I rolled up my dusting cloth. "I'm almost done in here."

"Maybe I should stay at the Hermitage today. You might need me later."

"What? I don't need no one. Definitely no watcher."

He rubbed his neck, and I regretted my words.

The gnawing pain to my back drew me from his gaze to the papers on his desk. Things had become awkward between us. He acted like my father when we first arrived, fretting over my sorrow and moods. Then he tried brotherly advice when my temper flared or I was caught leaving the Hermitage.

Now I was too big to slip away.

What was left for us? Nothing but employer and maid.

"Are you in pain, Dolly?"

"No." I tweaked his pile of parchments. His invoices and political letters seemed a safer place to put my attention. "I don't need special favors or anything. I'm trying to do better."

"You can be more at ease. Rest. I've more servants. My land here is thriving, much better than Montserrat. I knew it."

"More servants? Enslaved or free?"

He laid his coat on the chair, then carefully placed his hat on the desk. "I hire what's necessary. I always have."

That was his justification to own people? "I suppose you have to hire out often with all the settlers building up Demerara."

"Labor is in demand. The farther inland more so. This place will be a boon."

"And the status of owning land and people, that's power. Something an ambitious man needs."

"Nothing wrong with ambition. I remember you had ambition, too."

Had.

Did Nicholas beat it out of me? I hid night terrors from Kitty. My sister was a shell, quiet, barely there. I wasn't much better. Fear of seeing Nicholas's ugly face, that he'd jump from the shadows with slave catchers, should make me cautious, should lodge into my chest and make me settle.

But I couldn't be still. That's when the memories, the death masks came at me the worst. I couldn't breathe.

"Dolly—"

My fisted hand slammed the papers I'd stacked. "I had dreams, but I'm disqualified because of my mistakes. I whored. I did anything to forget the feel of him."

The blank look in his hazel eyes forced his lips to a line. He stepped closer. "You still have the world waiting for you. You're a little girl put in a woman's circumstances."

"Is that how you see me? I thought you said I was brave."

"You are that. Bold and daring, but sulking because I disagree with your choices shows your age."

"Almost fifteen, about to be a mother again, I'm old." I gasped from the needle-sharp pressure hitting my spine. "Maybe you're the child. You're mad at the things I've done. You can't forgive me."

He hovered, and I stayed in his shadow, unafraid. Cells wasn't Nicholas. He'd never strike me for saying my piece.

"There's a difference between disappointed and mad."

"Seems you get the luxury of that distinction."

Cells's sigh sounded exhausted. He moved to the grand window, tugging off his riding gloves. "I hate inclement weather."

"You mean bad weather?"

"Yes."

"Bad weather keeps your family from coming from Barbados."

His stare met mine, but his face was half fire, half hailstorm. "I built this house and rebuilt the one in Montserrat. But the Cells of Europe don't think it's good enough. My aunts in Barbados are too old to travel."

"Pity."

Now his gaze was full fire. "None required."

"I keep saying things wrong. You must miss your family like I miss Mamaí and Lizzy. Like I miss you."

"Me?" He tilted his head my direction then looked down. "I'm right here."

"We're at odds. I miss the friend I had in Montserrat."

He pressed his lips together, then shifted in his glossed black boots. "The one you couldn't rely upon. I think those were your words."

"Words of that little girl you're mad at? If you listened to her again, she'd tell you she was sorry."

He reached for my hand. I winced a little, but it was the pain in my back, not him. "I remember her being rightfully angry."

"She wants forgiveness. Forgiveness for drawing you into things you didn't want a part of. Forgiveness for going to the brothels, for acting wild, for being full of rage."

"It's done, Dolly."

"I've stopped going to the docks and can't huckster with this big belly." Agony, sharp and searing, hit my spine. I bent, bunching up my snug green pull skirt. "Sorry."

Cells slid one arm about my back, like he knew my knees would give way.

I fell against him.

"You're having pain, labor pains, Dolly."

"If I die, don't be haunted by my death mask."

"Don't believe in those things. Good Catholic boys don't. I'm still your friend. I'm helping. This baby's coming."

Cells scooped me up. "Polk! Mrs. Randolph."

His steward didn't answer. Nor did the fussy chef, Mrs. Randolph.

"Haven't seen them, Cells." My voice was a sad whimper.

My water burst. This didn't feel like the last birth, but I hadn't fought Nicholas as hard as I had in Pa's study.

"Where's Mrs. Randolph? Polk!" He carried me to my room.

My sister sat on the bed stitching a baby blanket. Her eyes were like saucers.

"Kitty," Cells said, "do you know where Polk or Mrs. Randolph is?"

She shook her head.

Cells strengthened his hold as every muscle in my body clenched. "Go get Polk for your sister."

Kitty didn't move.

"Please, sis." I moaned. This was hard for her. Poor Kitty stayed in this room. Fear kept her there, but I needed her to go, 'cause I might die. "Be brave for me."

My sister nudged forward, then ran.

Cells set me on my feet, but I leaned firmly against him with his arms about my middle. "I'm going to have to be a midwife today if Mrs. Randolph's not here."

"Oh, no you're not."

"We have to get that baby out. Who else?"

There was no one else. People died if the baby didn't turn. I'd seen that in the sick house.

I cried and Cells held me tighter.

"I don't want to die with dreams stuck in me."

"Dolly, you and this baby will be fine. You hear me? Now wiggle. That's how the Egyptians birth, especially their queens."

"Wiggle?"

"Make those hips work. I've seen you dancing as you dust."

My tears turned to laughs, and I held Cells like he was mine and this baby was his.

"I'm not going anywhere, girl."

Polk, the biggest, brownest bald-headed man I'd ever seen came into the room. "Massa Cells, what's going on? Oh, Lort. She's going to blow."

"I need you to find Mrs. Randolph, or you and I and Kitty are delivering this baby."

"No. I'll wiggle this one out first before I be showing you two anything."

Polk started laughing and slapping his foot. "She's out in the plantation. She left half an hour ago."

"Kitty, bring the sharpest knife from the kitchen. Polk, take the carriage and scoop Mrs. Randolph up and bring her here. If the baby can't wait, I'll use a chair and help that baby find the way. Matter of fact, go get one now."

Polk ran and brought one of the ornate carved chairs from the dining room.

Cells sat and put me in his lap spreading his legs wide. If anything dropped, nothing would get caught.

"Oh, Massa is going back to the slave field for this birth."

"Polk! Go!" Cells had a growl in his tone.

His steward fled.

"And Queen Cleopatra was known to do this, Dolly. I did a great deal of study when I lost my son."

"What!" I screamed again, part pain of the labor, part my surprise at Cells having a family. He never talked of one, never brought them here or to Montserrat. "Son? You had a boy and Mrs.?"

"I lost everything when he died."

Everything meant all was lost. I felt for him, but the next tremor in my gut had me wiggling.

"Don't leave me, John Coseveldt Cells. Don't talk about anything you see either. No gossip."

His fingers held about my belly. "I won't, Dolly."

If embarrassment didn't kill me, I'd live a long life.

Yet nothing seemed more right than Cells holding me, being with me for this birth.

DEMERARA 1771: NEW FEELINGS

Polk picked up his fiddle and played it in the yard behind the kitchen. Sitting on the steps with the last of the day's sun brightening the dusky sky, I admired the vast land of Cells's Hermitage. His fields had cane, beautiful green shoots denser than all Montserrat. The red rich mineral soil here blessed him more than the ash-gray dirt of home.

Cells made rum with his cane, not sugar. That seemed the right choice, one that would have been difficult in Catholic Montserrat.

Good cane shouldn't be for the devil's liquor, they'd say.

I missed the thick trees and hills, the outside worship of God. And the hymns. Cells sung to my baby Charlotte words to the hymn Mamaí had given to me and Kitty.

Rop tú mo baile.

Didn't know what it meant, but it made being at the Hermitage feel right and holy.

"Come on and dance, Miss Dolly." Polk had taken off the ebony mantle he wore indoors, exposing a brilliant white shirt.

Nice man. Full of life, his slick bald head perspired in the dry heat as he plucked that horsehair bow. I heard sorrow in his melody, then a peek at triumph—something distant and joyous.

I didn't know this tune, but I felt it gnawing at my gut, and I didn't want just a peek at joy. I wanted it all.

I'd started dreaming again, now that I knew Charlotte would live. My healthy baby loved music. She smiled as Kitty and I hummed over her in the beautiful mahogany cradle with filigreed sides that Cells offered.

Kitty guarded Charlotte always.

My sister was getting taller, but her mind didn't dream, not like mine. She was still a little girl, still stuck in yesterday, the day before the horror of the Marketplace.

My little swallow had begun to heal. She was a little more confident being outside, but I doubted I'd ever again see the bravery she possessed when she attacked Nicholas. Her sparkle had been stolen. I didn't know how to get it back.

"Come on now, Miss Dolly," Polk called. "Kick up those heels."

Mrs. Randolph came out of the kitchen. "Leave her be. Jumping about in the heat will make her wilt."

"I'm not that delicate, ma'am, but the music is good."

The housekeeper, a fancy word for cook, washerwoman, and everything else to keep a house, was a tall woman with short-cropped curly hair. She seemed suspicious of me, always eyeing me when I took Cells his supper. She didn't like when he and I had long talks about Demerara politics. She didn't want me here at all.

A few of the field hands and one of the young managers came up to this wide open space.

Polk played and played.

Soon, a crowd of people arrived from the fields and provision grounds. Everyone danced.

Cells spent over the clothing allotment. Women wore the more costly linen than osnaburg. No one was without shoes.

Some of his laborers were free, most weren't. Yet free and enslaved all joined hands, jumping and laughing. Cells was a good owner, if there was ever a thing such as a good owner of men.

Did these people not yearn for freedom? Many spent their leisure day fishing in Hobabo Creek beyond the fields, not trying to earn more money.

Polk stomped his feet and played on, his tune loud, proud, and joyous.

Was my tapping toe a traitor to what I knew? With a change in ownership or overseer all this perceived joy could go away.

Wouldn't I still be stupid and happy waiting on Pa, if not for Nicholas's lusts?

Mrs. Randolph picked up the scarf that fell from my braids and gave it to me. "With all the head swaying, maybe you should be dancing. You're not feeling poorly?"

"No, ma'am. I'm good." A sigh left me as I retied my hair. "They all look happy."

Maybe it wasn't my place to ask or cause trouble planting seeds when I myself wasn't free, when I couldn't provide for Kitty or Charlotte if I left Cells's protection.

Cells didn't own me. But if Nicholas floated up that Demerari River—

"Come on, girlie."

I jumped and almost fell off the steps when she touched my shoulder. "Mrs. Randolph, you frightened me."

"Your head was somewhere else. Are you sleeping more, now that the baby sleeps through the night?"

"A little more, but it's never enough."

She patted her hips to Polk's rhythm. Her white apron with frills swung from side to side and her long gray skirt stayed full and fluffy. "You can't sit like a bump on a log." Mrs. Randolph stretched her bronzed hands to me. "Polk is cutting a fine fiddle. You work hard, now dance hard."

Linking my palms to hers, we twirled. Round and round, until my lungs were full, heady. The rhythm felt good.

Except for the Egyptian wiggling I'd done to birth Charlotte, I hadn't done much moving. It felt wrong since I did that in the brothels.

Closing my eyes, I let the beat take over. The rhythm moved slow and silky along my skin, sweeping against my bosom, slipping to my thighs.

We whirled faster. My fine hair fell out of my scarf again. It whipped and teased my nose.

But this was joy.

Who knew my body needed this? To be happy, I needed to feel a tune from my crown to my knowing toes. So much healing was in the tempo.

The music stopped midspin.

Gasps.

Eyes moved to the kitchen door.

Mrs. Randolph released me and I almost fell.

"Mr. Cells," she said smoothing her apron. "We didn't think you'd be back this early."

Poking from his coconut-colored jacket were frilly white sleeves, the same hue as his long coconut-colored waistcoat. His tidy white pantaloons were tucked nicely at his stockings. He looked very elegant, elegant and stiff.

"The meeting was abysmal, ma'am. I made my apologies early and headed out before the dinner."

He tapped his foot. His sleek black silk slippers held shiny silver buckles. Shame such pretty things hadn't danced tonight.

With a hand to his brow, he scanned the area, shaking his head toward Polk. "Such temptation here. And alas the temptation of smuggled champagne was not enough to keep me."

Champagne? I'd heard it was something the planters coveted. Yet, he returned to us.

Descending the steps in a slow gait, he steepled his fingers against his lips. "This is what you all do while I'm away?"

The air was silent until Polk laughed. "Massa, you know how you were when you were young." He started plucking his fiddle. "You were wild and fun."

Cells wild? No.

Polk began another rousing tune, faster than the last. He stopped and put the bow string to his side. "I suppose you prefer this."

The man plucked the fiddle, moving his nimble finger across the chords; the thing now purred. The music had no regular beat. It could be a hymn. Yes, definitely something for church.

Then Polk bowed and spun like a puppet on string. His shirttails popped out. He looked like a rooster. "That's the music of your parties, sir."

Cells's face was blank, then he started to laugh. "You do a fine minuet, sir. I believe you missed your calling. You could be a virtuoso violinist."

He clapped slow and low at first, then it picked up speed. "Begin again. I'm not one to ruin a party."

Polk grinned, and there may have been a wicked gleam to his jet eyes. "Show us that fancy minuet, Massa."

"I'll need a partner for that."

His gaze was on me, but he turned a little to Mrs. Randolph. "Do you remember the minuet, ma'am?"

"I do, sir, but it's a dance for you young people. Try Miss Dolly."

He made a gracious bow to the housekeeper then slipped back to me. "Shall we, Dolly? Polk, do add a little allemande in the end."

Tossing his jacket to Mrs. Randolph, he waved at me to follow and centered himself on the flat ground. "Are you up to this? Dancing with everyone looking?"

The challenge in his voice was new. This was the second time he admitted to watching me dance in his study.

"Well, Dolly?"

I'd not miss anything that had him cheered. He'd started his day frowning in his letters at his breakfast table.

"Yes, I'll minuet with you."

"Good, do as I do but opposite. We are like a mirror, like two halves of the same. And when I draw near to you, you do the same."

That was an easy command. Life and death had bonded us. Mrs. Ben's death mask was ours, and watching him raise up my Charlotte, fingering the spittle out of her mouth to make her breathe, proud like he was her pa—that should make us inseparable.

"Wait."

His head tilted. "What?"

I reached for the ebony ribbon tying his dark hair. It swung free like my braids. "Now, we are truly a mirror."

His locks were shoulder length and ready to move. "Start, Polk."

The music began, but the rhythm, and Cells's haunted hazel eyes, had my heart racing.

He stepped back. "Watch and mirror."

I didn't need to be told that, not the way his cheeks flushed, not the way his gaze burned.

Could he be mirroring my thoughts of me and him and holding each other? Then there wouldn't be six feet between us.

"Show me, Cells."

"You . . . you stay there. Watch my feet, do the opposite."

He crossed his heels and came forward like he walked suspended on a thin branch.

I did the same.

"I'll stretch my hand to you, Dolly. Grasp it, but take it slow."

I did.

Our fingers touched, and we spun.

"Now, Dolly, we allemande."

Polk sped up the tune.

Cells bent to me and grasped my fingers, rotating me like the figure eight, arm over arm.

The beat matched my heart, thumping hard. One glance away from the heat of this man, I saw everyone dancing.

His grip tightened and my attention went back to Cells.

He knew I'd stopped concentrating, but he couldn't guess that it would be better for us if I didn't focus on him, the press of his lips.

Everyone kept moving and spinning. The blue sky turned purple and red. It was fully dusk, and I didn't want this to end.

Fingers laced with his, drawing me to him . . . I wanted Cells, but for Kitty and Charlotte's sake, I couldn't afford to reach for this distant star and miss.

"You're a good dancer, Dolly. I'll have to show you more sometime."

"Will it have more hand-holding like the allemande?"

That half-smirky smile showed, then he released my palm. "Perhaps. I'll be in my study working; bring me tea later when you finish here."

He bowed and wiped at his neck. He took his ribbon and jacket from Mrs. Randolph and went inside.

The housekeeper clicked her tongue. "I'll take him tea, Dolly. You go see about that newborn baby. Know your place and don't go trying to elevate yourself."

Her gape could swallow me whole. I stopped in my steps. "Yes, ma'am."

Yet my traitorous toe tapped the new dance I'd learned.

Mrs. Randolph saw the flame growing and burning in me. I wondered if Cells had, too.

DEMERARA 1772: NEW DUTIES

The music of angels filtered into my room, seeping beneath the crack in my door. The musicians for Cells's party had started. This rhythm like Polk's minuet had me swaying.

My one-year-old, Charlotte, finally went to sleep, suckling her thumb. The perfect baby with big mammee apples for cheeks, round and pretty. She had Mamaí's brown eyes. She was a little darker than Lizzy, or at least how I remembered her.

A wave of sadness roared through me. My Lizzy turned three a few days ago. Almost two years had passed since I last kissed her cheeks.

I wanted Charlotte and Lizzy to grow up together. I wanted Mamaí. I needed her to mother me and Kitty again. It was hard being a mother to my sister and my daughter.

Kitty was still nine in her head, or maybe younger. Her conversation hadn't grown up. At times it seemed she was stuck in the stocks at the Marketplace. Maybe she was when she closed her eyes.

I had no right to tell someone how long to grieve, but I didn't know if I was enough for my sister, that I'd done enough to help her grow and feel safe and want to live life outside our room.

My dreams hadn't left me. I wanted my own. I wanted to free us all and have a big house and land. Then Kitty could have the leisure of staying young forever.

"Dolly, you look sad." Kitty was on the floor playing with the polished wooden doll Cells bought her. It had moving rag arms and hinged knees. On its limbs hung the same boned corset and big-skirted petticoat that the massa of the Hermitage had given me to wear.

I swung my hips from side to side. This dome-shaped cloth swallowed my thighs whole. My new dress was big. I think I liked big.

No one would miss me when I entered a room. "I'm well, sis. I'm just getting used to all these clothes. I want to look right for him."

"You do. No fretting, Dolly. Tonight is Cells's party," she said. "You've practiced serving tea. You'll be fine."

Tugging at my jet skirt and off-white tunic, I watched the fabric billow. Cells procured this specifically for me, nothing handed down. *Procured* was one of the new words he taught me in his study. He shared many in his readings to us when he returned from church on Sunday.

An Anglican church, a building of wood and glass, not outdoors. He sought the English God like his British friends that arrived at the Hermitage tonight.

"You look very pretty, Dolly. Finish up and come back and play with me."

"Thank you, Kitty, but I don't know how long this will go."

I'd earned a chance to serve at one of his parties, not just spy on them from the kitchen. Cells trusted me, to allow me around these politicking fellows.

That meant more than dressing pretty.

I smoothed my starched apron. It made a snap sound as I tied the bands. "Kitty, you're going to be good and watch Charlotte?"

"Yes. No one will take her. Here, Dolly." Kitty gave me a necklace. "I made it for you."

The cowrie shells were glossy, painted red and gold and strung on a thin strip of leather. It looked like Mamaí's rosary beads that I prayed over, mentioning her, mentioning Lizzy. "It's lovely, sis."

Cells's other servers wore no jewelry, but I didn't want to be like the rest.

Putting on the necklace, I stared at my figure in the mirror. I wasn't skin and bones. My bosom was thick. My waist showed again, small and tight. This outfit missed the curves of my hips and thighs.

These colors, dull and dark, were dreary against my skin—it wasn't right. The skirt had no print or stripes. This couldn't be how to fit into Cells's world.

Charlotte awoke and pulled herself up on the side of her crib. She blew me a gummy kiss. "Mama."

Such a pretty voice.

Kitty leapt up. "She sounds like our mama. Like a humming-bird."

I fanned at my eyes. Charlotte sure did. Just like Mamaí.

Not crying or dwelling in my sorrow, I forced a smile and looked down at Charlotte. "It looks like a tooth is going to come."

Wishing I had Mamaí's knowledge of tinctures, I wanted to make something for Charlotte. I didn't want her in pain.

My baby lifted her arms, and I scooped her up and snuggled her close.

"Will Mr. Cells read to us tonight?" Kitty asked. "When his party's done?"

"He . . . he will probably be too tired."

Kitty's face held a frown, but it was a lot for her to look forward to Cells. Maybe my frets about my sister were just my own.

Charlotte smiled and dribbled and blew air through her lips. I was sure my baby liked Cells reading to us too.

"You were up late with Mrs. Randolph pressing tablecloths. You should be a part of the fun."

"No, Kitty. I work hard because I want to learn. Today, I serve. Someday it will be my party. I dream about us having a house like this."

"You should be a guest at this one. Mr. Cells should let you since you make him happy."

"He's happy with my work. I have to earn our ransom. I need to earn a hundred and fifty pounds more than the fifty I've saved."

Bending over the cradle, I put my Charlotte down. "Kitty's going to take care of you while I work."

"Work. Work." Charlotte put her thumb in her mouth again.

"Yes, your mother has to work. Thank you, Kitty." I saluted her and went to the kitchen.

Mrs. Randolph was tipping from this pot to that one. The smells.

When Mamaí cooked in the owl house she used one big fired bowl and cooked such wonderful stews of salt pork and potatoes. This kitchen had dozens of bowls and pots, each offering hints of onions or rosemary or ginger, or roasted meats.

Polk was in his spot by the cakes, fanning to keep the bugs away. "That planter's widow will be here."

"What?" I covered my mouth and wiped platters.

Waving her spoon at him, Mrs. Randolph had a big frown. "He can't be a hermit forever. No matter what he says. Men of his stature have two families, one in Europe and one here."

Polk swatted at nothing, but it made the smell of honey reach me. "Well, he likes playing family with you, Miss Dolly."

I shook my head like it would fall off. "Hush, Polk."

The crazy man tapped my shoulder. "Maybe you can convince him otherwise. That princessy woman gets in here and the place will be like everything else *they* touch."

"I'm here to work. I'm going to check the dining room. I'll take the soup tureen."

Grabbing up the fine white pot, I repeated that lie and walked down the hall filled with paintings of Cells's ancestors, pale white faces that surely didn't want the likes of dark me having thoughts about him. I stopped at the one I always did, the only portrait of a woman. Her features were unremarkable, but her happy eyes and the fine hat she sported told me she was somebody.

I wanted to be her. She looked as if she had power.

Hastening my steps, I went into the dining room.

The big, magical place made me gleeful. I had worked hard this week polishing the silver, positioning it perfectly around the blue plates. I set the soup in the middle for servers to reach and fill the bowls with ease.

The windows and double doors were open, allowing the cooler evening air inside. The bright white tablecloths lay on the three long tables, each sitting twelve. Many important people from across the colony would attend the Hermitage tonight.

Along with the planter woman who could change everything.

Was I ungrateful not wanting things to change or to hope no one could claim the most-sought-after bachelor in Demerara?

I went back to the kitchen two more times and carried the other tureens, placing them on the remaining tables.

Perfect.

Music. Music found me. It came from the adjacent drawing room.

I peeked through the open door. From this angle, I saw a man with fine sable skin plucking a bow across the fiddle.

Getting a little bolder, I stepped more into the entrance.

My eyes went to the lit candles and the large vases of pink and white lilies and cream-colored lotus flowers. The scent of flowers fought the fishy tallow smell of the burning wax.

The sweet fragrance might not be from the plants. It might be from the ladies.

I hadn't seen this many women, well-to-do stylish women, anywhere, all wearing bonnets or headpieces. One had a pile of straw . . . fake hair, powdered and curled.

I stepped back, again hiding myself in the dining room.

That was Cells's world in that room. His was fancy people, people with money.

My friend was seated in the last row of chairs.

A young blond woman, the planter's widow, slipped her arm about the massa of Hermitage. She was bold, sitting close to him, but he didn't seem to mind.

Her head bobbled with a pouf on top. The hat was made of satin with three swan feathers curled around it. Her big tresses might have powder too. There was no shine like when coconut oil dressed the hair.

I liked shiny, but those big curls might do well on my limp locks.

The widow's face was young with red dots on her cheek, but the white stuff in her hair made her look older. Was that what he wanted? Someone more mature and settled?

She leaned a little more toward him. She laughed at something. Probably one of his jokes.

Cells. Handsome, all in white.

A white frock jacket and long cream-colored waistcoat with silver and pearl buttons fell past his hips, covering his loose breeches. Only the onyx embroidery of spirals running down the length of his jacket held contrast. Mrs. Randolph complained something awful cleaning his white. *Rich folk white* she called it.

Cells led his guest through one of the massive doors out to his garden.

The woman on his arm stayed close as they walked. Would her hair powder leave a stain?

Probably.

She shouldn't be with him. She shouldn't.

I backed up, forcing myself not to run.

This was Cells's world, his night. I couldn't let my jealous thoughts ruin things.

DEMERARA 1772: NEW MONEY

Three months of the Hermitage hosting parties every week made me bone tired. Tonight's ball was no exception—demanding and tense, but I learned so much. My first moment to rest, I went to the porch. I breathed the cooler midnight air. Standing still after serving for hours, after watching Cells be attentive to the widow woman and toasting her, I felt numb.

Two men approached.

A young fellow slapped the other, the older one, on the back. "Foden, you all right? You need to get all the air you can."

"It's that perfume. Has my nose itching." He coughed and stood beside me near the railing and posts that framed the porch.

He looked to be choking.

"Sir, would you like me to get some water?"

The older man, the one with white hair who dragged a cane, craned his neck to me. "Yes, miss. And if you put some of Cells's rum in it, I'd be happier."

"You don't need rum," the younger man, a blond one, said.

"Thank you for your concern but this is between me and the young woman. Now, miss, please keep to your mission. Pay Captain Owen no mind. Half water, half rum."

I found a glass on the dining room table that looked untouched but saw no water. Thinking the man might choke while I dawdled, I went to Cells's study and got the bottle he kept behind his desk and poured half a glass. Not running, but definitely not shuffling, I returned to the gentleman.

None too soon. The old man shook his cane at Captain Owen, who I decided was handsome with his blondish-brown hair and scarlet jacket. "Sit, boy. Tell me about your latest scheme."

"No scheme, Mr. Foden, pure profit."

His voice was low and meant for Foden, but this captain's eyes were on me, following me as I brought the rum.

"See, this is what I call service. She knew I didn't really want the water."

The captain shook his head. "Do you remember what the physician said?"

"You mean the one I outlived? No. Miss, go get him a glass, too. Might make him settle and tell me his latest plan to use my money."

Owen's gaze stayed on my face like he knew me.

Fearing he recognized me from dancing at the shore, I looked to the floorboards. That was long ago. *Please don't know me from my sins.* "Did you want some, Mr. Captain? Rum?"

"My, you are beautiful. Your face has perfect symmetry. Those eyes are like painted glass."

My cheeks warmed not from embarrassment but joy. He liked the look of me. The old cistern song about not loving tar left my head, maybe for good. "Thank you. Is there anything I can get you, Captain?"

"Captain John Owen. And no, Miss . . ."

"Miss Dolly."

Owen hooked a hand to his lapel, fluttering his burgundy-cloth-covered buttons, and stepped forward. "Miss Dolly, maybe can you answer a question? Cells advises the council on the running of the colony. Has he mentioned a blockade?"

A blockade, one of those things Pa fretted. I shrugged then shook my head.

"See? No risk, Foden. The British won't cut the transport again. Everyone lost too much with embargoes during those last seven years of war."

From his emerald jacket with onyx threads anchoring bright silver buttons, the old man whipped a cigar, a fine roll of tobacco, then with the end cut and it stuck in his mouth, he patted his pockets. "Owen, your plan seems risky. You have a light, sir?"

The dinner was finished. Those candles on the table were wasting. "I'll get one and bring it to you."

Walking past Cells's study, I saw the door ajar. I heard voices, Cells and one, two other men buzzing.

"Mr. Van Den Velden," Cells said, "I'm simply making an observation or using common sense, as the American Thomas Paine might say. 'A long habit of not thinking a thing wrong gives it a superficial appearance of being right.'"

"You sound as if you oppose slavery, Cells."

This voice sounded more nasal than his other guest.

"I think it interesting that the Americans go to war for freedom. The Catholics want freedom from the restrictions the Anglicans have placed on their services and worship. They serve the same God but differ merely on administration."

"It's more than that. That pope can't be trusted."

"The Americans would say that about King George." Cells pointed his fingers. "Yes, where was I. Neither religions want to be enslaved themselves or to allow slaves to have autonomy over their bodies. Did you know what they call manumission? A ransom. You pay a ransom to free something captive, imprisoned."

Peeking, I saw Cells offering a brandy to Van Den Velden, a man with a rough iguana's nose.

Leaning forward and wearing a high powdered wig that surely itched, Van Den Velden took the glass. "Thank you. That seems a might pompous for a man whose numbers of enslaved are as many as mine. You're going to free them all right now to prove your point?"

Cells sat against his desk. He'd powdered his hair this evening too. It looked stiff and frizzy, like the others. Yet the embroidery on his waistcoat, down the length of his jacket, made him appear princely and handsome.

"Why would I do that when you two will just buy them up and use their talents to outproduce me? My rum is king, gentlemen. I want to keep it that way."

A second man, the nasal speaker, poked at the bookcase. "Then why talk of these radical things?"

This one wasn't Dutch or even Irish. It had to be one of the British men Cells sought to influence.

He tapped his writing blotter. "Just thinking out loud with two of the brightest men of my acquaintance. You both know I'm always looking for a way to increase efficiency. I think if we paid workers for their labor, that would bring more value as opposed to enslaved men slacking in their tasks to lower their ransom."

Van Den Velden finished his drink and stretched with his short arms to put the empty glass on the desk. "That's a radical idea, Cells. You sure you're not trying to get us to endorse upending our way of life?"

"Nothing of the sort. I believe in adhering to principles and good sense. I know things can become difficult for planters that *rebel*. I've watched the difficulties a few of the free colored planters have had when they resist becoming slaveholders."

The man at the bookcase blew smoke rings. "Cells, everyone knows you're liberal, but you take your questions too far."

They were making threats, but my friend was too kind to know it. I had to help him and burst into the room.

All the men stared.

Frowning, Cells waved me forward. "Yes, Miss Dolly, is there something you want?"

"Ummm. One of your guests, sir, needs a light for his cigar. I was going to get matches from the kitchen and wanted to know if there is anything you gentlemen needed."

"Well, look at the efficiency of this one," the bookshelf man said. "Maybe you have a point, sir."

With his sly half smile showing for a second, Cells reached into his desk and pulled out his silver box of matches. "Here you go. Return it and bring a service of tea. Does anyone need anything else from Miss Dolly? I employ her."

"She does seem efficient," Mr. Van Den Velden said rubbing his chin.

When no one responded, I curtsied like Mrs. Randolph taught me and backed into the hall and kept going until I was with the men on the porch. I took a match and struck it along the rail until the flame ignited. "Here, sir."

"Thank you again, Miss Dolly." Foden puffed on his cigar. "No wonder Cells is such a settled man. A housekeeper who can anticipate his needs before he asks. Delightful."

"I'm not the housekeeper, but a helper."

"Oh. Seems you've been trained well. I wish Cells hired out his Negroes. I'd have you at my estate in a second."

"Cells doesn't own me. I'm . . . employed. I can hire myself out."

Foden's bushy brows shot up. "Then name your price."

"Wait," the captain said. "I don't want Cells upset. He'll be my next investor after you."

The old man held his hand out to me. "When you get a chance, Miss Dolly, come to parcel 18, the Anna Catharina. Pass the Hobabo Creek's bend. If you hit the canal, you went too far."

"I'll make sure it's fine with Mr. Cells. Don't want you to be one of his enemies. I'm loyal to him."

Captain Owen came a little closer. Tall, assured in his stride, he stretched and folded his arms. "Cells has a loyal helper?"

"Don't all rich men?"

Owen started laughing. "Should've known you'd be smart. Everyone knows Cells has exquisite taste."

The smile the captain offered gave away everything; he thought I did more than housekeeping for Cells. He almost seemed jealous.

"Housekeeping. That's what I do. That's all, Captain."

"Easy, Owen," Foden said, still puffing away like a chimney or a volcano cone. "This young woman does her job. A good one from how Cells brags. I'm glad to have met Miss Dolly."

Music started up inside.

Foden rubbed his skull. "Oh, Lord. That Haskel woman is going to sing."

"No, she won't," the captain said. "She's trying to catch Cells, not chase him off."

The widow woman.

I couldn't stand here and let these men talk about Cells marrying. Yet maybe it was a godsend. No wife was going to let me stay while I made eyes at her husband.

"I've thought about it. I'll be at Anna Catharina estate on Saturday. I'll work the whole day. We'll discuss wages then. I must go get Mr. Cells's tea."

The older man nodded. "Oh, capital. A good housekeeper or helper is hard to find."

I curtsied and went inside. When I carried the tea past the drawing room, I saw Cells dancing with the widow in the center of the room, the only two dancing.

I wanted to be her. I wanted Cells to look at me like that.

But he wouldn't, not to an enslaved woman with no power or money.

Cells would marry again and that would be the end to my second family. I resolved to start building my *fhortún* faster. It was the only way to ensure that me and my *girls* would be fine.

DEMERARA 1773: NEW SPARK

Walls of water fell.

From the porch, the Hermitage must look like a castle set in a moat. The Demerari River might flood. Last year, Cells's Barbados was hit bad by the rainy season. Nevis, too.

He left several times to check on his property, but he came back hungry to see me. Well, it seemed that way with each lingering look.

He hadn't married that widow, but I needed to stop hoping to see love in his eyes.

Footfalls fell behind me. Cells. Had I dreamed him here?

The massa of the Hermitage came with a lantern onto the porch. "I thought you were here."

He was in his nightshirt. Long and flowing in the breeze. He looked tense, maybe flustered, with his face pink like he had a fever.

I held my breath and waited for him to tell me news of his engagement.

"Did you get Charlotte to settle, Dolly? She doesn't like storms."

My two-year-old ran through the halls like she owned them, like she was Cells's daughter. If I could build my coins, the child might never know she was born enslaved.

"Dolly, did she settle?"

"Sorry. Yes. She and Kitty are snuggled into my bed all covered up."

He set down his lantern and rubbed at his chin. His perfect mustache had curled, but his chin had bumps from his close shave. I noticed those now and again.

"Shouldn't you be in bed, Mr. Cells? You probably have a lot to do in the coming days."

He looked out in the night toward the river. "If it weren't raining, you'd see the fireflies dancing, flickering their lights about the far cannonball trees."

Those trees had pretty pink flowers and big bunches of brown fruits that grew like cannonballs, cannonballs caught in nets aboard the frigates. "Fireflies? Must look like embers from a blast. I remember those big ships near Montserrat shooting in the distance."

"You miss home, Dolly?"

Clasping my elbows, I nodded. "Mamaí and Lizzy."

"It's better that you're here. Safer. More fireflies, too. Their glow reminds me of your eyes, bright, buzzing."

The restless energy between Cells and me was as thick as the steam in the air.

I pulled my heavy apron off. I needed something to do with my hands, something other than reaching for his collar and shaking him. Why was he destroying our family?

"Dolly, I have something to tell you."

Twisting my apron almost to breaking, I dropped it. "Don't fret about me. I've been working for Mr. Foden. He says he'll let me and Kitty and Charlotte live with him."

"You're leaving?"

"I'll still work for you if the new Mrs. allows."

The thunder in his face cleared. "I'm not marrying again. The first was disastrous."

"Does the widow know?"

"She knows now."

I stared at the lantern he'd set by his bare feet. "But she's been attached to you for over a year."

"She was attached, but I wasn't."

"Seems a little cruel, Cells, to lead her on."

"Really. You truly think this? You're not happy with me either. Or has old Mr. Foden finally persuaded you with his money to be his?"

My head spun like he'd twirled me in the allemande. "He's a kindly employer like you, nothing more."

"That's the problem, Dolly." Cells put a palm to my cheeks. "I want more. I haven't been able to stop thinking of more. You're always on my mind."

I know I moved first. I reached for his shoulders. On tiptoes, I pressed my mouth to his. He held me, sculpting me to him. The chest that always offered comfort, offered heat. He kissed me slow, tasting my lips.

Then he moved away.

"Cells, is that what you've been afraid to tell me, that you want me? Afraid that I didn't want you, too?"

"No. I know I've turned you to me. But I'm older and allegedly wiser. You don't trifle with a friend, no matter how dear the woman."

"At least you see me as a woman."

"Goodness. Yes. Your beauty is beyond compare. But your spirit and drive is a flame. I've tortured myself wanting to be burned."

I wrapped my arms about his neck, reaching to capture his height, his heart, but he patted my hands away. "What I want is not good for us. You have dreams. I do, too. I could be a leader of this colony. I want power to match my wealth."

"You can't have that and me?"

"Men with Black wives or concubines don't gain power. Black doesn't gain power. It's a target. That's why the rebellions fail. The British, the Dutch, the French—all believe the same."

"Being with me means you don't get your dreams? I didn't think I was more powerful than you."

He bit his lip and looked away like the rain was more interesting than the passion in my eyes. "Dolly, I have to consider things long term. How does anything benefit me . . . or you?"

"You need to know what's in this for you to give in to desire? Lack of sleep is not a benefit."

"I don't sleep now." He sighed, his hands reaching for mine before he slapped them to his sides. "I need you to understand. And I don't want to push you away."

No. He'd just walk away.

"I'm lonely, and it's raining outside, and I have visions of touching you through the night. *Clagarnach* is Irish for the pounding of a storm on the roof. It's a lonely sound unless shared by two."

He ran his finger along his cloth buttons. "I know me. My wife said I was selfish, that I didn't think about the ways I hurt her. Dolly, I don't want that with you. You're the one bright spot in a great deal of darkness. My one best decision was to bring you here. We've been friends a long time. Desire will ruin it. Sometimes friendship is more."

He used a lot of words to say he wanted me, that he didn't want me, and that he was white and I wasn't.

I knew it.

I knew from the beginning. He was of one world and until I made my *fhortún*, I wasn't allowed. I'd always be looking and serving. Those weren't my dreams.

The sharp knot in my stomach didn't care much about his arguments. Yet I couldn't move from him. If I took a step, I could touch him. Like shaking a burning log or those cannon blasts, embers would fly.

"I'm going away. I have things to attend to."

"What? Where?"

"To England and Scotland. I'll return in a year."

"A whole year without you."

He picked up my palm, kissing it, then each knuckle. Those lips were soft and warm, tightening that knot inside me. Something would burst. Didn't want it to be my soul.

"When I return, if I'm in this same place of wanting you badly, needing to savor the taste of you, then politics be damned."

"Then I have to be in this same place, too, waiting on you?"

"It's selfish. I know. Much is at stake."

"Like what?"

His mouth opened, then his lips pressed closed. Something, some secret, was on his tongue. He looked at the rain and gripped his collar. "I need to be sure. You too. Seventeen, after all you've been through, is still young."

Eighteen to his thirty years would make things different? "Planters marry off their virgin daughters at fifteen. Colored girls have to wait for a kind lover? Sounds like you're testing my feelings."

"I'm testing me, Dolly. All the calculations and sacrifices I've made to secure my position can't be undone by a scrawny miss."

"Not scrawny. And you're calculating all the time, nor stiff either. You dance well enough when you're not politicking."

Something was hurting him. I saw it in his eyes. This was my chance to help him, to show him I could save him from these burdens. I stroked those buttons of his nightshirt. "You'll be everything that you want. You've made a name for yourself in Demerara. You'll be an adviser to the commanders or whoever leads the colony."

He clasped my hand, pressing it into his chest. "What gives you such confidence?"

"I overhear them speaking of you at your parties. And Mr. Foden thinks the world of you."

Cells's smile faded. "Foden thinks the world of you. He's in love with you."

"I hope he isn't the only man."

He chuckled with me, but I had begun to understand my power. Men, all men, saw something in me that they needed to possess. I'd only started to learn what I needed. "Foden's a nice old man, older than my father, but at least he's around."

"Foden would marry you and pay whatever you needed to free your family. I can give you the money, too."

"I have to earn it, or I'll just be an agent. An agent ain't free. Working for you and Foden has made a way for me to do it myself. You need to know I want you for you, not your means."

"You could be with Captain Owen. He has made no secret of desiring you."

"I'm not that little girl you befriended. I'm a grown woman. If I want companionship, I can get it."

He drew me close. His heart beat fast. The rhythm between us built again. "But you haven't."

"I haven't wanted anyone but you. I will have my own, independent of you. Your rum money can't last forever."

"Bite your tongue, Dolly."

I wouldn't back down from these feelings, and if he were going, I wanted him to remember why he had to come back.

Reaching up, I touched Cells's lips, traced the top and the bottom. The tender flesh went pink, then reddened like a red rose when my pinkie lingered.

His intake was sharp. He pressed a kiss to my palm, then to my wrist.

"It's raining, Coseveldt. The children are sleeping. We're two adults, awake and restless."

Drawing his head to mine, I tasted that mouth I teased.

Wanting all of him and needing no other woman or his dreams to take him away, I wrapped my arms about his shoulders. His palms lifted me high, sliding about my hips, dividing my layers of petticoats. He found my thighs, all my hidden curves.

The taste of him, rum and molasses was good. The pressure of his kiss was wonderful. His hold was tight, perfect.

Gobbling air, he set me down. "No, Dolly. No."

He wiped at his face. He was red, painted by my passion.

"Dolly. I have to take care of things. Then, if . . . when I come back, we can give in to these feelings."

"Dolly?" My sister's voice. Kitty stood at the door.

"Sis. Don't be scared."

Cells schooled his face like nothing had happened, like nothing had changed. "I leave in the morning, Dolly. Polk's taking me to the docks."

I hugged Kitty, putting my face into her braids. Her scalp smelled of coconut oil. "I'll be here a year, no more."

That was bold to say, but he had to know I wasn't one of those women who'd wait forever. And I wasn't Mamaí forced to let Pa into her bedroll.

"Take care, Dolly." His bare feet slapped away.

I had a piece of his heart. I knew it. I gripped it in my hand. Didn't know if I'd have to give it back.

DEMERARA 1774: NEW DAY

Mr. Foden had his spectacles on his nose in his huge poster bed. He'd finally drifted to sleep. I ran my polish cloth over the indentations carved in the walnut frame, something he'd imported from Europe.

Putting the rag in my pocket, I went to the silver service on his bed table. Heavy and solid, the filigreed metal was etched with a design of roses. I slipped my thumb along the initials at the bottom.

"You're smart enough to read better than you do."

"Takes a lot of concentration. Don't have time for all that. I've learned to manage."

He reached for my hand, and I gave it to him. He wasn't ashamed of things I didn't know. I understood many words, though most looked like squiggles, but I could read and write numbers.

Foden made my math sharper. He taught me about contracts and how to make sure they were good. He was better than my pa to me. Foden was my dearest friend.

"You need to rest, sir. You'll get over this cold and be ready for the harvest."

He sighed long. "I'm not afraid to die because I've lived. And don't fret about me. I have a lot more living to do. And I have plans for you, more bookkeeping. I'll see you tomorrow."

I nodded and picked up the tray. Easing out of his bedchamber, I took the service to the kitchen, to the servants who would watch him through the night.

With all my chores done, it was time to head to the Hermitage. The walk was an easy one. I did it twice a day and enjoyed my best thinking along the route.

The Demerari River stirred today, kicking up a soft breeze that cut through the heat. These layers of petticoats and the stays and chemise under my tunic added to my misery, but these were the clothes that freewomen wore. I'd earned the money for all of us. My family would be free. Mr. Foden would negotiate it. I'd ask him next week.

My pulse ticked up. It had been four years since I left Montserrat. I'm sure I could see Pa and not crumble. Nicholas, too . . . with Foden or Owen with me. They were dear men. Their attention kept my mind from missing Cells.

A year, one month, and two days had passed since he left.

We were done. Once free, I'd move forward. Sweet Captain Owen might be the one. If he weren't blond or told stupid jokes, he'd definitely be the one. His sad humor might be forgivable if he read like Mr. Foden.

I liked a man who read as much as I liked them smart. I wanted to learn. Cells wasn't the only smart man.

Demerara's sun cooked the dirt under my sandals. The light wind lifted the red dirt, and the grit tickled my feet as it flitted over my toes.

The clip-clop of horse hooves sounded behind me.

A carriage slowed, then stopped beside me. It was Polk. "Miss Dolly, can I give you a ride to the Hermitage?"

"My feet won't turn you down." I climbed in and pulled out the fan Cells sent six months ago. The lacy thing moved the air, keeping my layers of shifts from sticking to my skin.

Polk was an interesting man. He was free, freed for almost twenty years, and had worked for Cells almost as long. He had free sons and daughters who were artisans and blacksmiths.

"Miss Dolly, you determined to move out to Mr. Foden's?"

"Yes, Polk. I think I've used up enough of Cells's kindness."

"I don't know, Miss Dolly. He can be awful kind. How is Mr. Foden? I heard he's been sickly."

"Better. A little nursing and hot soup seemed to set him right. He wants a full-time housekeeper."

"You could be that at the Hermitage."

"Replace Mrs. Randolph? Never?"

"You got that right, Miss Dolly. It would just be nice to have you and the children and Mrs. Randolph."

I breathed a heavy huff. "Nice doesn't last."

My friend frowned something awful. I didn't like a sad Polk. I leaned forward and tapped him with my fan. "Mr. Foden has taught me more about working a ledger."

"You're going to have your own, Miss Dolly. Haven't seen someone work this hard, but you need to slow down. Between cleaning the Hermitage, caring for Miss Kitty and Miss Charlotte, and taking care of Mr. Foden, that's too much. You need more fun."

"Ah, Polk, who needs fun when there's money to earn?"

"Still think you need more fun, Miss Dolly."

He stopped at the front of the Hermitage's grand porch. Another carriage was in the drive. Portmanteaus were on the porch.

"Polk?"

"Oh, I forgot to tell you. Mr. Cells came back today. He sent me to pick up a few things from the docks and then to hurry you up."

My heart wasn't supposed to race like this. "No. No. No. Polk, you should have warned me."

"Sorry, Miss Dolly, but he pays me. And Massa Cells gave me a shilling to keep it a secret."

"I'd give two for the truth."

He started laughing and adjusted the straw hat on his head. "I wouldn't take your money. And I need him to convince you to stay. You and Cells need more fun. He's waiting for you in there."

Holding my breath, I leapt out then marched up the steps. My plans weren't changing 'cause Cells done slunk back.

I picked up my long papaya skirt that belled out around me and went inside.

Chatter came from his study.

From the door, I saw him sitting at his desk. His head, with that thick black hair, was down in a book. Charlotte was on his lap and Kitty at his feet. A pile of new books lay on his desk. The gilded spines glistened next to his hat, the black tricorn I missed every day and every night.

The hat my little girl looked for each time she passed this room.

The missing hat made Kitty cry for weeks.

The thing had returned to upend my world.

"Mama!"

Charlotte hugged Cells then ran to me. "Papa Cells is back."

"Papa?" I wanted to scowl.

He had to know it, for he offered me the sheepish smirk he had sometimes. "Kitty, why don't you take Charlotte and go play with the gifts I brought you. I need to talk to Miss Dolly."

"Don't untidy that room. It won't be ours much longer."

Kitty frowned big. "Dolly says we have to leave. And you've just come back." My sister put her arms about Cells's neck.

That meant a lot. She didn't trust men. She'd grown comfortable with Polk and Cells.

I tried not to grit my teeth. "Kitty, take Charlotte and go."

"Papa Cells, you stay?" My daughter had tears in her eyes.

"I will, darling."

Oh, the smooth man must've been here working them for hours. He wanted us to be here. He'd decided.

My sister took Charlotte and fled. Maybe she saw the tightness in my face. I was no hummingbird or swallow when I was mad.

Cells left his chair. He had a little tan from his travels. The cut of his coat was different, a little straighter, fewer pleats. His light blue waistcoat had a sheen, and was that silver thread about his buttonholes?

His pantaloons were his customary cream.

He stopped in front of me. "Dolly, I'm glad you are here. I've—"

"We move out at week's end. Mr. Foden wants a live-in housekeeper. The pay is good. He doesn't mind children."

"I just returned."

"Good for you."

"I thought." He rubbed at his neck. "Have I lost your love?"

"Love? Didn't know you cared for me like that. My feelings sure didn't stop you from leaving."

"It made me come back, Dolly."

I lost a bit of my anger at his repentant tone, but not all. "Well, let's see how long you stay."

When I turned to walk away, he grabbed my hand. My fingers curled to his as his palm wrapped about mine.

"I had to do some things, Dolly. Things to finish. I did that, and now I'm back."

"You left me once. I'm not prepared to depend upon you again."

I sounded brave, but my fingers were still locked in his, still feeling the warmth of his skin, the thudding of his pulse.

"Dolly, we can move forward."

That wasn't good enough for me now. With a hard shake, I freed my hand then stepped into the hall. "I need to make sure Charlotte's not too upset. She missed you a great deal. I don't want her confused or reaching for something that's not true."

It took everything I had to walk away, to leave a man who sounded like he wanted to love me. As Mamaí could attest, just 'cause a man was here today, that meant nothing tomorrow.

DEMERARA 1774: NEW CARE

I couldn't get out of bed this morning. I wriggled my tired limbs, but the will to move abandoned me. My foggy head could do nothing but turn deeper into the bedclothes.

Tuesday night, Wednesday, and Thursday, Cells, the great politicker, let everyone in Demerara know he'd returned by holding dinner parties.

The past three days, I rose early to polish the new silverware, a luxury of four-tine forks. Four, not three. In the afternoon, I'd run to Foden's to take care of his needs, then come back, wash away my perspiration, and get ready to serve.

I hadn't seen my bed or my girls since the wee hours. It made perfect sense not to leave this room . . . ever.

"Dolly, you have to get up."

That was Kitty, trying to shake me awake.

"Friday, Dolly. You have to work then take us to the Anna Catharina Plantation."

Hot and achy with everything hurting, I had no strength to rise. Part of me wondered if I should go to the sick house, but that was for slaves in the field. Where did those not technically free go?

Kitty poked my cheeks. "You look awful, Dolly."

Charlotte still slept. I didn't have the energy to touch her or push her toes from my knee.

"Kitty, go tell Mrs. Randolph. I don't feel well."

My sister leapt off the bed and I shut my eyes.

When my eyes fluttered open, Cells hovered over me.

"Yes, Kitty, she does look ill." He put the back of his hand to my forehead. "You are burning."

"Mr. Foden must truly be sick this time."

"Well, you can't take Kitty and Charlotte over there. They can't get ill."

My throat burned. I coughed and watched Cells's scheme. I didn't have the strength to fight. "Next week then. I'll be better soon enough."

"Well, Dolly, I intend to make sure you are well. Now that I've returned, I'll see to it personally."

Mrs. Randolph poked her head in. "Sir, what's all the fuss?"

"Send notes of apologies, I'm canceling tonight's party. We have a very sick girl here."

He put his hands to his hip, his emerald waistcoat shimmering with gold threads. More extravagance from across the sea.

"I'll be up. You don't—"

My chest erupted in coughs.

"The young ones can't get sick. Coughs are dangerous." He bent and scooped me up, along with the sheets, all the bedclothes.

Charlotte tumbled and rolled but didn't awaken.

"Put me down."

"No. You will sleep elsewhere."

"I can walk, Cells."

The world swirled as he moved out of the room with me bobbling in his arms. "You'll not fall and add a bump to that stubborn head."

He carried me to one of the guest rooms that never had guests. "Mrs. Randolph, open this one. The bedchamber near mine."

Cells laid me on sheets that were cool on a big bed that was empty.

"Mrs. Randolph, get her something to drink. Her throat must be dry. You shouldn't talk, Dolly. Save your strength."

I shut my lids and waited for the world to stop moving. I needed off the dray.

When I opened my eyes again, I had a window. It was open and I could see the night sky. My stars. Oh, I missed a window with stars.

I blinked again at Mrs. Randolph, who sat in a chair by the bed. She mopped my forehead with a wet cloth. "Looks like your fever broke."

My mouth was dry. "The party, I should—"

"Girlie, that was two days ago."

Two days? "Kitty, Charlotte?"

"They're fine. Mr. Cells has been entertaining them. In between checking in on you."

I rubbed my face. "I never get sick."

"You've been working too hard. Something like a cold can get much worse if you're too tired to fight."

My nose wrinkled. "What's that smell?"

"Mustard plaster. To break up the cold, he said, to help you breathe better."

"You had a doctor out here?"

"Mr. Cells called a physician, but he wasn't satisfied and came up with an idea from an old woman close to his family."

"Mrs. Ben? Nice woman."

She dabbed at my cheeks. "You knew her?"

A knock on the door drew my eyes. Cells stood there with Charlotte in his arms.

"Mrs. Randolph, is she better?"

"Yes, sir. She's awake."

He came inside and made Charlotte fly like a bird. "See, my dear, Mama is better."

She clapped and hugged his neck. "You said you'd make her better. I'm glad you're back, Papa Cells."

"Me too. Miss Dolly, you keep listening to Mrs. Randolph and get better. Charlotte, let's go get Kitty and read. Dolly, I'm going to hire a tutor. Charlotte will learn. Education is important."

If I started to cry, he'd know how this touched me.

So I couldn't.

I clutched the bedclothes, tugging the mustard smells and the sheet to me. "Cells, I don't know what to say."

"Just get better. I have the family."

He walked away with Charlotte giggling like she hadn't in a long time. For a moment, I was five and that was Pa bringing a treat from his travels.

A tear leaked and I turned my face from Mrs. Randolph. Charlotte claimed a papa. How could I leave and deny her, when I would've done anything to have my pa make me fly like a bird, to give me a spot in the owl house?

Mrs. Randolph washed my face. "Listen, girlie. Planters have two families—one here, one away. Seems as if your little girl has helped Cells make up his mind."

"I don't know what . . . I thought you didn't want me for him."

"No, Dolly. I didn't want you hurt. A lot of women have tried to catch Massa Cells, but seems he's caught you. What are you going to do about it?"

"Like I said, nothing. I'll still work for him and Mr. Foden."

"You keep your butt here. Cells is happy with you. Then he won't be courting no widows or anything else. Nothing at the Hermitage will change."

Craning my head, I squinted at her. "What?"

"Girlie. If the widow or one of those planters' daughters gets a hold of him, do you think there will be dancing out back of the kitchen? Or cotton not just osnaburg for the folks in the field? One of those society women will take him and make him cruel. They care nothing for us. Black and brown bodies are nothing but to be broken for profits."

She wanted me to go after Cells, to be a whore or a concubine wife. I rubbed my head. "I need you to be clear."

"If Cells chose you, girlie, let him choose you. I've seen how you looked at him before he left. Now he's playing papa to your baby. Accept him. Then we're all saved."

"What I do affects everyone else? That's not fair."

"Life isn't fair. You know that. But this is something you can do to keep things good for everyone just a little longer. Think about it. You were burning for him before. This can't be too bad."

That was the most elegant argument for lust I'd ever heard. Mrs. Randolph was crazy, and I wouldn't sacrifice my peace for things that didn't last.

DEMERARA 1774: NEW CHOICES

I sat up in my bed, the one in my old room. I couldn't sleep. It seemed staying by myself was something a body could get used to. My bones did, stretching out fully on a wide mattress.

Easing away from Charlotte's kicking foot, I lit a candle and moved into the hall but stopped at the line of portraits. With my finger, I swiped at dust on the gilded frame of the lady. In the paintings of the males, the eyes of noble-looking men looked down on me, but the lone woman's gaze demanded I stand up straight, smooth my chemise of wrinkles.

And own what I wanted.

The knot in my stomach had a name; just couldn't say it aloud.

Bumping into the polished table in the dining room, I caught the edge, but my hip moved backward like I danced. Setting down my candle, I admired the mahogany grains I buffed yesterday. The orange oil I'd rubbed into the wood smelled sweet and made a shine, almost like glass, like twinkling stars.

Circling it, pushing chairs in, pulling them out, sliding them left, then right, I made a turn about the room.

The rhythm in me needed movement. I twirled. My braids slipped down my neck. Freshly washed, the springy curls feathered between my fingers. They wanted to be free. They wanted me to be bold and wild.

Imagining Polk's fiddle, I hummed and opened the doors to the drawing room. My single candle shed light for my feet. Heel to heel, swaying with my hands, I twirled and did the steps of the minuet.

Clapping. The sound made my heart slam against my chest.

"Your allemande needs a partner."

Cells.

I wished I had imagined him. My arms floated down to my sides. My chemise of fine cotton slowly lost its air and fell to my hips. "Sorry. I didn't mean to be loud."

"No, don't stop," he said. "It's good to see you up and spry."

The man was at the door. He looked casual, his black jacket gone, his cravat missing. "Yes, I think you'll do nicely with a partner."

"Don't need one." I pulled at my sleeves, the soft satin ribbon threading my cuff. "Have fun at your friend's party?"

"None. Kept wishing to be here." His gaze sank upon me and lowered to the floor, my bare feet.

Self-conscious, I ducked one behind the other.

He laughed. "Your feet are fine, as is the rest of you."

It was silly trying to hide. "You make me want to check to see if everything is perfect."

He stepped closer. "You are perfect, Dolly, as you are."

He cupped my elbow, then slid his palm to my shoulder. "Amazing. Fine and fit."

My skin could feel the heat of his touch through the fabric.

"Did you see Van den Heuvel, the duchy commander tonight or was it Van Den Velden?"

"Van Den Velden is a fool. But Van den Heuvel, the old commander, is no longer in charge; Van Schuylenburgh is the commander of the colony, but the Dutch are too distracted. This colony will go to the British."

"Was that one of the things you checked on when you left me?"

His lips thinned, then he bit the lower. "One of many. I must know the way the wind blows."

"Doesn't blow enough here. The air's too dry."

He fingered one of my curls. "You should wear your curls free close to your face. It will make your eyes stand out even more."

He claimed both of my hands and we twirled together. His allemande had me spinning.

"We are alike, Dolly."

"That mirror, Cells?"

"Yes, but you are on the true side of the glass, the clear face. I'm hiding along the silvered back."

"That makes us both shiny."

Cells turned me fast, and I fell against him. "Don't make me noble. I'm not. I've been known to do what's in my best interest."

"You're a man, it's expected."

"Merr Merr Ben did not expect it. She always wanted me to be a better man."

His friendship with my old *damfo* sounded as strong as mine, maybe more. Maybe he missed his encourager.

"You're the best man I know."

"You don't know enough people." He sighed and righted me but bent to keep our faces near.

I saw flames charring his hazel eyes, those heavenly lashes.

"Dolly, I owe you an explanation. I owe you an apology."

"Thank you for caring for me while I was sick."

He bit his lip again. The pressure made the crinkles a brighter, tastier pink. "Since I'm forgiven, I shouldn't tempt fate. I should send you back to your room. But that would leave you untouched, unspoiled by my desire."

It was now or never to stake my claim on Cells, or be damned to my fears and those of all who worked at the Hermitage.

I put his hand to my bosom, letting him cup the fullness that the years and motherhood had wrought.

"Now, I'm touched. What should we do about it?"

His laugh was low and easy, but he didn't take his fingers away. The pressure increased. His pinkie slipped the button placard and searched my skin like I was a bundled gift.

That caress called to my restless soul. His stroke to my flesh was gentle, making me like the bud of a lotus flower ready to open.

He kept undoing layers and sliding away buttons until he had me panting.

His head dipped and he pressed demanding lips to mine. The

wine of his vintner was on his tongue, berry and tangy. I could become drunk in his kisses.

"More, Coseveldt. More."

He angled his face, the half smirk broadening. "Only Merr Merr called me that."

"Maybe 'cause you let her see the true you."

He closed his eyes, for a moment, a second. Then he drew me fully into his arms.

"No, she knew who and what I am."

"I think I know my worth. To be with a man who's gentle, who cares for me. You do care for me?"

He kissed me. It was soft, then fevered.

In a blink, he carried me to his bedchamber. Cells draped me on his bed, like one of his fine coats.

When the heat of his body left, I sat up with such a disappointment it hurt, but he lit candles then went to open the window, adjusting the louvers to let in stars.

Then his waistcoat and shirt fell to the floor.

Nothing compared to Cells. Lean and muscled and drawing near, he was a thing of beauty.

He held me. His kisses went to my ear, then down my neck. It took a slight chill to notice the circles he wrought on my spine made my nightgown and corset disappear.

There was no going back to mere friends, to hero and the lass he rescued, not even mentor and student, unless you counted this lesson in love.

His mouth drew down on me slow. Again, building those knots, making me ache, making me arch to him.

"We end up here? Dorothy, this was nothing I planned."

He said my birth name. I liked how it sounded, tasted on his tongue. "Not planning is a first for a man like you."

"I'm not as calculating as you think, but some things seem to add up to right."

The man who hurried for nothing devoured my kiss.

With my palms to his back, holding him, I closed my eyes and waited for this tightness to find release.

His bed was smooth, his sheets cool to my skin, but he lifted from me and rolled to my side. "This is a choice. Not for a moment, and we can't change back."

I opened my eyes and found his face a mash of contrasts. Half smirk, half frown, his long lashes, lazy and shadowing cracked lids. "You're stopping?"

"Perhaps. You're my choice, you know, mine to concubine as wife here in Demerara. I'll work harder to have my power and you. You ready for the sacrifices, the parties and politicking?" He fingered his mouth, then rested a pinkie on mine. "Forever, for us, is a long time for someone still so young."

Eighteen years living mostly enslaved wasn't young and that was an attitude to take with me naked in his bed. "Make me ready unless you have something better to do. Or I could just sleep here. Charlotte kicks my knee. I don't suppose you will."

A full smile beamed. He reached for me and took his time, kissing and touching. I looped my arms about his neck. I wanted to rush, but bit back my begging.

Cells, typical frustrating man, made time go slow.

He kissed me, working my body into a fever.

I was slick and wet and waiting for the answers to the desire echoing in me. *End the knot, break it, split it wide.*

He hovered above. His beautiful mouth held chuckles. "I think you need more kisses than anything else. Seems you've yet to learn how to do it right."

I lifted up and took his lips, trying to gain his world—all his secrets, his scent, his whispers of hymns.

"Not sure what you mean, but you'll teach me. I'm confident you can."

"Dolly, I'll teach you everything. We choose each other."

I didn't know what he meant, but I wanted this, him and me and fire.

My friend touched me where I hated until I didn't hate it. I let him take his time sending me, spiraling like I could fly. When I didn't think I could take more, he showed me there was. His hands covered mine, stretching me when I wanted to shrink, sinking me when I wanted to stay afloat, not drown in his rhythm, his song.

We were entwined, fitting together like missing pieces of a puzzle. I cried out in Irish, *maológ*, for I was full, overflowing in love.

I burst.

I melted.

In this heat of ours, I needed him to take me again before reason or rules ruined us.

And he did.

This act of him possessing me and me him, I knew would leave us broken for anyone else.

I stood in front of Cells's dressing mirror, measuring how my waist had begun to disappear. Being Cells's concubine wife these past six years, I should've guessed that the regulation of my menses would eventually fail. How could tea keep at bay all the love we shared?

Mrs. Randolph came into his bedchamber with the linens. She glanced at me. She didn't have her practiced scowl. Her face held questions.

She put down the bundle. "You going to tell him?"

Of course she would know. She and Kitty laundered the linens.

"Today."

She put his shirts away into his dresser. "It changes things, you know? You've been good about not changing things."

I know it did. The Hermitage had been a happy place. Cells had nine-year-old Charlotte reading. Still very shy around everyone, Kitty had become quite an artisan. My dear Cells shipped twice the number of barrels of rum than he'd done two years ago.

And I had the money for manumission for all of mine, including this babe in my womb. I wasn't free. I hadn't pushed for it. Slave ships still came monthly to our shores. The crime of aiding runaways was subject to severe fines. I feared that my circumstance would reflect badly on Cells and his drive to influence the colony.

Mrs. Randolph lifted my chin. "The way he loves Charlotte, how could he not love this one?"

I clasped her hand. I thought she didn't like me, that she was like the women at Pa's cistern, or the women I'd met at the markets along the riverfront. Many thought I lied about being a mulatto because of the darkness of my supple skin. Others thought I should be content living off Cells's means. Their lovers' dreams meant more than theirs.

Both his and mine were important.

She gave me a hug. "He will love the baby, Dolly."

"You think so?"

"I do."

Bolstered, I went out of our bedchamber and moved down the hall. I straightened my shoulders and went into Cells's study, but he wasn't alone. Commander Van Schuylenburgh, the leader of the colony, was in my chair.

Mine. Where I sat listening to my dearest talk of his plans, cheering him on when things didn't go as planned, yet both men looked as if I didn't belong.

"Yes, Dolly," Cells said.

"I didn't know you were busy . . . entertaining."

Van Schuylenburgh had a hook nose like my pa and he looked me up and down, then dismissed me. "*Je chattel is knap.*"

He laughed and Cells did too.

I'd picked up some Dutch from the market and from the planters at Cells's dinners. Handsome chattel or slave . . . I should take that as a compliment, along with the leer that reduced what Cells and I had to something dirty. I wasn't Bilhah, a concubine wife to Jacob. Something much less.

Cells's smirk faded. "Miss Dolly, is there something urgent I must attend to?"

"No."

Van Schuylenburgh gawked like my shoulders were bared. I dressed as a woman of leisure, something befitting Cells's stature. My embroidered gown was a pretty dress of olive satin that shrouded white linen skirts.

But the commander's sneer exposed the enslaved osnaburg wrapping my soul.

And my Cells let him.

Careful not to slam the door, I backed out and returned to my old room.

Kitty was at a table, pressing her thumbs into clay.

"Where's Charlotte, sis?"

"With Mrs. Randolph, learning cooking."

"Oh."

She swiveled and gaped at me. "Look." Kitty lifted the vase she created—smooth walls, a big curled lip. Sketches in charcoal lay at her feet of how she'd paint the finished creation. Dancing women celebrating music like they did at Pa's cistern.

"Are you all right, Dolly?"

Used to lying to myself—like how my feelings mattered less, how I drank tea to control my menses for me and not the fear that being with child would make me lose Cells; and how in small ways I'd made his dreams more important than mine—I nodded to my sister. "All is good."

"Mr. Cells can solve problems, but you can too."

My sister turned back to her vase. I wished I could talk to her and make her understand how fragile our position was.

I couldn't.

Kitty's soul was trapped, still young, nothing of the nineteen years she'd lived.

Yet this was my promise. She didn't have to be grown like me. I came behind her and hugged. I might've cried into her braids.

Kitty kept making her vase. It would be another treasure when she was done.

I nursed my little Edward as I sat in the rocking chair. Solid spindles, chiseled curves of mahogany, and a caned seat that offered gentle padding. Rocking in it was perfect. Cells sent it to me.

He had left on urgent business a month after I started to show, first to Barbados, then to Europe. Though he sent letters that Foden read to me and said he missed me, it didn't take away the hurt. Like my pa, maybe this coming and going was the way for men, especially those who lived pieces of their lives across the sea. What was it about the waters, the distant shores that drew them? I'd have to find out. I promised myself I would.

Tears streamed down my face. I don't know why. I was mad at Cells, but this feeling, this darkness was different.

Edward's birth had been difficult. Mrs. Randolph, thank goodness Mrs. Randolph was here. The cord . . .

Doing too much. Fretting too much. Waiting too much on Cells. My body was different. That's all. Mamaí used to help women with the birthing lows. I wish I remembered how.

My boy's head of dark hair bobbed on my bosom. His skin was warm and smelled of lavender and coconut. This baby was born of love not hate. *Remember that, Dolly.*

I tucked Edward into the cradle and left the loneliness of Cells's room to peek on my girls. Kitty hogged pillows in the big poster bed and Charlotte sprawled into the space that once held us both.

I started weeping again and pushed from the bedroom unnoticed.

Mixed up, spinning like a top, the scent of fresh baked oattie bread hooked my nose and led me to the kitchen door. Cracking it, I saw Polk stuffing slices of the loaf into his mouth. "What you think Massa Cells is going to say about that boy?"

Mrs. Randolph wiped her hands on her pressed white apron. "Nothing, that baby is beautiful."

"Mighty dark, this one."

"Her skin is dark. What do you expect, Polk?"

"Her pa is white. I hear her other daughter is like lil' Charlotte, white as a ghost."

"Polk, you're talking foolish. You trying to say that baby isn't his?"

"Well, no. Not—"

"They're rabbits. Always in each other's company. The only time they aren't is when she's working for Foden. That boy ain't no old Foden's."

Polk cut another slice of the bread. "Then maybe the old rumors are true. Barbados Creole skin my eye. Cells was a slave baby taken and raised for a stillborn."

Mrs. Randolph picked up her butcher knife and swung at him. "Boy, don't let none of that come out of that mouth again. You hear me?"

I backed away. Merr Merr . . . Merr Merr Ben . . . Grand Mama Ben. Was that why he'd helped Mrs. Ben long ago?

Passing as white?

Polk's story of an enslaved baby being taken by massa wasn't unheard of. When island heat made white women so delicate and surviving childbirth so hard, things happened to keep inheritances in families.

Was that why Cells pushed himself so hard? Why gaining power was everything?

Nooo. Maybe?

It would explain why weighing consequences was his first notion, not right or wrong.

I ran back to my precious Edward, peaceful sleeping in skin a little lighter than mine. I was jet, he was deep, deep topaz.

If being colored, a mulatto like me, was Cells's secret, why didn't he tell me? I'd be proud of how clever he'd been conquering the white world, commanding their influence. He was the equal of any man.

Easing to the bed we shared, all I proved was I was a rabbit to match his lust. This rabbit bore children to men who didn't want them.

Nicholas's laugh, death masks, every bad thought I'd ever had flooded my head. Humming my mother's hymn stopped the room's spin.

Cells was my concubine husband. He loved me. He said he chose me. How could he look on this boy, his boy, and not want him?

I glanced at the mirror.

My thin hair curled from sweat. My cheeks puffed and reddened. My perfectly round face was fevered and tired and wet.

My strength had to recover. I had another babe who might only receive one parent's love.

DEMERARA 1781: NEW WAY

The fiddler played a jaunty tune. It was the first party at the Hermitage in over a year. I dressed in my best gown, a linen overskirt of sky blue and a gown and bodice of fine muslin striped in red and cream.

Cutting two of my tendrils closest to my face, I let the short curls show.

My straight hair was one of the first thing Cells and other men noticed about me.

I wanted Cells to notice me.

He'd been back for a month, and other than pleasantries and a short peek at Edward, there wasn't much else.

None of the passion we had before.

Nothing.

I slept in the bedchamber next door last night. He didn't seem to care, almost relieved as if some measure of guilt had been removed.

Near the dining room, I bumped into Captain Owen. I hadn't seen him in ages, not since he'd left for an adventure in Barbados. I heard he was from there.

The look on his face—pleased and smiling—said exactly what I'd hoped. That even with a little more weight about my middle and thighs, I could catch a man's attention.

"Miss Dolly, you're always a vision." He kissed my hand. "Do you know where a man might find a good housekeeper? I see how satisfied you keep Cells. His house and his parties are quite immaculate."

"Yes, she does quite well." Cells came from his study. The stare he offered the captain chipped away the fellow's cheeky smile.

Then Owen laughed. "Cells, everyone knows Dolly's taken. But there has to be more Dollys around. You can't always be the lucky one."

Cells nodded, but he drew me away. We stood close to the portraits of his ancestors, to the lone woman who'd make him confess here and now.

"Dolly, I didn't think you felt well enough to join us."

"I feel quite well, John Coseveldt Cells. I can still run your house, like always."

"You should be with our son. You're nursing him. He should be your priority, not business ventures with Owen."

What was this? Jealousy over the captain or my thoughts of starting a business again? Or was this something worse, a rejection of our dark-skinned son. My heart hurt. "Who is this portrait of, Cells? Who is this woman who seems in control? I've always wanted to know."

"An aunt. Carolyn Cells. And yes, she always made her opinion known."

"A woman with opinions is not horrible to you?"

His lips pressed tight, so I poked more. "Carolyn Cells is on your father's side, not your mother's people. She doesn't look as if she's accustomed to working . . . managing the fields."

His gaze burned. He tugged hard on his white dinner gloves. "Dolly."

Foden entered the Hermitage with his black-and-white coat and pantaloons, cane bopping on the floor. "Cells. Dolly. Oh, my angel is back on her feet."

"I am, Mr. Foden. Thank you. I'll be back at work soon."

"Oh, good." Foden clapped. "How's the boy? What did you call him? William, I hope."

The old man laughed, but Cells's brow raised and that look he'd given the captain returned. "Yes. William is an excellent name."

Breathe, Dolly, I said to myself. "The boy is Edward. Excuse me, I need to go to the kitchen."

Mr. Foden wrapped a palm about my arm. "Can't this angel take part in the dinner? She can be my partner."

"Seems you get to be elevated, Dolly, courtesy of Foden."

Cells spun and walked into the dining room.

Oh, Bilhah gained a seat at the table, begrudgingly. The man whose son I'd borne, the beautiful brown boy I gave my concubine husband, he wanted to be someone else's.

Cells brought a new dance from Europe, the contredanse. Couples in sets of four formed lines in his ballroom. It had movement and twirling, lots of hand holding. Polk could definitely master these fast-paced tunes.

The rhythm, which had always been my friend, seemed far away. I needed it to pour into me, to make me feel normal. Dinner was stiff and formal, but I'd learned my forks and my water glasses long ago.

I forced myself to appear at ease and offered polite conversation, things I'd learned from Foden and Cells, but I stayed at the table. Bilhah was lost, not stupid.

"Miss Dolly"—Mr. Foden had his pipe in his mouth—"I've missed you."

"And I've missed you. Mr. Foden, I need you to do something for me."

"Anything for you."

I raised my gaze to his fatherly eyes. "I need you to—"

He eased from the table. "Go on a walk with me."

We went arm in arm to the porch. The torches lit the lawn. I could see down to the river. The rosy scent of the cannonball tree blooms filled each breath.

"My dear, you don't look happy. You don't look confident. That's not my Dolly."

"Mr. Foden, I never told you something. I'm not free."

He laughed. "Of course. You're with Cells."

"No. Well, yes." I claimed a breath, drawing the strength to say the next part. "I need you to find my father, Andrew Kirwan. I have the money for manumission, for my mother, my sister, my daughters, and my son. Help negotiate our ransoms."

Eye wide and alert, he stepped back. "No wonder you stay with Cells. You're trapped."

Stunned. Slack jawed. Silent. Foden laid my life, my heart, bare.

He took my hand, my dark jet one, into his palm. His gloves were in his pocket. I felt his strength.

"Is he hurting you, Dolly?"

"No, but nothing lasts, Mr. Foden."

"Dolly, my house is open to you."

"I'm grateful for that, but I have to be in a position to take care of my family. Tell Owen I'll find him a housekeeper for a fee. If I've trained her, he'll not be disappointed."

"A finder's fee? Capital. A new businesswoman in my midst. Capital. Good evening, Miss Dolly."

After helping Mr. Foden into his carriage, I watched it journey down the drive, then I returned to the Hermitage.

Cells stood in the hall, almost like he waited for me. "You see Mr. Foden off?"

What had I missed? Why was he jealous? I folded my arms and glared at him. "Yes."

"Have you two become closer in my absence? Or has the captain—"

I reached and straightened his ebony cravat; I fingered his sensitive Adam's apple. "I have secrets too."

My faithfulness shouldn't be in question, though I wondered about his. I walked away with his gaze on me, but I didn't care.

"Dolly, wait."

Cells came to me. "Go to Edward and retire for the night. He needs you. Charlotte, Kitty. Me. We all need you. You don't need to be thinking of business. It's not necessary."

"I should've kept the man who believes I can do anything and be anything."

His face tensed, reddening. "I've advanced you as much as I can. But these are places of negotiation sometimes. Investors are here, bankers from London. Thomas King is the most influential. I might be their agent in Demerara."

"Thought you wanted to run the colony?"

"I did, but as long as it remains Dutch, control will stay in Dutch leaders. I calculated the British would take it by now. Thus, I have a new goal to be the wealthiest man in Demerara."

"You can just switch a dream? And you still need *their* goodwill."

His gaze narrowed. "I'm one of them. Perhaps a bit too liberal."

Lies. He wasn't a liberal, but he was passing for admission to their parties and politics. "If you say so."

"Dolly, keep your opinions to yourself. There are people I must impress tonight."

"Yes, Cells, you must keep your chattel, *Je knap chattel,* in line."

His breath steamed over his lip. "This night can't be ruined."

"I'm not going to ruin a thing. You should know me better than to think I'd cause you trouble. I'm a better keeper of your secrets than you know."

Darting, blinking eyes, he clasped my elbow. "What do you mean?"

"I figured out why it benefited you to help Mrs. Ben, Merr Merr Ben. We are a mirror, Cells, two people who want the world, but I live in the truth. I live in my skin. My *black* skin."

I knew Coseveldt. I knew when he was pleased; I knew when he was so full of emotion he'd burst. I'd come to even appreciate the tight control he put on his life.

Now I knew I had to leave him. Mirrors exposed my soul and all my fears. I wasn't convinced that he'd resist using my weaknesses against me.

He caught my palm, and my fingers curled with his. It was awful to be furious at him and still respond to his touch. "Dolly—"

"Cells, there you are."

Coseveldt dropped my jet hand as if it was a sin to hold. Maybe for a man wanting to be white, wanting to impress people, it was.

"Yes, Mr. King," Cells said. "The Hermitage is a success."

A tall, stocky fellow with a receding hairline came toward us. Elegantly dressed in a black jacket similar to Cells's—a high collar, but no pleating about the waist, very short and smooth in front—he stopped and stared at the paintings. "The Hermitage is everything you said it was. Your tastes are exquisite."

The man glanced at me, a little too long.

Not feeling flattered, I curtsied. "Well, King. I hope you like your colony."

"Oh, she's funny, Cells. Where did you transport her from, one of the islands or Africa?"

"He didn't buy me. I hired myself out. Excuse me, sirs. I'll retire now." I did a half curtsy and went down the hall to my room. The temptation to slam the door almost overcame me.

But I wouldn't be spiteful and hurt Cells's new idea. He needed his dreams, not me.

I'd never leave Cells in a bad way.

This woman, the mother, this abandoned Bilhah, would just leave.

I counted my coins as I walked back to the Hermitage. The sun lowered on the horizon. The temptation to dance at the harbor was great, but the brothel owners were wary of me. I'd taken six girls out of that life and trained them in housekeeping. My business was growing. Even Thomas King employed one of my protégées for his estate, the Friendship.

"Mrs. Dolly, might I walk you partway to the Hermitage?"

"Yes."

D.P. Simon lived on a plantation close to Cells's. He was a nice Creole boy, a pretty mix of Sephardic Jew, Spanish, and a little Black. The swarthy young man was from a good family and seemed to have fallen for my daughter the moment he met her.

"Is Miss Charlotte well?"

"She is, D.P. I'll tell her you asked about her."

The boy ran down the lane. Charlotte was too young, barely eleven. I doubt he'd stay in love with her eight more years.

Hearts were fickle things. Such hope one had to have on things lasting. I quickened my steps, determined to talk with Cells. We needed to settle our future.

A French officer who I'd hired a girl out to last week passed me, tipping his tricorn. His long blue jacket over bright red breeches looked smart. He headed toward the market. The French now controlled Demerara, wresting it from the Dutch. Governor Kingston, who took over from Van Schuylenburgh, had surrendered.

Salut to the French.

My Catholic faith didn't have to hide any longer. I would celebrate, but poor Cells, he'd cast his lot with the Dutch, and he'd lost. He no longer had influence. He'd chosen the wrong side. Watching his politicking crumble stung.

He took it hard and became more withdrawn, a hermit to the outside world. This was the Hermitage's gain. The past three months, he was Papa Cells loving on Charlotte and caring for Edward. It started slow, but there was no doubt in me. He loved our son.

Polk met me on the porch. "Miss Dolly, you're back. We've been in a state."

The drooping frown on the big man's face frightened my soul. "The doctor just left. Massa has lil Edward."

My heart stopped then jolted out of my chest. I ran through the hall to my bedchamber. "Cells!"

He put his finger to his lips. "He struggled to breathe, Dolly. I didn't know what to do."

In my rocking chair with Edward in his arms, he focused on our baby as if he could will the boy's lungs to work right. "We almost lost . . . I prayed. God answered with a miracle."

I fell at my husband's lap. My son, my babe, was alive. His little chest pumped so hard, but air was going in and out. His little snore sounded like a harsh whistle.

Cells reached out and stroked my cheek. "He's better now. Edward's a handsome boy, Dolly. Has my noble chin."

"That he does." My eyes stung. I was away gloating about money, not staying where I was needed. "Good that you were here."

He put my yawning Edward into the crib, the lovely one that once held Charlotte. "Such a sweet boy."

Tears were on Cells's face. He knelt and hummed the tune Mamaí sang to get me to sleep.

Rop tú mo baile.

His Montserratian Irish roots showed. He'd been a good Catholic before flirting for Anglican power. My heart broke for him, the guilt staining his reddened cheeks.

He'd lost his dream, but maybe he discovered the power of us.

Rop tú mo baile.
Rop tú mo baile.

He was on all fours and he kissed Edward's brow. "Rest up, my boy."

"What does that song mean, Coseveldt? It's chased me all my life."

He stood and lifted me; our fingers entwined. "Be thou my vision. Be thou my father, be I, thou a son. You're a vision, Dolly. You've given the Hermitage a family. That's why I built it. I guess I was blind to it." He kissed my forehead and held me, just for a moment. "Thank you."

Cells moved to the door. "I didn't reject Edward because of his skin or the fool notion he'd expose me." His voice trailed off, wet and throaty. "My first son surely died because of the lies I've lived." He wiped his cheek. "I didn't want that curse on Edward."

"You're not a curse. You saved him today. And look at the Hermitage and your rum business. You built those things. They are successes."

"Forgive me, Dolly, but nothing feels like a win when I make choices that cause ruin."

Charlotte ran and hugged his waist. "Papa Cells, is Edward better?"

"Yes, my *cailín beag*, my sweet little girl. He's sleeping and his beautiful mother is here to make things perfect."

"You make everything better, Papa. Can we read one more chapter? I've finished my chores."

Cells looked hesitant to leave, but I nodded. "I'll watch him now, Papa. Go with our girl."

Half smiling, he took Charlotte's hand and left.

Sinking by the cradle, I hummed to my son and put his small thumb in my palm. What were my dreams if they put my family at risk? Or if I had to choose between reaching for stars and touching my baby's warm fingers.

On my knees, I prayed for the family I built. It had to live and thrive with my dreams, not instead of them.

DEMERARA 1782: FORGIVENESS

Swiping at his books, I moved about Cells's office making sure everything was up to my standards.

"You're working too much, Dolly."

Books aligned, spines showing, I ignored the man sitting at his desk. This was his common complaint.

"Nothing is neglected here. And I have three more housekeepers."

He sighed, brooding over his letters from Scotland. The rum and limes from the glass he put to his lips scented the air as much as his cedar cologne. "Neglect is an odd term."

The sound of precious footfalls bounced outside of Cells's office.

"Sorry. The children. I should stop them from running."

"No." He crumpled a piece of paper, his foolscap. "Let them. My father was very stern. He wouldn't allow for children to dance or play in his halls. Let Charlotte and Edward be."

His voice sounded sad and deflated, not the happy planning fellow I knew.

I missed our conversations, his laughs . . . him. "Talk to me, Cells?"

He glanced up. His lips pressed tight. "King has decided not to invest further in Demerara. He sends his compliments for your business affairs. A pretty woman providing essential services is always a winner."

His voice was low. He'd lost again and, in his eyes, it seemed I won. A few contracts didn't surpass his rum sales. Maybe this was his way of ceding to my potential and that I could one day earn as much or even more than him.

Ignoring the sourness of his tone, I focused on what was important. He remembered I was pretty. It was my choice to avoid his bed, to sidestep his touch at every turn. Weren't we different being ma and pa to our children? Shouldn't we put our pieces back together?

I clutched my lacy bodice and satin stomacher of papaya yellow. "Should I have your dinner brought to the dining room?"

"What about a small supper for two, here, for you and me?"

"I'm not hungry."

"Then I'm not either." He thumbed his chin, his index gliding on the cleft I missed kissing. "Dolly, your dress. It's lovely."

I wore the full petticoat underneath my gown. It was a present he'd sent from his last travels. The white muslin of the skirt and the satin overdress draped my curves.

"You do look . . . beautiful."

"Thank you."

He didn't turn away. Maybe I'd become more interesting than the squiggles of ink that had him angered.

He lifted his quill then set it down. "Am I still to be punished?"

I wasn't punishing him much. "Is it punishment if I suffer, too?"

"Yes. Just not an effective measure."

The quill was in his hand again, balancing on the curve of his fingers.

Like before, like always when I wasn't lying to myself, I felt his touch, the stroke of his strong fingers from across the room.

I didn't want to be this weak. Things weren't quite right between us, but it had been a long time since desire found me. At twenty-six, I was old enough to be scared and to admit to being in want of man.

"Is it folly to let a man who's hurt me come close so he can break me again?"

"Break you, Dolly? Never you. A little bending, maybe."

Cells moved to the front of his desk. Arms folded about his waistcoat—fine ebony silk patterned with scrolling, he hummed my hymn, changing it to English. "You are my vision."

Holding my breath, I put down my cloth and lifted my palm to him. "Come to me, Coseveldt, if you want."

With his waistcoat open, swaying at his hips, he did.

Face-to-face, he tugged at a curl, stretching it to my cheek. He released it and it snapped back, a tight ringlet. "I think supper for two here or in my bedchamber would be nice, just you and me."

"No supper. I'm not hungry for food."

That smile, that slight smirk, showed, then it disappeared with the world when he kissed me.

It all came back, the press of his hands against my bosom, the sound of the satin crinkling giving way to the heat of his palms. His finger touched everything that needed him.

Eyes closed, I became a flame at the unpinning of my gown. He held me, searching me through my lace and silk. Found, found wanton, and in such need.

"Dolly, we should—"

I kissed him, hard then slow. "Actions, not promises."

Up in his arms, I tasted wild, sweet rum on his tongue, then I felt us sinking.

My arms tightened about his neck, my face, my tears buried in his starched cravat. "Not the floor, never the floor."

He righted me. My heart gonging, meeting his.

"Not sure we'll make my chambers without being stopped by Polk or our children."

Ours. Ours. We could rule the world together. "You're strong. I believe in you."

He laughed and the lush sound vibrated against my throat. Cells locked the door, then drew me over his shoulder. It was a wild dash to his desk.

Knocking away ledgers, he laid me atop his precious paper.

"I believe in us, Dolly." He crowded me. We became a tangle of arms and legs, of satin and silk, of flesh and forever. "No one knows me like you. I'm free when I'm with you."

Coseveldt hummed my name and claimed me, claimed everything I had inside. A whisper I couldn't suppress gave him three little words I hadn't meant to say, hadn't ever said aloud.

The three words he didn't repeat.

DEMERARA 1783: FAULT

I was dressed, but I had no energy to rise. My heart was heavy.

Mr. Foden passed last night.

I'd finished nursing my new baby when Cells took me to the Anna Catharina Plantation. At his bedside, I held Foden's hand and memorized my friend's death mask. I made it a part of my heart. No man had been as good a pa to me, not even my own.

Easing into the rocker, I looked into the cradle. This bundle of joy slept suckling her thumb. Birthing my daughter was easier than my son. Cells stayed by my side. He and I watched this baby breathe air and grab for me like the world was owed to her.

I liked that about her.

I liked the notion of my daughters owning the world. I'd convince Cells to call her Catharina. The way he doted on little pink her, I had no worries that jealousy would deny this request. The way he looked at me, holding me in our bed so gentle and tender, I knew he'd understand.

The happiest four months of my life passed in a blink of my eyes. Catharina was healthy and Cells was good to her and Edward and Charlotte.

And to me.

I fought the shadows of birthing sadness and fretted over fears of the strangest things. Said stupid things about dying and hating childbirth.

Coseveldt understood my nerves. He was so loving and dear.

We had small squabbles when his letters arrived making him cross. Some deal or something hadn't worked as he intended, but a day wouldn't pass before he was reaching for me and making amends at night.

With my papers to become manumitted rolling in my palm, would everything change? I waved good-bye to Captain Owen on the porch. He gave me these this morning and lined out all the monies agreed. Foden's last act of kindness was to get Pa to settle for forty pounds apiece for the ransoms. I had twenty times that two years ago. If Pa had been easier, I could've borne Catharina free.

Poor, dear Mr. Foden. Gone. The way he loved life, it was so hard to accept he was gone.

My eyes leaked. Another full-on sob seized me.

Kitty swooped in, dancing. She sat on the floor toying with my open portmanteaus, flipping a lid, tugging a buckle. "I can go with you when you tell Mr. Cells. I don't like you sad."

My sister hated me being weak. Her stories of getting neat Polk to mix muddy clay for her made me laugh.

Kitty's childlike joy, her art, helped me escape most of the heaviness of my heart.

Still my sorrows shouldn't be on her shoulders. I planted Mamaí's smile on my face. "See about Edward. I need him strong when we go on the boat next week. Charlotte and I will be minding Catharina."

Kitty offered me a hug. "Cells has the baby now. That should bring you cheer." Her grin widened. "He can't get enough of that baby."

Good. It was good he was that way with our second child.

Then he shouldn't be too angry about my friends helping to arrange our manumissions. When I tell Cells about going to Dominica to certify my freedom, maybe he'd come too. Crumpling the papers in my palms, I went down the hall.

My knock on the door was light. Then I barged inside.

Cells reclined in his chair, humming to our daughter.

Catharina was pink with a fuzzy head of thick black hair, not thin like mine and Edward's. Her eyes were a darker hazel than Coseveldt's.

"Dolly, she's beautiful."

"Mr. Cells, I'll take Catharina back to her cradle." Kitty had followed me and poked her head into the doorway. "Then you two can talk."

He gazed at me, then gave Catharina to Kitty. "Good night, my princess."

Kitty brushed past. The door to his office closed. Cells and I were alone.

He stared at his hands, then the stack of documents on his desk. When he looked up, his eyes seemed distant. "Polk said you're going away?"

"For a little while. Mr. Foden negotiated with my pa. The terms of manumitting me, Kitty, my mother, and our children have been settled."

"Oh, I thought it was an expansion to your business. King has said how good your services would be across the West Indies."

Cells was in one of his moods. Something in his papers must've done it. I offered him mine. "Why don't you come to Dominica with us? Then, once my ransom is done, we can go across the sea together. As a freewoman, there's no better dream than being with my family. Sailing with the man I love. You can show me England and Scotland."

"I can't—we can't." Cells plowed through my pages then dropped them on a pile next to a goblet. "I never did this for you. Foden did. I've let you down often."

Bending behind his chair, I put my arms about his neck. "You're busy with your dreams. Rum sales are up. Cells, we're good. We've found each other despite difficulties."

He clasped my hands then gently tugged free. "I'm . . . I'm not going to be here when you return."

His stutter was soft. His leaving wasn't business. Rounding in front of him, I stared into his eyes. The windows of his soul said I didn't have his love, not anymore. "Why don't you tell me about *her*?"

"Her?"

"Yes. Why else would you have to go away? Whenever you do you come back different. Your mood becomes sad and guilty when you read your letters from abroad. Has to be a *her.*"

He rose and slurped his rum. "The her is Fanny, my wife."

"Wife? I thought she died when your son—"

He shook his head. "No. We've been separated a long time. She wanted her parties and London society. I wanted adventure. I had to make myself a success."

"Wife. You've been lying."

"Not saying. Omitting."

"Lying, Cells. That's *lying.*"

"I asked for a divorce. She agreed. We did the paperwork. I was free. My vows said to God were done. That's why it took me a month longer to return to you before. I came back free."

I put my arms about his waist. "You're divorced then, so she has no hold on you."

He moved from me. "Fanny went to the Sheriff's Court, then the Scottish Court of Sessions to seek redress. To stop our divorce, she filed a Declarator of Marriage to overcome our Declarator of Freedom. It's been dangling over my head since Edward's birth. Fanny is ruining my chance at happiness." He picked up a folded piece of parchment. "The court has ruled in her favor. I'm still married."

"Filing paperwork did this?"

The yellowed thing with creases fell to the floor, gliding like a creased cracker leaf.

"Fanny and I wed when we were young. She didn't know about me, nothing of my race, just my family. When our son died, I confessed. She hated me. Now she's sick and doesn't want to die alone. Her priest keeps writing me to make things right."

"You're Catholic again?"

"Always was, but I can sit through any church service." He put his fingers in his black hair like he wanted to crush his skull. "Her last months should be of peace. Now I can make things right for her. Offer her what we never had."

My breaking heart stopped cold. "Offer her what?"

"I'm going back to Fanny. I'm taking Catharina with me."

I fell into my chair, the chair I stupidly sat in to sup, to discuss our days, our children. "No, Coseveldt. No."

"Dolly, she'll fit in my world. She'll be educated and have everything, even the things that I can't."

"You want Catharina to pass for white so she can live with your fears of being rejected?"

He winced. "It's for the best. You can go build your dreams. You don't need a baby whose birth makes you so sad."

I popped up and slapped him, as hard as I could. "You bastard. You think business comes before my children? You think my being sad means I don't want my child?"

"You've sacrificed time with Charlotte and Edward and me to grow a successful business. To get what you want you must. I understand that now. I won't ask you to give up what you love or to slow down. If you were a man, no one would think to ask."

Cells was smart using every fear—from the birthing sadness to failing my dreams—against me. I gripped his waistcoat, ripping at his buttons. "Don't do this. If you must go, go, but don't take Catharina."

"This is best. You'll never have to explain the past to Catharina. You've let Charlotte believe she's mine. You never told her who her real father is. You want to hide just like me."

"I never lied, Cells."

"You never mention the truth, but I love Charlotte. I wish she was mine."

"Then you'd steal her, too?"

He bit his lip and looked down. "Catharina Cells doesn't need to be manumitted, doesn't need to know any of the horrors you've lived. She'll be mine and Fanny's free daughter."

His words echoed, plummeting down the hole in my soul. White or Black, Cells was a man. He had dominion over the child he claimed and the one he didn't. "How can you do this?"

Cells rubbed his jaw, which still held my red print, red on his light skin. "Catharina will have a real future in England."

"Because she won't be a concubine wife, like me."

He went back to his desk, pulled out his purse, and dumped coins. "For Edward's manumission. I love him, but he will stay with you."

"Because his skin is dark. And this money is your forty pieces of silver?"

"Don't hate me. Don't let my boy hate me."

My lungs gasped now. "Then what am I to say to him?"

"That vows said to God matter."

Had to remember I was still standing, not falling through the floorboards.

Cells clasped my shoulders. "Dolly, this is not what I wanted or planned."

How could he look so hurt when this was his doing?

The last time he shoved coins at me I had batted them away. This time I scooped them up for what he owed our beautiful son. "Pocket change for Edward. My earnings will free him. Mine."

"Live at the Hermitage, Dolly. I'll leave you in control. Your business is doing well. Stay here."

"You want me here, waiting for your return, waiting for some woman to die to regain a life that was a lie? Never. You chose you and Fanny, not us, not the family we built."

He tried to hold me, but I ran.

Cells's footfalls followed.

I locked myself in the nursery and dropped to Catharina's cradle.

He pounded the door. "Mrs. Randolph. I need the key!"

Time had run out for this dream. I was to lose another daughter. "Catharina."

She smiled and puckered her lips.

I gave her all I had, a blessing. "My *pickney dem*, my little, littlest girl, I love you."

The door creaked. In silence, Cells slipped inside, put my papers in my hand, and stole our daughter away.

PART THREE

The Stand

I stood for my family and my truth.

DOMINICA 1784: FLOUNDERING

The sun felt different in Roseau, Dominica. It was as hot and bright as any day in Demerara, but the air was less dry, more forgiving to my skin. The shores on the western side of Dominica weren't swampy like Polk had tried to convince me. He wanted us to stay at the Hermitage.

The dear man was right about the singing in the bay.

Yo-yo-yo. Male voices of the deepest accent merged with the breeze. Clothed in just tan-colored aprons, enslaved men stood in lines of two along the sides of the deep-bellied boat.

Yo-yo-yo.

Their sorrow tore into me. Their plight would worsen. They didn't know the misery to come.

They'd yet to be sold like animals.

They'd yet to know the overseer's boot.

They'd yet to learn and earn their ransoms.

Yo-yo-yo.

Fourteen years it took me to awaken, for me to come to this free port and certify my freedom.

"Miss Dolly?"

Captain Owen approached. He'd said his good-byes to Edward and Charlotte. Kitty shooed him toward me.

The captain, the happy bouncy man, didn't notice my sis's hiss. He led me closer to the dock. "Dolly, Captain Thomas is bringing your mother and daughter from Montserrat. He should've been here by now. I can't wait any longer. I have to head to Barbados . . ."

My mind drifted to the singers, the kinship I felt to their pain. I temporarily forgot Owen's renewed proposal. I brushed sand from his lapel. "I'll be fine, sir. Go on. Thank you again for bringing us here."

"Think about what I asked you, woman. I'll be back in a month. Maybe you'll marry me then?"

If I asked him how a Catholic and an Anglican could wed, he'd think I took his offer seriously. Instead, I patted his arm. "Let me get used to being free, Captain Owen, completely free."

I waved good-bye as he walked toward his tied-off sloop with all the enthusiasm of a woman who'd bedded a friend and discovered the experience lacking.

I don't know what I was thinking, lying with him.

That wasn't true.

I knew exactly what I did and why. The captain liked me, and he seemed the easiest route to getting Cells out of my blood. He'd also be a name to place on a birth register if my menses came up missing. John Coseveldt Cells would never take another of my children.

"You actually like Captain Owen?" Kitty paddled to my side. Wide sandals, tan skirts, and a bamboo green tunic, my sister seemed different, a little more grown-up voicing her opinions. She did more of that since we left the Hermitage.

"He's pleasant."

"Polk says he wants your share of Foden's estate. Polk is a good man. They aren't all bad."

She'd mentioned Polk again.

A third time this week. I hadn't noticed that they'd become friends. Too caught up in Cells or business or the birthing sadness, I hadn't noticed much.

"Dolly, I think Polk is right."

Five thousand pounds left to me by Foden was a small fortune. A fortune that would be gone quick, paying for food and clothing and lodgings for my family.

I scrunched up my sleeves to absorb more of the rays. "Mr. Foden told me to be careful. I'm using his solicitors." His expensive solicitors. Once everyone was free, I'd figure out how to start my business here in Roseau.

Kitty leaned into me. "I miss Cells and the baby. I like babies."

I nodded, but I was beyond missing. The loss rattled in my hollowed-out lungs every time I breathed. "I . . . We have to deal with Pa now. You ready for that, my swallow?"

Her head dipped and I kissed her brow. "Before we left the Hermitage, Charlotte and Edward's tutor taught me the word *freedom*. I'll be able to read it on the official papers."

The shadows in her eyes made me fear for Kitty and the safety of her still nine-year-old world. To make her smile, I spun her and pointed to the black sand beach of Roseau, then up to the hills. "Look at those mountains. They say it rains a lot up there, but only a little here."

Fog floated like a collar about the peaks. "There's steam. It comes from broken cones sending hot breath from the earth."

"That doesn't sound good, Dolly. I think we need to stay at the shore."

I twirled her in the allemande, faster and faster until she laughed. We stopped and walked to Charlotte and Edward.

They were miserable.

My daughter didn't want to leave the Hermitage. She cried when I told her we may never see Papa Cells again. Edward, my stoic four-year-old, wiped a few tears. I thought Cells loved him, but he sacrificed knowing our Black son to give our white-skinned Catharina a lie.

A crowd of women passed behind us, beautiful women with faces of brown, topaz, and henna, smart women with beads teasing their throats and hats topping their heads.

"I want to craft necklaces, Dolly."

"The one you made me is a treasure. Kitty, I'm going to buy us hats."

Edward touched the top of his head. "Me, too, Mama."

"Of course."

"A black one, Mama." He jumped up and down.

Charlotte rolled her eyes. She didn't know the significance of wearing a hat, only that Cells's black one was gone.

Sighing, I turned back to the sea. The rippling waves exposed hints of green and gold.

Yo-yo-yo.

"You think Mama has changed much? Dolly, you think she'll recognize us? Lizzy, too?"

That question about Lizzy haunted me, and now it would torment me with Catharina. Would my babies, either baby, ever forgive me? Oh Catharina, I didn't fight harder 'cause . . . ?

Yo-yo-yo. Yo-yo-yo.

'Cause deep in my chest, I thought a white world and a white mama who'd never suffered enslavement was best.

I'd never forgive myself. Never.

"Dolly? You're crying."

"No." I wiped my eyes. "Just some sand."

Thirteen-year-old Charlotte came to my side, dragging her sandals almost stepping on her dress of white linen with embroidered lotus flowers, a dress meant for floating or dance. "May I write to Papa Cells?"

"I'll get an address."

Edward wheezed. It sounded heavier in this humid air. "Much longer?"

Dipping to my knees, I straightened his olive-green jacket. "Mamaí will fix you up. She has many medicines."

Kitty put her hand on my shoulder. "Yes, our mama will."

I looked at my sister's approving smile and feared my mother's reaction. Would she love the easy spirit Kitty was now or mourn the warrior Kitty who'd disappeared?

DOMINICA 1784: FAMILY

A boat appeared on the horizon growing bigger. The people on board looked like ants.

Mamaí, my Lizzy, and Pa?

And Nicholas?

No. No. No.

Kitty tugged my arm. "A boat, Dolly!"

I nodded but my heart stuck in my mouth.

Knees knocking, betrayal pooled like spittle on my tongue.

A gun vomited. It cut short the haunting yo's. The enslaved were pushed below, buried in the belly of the boat.

Dead. I was dead if Nicholas came, or he needed to be.

Until my papers were certified, I couldn't swallow, couldn't get my gut to settle.

The boat, a sloop, navigated the sandbars and pushed close to the docks. Big white sails hooked to a blue-painted pole—it looked like the sky or a piece of it.

On the deck was a captain, my mother and my pa, a young woman and a young man . . . no Nicholas.

No Nicholas.

I gulped air, rubbed my heated stomach.

The boat kissed the docks.

My mother, my Mamaí, waved.

An orange osnaburg woven skirt draped her thicker middle. She was a little grayer beneath her orange knotted headscarf. Her feet were bare.

I'd change that.

The young woman sitting next to her, almost hiding, my Lizzy?

Had to be the now fifteen-year-old daughter I left all those years ago. I started moving.

My pa climbed out of the boat. He whipped off his straw hat and exposed a head full of white hair. There was a scowl on his face.

My low heels skidded. It took a great effort to stay upright.

Had he changed his mind? Did he see my fine clothes, my shoes, and think he could charge a higher price?

The man piloting the ship hooked rope on the deck post. He stepped onto the dock and finished tying it place. "Yuh dey? Spectator?"

His rebuke sounded mild, almost calm. He eyed me and smiled. "Ma'am. Stay back. It's slippery."

Finished with his knots, he reached into the sloop and helped my mother onto the dock.

Ignoring all, I ran to her. Years of tears stung my cheek. "Mamaí."

"Dolly. My Dolly."

Buried in my mother's arms, I gobbled the sound of her heart, her voice, her strength. Her keeping herself bottled up, I understood it all. Then I heard a young woman thanking the captain.

"Mama?"

That small voice was meant for me.

"Lizzy?" I broke from my mother to the young woman standing a few feet away. Slim, gold in coloring with a small hook nose. Her pull skirt was red and green wrapped under a blue tunic with yellow flowers. She had shoes. Pa had purchased her light-colored slippers.

"My little girl? My Lizzy."

A tall dark-haired fellow released her. I tugged the lithe little thing up in my arms, but she wasn't little. She was flesh and blood, with a figure her tunic barely hid. She was older now than I was when I bore her.

"I love you, girl."

I must have said this a thousand times. A thousand and one.

"Mama. Grama, she told us . . . Grampa told us you were alive."

Caressing her pale cheeks, I nodded. "All these years apart." She was an Irish rose with my deep-set eyes, my pa's nose, and nothing, nothing of Nicholas. "If I could've been with you, I would've."

"Yes. Grama said *you* had to go."

Mamaí moved to Kitty and Edward and my Charlotte, giving them hugs and kisses.

"Hmmm. Hmmm." The boy with the dark hair made noises like he was important.

Cells had introduced me to colony governors and financiers. They didn't harrumph with their throats. Power projected in the quieter things—silver buttons, silk, soft politics.

"Mama," my daughter said. "This is John Coxall. He's the son of John Cavelero Coxall."

The young man was from a wealthy Montserrat family like the Tuites.

Lizzy blushed as this young man put her hand on his arm.

"When your business is done in Roseau, call on me at 22 Long Lane. Where shall you be?"

"She'll be at Hanover Street. A house I rented. You may visit."

"Thank you, ma'am." Coxall dipped his chin to me then turned to Lizzy and bowed.

I liked that. I liked his sign of respect, reminded me I was worthy of it, even with my mistakes.

"May I walk you all to your residence?"

"Let him, Dolly, but I must speak with you," Pa said.

My gut started twisting, but I needed to hear his changes before he hobbled me at the solicitor's. "Yes. Kitty, lead them. Pa and I will catch up."

"They make a nice couple." Pa's face held a grin full of pride. He stood at the edge of the dock between me and the endless sea. He'd aged. His eyes looked strange hidden behind lenses as thick as bottled glass.

"Pa, let's catch up to the others."

Shifting too fast, I slipped, and I braced to hit the dock.

Breath stuck in my craw as I was caught and lifted like a prize fish.

"Easy now, woman." The brawny boat captain had me. He turned to my pa. "She's a beauty. Fiery like your granddaughter."

"Put me down, before my fire eyes consume you."

"They already have, ma'am." He steadied me on the dock. "Just a lil' *helpin han.*"

His whisper had a slight Creole pitch to it, like a British tongue that mocked the islanders. Then he laughed, full bodied and rich, like sweet claret.

I straightened my overdress, smoothed my satin skirt. "Captain—"

He lifted a trunk out of the boat, my father's traveling trunk. "Thomas, Joseph Thomas of Grenada, ma'am."

Pa put his foot on the leather-skin box. "You're moving too fast, Dolly, but you always have."

He and Thomas chuckled. Both men could go to the devil.

"My Dolly, you've done what I could not."

Could not or would not?

Pa put his hand under my chin. Could he feel the steam brewing in me?

"My little doll has nothing to say? It's been a long time."

My fingers fisted. I should curse at him for leaving me to be abused by my brother.

The captain nudged me. "I think you need to leave and be ready for that big meeting tomorrow at the offices of Brayshaw and Bates."

Pa moved and began fussing with his trunk, no longer paying attention to me.

"Good girl."

The captain's mocking endearment made the taste of vomit rise. When I turned to tell Thomas to go jump off the docks, I saw something in his squinting sea-blue eyes.

A warning.

Pa tipped his trunk, put his foot up on it. "Tomorrow is big. I don't know how you did it, coming up with the money. And it's a big step to be independent and take care of your mother and the rest."

"I'll manage, Pa."

"Miss Doll, what a spirit you have." Captain Thomas stood up after making a final knot in the boat's rope. "I've gained an earful from your mother and my old partner, Mr. Foden. He described you very well—light eyes, skin pretty like midnight."

"She is. My Dolly has always been special, special and bold. And she has a head for numbers, just like me." Pa had his boastful grin showing, and for a moment I was seven in the back of his dray loving his praise.

Praise that made Nicholas hate me.

"A week," the captain said. "That's the earliest I can get you back to Montserrat."

Captain Thomas glanced at me again. "Seven days is a long time for minds to be changed."

This time I understood. The captain definitely warned me about my father.

"Pa, I'll see you at the solicitor's office tomorrow."

His hand touched my elbow before I could withdraw. "Dolly, wait. After this is done . . ." He clutched his neck. His face had another sugary grin. "I want Betty to return with me. Lizzy, too. I think it best. Convince your mother."

I offered him kind eyes, the kindest I could, but I would do everything to make Mamaí and Lizzy's visit permanent.

I woke up crying in my sleep, reaching for Catharina. My babe, did she look for me, or had she stopped?

Kitty and Edward slept with me in the bed, a four-poster one like I had at the Hermitage.

My sis, whose face had been beneath a pillow, bounced out of the bed and hugged me. "Dolly's day. Freedom. We'll do something fun when you get back. I wish Polk was here. Then he'd play his banjo and you'd dance."

I took my time dressing in a mango-colored tunic. Tightening the corset front strings over the linen, I forced a chuckle. "You never go dancing."

She climbed back in the bed and pushed Edward's feet to my side. That boy snored louder. "Maybe I would if Polk was here."

I scooped up the hope in her voice and filled the hole in my chest. "We'll see."

Plodding out into the hall, I checked on Charlotte and Lizzie in one bedroom, then on Mamaí in hers. She was asleep, stretched out in bed.

I wondered if Mamaí had ever slept in a bed unless Pa had sent for her. I was glad to give her the best bedchamber.

She couldn't go back with Pa, not after I'd freed her.

With my scarf in hand, the signed papers for manumission in my sack, the deep bag I'd left Montserrat with, I headed to Mr. Bates.

The morning sun reflected off the glossy painted red shutters of the buildings. Roseau, Dominica, was an endless grid of streets. Would a home here be as fine as the Hermitage?

Clutching at my chest, I stopped in the middle of the cobbled street gasping like I'd been overcome by the heat.

Why did I have to miss Cells more than he missed me?

Why on this, the biggest day of my life, did I have to face it alone?

"You looking to buy, miss?"

An old woman at her vendor's table stacked fabric rolls like a rainbow come down to earth.

Pretty, but I saved my spare pennies for a hat to show off our new status. "Do you have tricorns or bonnets?"

The sable woman wore a headscarf of gold with a knot in the front. The end pulled through was shaped like a spear's point. I'd seen women done up like this. "In the Demerara's markets, women with sweethearts wear scarves like yours, but I want hats."

The lady smiled. "*Wacht me op de hoek?* Your birthday?" She stood and pointed. "*Drie hokjes beneden.*"

Her Dutch was beautiful and I missed Demerara more, all my customers. "Yes, ma'am, I'll check three booths down."

I turned and bumped into Captain Thomas. "Sorry."

"No problem, Doll. Enjoying the Old Market?"

His smile managed to be both bright and lazy.

"Yes. Most call me Dolly. Miss Dolly."

His tan coat looked twice his size, hard to do on a big man. The jacket was straight with no pleating or embroidery. "Hmm. Dolly is such a diminutive name, one fit for a child."

His gaze went up and down my dress. I had to check if my tunic strings had come undone.

"I'm particular about what I'm called. Add Miss. We're not that familiar."

"Pity about that, not being familiar." He laughed. His cheeks held stains of red from the early hour or a night of drinking.

"Nice bumping into you, sir."

Captain Thomas followed me. "Miss Doll, do you have your documents?"

"Yes." I pulled my copy of the signed agreement from my sack. "See."

"Is that all, lady?"

I poked him in his solid chest. "What more do I need? These are all the documents Foden gave me."

Thomas put his palm on mine. "Now calm down. No one said that wasn't enough. And no one is telling you that if a person wanted to invalidate this agreement, they might try to say it wasn't your money that paid but Foden's. That would mean no agreement at all."

It took all my strength to keep my breathing even.

"Calm, Miss Doll." His fingers tightened, steadying me. "You didn't *come with two long hands.*"

"What?"

"A saying from home." He waved empty palms. "I meant you earned your money. You need proof of earnings."

"Like a ledger, sir?"

"Exactly like that, but nobody's telling you this."

Sandy brown hair, sea-blue eyes, a little taller than I remembered from the docks—Captain Thomas seemed a good man, a nice-looking one. "Be careful, Miss Doll."

"It's not fair. The monies paid are my own, by my sacrifice. My word should be enough."

"Not in a court of men who can twist legal precedents for their purposes. I should know, being a man and a scholar of the law."

If he meant his words as a joke or an omen, I wasn't sure. "Why is nobody being helpful, especially since he's a man?"

"Foden was my friend, too. He told me about a hardworking, caring young woman who had big dreams. Seems a shame for fools to thwart her now."

"Thank you. I have to go home."

He tipped his hat, a slim cap of brown felt. "Good luck, Miss Doll. Don't be late. Solicitor Bates likes to start on time."

After offering Thomas a parting smile, I scurried to the leased town house. My ledger was all the proof I had. It needed to be enough.

My family was still asleep in the town house when I returned to retrieve my ledger.

Except Lizzy.

She sat in the parlor with her feet curled on the sofa. "Is it done?"

"Not yet."

She ducked her face onto her knees. She looked dainty in Charlotte's lacy nightgown.

I moved to the desk and grabbed my book, tucking it under my arm. I didn't need to turn to know she stared at me. Didn't need to search very far to know her questions. "It was a matter of life and death. That's the only reason I didn't take you with me or come back."

"You chose my aunt over me. And all these years, was it still life and death?"

Her words were muffled in the lace, but I heard the ache in them.

The years away.

We'd never have them back. I had nothing to soothe her, nothing but the truth. "I had to earn the money to free us."

"My pa said you were wild. You didn't like being told what to do."

"Why would my father say that? He knows I was a good daughter."

"I said my pa."

My gut clenched tight, twisting. She meant Nicholas. "Your pa's the reason I left. Whatever he said is a lie. My brother is a liar."

Lizzy didn't say anything, but she didn't look at me either.

"I have to go do what I set out to do, free us today. Then we'll talk."

She didn't respond, not till I was at the door.

"If you come back, I'd love to hear."

Her voice had bitterness, but she had fifteen years of Nicholas's poison to sour her.

I didn't slam the door but closed it with a soft click of the lock. I understood Lizzy's feelings, even if they meant she hated me.

More people were out in Roseau. My joy of seeing brown women in hats, freewomen, walking alongside the others, leaped in my heart. Lizzy would take her place with them. Then she'd forgive me. She'd have to.

All my daughters would forgive me, one day.

My steps picked up as I passed the government building. Soldiers were everywhere. These men ate and drank and danced through the night.

Better that than starting up a war.

The Holy Father needed to keep them calm and stir no rebellions. This place was special, more liberal than Demerara. Last week, I attended my first service in a church, Notre Dame du Bon Port.

Indoor worship with a priest.

I went at eleven for the enslaved, next week I'll go at nine with the free people.

God was closer to me here than anywhere. This had to be the place to start over, start over my business, start over my heart without Cells.

Turning down one path then another, I stumbled near a well in the middle of the cobbled market. A stone wall supported a thatched roof and a bucket. The water looked cool, but on this hot day, no one drank.

That had to be an omen, a bad one.

I backed away, the heated air whipping my face. I made my boots follow the wind. It led me down an alley to a small building with blue shutters.

The hand-painted sign looked like squiggles, but the number on the door was twenty-four. With a quick knock, I went inside. A young man at a close desk sprung up. "Can I help you?"

"I'm here to see Mr. Bates. Mr. Charles Bates."

"You're Dorothy Kirwan?"

"Yes."

The man looked stunned.

"Is something wrong?"

"Miss Kirwan is mulatto. You're not—"

"Tell that to my pa, Andrew Kirwan. I suspect he'll be here to finish the paperwork for my ransom."

The man kept staring. I suppose I was used to it, how aware folks were of my skin, but my black was beautiful, supple with coconut oil, and now adorned in fine linen and silk. Respect. Today, going forward, I'd remember I'd earned it. "Go tell Mr.—"

Pa came through the door. "Dolly, you're on time. Of course you would be today."

The young clerk backed up; he may have even bowed. "Sorry, miss. I'll go tell Mr. Bates."

The fellow ducked into a room and closed the door behind him.

"Dolly, is there a problem?"

"No, Pa. They just don't know me here. I'll have to fix that."

"You plan on staying in Roseau?"

The wind, the church, Foden's influence said this was for me. "Yes."

The clerk stepped out of the room and said to us, "They'll see you now."

I started down the hall, but Pa stepped in front. "I want you to convince your mother and Lizzy to come back to Montserrat."

"Kitty and Charlotte and Edward haven't had enough time with them. Me neither."

"Then all of you should come back."

Did I shrug, did my face fall off and shatter? Not sure. I'd watched

Cells hold his tongue with his politicking, but I wasn't him. "Can we talk of this later?"

"Fine." His heavier footfalls passed mine. We headed into the room.

Then my world ended, shattering like it had years ago.

Nicholas sat at the table, waiting for me, smiling like he'd won.

Blinking, I held on to Mr. Bates's long pine table and dropped into a chair. The pea-green walls seemed to close as my gaze locked with Nicholas's.

The scar Kitty left on his cheek was jagged and long. Time had darkened it, marking him with ugly, more ugly. At least we left him something to memorialize his evil. I'd cut him again for the lies he told my daughter.

"Let's proceed." Mr. Bates, a man with small eyes, no jacket, just a shirt, a gray waistcoat, and pantaloons, stacked papers with his fat fingers.

Nicholas sneered and tugged his thick shirtsleeves. "This gambit is illegal. Pa should keep her money and the chattel."

Why was my rapist here, speaking?

Before I could spit or curse or scream, the door behind me opened.

In strolled Captain Thomas with another man. "Mr. Bates, I'm sorry to be late, but the second witness to these transactions, Mr. Frasier here, was a little lost."

Frasier was a round, older man. He sat beside me on the left, Thomas on my right.

The captain looked different from this morning. With his hair parted in the middle, combed and tied back with an indigo ribbon, he looked like a gentleman. I approved of his matching waistcoat and shiny brass buttons.

He scooped my ledger book from my sweaty fingers, then caught Pa's gaze. "Good to see you, Mr. Kirwan. This must be your son Nicholas, the former owner of Miss Dorothy."

"Nicholas never owned me, but he tried."

My brother's green eyes flashed, but the captain laughed.

"Miss Kirwan, you've met Mr. Bates, the head of the practice."

I stuck my hand out to him, but he didn't grasp it. "Mr. Foden spoke well of you. I hope his faith was not misplaced."

Burly Mr. Bates sat back, his gaze narrowing behind his brass spectacles. "He was an excellent man."

Nicholas pushed back in his chair. "Bates, your partner, Bradshaw, should be here. Let's push this off until Bradshaw returns."

"No, Mr. Kirwan," Mr. Bates said. "Frasier is capable of conducting this. He's assisted on others."

"This is a farce." Nicholas pounded the table. "There's no way she paid with her own money. She has none. And she couldn't make enough whoring."

"Stop, boy." Pa caught the fool's shoulder. "Let Dolly have her say."

"She's a runaway. She should have no say. Any money she's earned, even the fortune Foden left her, should be ours."

"I can't be a runaway if Pa knew where I was. Right, Pa?" I stared and begged with my eyes. *Show them all the father who loved me. Be a fair man today.*

In what felt like a year's time, he slowly nodded. "I knew where she was. It was safer for her to be in Demerara, until everyone had cooler heads."

"Cooler heads? My brother had violent lust for me. He tried to sell off my sister. How could anything be calm?"

Pa dropped his head. "Please say no more. It's the past."

That's how planters escaped consequences? Just put enough time between their crimes? "All is not forgiven. It never will be."

Nicholas gripped the table like he'd turn it over. "The whore didn't pay us. That was Foden's money. She's using his death. She'll say or do anything to cheat."

Thomas took papers from his jacket. "It states plainly that Foden was of sound mind when he wrote his will. He left her a third of his estate and worldly goods like his teapot."

"A lovely silver service." My anger became awash in sorrows.

The list in my head of the wrongs done, done to me, by my blood was so long. "That man was better to me than my own flesh." Better than the man I loved.

Mr. Bates rotated a piece of parchment and pointed to a clause, some squiggle of ink. "We don't have proof that she paid the funds. It has to be separate from the monies of Foden's estate."

They all looked at me with judgment in their faces. Nothing black like me could have power or earn money or deserve freedom.

Thomas thumbed through my ledger. "The money was paid. The amount agreed to by all parties. There should be no question of the validity of Doll's . . . of Dorothy Kirwan's claim."

Mr. Frasier shook his head. "That's a nice sentiment. Admirable that Andrew Kirwan the father agrees, but Nicholas Kirwan raises valid objections. If the money was not hers but actually Foden's, then she is property of the late man's estate."

"The estate in which she was left a third?" Captain Thomas laughed. "You're suggesting she inherits a third of herself? Come now, gentlemen."

Men were talking, pointing to squiggles like I wasn't in the room. But I was.

I took my ledger back from Thomas and slammed it to the table. "I have proof of my wages earned as Foden's housekeeper. Every bit and fourpence, for you British, guilders for those that know Dutch. You can see my entries of payments and even Mr. Foden's initials, everything earned as his housekeeper plus the income from the housekeepers I hired out."

Nicholas drummed the table. "You illiterate whore. How could you ever have a ledger?"

"Because of my pa. He taught me figures. Pa, tell him of your dreams for me."

"She's right," my pa said. "And now I want for you all to come to Montserrat."

"See, Nicholas, you *adharcáilí* fool. You couldn't hold up your part of the bargain. You couldn't do school right. You couldn't do right on Pa's plantation. Everything you try, may it always be a curse to you."

He sputtered and made a fist as he leapt up. Thomas bounced up, too, and shielded me. "Kirwan, get your boy under control. We're conducting business."

Frasier pushed back in his chair. "Sounds like a lovers' spat."

The ugly laugh falling from my lips made Frasier wince. "Is a man a lover if he beats you bloody, cursing at you to hold still? No wonder you men pray so much to soothe your little souls. Calling rape a coupling, a lovers' spat? May God have pity on you and your households."

Frasier looked down; his fingers clenched the chair arm. "I . . . I heard you bore him a fine daughter, barely any color in her."

If I slapped him, I'd be imprisoned. Better to hurt him like the priests did. "Mr. Frasier, when your days are up, remember to tell God why you ignored the screams of women. See if He thinks the *pretty* children make it all right."

"Miss Doll," Thomas said. "We need to proceed. How these gentlemen sleep is not your worry."

His eyes pleaded for calm, but this still needed to be said. "If my rights are to be denied by these men, I want them to burn for their sins." My gaze locked on Pa. He wasn't to be spared. Never would I set foot on his plantation again, unless it was to set it aflame like I'd wanted all those years ago.

As if he'd heard nothing, Bates lifted his head from my ledger. "This is a tally of wages, but the numbers are wrong."

My heart stopped.

Nicholas's laugh punch into my chest. "That chin will lower yet, Dolly."

Bates passed my book to the captain. "Seems as there's an underpayment. She's owed an additional fourpence by the Foden estate. You didn't receive your payment for the week the good man died."

Breathe, I could do it again. The past, the nightmares of my suffering unwrapped from my lungs. I sounded like Edward's whistle snores. "A lot happened that week."

I shoved the ledger to Mr. Bates. "But my numbers are right. You need to count again."

The captain tugged my hand. "Dolly, he just said—"

"Count again." I didn't lower my voice, didn't defer to the captain. No more to any man, I pressed forward.

Bates did. I heard him counting. "She's right. Though she's due an additional fourpence, the amount Miss Kirwan tabulated is right. Foden's mark is noted where she loaned him two hundred pounds."

I smiled and showed off my teeth. "That's 441 guilders."

Pa slapped the table. "Of course she'd have those numbers right. My daughter would."

A glance at his smile made me clutch the chair arm. All I knew was Pa left me, left me when I needed him, left me like Cells.

Nicholas groaned, his red face burning. "This is illegal. Father, stop her. Rescind—"

"Hush, fool." I turned to Bates. "Now that the challenges are done, I need deeds for Edward Cells, Charlotte Kirwan, Elizabeth Kirwan, Betty, and me, Dorothy Kirwan. And I paid the fees to manumit Kitty Kirwan. I had an agent buy her at auction for me. The receipt is in the front of the ledger."

Mr. Bates shuffled his paper again. "What's Betty's surname?"

"My ma was never given one."

"Kirwan," Pa said slow, as if he'd thought long and hard. "Kirwan should be the name."

Pa's dimples had sunken, wrinkled with years of regret. If he'd loved Mamaí more than himself, he would've given her that name proper.

Thomas inspected Mr. Bates's documents. He signed and had Frasier do the same. Then passed them to Pa.

When he was done, the pages slid to me.

It had many squiggles, but I saw a word, not *freedom* but *manumit*.

It was good enough. I took the quill, dipped it freshly in the well of ink, and put my mark to the paper.

The captain took the documents and gave them to Mr. Bates. "The deeds are done, Dorothy Kirwan. You are a freewoman."

Mr. Bates arose. "The witnesses have now formally attested. Congratulations."

Part of me was afraid to touch the parchment he extended. "These deeds will be recorded, Mr. Bates? The British government will know this has happened?"

"Yes, ma'am. This is proof for all the king's colonies."

"That means Montserrat, too, Dolly." Pa's voice sounded sad, but I had no care of it. He should've done this years ago. He should've been the one to make things right.

Nicholas tore away from the table. If he thought about hitting me, the way Thomas leapt up made the fool back up.

A curse was on Nicholas's lips, but he kept it to himself. He pounded through the door and never looked back.

I wouldn't fret about him anymore. I was free. Mamaí too. All my children, except Catharina, were legally free, but Cells's deception took care of that.

"Gentlemen." I took up my ledger and the copies of our deeds, stashing them in my sack. "Mr. Bates, you can send me the fourpence."

Thomas held the door for me. "Miss Dolly, may I escort you back to your residence?"

"No," Pa said. "I will. Let's go tell your mother together. Betty will be thrilled."

"You both can. Mr. Bates, thank you. Make sure your people know me the next time we do business."

"I'll do that. Mr. Lionel, my clerk, will definitely know." Bates looked me in my eyes and shook my hand.

I marched out of the office. I'd bested Nicholas today, but I was no fool. His hate had grown. Until he was gone from Dominica, none of my freed family was safe.

DOMINICA 1784: FINE HAT

I sat on the sofa in the parlor. That's what I called the front room of my leased town house. It was the best seat to look through the window at Mamaí and Pa.

Their conversation was animated. Tears streaked her stoic face.

She did care about Pa.

He did love her.

I thought it rare for a man to say such.

Kitty flopped against me, and I put my arm about her.

"Dolly, I want Mamaí with us now. I'm selfish."

"Not selfish." I snuggled her closer. "I want her here, too."

Lizzy came down wearing another of Charlotte's dresses. Lizzy seemed to have lost her love of waist-hugging tunics and pull skirts. This draping cream gown sculpted her, putting embroidered flowers on her slim shoulders. Remembering the Hermitage, I could almost smell the sweet lotuses.

She swept in front of us. "Mr. Coxall wants me to be his wife. I want to, Ma."

"What?" I sat up from the sofa, almost rolling Kitty to the floor. "You what? I thought maybe you'd want to stay with me awhile."

Her lips hadn't poked out, but she offered a look that made me shudder. "Say it, Lizzy."

"I don't know you, Mother. You chose to be away. You look like you've done well. Me and Grandma were left to famine and hardship. I don't want to stay with you now."

Kitty stood and smoothed her blue-striped skirts. "She's mean, Dolly. You sure this is Lizzy, that sweet little baby? I don't think so."

"Sis, go upstairs. Check on Edward. He coughed a lot during his sleep. Let me talk with my daughter."

When she left, I pointed to a chair. "Sit and say everything."

"My father says he was drunk and you confused him. You led him on 'cause you wanted him. Look at all the children you have. You must be wanton."

I didn't want to explain to her about the beginnings, not that she would believe me. "That's not what happened. I never wanted him. I wanted nothing from my brother."

"Then you must despise me because I'm my pa's daughter."

She was going to make me say aloud she was a child of rape. I swiped at my mouth, my stomach turning. "If your pa is such a good man, why didn't he free you?"

Lizzy shrugged. "He says you're not his sister."

"You think your grandma would lie who my pa is?"

"No, but they both can't be right." She started to sob. "Are you saying he forced you?"

Cells was right about how hard it would be to talk of the horrid things I'd survived. Even worse—to say it, and for her not to believe me.

Kneeling beside her, I cupped her chin and wiped her tears. I hummed our song, the one I put her to sleep with every night, *Rop tú mo baile.*

"I made peace with what has been done, Lizzy, but Nicholas always knows how to hurt me. He knows how I loved you, how I begged him to take responsibility for you. I left because it wasn't safe to stay. I never wanted to leave you."

My cheeks were wet. Didn't realize I was crying. I let go of Lizzy but she clamped on to me. She sang too. Maybe there was some forgiveness in her heart.

"Listen to me, Lizzy. I'll always do right by you. You want this boy? Then I'll see about a marriage contract. You're free. You deserve promises on paper. I'll have my solicitor, Mr. Bates, draw it up. I'll give you a dowry to protect you."

"You would do that after what I said?"

"It's too late to be your mama. You had the best, Mamaí. I want us to be friends. As women, we should be friends."

Lizzy swiped her face. "You'll see, Mama. John will never hurt me."

"Nothing looks as good as the beginning, but paperwork makes it good in the end. I don't want you giving him all your love and care, and he decides he wants someone else."

"That won't happen. Just because no man loved you doesn't mean the same will happen to me."

She took off running up the stairs, passing Kitty, almost pushing my sister into the rail.

My sister came and offered me a handkerchief. "Edward's sleeping. Sorry about Lizzy."

"The girl grew up with my temper. Didn't even need to see me to have it." I whirled Kitty around. "I want to go dancing. I want music. I want—"

Through the window, I watched Mamaí kiss Pa, then she slapped him.

Kitty and I sank on the sofa again. Neither of us could stop watching the shadows on the veranda.

"Let me do your hair, Dolly."

I nodded and put my head in her lap, still watching the antics outside.

"Charlotte's working on a letter to Mr. Cells. He left her addresses for London and Scotland."

The groan I released came from the bottom of my soul. "You and I, Kitty, we'll own the world. But first we should get material to make hats."

Twisting and flicking my tresses, Kitty undid my braids. "You rest, Dolly. You've done enough. We have tomorrow."

I hadn't done enough, not near enough. We were free, but I had to start all over. This time I wanted my mother with us. Gawking at the window watching my parents argue, I selfishly hoped she'd break from him. No woman needed a man who wasn't worthy of her heart.

DOMINICA 1784: FORWARD

Convinced that a defeated Nicholas had fled Roseau a week ago, I went to the Old Market without fear. Taking my time, I palmed yams and yellow squashes in a cart of a woman in a bright white turban.

I didn't realize I was hungry until the scent of cooked meat, a savory squab, surrounded me, made my mouth to water. Then I became sad wondering about Mrs. Randolph, and if she missed cooking for us. I knew she loved the daylong roasting of wild onions and partridge for Cells's parties. With him going back to his life in Europe, the Hermitage wouldn't see a big celebration, not for a long time.

"The plantains are nice, miss, but try the callaloo. Make coconut callaloo, throw in some fresh crab," the seller said.

The big green leaves, callaloo leaves of the taro root, looked lush and the soup she talked of would be hearty, but my eyes were drawn to the fine hat she wore. Delicate folds of satin made the base crowned with dried flowers and dainty berries a regal display.

"Miss, you want some callaloo?"

"Your hat is lovely."

The woman touched her head. "My pouf? Thank you. Try the vendor in the middle. The milliners make pretty ones. Good for you."

Her gaze locked with mine. An unspoken solidarity passed between us. I didn't need to ask her story or share mine. She was free like me.

Almost curtsying, I smiled and headed to the milliners.

Two women set out their wares on a table formed of boards resting upon old dray axles that were hewed from strong neem. In Montserrat, Pa harvested that wood for his carts, bragging the heavy grains built the best foundations.

With Pa still trying to sway my ma, the foundation I wanted to create here in Roseau was at risk. Mamaí couldn't return with him, but Pa kept coming and courting *his Betty*. She'd yet to answer his beggin'.

"You like what you see?" The older of the women smiled, and I pushed my fretting to the back of my mind. Lifting a bonnet, a white satin one with a shiny bow, I studied its beauty. It was art, as fine as a painting.

"Miss Doll, why not try the straw hat with the jade feather? It would go well with your eyes."

I peered over my shoulder at Captain Thomas. "Hello, sir. Glad to see you."

His smile turned a little wicked. "I like being seen."

White shirt, emerald-green waistcoat, and black pantaloons was his garb today. "What are you looking for, Miss Doll?"

Tugging my pale-yellow tunic by the corset strings that felt snugger than I remembered, I sighed. "I'm on the hunt for a perfect hat."

"Hmmm." He folded his arms behind his back, puffing up his broad chest. "That's an important decision." He hovered over the table, poking and tapping until he picked up a straw one and put it on my head, atop my braided chignon. "Yes, this would be lovely on you."

The brim felt too pointed, offering no shade for my eyes. I had to squint up at the captain.

I didn't like that.

Made me feel as if I were angling for something. I wasn't.

Returning the hat, I studied the other selections.

His lips pursed. "Is a tricorn to your liking?"

"No. No tricorn." I walked away from the stand.

He caught up to me. "Miss Doll?"

Suddenly feeling winded, I rubbed my brow. "You did me a great favor at Mr. Bates's. I'm in your debt."

"That's a dangerous place to be for a woman who knows numbers." His broadening smile gave me comfort. "Think nothing of it. I have a weakness for justice and light eyes."

He teased and I wanted to be teased.

"Let me show you Roseau." He placed my palm on his arm with no hesitation of being out in the open showing affection, putting my dark hand in his pale one.

The captain was good-natured, waving here, tipping his hat there. He knew a lot of people in this city. That might be helpful for a woman trying to conquer a new world.

"Captain—"

"It's Thomas, Mr. Joseph Thomas. Upon occasion, I'm a captain of a sloop, the *Mary*, of which I own a portion."

"The boat with the blue pole has a name?"

"Yes. *My Proud Mary. My Bonnie Mary* for my Irish friends."

Pocléimnigh pals? Well, Thomas was nice and a talker.

Walking through the Old Market, his boot heels clacked on the cobbles. We stopped at the well.

"Is the water poisoned? No one seems to ever drink."

"Well," he whispered in my ear, "they put the gallows near the well sometimes. Some think the well holds the pain of death, the suffering of those killed here."

I peered down the well. It seemed bottomless and black. Thomas lobbed a pebble. Long seconds passed before I heard a plop into the well water. "The hole of all that suffering is deep. I think I understand."

He clasped my arm and steered me away. "You shouldn't have to, Doll. Not at all. I'm sorry for your loss, Miss Doll. Foden was a very good man."

"The way you say that, it was as if I was his widow. I was his housekeeper and friend."

"Oh. Many women in your position look for benefactors."

"Is that a fancy way of saying I'm a whore?"

"Umm. No."

"You men are terrible. You can't accept that two people can be friends or that a good man like him can look at me as anything other than a wench."

I glared at Thomas and the other women, planter women, passing by and staring at my uncovered hair. "I'm not ignorant about colored women looking for white men *to take them far*. But I'm free, I can get there on my own."

He took off his hat, slammed it to his chest, and stepped into my path. "I . . . I am sorry. A thousand pardons. May I make amends by walking you home to Hanover Street? Give a fellow a chance."

The furry brows above his sea-blue eyes wriggled at me.

I yielded a little and offered a nod. "Fine. But answer questions as we do."

"Hmmm. Sort of a confession? I am trained in the law and evasion."

"You're honest. I'll give that to you. How do you own part of a boat?"

He gripped his jacket by the brass buttons. "I dabble. Dabbling is a costly enterprise. I get investors to support my dabbling."

"So you're looking for white men to take you far."

His mouth fell open, and I laughed.

"I wouldn't put it—" Thomas looked back then led me across the street.

"What? What is the matter?"

"The younger Kirwan. He hasn't left. Made quite a stir in the tavern last night. He's dangerous, but you know this."

My feet felt mired in place. "I thought he was gone. I don't want to think of him ever."

I pulled away, wanting to turn and search and hide, but Thomas blocked my retreat. "Nothing will hurt you. You deserve peace. I'll make sure of it."

Those large eyes of his saw me, saw me as the woman I was—a survivor of the worst, not damaged goods, something worthy to be protected.

"Kirwan probably won't leave Roseau until your father goes. Be careful."

"I'm free. I can't act as if I'm a captive."

"I agree, ma'am." His smile returned, dissolving the tension in his high cheeks. "Let's walk to the church. It will give you time to come up with more questions."

Not ready to be home, I wrapped my palm about his arm. "Tell me of the Coxalls. My daughter Lizzy has caught the son's eye."

"Well, John Coxall is the heir to the Coxall fortune. The family owns a successful merchant practice. Their business rivals Tuites of Nevis."

"The Tuites are powerful. They brought priests to Montserrat and made God meet everyone in the woods."

Thomas chuckled. At the church he tugged the locked gate. "Notre Dame du Bon Port is glorious."

"I love this church. The stone tile floor and beautiful stained-glass windows. If it was allowed, my Lizzy should marry Coxall here. Thomas, I want her protected with a contract. Can you help me with that?"

"I could if you answer a question for me."

Lifting my chin, I braced for the worst. "Yes."

"You're beautiful and sad. If not for Foden, whose love are you mourning?"

"Sir, you can tell all that from a walk?"

"You're forgetting I held you on the docks. You curled into me like you missed a man's touch. Yes, I can tell a lot by listening and looking, caressing."

"I did no such thing. I—"

The smug look on his face. He baited me, and I'd given him this power. "I think I can walk back by myself."

"Now, Miss Doll—"

"Miss Kirwan to you."

"No, not formalities. You have my curiosity spinning."

"Then be like a cooper's hoop and keep rolling down the road. Don't stop till you hit the water."

"That's harsh, Miss Kirwan. I'm sorry. I'll make it up to you."

I started down Virgin Lane.

"I can noodle out a marriage contract for your daughter and negotiate on your behalf. I'll personally ensure it to be complete and have the protections a freewoman needs."

I turn to him. "How much?"

"Another walk on the day of my choosing?"

The legal fees for Brayshaw and Bates were hefty. I needed to save my coins for Lizzy's dowry and our living expenses until I decided what to do to earn money.

Thomas's wide eyes seemed to beg. Nothing wrong with a man who can humble himself. We took our time walking to Hanover Street. He showed me more vendors, had me laughing and sampling buns filled with saucy saltfish until well into the evening. Such a pleasant fellow, this Thomas. His beggin' wasn't bad. It could sway me if I wanted to be swayed.

Finally, we arrived at my rented house. "Well, Miss Doll."

"I accept your offer . . . for the contract."

It took a second for a grin to pop onto his pursed lips. Was he looking for a different answer or had he forgotten what he'd asked?

Thomas nodded with vigor. "My pleasure to offer you my free legal services. I'll have the first draft by the end of next week. Night, Miss Kirwan."

He tipped his hat, whistled, and went away.

Shaking my head, I went inside. Edward was on the floor playing with the pull toy of a carved lion. Kitty sat on the sofa, braiding Charlotte's hair. The fragrance of coconut pomade filled the room. Lizzy was in the corner, a book in her lap.

My Lizzy read. Lizzy was a reader. Pa did right by her.

When I moved closer, I saw her eyes were puffy.

"Lizzy, what is it? What has happened?"

"Grandpa left. He took my pa. They're gone for good."

I turned to Kitty. "What?"

"Mama sent Pa away."

Mamaí?

Lizzy leapt out of chair. "She's staying 'cause of you. Now, I have to too."

She tore away and ran up the stairs.

Though I wanted to gloat, I couldn't. It would hurt my daughter. I'd hurt her enough. "Lizzy, stop right there."

She did and leaned over the landing.

"Dry your eyes. I told you I'd take care of things. I'm working on a contract for you and your young man. Once it's negotiated, you'll start your own household."

"You're going to let me go?"

"I'll hold none of you back if I think you're ready. You're ready, ready to make every mistake a wife can afford. That contract will be done. I freed you. I won't let you be unprotected."

Lizzy covered her mouth. I could see her crying harder.

She launched from the steps and hugged me. It was a big embrace, the biggest since our reunion, but this love was because I gave in to her.

Nothing but time could fix us. I hugged her back and accepted the love she offered. I prayed this headstrong girl wasn't making a Dolly-sized mistake.

DOMINICA 1784: FAREWELL

Sleep refused to come to me. It was hard to get comfortable on this crowded mattress.

I slid out of bed, making sure not to wake Kitty or Edward.

He'd stopped coughing. Mamaí had made him something from the garden she'd started out back.

Wrapping my blanket about me, I went down the stairs. The town house had a rare chill.

Something was off in me.

I felt buffeted about like a boat in the sea looking for land in a storm. Lizzy and I weren't any better unless we talked Coxall. She didn't want a mother, or me as a friend either.

Through the parlor window I saw Mamaí on the porch. She burned a candle, and the flame cast her shadow on the rail.

I went out and sat in the empty chair, the one Pa used to court her. "You couldn't sleep either, Mamaí?"

She nodded. "I missed you calling me that."

She sipped a mug of tea and stared straight ahead.

From our position on Hancock there wasn't much to see, just more walls of town houses.

"A soldier marched past again." She tapped her fingers. "That makes four tonight. That war in the seas has put everything in British control. I like the French better."

How would Mamaí have a side in war not fought in Montserrat? Cells always sought to be on the British side. Maybe they'd prove him right in Demerara in time. "More soldiers could be a good thing. They need goods. Remember when you made blankets for me to sell?"

"You're free, Dolly. You can't be huckstering."

"Mercantilism. I made a lot of money hiring out housekeepers."
Mamaí stared forward as the redcoats passed.

"I'm not going to fret about them. I have our papers. We are
free."

"Dolly, you think men with guns will take the time to read?"

"Then I'll have to become important, powerful enough they'll
know me."

"If anyone could do it, you will." Mamaí sipped on her tea.
"They don't put their estate houses on much land."

"Farther into the hills are the plantations. We're too close to
shore. I don't want an estate until I can rival the Hermitage."

"That would be John Coseveldt Cells's Hermitage?" Her voice
was low, but I didn't miss any of the sharpness in saying that man's
name.

"Demerara, Mamaí. Cells took Kitty and me to his plantation."

A long silence enveloped us, before she grasped my hand.
"Charlotte and Edward are lovely."

"I've chosen to give myself to men, but nothing was taken. Edward is Cells's. Charlotte's not. She's a Kirwan."

"Tarn bastard makes pretty children. The fool should rot in
hell. When he discovered that you'd gone and that Cells bought
Kitty . . ." She folded her arms about her. "He'd have killed you if
he caught you."

I'd never heard her say harsh words. I sort of liked it. "Did
Nicholas hurt you? Did he touch Lizzy?"

"No. Your pa came back and moved us into the big house.
Massa Kirwan was good to us when famine hit Montserrat."

Famine? Thinking of Cells's decadent parties, even the waste-
fulness made me nauseous. I held my stomach. "Mamaí, how do I
make it up to her?"

"Don't try. She's unharmed. She's had tutors and can read and
write. When she caught the eye of Coxall's son, your pa made

them understand she wasn't for sale, made sure she knew British etiquette. She'll make a good wife. The boy loves her so."

There wouldn't be a marriage. Thomas had explained what I knew, that the Catholic Church, our church, hadn't legally sanctioned marriage between races. If Coxall had a little Black blood . . . "A contract will keep her protected."

"You could've freed yourself a long time ago, Dolly. Your dreaming made Lizzy's world better."

The press of her lips trembled. A lone tear trailed her cheek. "Kitty. My youngest. She—"

"She's happy, Mamaí. She's safe in the world she built."

Mamaí drew me to her, kept me from falling down that hole of guilt. It was bottomless in my chest. "She doesn't have nightmares anymore, none like mine."

She kissed my crown where my braids had fallen. "You going to see Cells again? You have a child by him. At least he let you grow up before he started in on you?"

"He never forced me. I loved him, but he has a life in London he had to return to." I wanted to tell her of Catharina, but shame kept that secret buried on my tongue.

"Cells couldn't have you in his world and keep his."

Mamaí knew? Of course she would, being friends with Mrs. Ben. "Who birthed him?"

"Mrs. Ben's daughter. She died in childbirth. Mrs. Cells mourned her own stillborn and forgave her lousy husband with that white-as-a-ghost babe."

"He was taught to lie. And that pale skin matters more."

"It's how it is. It's survival."

I raise my head. "Then I need to prove skin don't matter at all."

"That sounds like my Dolly."

I closed my eyes, savoring the comfort of her warm weathered hand on my brow. I could win, win bigger with Mamaí here supporting me.

"You're the leader of our family, Dolly. I'll help you all I can with the children and this next babe."

"Next?"

She slid the union of our fingers to my stomach. That heaviness I'd been feeling for weeks, a parting gift from Demerara, but from whom—Cells or Owen?

It didn't matter. No man would take from me again.

DOMINICA 1785: A CEREMONY

In my bedchamber, I pinned up my hair, leaving a few curls to frame my face. The Coxalls would gather soon. This was Lizzy's special day.

Like I'd done for Cells's parties, I rolled big sections of my hair around plantain-shaped cushions to achieve height and jabbed them in place with the buckle pins. I used to think my hair was too thin, but the way my new solicitor, Mr. Thomas, seemed to notice, it was perfect. He visited often. Didn't mind that.

About my neck, I put on Kitty's colorful beads and picked up my hat, the perfect one for Lizzy, a pouf of creamy white satin surrounded by tiny pink and red Bwa Kwaib flowers.

I went inside the bedroom the sisters shared and stared at my daughters; they looked like twins except Charlotte had Mamaí's coloring and Lizzy's hair was thicker. Her lovely braids were magnificent pinned in circles and stacked like a crown.

"This is for you, Lizzy. When you walk out with Coxall and he takes you to his family, wear this and be proud."

Lizzy bounced up from the bed. The hem of her yellow gown with silver threads swirled about her. She reached for the hat but stopped and ducked her face into her small hands. "I don't deserve this. I've been unkind and you have given me the world."

I kissed her cheek, and we hummed our hymn.

Charlotte joined us. In the circle of our arms, we'd found each other as sisters, as blood.

When the tears cleared my eyes and I could distinguish the fine embroidery of shells on Charlotte's gray bodice, I let them go. "You two are my vision. You both are hope and peace. I want that for you."

With the hat pinned to Lizzy's locks, we went down the stairs.

In my parlor, Thomas hovered about the table, pointing to sections in his drafted contract for the senior Mr. Coxall. The man, with the pinched nose and balding head, had his face close to the pages.

When Thomas visited, he spent time with Edward, claiming the boy was outnumbered in a house of women. I think the man liked me, the look of me with dark cheeks beginning to puff, my figure getting thicker.

But I needed a friend, nothing more, especially with another man's babe in my gut.

The younger Mr. Coxall claimed Lizzy's hand. His gaze never left her.

"Done." His father put down his quill and turned to the lovely couple. "Congrats, my boy."

They did look fine together. Coxall was of good height and enough muscles to protect Lizzy. 'Course his father's money would do that, too.

"This is done, Miss Kirwan. You've handled things well." The father's face had that look of tolerance, like he'd given his boy the birthday gift he'd hoped for the whole year.

Lizzy was a gift, despite how she came to be. I knew the younger Coxall saw it. That was all that mattered.

Thomas caught my arm. "You need to make your mark."

"Show me where to put my signature." I'd practiced for the manumit documents. I was ready.

I sat down and inked every spot that read Dorothy Kirwan.

Thomas took the quill. "Now we're done."

The way he said it, sharp and final, stabbed at my chest. I realized I didn't want to be done with him.

Mamaí served sorrel punch. Kitty dished black cake onto plates. My little Edward had a small bouquet he'd made from my mother's garden. More red Bwa Kwaib, pink hibiscus, and orange peacock flowers.

My mind was a little taken aback by the addition of the menses flowers. That was the flower of hate.

A knock upon my door set my heart beating fast. Everyone who was supposed to be here had arrived.

Thomas sprinted to the door. "I'll answer for you, Miss Kirwan."

I braced, holding my wobbly insides, hoping that Pa or Nicholas hadn't come to cause upsets.

The door opened. A man I'd never seen—brown hair, young face; he was wearing priestly robes—stood.

"Come in," Thomas said, grinning like he'd won a prize. "It's my minister, Mr. Johnson. I thought he'd offer the couple a blessing."

My eyes felt a little weak and wet. My friend had found a way to bring God to this union. "Thank you, Thomas." I said in a whisper and stood at his side. "It's Miss Doll to you."

The minister leafed through his book. "Join hands, Coxall and Miss Kirwan."

His voice was clear, and the couple obeyed, smiling so hard I thought their teeth might fall out.

The shared vows were crisp, saintly. The minister wrapped his stole about their linked hands. "You will forsake all others and be only to one another."

"I do." Coxall's and Lizzy's voices blended.

Then Johnson prayed for the couple's fidelity, their love and joy.

Thomas clapped. "That will do, Johnson. Congratulations, Mr. Coxall, Mrs. Lizzy."

I kissed my daughter's cheek.

"Mother, don't cry. You've given me what I wanted. My freedom and my love. We won't lose touch again."

"No, we won't."

I did what was needed. Now I waved good-bye. Lizzy belonged to Coxall, not as property but as a free person.

The door ripped open and the devil himself stood there.

Nicholas had found me.

If he'd come to steal Lizzy's joy, I'd kill him for sure.

DOMINICA 1785: A CANCER

Nicholas—the man who haunted my dreams and tried to block my grasp at freedom—charged into my house.

"Father," Lizzy said. She went to him and he embraced her. "I thought you went to London?"

"Not yet. When your grandfather told me of your union, I had to come and offer my congratulations. Didn't Dolly tell you I was here on the day you were manumitted? No. Well, she never wanted me to wish you well, Lizzy."

I held off my strangling rage and stepped out of Thomas's shadow. "Lizzy, you and Coxall go on. This is your day."

Coxall's father looked at me and then Nicholas and must have decided it was better to leave and did so.

"Pa, have some cake. Greet my husband again. Ma—"

I glared at Lizzy. "I love you, but this fool isn't welcome in my house. He'll have no part of this celebration."

"But Mother—"

Mamaí's eyes widened but then she gave me a nod. The truth would out.

"The liar's paid nothin' and even tried to block me from freeing you."

Fire hit her cheeks. "Pa, that's not true. Tell everyone the truth."

I took Lizzy by the shoulders. "Long ago, he didn't want to put his name on your birth records unless I allowed him to force himself on me. . . . Say nothing of the rapist and his truth in my house."

Lizzy's mouth dropped open.

I held her for a second then shoved her to Coxall. "Take my

daughter. Go be happy. Comfort her because she is a jewel no matter her beginnings."

Coxall sheltered Lizzy with one arm but stepped forward. "Yes, ma'am, unless you need me here."

Thomas stepped between me and Nicholas. "No, Coxall. Take your wife."

My son-in-law escorted my crying Lizzy out of the door.

Nicholas laughed. "She'll always love me. I'm the one who stayed."

"Mamaí and Kitty, take Charlotte and Edward upstairs."

My mother grabbed my youngest and took him to the second level. But Charlotte stood still, staring with the tray of cakes in her hand.

Did she see the likeness and know that this horrible man was her pa, too?

Kitty took up a knife from the table. "Go away. Don't hurt no one."

"Ahhh, sister," Nicholas said, "that's not nice."

I took the sharp thing from Kitty and waved it toward my brother. "You want another scar for your right cheek? I strike harder than Kitty."

The minister waved his Bible. "Everyone needs to calm down."

"Kitty, take Charlotte upstairs."

Kitty clasped the tray and dropped it on the table. Then she towed my stunned girl up the steps.

Nicholas plodded past Thomas and plopped onto my sofa and fingered a piece of cake in his mouth. "Nice place you have here. How much whoring does it take to maintain a place like this?"

I laughed. "That's your best, you little worm?"

"Miss Doll, let me just get him out of here." Thomas stepped again between me and Nicholas.

The minister tried to reason with words of calm.

But I was done. I went to Nicholas and put the knife to his neck. "Thomas, you want me?"

"Yes."

"I'll let you have me, if you kill him and make sure no one finds the body."

Nicholas tried to grab the knife, but I'd cut into his flesh. He stilled. "Are we agreed? Since this fool thinks I'm a harlot, I might as well use my body to get rid of his."

The minister looked faint, all red and pink in his cheeks. "This isn't right. I can't. Thomas, I didn't—"

"Sit down, Johnson," Thomas said. "She's not serious, 'cause Miss Doll knows I'd kill for her without a second thought."

Nicholas's eyes became wide like plates. My brother didn't think I had a friend to defend me.

The fool was sweating. He knew I'd kill him, that he deserved it.

His throat vibrated as a lump went down. "I had to see our little girl. Then I had to see you. I've actually missed you. Have you thought of me?"

"Only in nightmares." I gave Thomas the knife before I did stab the fool. I might be free, but killing a white man had consequences. "Make him go away, Thomas."

Nicholas slipped to the right, and the fool minister blocked Thomas from putting his hands on my brother.

He was at the door. "You think you've won, Dolly? You haven't."

My laughter fell heavy. "I'm in your head, Nicholas, controlling you, your thoughts. You'll not be free. You'll always know you tried your best but couldn't defeat me."

"Shut up, Dolly. You whore. You *N'girl*." He ran at me, but Thomas punched the fool in the face. The big man dumped my brother to the ground and put a knee in his chest. "You're here to start a fight. That's incredibly stupid. To hurt a woman. That's evil."

"Oh, your new lover? You're stupid if you think she's worth the time."

Thomas hit him again, bloodying Nicholas's mouth. "I've heard

Kirwan's son was a belligerent drunk. Should've known all that meant was stupid."

"She's evil. Dolly is evil."

"I can't help that everything you've done has failed. That Pa knows I am the more successful of his children. Get out of my house. If you come back, I'll have you killed on sight."

"You wouldn't dare touch a white man. That's illegal."

"Then I'll have Thomas kill you. He's already agreed."

Thomas grumbled, sputtered a curse then a sigh. "And the terms are to my liking."

The minister was at the door. "I don't know what's going on, but this is more than the favor, Thomas."

My hero punched Nicholas hard. Blood splattered on the floorboards.

The evil man's head fell back.

"He's out cold. A new version of *helpin han*. A firm punch." Thomas shook his fist, then signaled to the minister. "Johnson, you're not done here. I need help getting him out of here. The streets are full of soldiers. They'll ask questions."

Johnson mouthed a prayer, but he came back into my parlor.

Looking at Nicholas still breathing, I pulled my arms about me. "Get rid of him."

Thomas jerked off his coat. "I'm not killing him, if that is what you want."

"Take him from my life."

"I can do that for you. Get me something, a sheet. Need to tie him down."

I ran up and grabbed bedclothes, rushed back downstairs, and tossed them to the minister.

He ripped one in shreds, then he and Thomas tied Nicholas's hands and feet.

Thomas went to the door and peeked out. "We didn't bring a carriage. We'll take him out back, then to the docks, to the *Mary*."

He and Johnson took the second sheet and wrapped Nicholas like he was a bundle. Then Thomas threw him over his shoulder.

I grabbed Thomas before he made it out my back door. "What are you going to do?"

"I'm going to dump him back in Montserrat, back with his father. I'll make sure he ships him off to London where he can do no more harm."

"Thank you." I kissed Thomas's cheek. "Thank you for everything."

"Remember what you promised. I should collect something for wanting him dead for hurting you."

I put a quick peck to Thomas's mouth. "We'll see how long you stay in Dominica. That boat and those investors might have other plans."

"Always ratcheting up the stakes. Murder. Now a residency clause. I'll have to see, 'cause you're in my head too."

The minister opened the back door. "This is highly irregular, Thomas."

"You can preach at me and this fool all the way to Montserrat. Unless you want me to throw him overboard with everything bound. That might get me free of Miss Doll's residency clause."

Johnson sighed. "Oh, Lord. Thomas, what have you gotten me into?"

"Minister, keep praying. Miss Doll, close the door behind us."

Standing in the threshold, I wished he was the type to kill for me.

Mamaí came down. "All gone?"

"Yes."

She hugged me. "If Nicholas knows we are here, the better for us to leave. Maybe go to Grenada."

"No. I stay for Lizzy. The Coxalls are residing in Roseau the rest of the year. Need to make sure Coxall treats her well, especially after tonight."

"Nicholas could come back and Thomas won't be here."

My brother's blood stained my floor. My nose filled with the scent of the smothering peppermint water that would be needed to clean it. Stomach turning, my hand pulsed. It wouldn't stop. Everyone who hurt me wanted me to not breathe, to be shaken and quiet and gone.

No more.

"I'll succeed here, Mamaí. Roseau, all of Dominica will know my name."

Her hold didn't slacken. "It's going to be all right."

It had to be. I couldn't let him win, none of 'em.

PART FOUR

The loving

I overcame my weaknesses by claiming theirs.

DOMINICA 1785: A CHARMER

I looked down in the cradle at my little girl. Frances Owen was cute, a natural charmer. Her ears were darker, a nice color, like toasted wheat. That would be her color, her complexion, not like my palest children, Catharina and Lizzy.

Frances had pinkish-brown hands, eyes of yellow topaz, and the cries of a banshee; I loved her, every inch of her.

Even the cleft in her chin.

Yet it took all my energy to get to her. Flopped on the floor, I didn't have it in me to pick her up. Luckily, this sweet little thing lulled herself back to sleep.

Kitty came into my room. Sat behind me and tugged at my braids. "I should do your hair before it knots."

"Sorry, I'm not of any use."

"Dolly, you've had a baby. Before your confinement, you trained two women to work as housekeepers for new clients while carrying the load of five coconuts on your stomach. You need to rest."

I rose up from my crouched position on the floor. "Frances is asleep now. Kitty, my milk isn't right."

"Mama has taken care of that. She has a wet nurse coming." My sister led dizzy me back to bed. "You don't have to fret. We'll take care of everything."

"Serves me right, having a baby when I'm old. Almost thirty."

Mamaí stuck her head inside. "Well, most don't make it to thirty."

She tucked me beneath the covers and a fine new blanket of silver and blue, one of our mother's best. "We should've saved this to sell in the market. I'm wasting goods. I'm terrible."

Mamaí put a palm to my forehead. "You don't have the birthing fever. This is the sadness, comes sometimes when you have children. The pain mixes things. You will be fine in time."

She walked back to the cradle and poked at the covers. "Little Miss Frances has been born free. You did good, Dolly."

This one was born free. Maybe I wasn't terrible.

My mother sat next to Kitty on the bed. "You going to tell Captain Francis? You gave this child his name."

Mother wasn't sly. She saw the resemblance to Edward and knew what I was doing.

"Owen saw I was with child on his last visit. That's why he left quickly. He doesn't want children. He's married to the sea. And I don't want him. Frances is mine. No one will take her away."

Mamaí squinted at me. Kitty kept untangling my sweaty braids.

Yet I heard the roar of guilt welling in my gut. I was guilty. Catharina was two and I hadn't seen her, knew nothing of her.

Mamaí touched my brow again. "I'm going to make you some tea."

"No one is strong as you, Dolly. Please get better. Sister, you have to."

Kitty's eyes had tears. Seeing me sickly made her scared.

That was a bad place to be, where your weakness made others weak.

I pulled her close and held her so tight. "I'll be fine."

Mamaí moved to the door. "Mr. Thomas visited again today. He said Nicholas is gone for good. He's in London."

Was that good enough? I covered my face with my arms. The sleeves of my nightgown fluttered like wings.

Kitty nudged me, which meant I needed to stop fidgeting if she was going to dress my hair.

With my braids done, I might try to leave this room. The Obeah shadows and the death masks of Mrs. Ben and Cudjoe haunted my eyes.

And I was weak, and I didn't know why, didn't know how to return to me. I wasn't ready for a death mask. I had a business to run, money to make, and another child to raise with no father.

DOMINICA 1785: A CHANNEL

I sat in my parlor with Thomas King. He wasn't an old friend exactly, but he remembered me from Demerara and was one of my first clients for my housekeeping services. Upon arriving in Roseau, he searched for me and came to see me at Hanover Street.

"Miss Kirwan, I'd heard you'd moved here and have been doing quite well."

I nodded and stirred my tea, fingering Foden's crest. "Business is booming in Roseau as more soldiers pile into Dominica. The demand for reliable housekeepers is high. I employ fifteen now."

The man nodded, but I could see him calculating. Four shillings a week, netting three per housekeeper, was a good start.

"Miss Kirwan, I have a business proposition."

What? I set down my spoon and collected myself. "It's not often a man like you would seek me out."

"Well, you're a good businesswoman. When I saw Cells—"

My heart beat fast. "You saw him?"

"Yes, I visited him in London, a few months ago."

I tried not to sound anxious, but I couldn't help myself. "How's his family?"

"His wife is still poorly, but his little girl is precious. I've never seen a man more smitten by his daughter. He throws a party for her doing the smallest things like sounding out words or walking."

My two-year-old Catharina was walking and talking, perhaps reading like her pa. I took this wave of good news. It poured into my chest. It echoed, hitting the bottom of my sorrows.

"Miss Kirwan, are you all right?"

"Yes." I wiped my fingers on a napkin and hoped I seemed calm, not brokenhearted or scared. "It's good he's well."

"Next time I see him, I'll tell him you asked about him."

My false smile must be broken. He looked down and finished his biscuit.

I leaned in closer. "Mr. King, what can I do for you?"

"You have a network of clients in Roseau. I have a network of clients with goods in Scotland and England. They want access to sell to the island. I think we can be beneficial."

I chuckled. "That word usually means you'll make more money than the women involved. I'm not the woman for you." I stood. "It was good of you to stop by."

Mr. King didn't move. He peered over his spectacles. "Miss Kirwan, I understand why you might be skeptical, but I need a trustworthy partner. I won't risk my clients to anyone."

"You're choosing me because I'm trustworthy. How do I know you are trustworthy? I met you through Cells. You paid your bills on time. Does that make a criteria for trust?"

"I'm reputable."

"You have a reputation. You manned slave boats. Did you ever make your cargo sing on deck?"

His face blanked then went orangey red in his cheeks. "I'm a blackguard. I've killed a man."

Where was he when Nicholas was here? I dipped a lump of sugar into my chamomile tea. "This isn't helping me today."

"I'm trying to change Camden, Calvert and King to do more banking and merchandising, but I have to show successes."

"Trading in people and broken lives made you wealthy. I want nothing to do with that. Didn't Cells tell you my background? I'm recently manumitted."

"I wouldn't bring that to you. None of those deals. I need to prove that money can be made other ways. You can help transform the firm."

His face seemed consumed in shadows. Good. Making a fortune stealing proud people should eat him alive.

"No, thank you. Mr. King, it was nice seeing you."

"But you could make money."

"I am making money."

His upper lip sweated. It was rare to see a man do that. Full damp face, arms wet from exertion under the sun, but that upper lip thing, pure nerves. He was desperate.

"My references are impeccable."

I looked at him and his big words. "You need me more than I need you, Mr. King, and as you said, I'm doing fine."

"If you have more goods to sell to your clients of the finest qualities, you'll do better than fine. You'll be rich."

"What's in it for you? Never met a man or woman who did something that wasn't for his purse."

His lowered his chin. "Death. I have to do something to right my scales. I built a vehicle on financing. I need a vehicle built on something else, something that doesn't involve selling humans. I see this now as I see you. I sold humans."

"You can quit."

"Then nothing changes. But if my partners see that money can be made in other ways, they'll change. My bishop, Dr. Porteus, he's challenged my church to cease involvement in the slave trade. He's trying for hearts. I'm trying for purses. We'll see who wins more souls."

King had some conviction on him. He definitely wanted to prove something. If not me as a partner, he'd find another. Men on a mission did. Goods from England, like the finery Cells brought back, would give me the competitive edge in Roseau.

"I tell you what, Mr. King. Let me think on this. I'll be in touch."

He stood this time. "Please do."

I walked him to the door, but Thomas was there knocking. "Mr. Thomas? Mr. King, this is my solicitor. He'll be the one to finalize any contracts, if I decide."

Thomas wore a big frown. "Yes, Miss Doll." His tone was sharp.

King went on his way and my free legal resource came in.

He looked good. His hair was combed and topped with a brown bicorn hat hosting a copper-colored cockade of ribbons. It was as fine-looking as was his jade coat. His gaze, respectful and heated, already held me close.

"You're doing better, Miss Doll. Up to seeing people?"

"Yes, yes, I am. But having a child is not an easy thing." It was getting less easy. "Please be seated."

He tossed his hat on a chair then stared at me for at least two minutes.

"Do I look the same?" I touched my cheeks. "I put on some weight."

"You were beautiful before. More beautiful now."

Such a flatterer.

That made me want to smile, but I bit my cheeks not to. "What brings you about?"

He surveyed the room as if trying to inventory things. Same indigo-blue sofa, one additional chair covered in gold tapestry fabric, a gift from the Coxalls. Lizzy and her husband had good taste.

I hoped it was a sign of mother and daughter rebuilding.

Thomas didn't sit. He stared. "Well?"

"Well, what?"

"The last contract I made for you was a concubine marriage. I hope that's not what you want with King?"

With a shake of my head, I dismissed that. "No. Are you always the jealous sort?"

"Thomas King is a slave transporter. He's too old for you, and he's married."

"He came with a business proposition, not the other kind."

"Oh." Thomas gazed at me with that lip-biting smile. "Look, I know this might be an inconvenient time for you, but I have an interest in you. I fear that this condition is not going away. I think we need to do something about it."

"Sounds as if *you* have a problem, sir. I have none except . . ."

Thomas leaned forward like I was about to share a secret. "What?"

"I'll need you to review a few contracts for me. I'll pay."

"You want to use me for my legal opinions. And you wish to pay me in something other than affection." He put his hand over his heart. "I feel used. That certainly cheapens my declarations."

"Then never mind, I'll ask Mr. Bates."

"No. No. Let's not be too hasty. I'll work for you. Maybe you can offer incentives."

"Inc-cent-whats?"

Thomas sat close to me. "Incentives are nice things that you do to keep one motivated to serve."

"Doesn't seem as if you need much motivation, not with you sitting this close."

"Doll, do you like me, even a little?"

"You know I do."

He folded his hands behind his head and leaned back against the sofa. "That's good. I've never second-guessed myself so much in my life."

"I don't want you guessing anything. I like you. I think you're a good man."

He stood. "I'm back in Roseau for a few weeks. I intend to come and spend some time with Edward. He's still outnumbered. I heard you had a beautiful baby girl."

"Yes. And Edward misses you. Thomas, right now I need a friend, nothing more. I trust you. I trust you with my children. That means more than affection."

"Don't know about that. You've never had my affection."

"Trust me. I know that we won't work, Thomas."

I followed him to the door. "I like a big family, always craved one. There's the makings of one here, with me and you."

"Thomas, please."

He smiled at me. "Fine. A hug, friend?"

I went into his arms quite easily.

But that man held me, tight and close, with palms stroking and soothing my back.

I didn't know I missed a man's touch, not till this moment when Thomas wove his fingers in mine and my heart found the rhythm of his pulse.

DOMINICA 1786: A KING'S SON

Mamaí stood in my bedchamber making me dress in pink and red. My gown had a festive border of hibiscus flowers at the bodice.

"Hurry," she said and fussed with my braids, the curls I wore that framed my face. "No more talk of business."

Mamaí walked, swaying like a church bell. She'd finally started to wear the full petticoat, a sage-green dress with beige tunic puffed. This was the fashion of freewomen in Roseau. "Your legal man Thomas keeps reviewing your contracts. Funny the words sound like poems."

Well, he did slip in a line or two. The man was sweet and attentive and looking for forever. I was good with today. "He's away in Grenada. He'll be gone for a while."

Kitty came into the room. She was dressed in a light blue gown of stripes. The overdress was a solid satin of deep indigo. Did Mamaí get her ready to go out too?

"Sis, you look pretty."

"Polk is here in Dominica. We might see him at church tonight."

My Charlotte sat at the table where I signed the housekeeping contracts. She added up invoices. She had a head for numbers.

"Mama," she said, "we're doing well this month. We'll need to hire two more girls." She glanced at me with an approving nod. "Glad you're going out."

"Mamaí is sending us to church."

Charlotte was shy, but she wasn't stupid. It was Tuesday. There was no Tuesday service at Notre Dame du Bon Port.

My daughter shook her head and then brought her palms together, steepling her fingers. "I pray that your mood stays lifted."

Kitty and I left the house. The night air was hot and sticky. We headed to the shore.

My sister's locks had coiled tighter, frizzing in the humid air. Then I heard music. It was fancy, the sound of banjos, a flute, and drums.

The ground swayed with the rhythm. The sea roared in the distance.

The salt air smelled good, felt good. The heat felt good.

I was good.

"This is not Notre Dame du Bon Port, Dolly. I don't think Polk will see us here."

"When Mamaí made us go, I sent word to his ship. If he can, he'll meet us here. This is a new church. It's for the temple of the spirit." I took my sister's arm and we danced, danced until my hair fell, danced until my locks were as wild and as puffy as hers.

It felt good to twirl, to kick up dust beneath my slippers. I was free. Today was the first day I felt it.

We flopped onto the beach. Sand gathered in our fine skirts, rubbing into our hot skin. "See, we did have church. I found peace by the water."

Kitty laughed and pinned up my braids. "This is wonderful. I like this, Dolly. I like you having fun and playing with me."

I lifted my sister. The wind swirled about us like fairies cleansing us of sediment. I craved the healing of movement. "We're not done praying, Kitty."

Taking her arm, we headed to the ballrooms by the docks.

Sailors dressed in sharp red uniforms came in and out of one building. That had to be where the ball was tonight.

"Miss Dolly, Miss Kitty, is that you?"

Booming baritone. No one had a bigger voice than Polk. I cupped my eyes until I saw the tallest, blackest man in the world.

It was him. I waved.

Dressed in a slate-colored mantle and breeches, he ran to us. Kitty leapt into his embrace. He whirled her around like a rope swing. "Miss Dolly, Miss Kitty, you both look good. It's been too long."

"This is church, Dolly. Dreams come true. My *damfo* is here."

Polk, sweet Polk looked down at my sister with such tenderness. Then he looked at me.

He knew.

He knew Kitty was delicate and younger than her years. He knew.

And Kitty was right. Polk was the best of men, befriending and loving a girl who didn't have the mind to love him back. My heart hurt at her choice of safety, of keeping her mind young rather than aging and loving and risking, maybe losing.

Had I made that same choice by focusing only on my business and my family?

Yes.

Yes, I had. No more being afraid.

Grabbing Polk's other hand, I led them. "Let's go into the ballroom for a baptism in music."

The air sizzled, awash in cologne and flowers and sweat. The place was packed with people, and I watched blue-eyed and brown-eyed men beam down upon us.

They backed up.

Polk's height made them reconsider. I loved me some Polk. We could hear the music, dance, and not be bothered.

We planted in a corner. Hundreds of fishy-smelling tallow candles burned about the room's perimeter like stars. Festoons of pink hibiscus paired with fragrant white lilies. Fish or heady perfume—wasn't sure which would win.

Kitty nestled closer. She was here for me, my love of music, and Polk. My sister was a true hero, my soft heart. I leaned to her ear. "We can go anytime you want. I like the feel of the rhythm."

She gazed at me with her soft eyes. Then with her finger painted a smile along my lips. "Every moment is borrowed time. Enjoy tonight. Dance. Dance for me."

Her words stung with the weight of our truth. We were living borrowed lives.

"You're my strength, Kitty. Know that."

"So dance." She tapped a man on the shoulder and pointed to me.

The fellow glanced at me. I thought he'd turn away, but he grinned and towed me to the center of the room.

I remembered every dance Cells had taught, flourishing my contredanse.

The hours passed and I went man to man—all faces, all shades of the rainbow.

Only a few headed to women whose skin was bright like my daughters. Didn't bother me none. A dance or rejection didn't last any longer than a song.

Patting the last fellow's groping hands away, I started back toward my sister.

Before the music started again . . .

Before I caught my breath . . .

A tall man with sunshine hair who'd held court in the back of the room moved to me. "You're an exceptional dancer. Many island girls don't know the European steps let alone a successful allemande."

He bowed a little. "I will dance with you. The minuet."

"With such an invitation, how can I refuse?"

His laugh was hearty. Weaving his hand with mine, he returned me to the center of the floor.

As if he owned Roseau and everyone in Dominica, the crowds parted. Me and him were all that was left, that and the music.

The rhythm, the blessed rhythm took over me. His steps were perfect. Very skilled, not sloppy or grabby or drunk—the kind of touch that left one wanting more.

The banjo and drums could play forever.

The gold braiding on his coat looked as if coins had been melted to make it.

Except for a stare, his expression was blank.

The song ended and I moved toward Kitty and Polk, but he kept me close.

"Sir, the dance has been nice, but I should return to my party."

"Of course. But your nose."

I willed my fingers to stay at my side, to not check my face. "What of it?"

"It's mine I dare say, same as mine and my mother's, flat and wide with no flare. Even thin at the bridge."

"It's a nose, the blessed features of my mother. My father has a dreaded hook in his."

He lifted his hand toward my face, and I stepped away. "No. No."

"Sorry. You just have extraordinary features for a Negress."

"Why, because my nose looks like yours? I would say we're both blessed, then."

He chuckled harder. "Dance with me again."

That didn't sound like an ask but a command.

Fool that I was, I gave him my hand. The music began when he looked at the musicians.

This time he stepped closer and every turn of the contredanse that required me to be near him, he made sure we touched.

It took great skill to dance and ogle in time to the rhythm. Great skill.

When the tune ended, I moved away, ignoring the whispers of the crowd. I checked my clothes, my hair; everything was in place.

"This is my second Tuesday here," he said. "I'll be leaving soon. My ship will sail to Grenada. I wish we'd met sooner."

"Well, you've seen me now, but it's time for you to go."

"What's your name? I heard your friend say Doll or Dolly."

"It's Dorothy Kirwan, but some call me Doll."

"You're a doll, but I shall call you Miss Kirwan, until we are more intimate."

"You said you were leaving. No time for that."

His lips ripped open and chuckles fell out. "But I do come back. My command sends my orders here."

Seems all the fellows I liked went away, but this one promised to come back. That was new.

"Miss Kirwan, I'm William Henry. Captain of the *Pegasus*."

Another captain too? No. Were they bees and I some sort of flower? "Captain Henry, you're a fine dancer. But my sister is yawning."

"That is a new excuse to not claim all my dances. Until we meet again."

He bowed and I balanced in a perfect curtsy.

Kitty came and possessively locked arms with me.

She didn't need to fret. No matter how wonderful it felt to spin in strong arms, you go home after church, cleansed of your sins. You don't try to find new ones.

DOMINICA 1786: A KISS

Edward and I walked to the shore. Ships moored at a distance bobbed in the waves. My dancing friend had invited me to see his ship. No one had been more shocked than me to discover that the captain of the *Pegasus*, Captain Henry as I'd called him, was actually Prince William Henry, son of England's king. Me, Dolly, freed two years, kicking up my heels with the son of the man who owned the world, well, most of it.

Cells once said that a man couldn't have power with a Black wife. Yet here was a man with power using it to extend his time in Dominica to court me.

Humbling, exciting, the sheer pleasure of it trembled my soul. I had no choice but to go to my prince and see his *Pegasus*.

"Mama, look at the big boat, the one flying the English flag."

Red, blue, and white, the square hung from the forward sails and flopped in the breeze.

Edward knew his colors and the flags of the nations from the flood of visitors coming to Dominica.

"That big one looks fit for a prince." I peered at my little prince, my six-year-old son. He was getting taller. Mamaí's mixtures had made him stronger. His wheezing only happened in the wet season. "Come on, Edward. Polk is waiting."

My Demerara friend waved at us and we climbed into the *Dolus*.

"Miss Dolly, Master Edward. Morning. Ummm . . . You sure about sailing close to a frigate? They have guns, Miss Dolly."

I patted the side of the boat. "Yes, take us to the *Pegasus*."

"Our people don't do well on those big 'uns. Don't be going below."

"It's not a slaver boat. The only man singing from the deck is a prince."

Polk shrugged and straightened his wide-brimmed straw hat. "Come on, Edward, you row with me."

My boy's face lit up as he grasped the oar.

"Mr. Cells asked about you and Charlotte and Edward."

The look I threw Polk must have been sharp. He threw up his hands as if to protect himself. "I'm just doing what Massa wants."

"Tell him we're fine and I'm visiting men on frigates."

Polk shook his head. "Not sure he'd like to hear that."

My shoulders lifted and I stared again at the *Pegasus*. It was huge, enormous. It could swallow Polk's sloop whole.

The guns on the side—intimidating. The three massive pole heads stood like giants. Hooked to it, yards of tanned fabric rolled up as if it could hide from the wind.

The whipping air swept away the scent of salt, even the perspiration from my brows. I could see how those big ships could fill their sails and travel the world. Thomas's *Mary* had caught some. I last heard, he was in Scotland.

The closer Polk's boat came, the more we were gobbled up in the ship's shadow.

I saw Captain Henry looking down at us through a scope.

Blue jacket painted in gold braiding, he looked regal, standing at his wheel.

A raft with women passed us. They were heading back to shore.

I almost wanted to cover Edward's eyes at the scantily clad souls. Such pretty brown and white faces with tunics showing off their bosoms—prostitutes. I'd heard that they visited soldiers at their boats. I thought it a joke.

I looked down. Didn't want these women to think I judged them. I didn't. They did what they had to do. I was lucky my path changed.

"Miss Kirwan." The prince's voice boomed. "You coming aboard?"

"I was invited."

"That you are, lass, but I didn't think you'd show."

He put the scope into his jacket and waved to a fellow who tossed down a rope ladder.

Polk piloted the *Dolus* closer until I could clasp the last rung. "You sure you about this, Miss Dolly?"

"Yes. I'm going to show Edward that there's nothing scary out here in the water."

"Mama, I'm not afraid of much. Mr. Thomas used to take me." My boy's head fell back as he eyed the frigate. "Mama, this doesn't quite seem safe."

"It's high, Edward. But I'm going to do it."

I had my boots on. My striped dress was short, exposing my ankles. I used to climb trees in Montserrat, until Nicholas showed me Cudjoe's feet.

The niggling fear of my brother's terror was mostly gone. I climbed the wobbly thing like I was Mamaí's powerful goddess, Èrzulie Dantòr, one she'd learned about from neighbors.

Edward needed to see me brave again. "Polk, you journey about the coast. Be back in an hour."

He grunted. "Not a minute longer, Miss Dolly."

When I made it to the top, I knew daring me had returned. I waved at the *Dolus* as they floated away.

The prince held his hand to me. "Welcome aboard."

A few men seemed to laugh. Others stared, but I wasn't there for them.

"Captain, you have a very big ship here."

"Better to sail the seas than your little boat." He took me along his deck and gangplanks. "This is a frigate, one of His Majesty's most powerful weapons."

It was beautiful, a celebration of wood and fabric and metal.

"The foremast, main mast, and mizzen harness the power of the wind, Miss Kirwan."

My heart couldn't imagine what it felt like crossing the sea. "Where's the farthest you've been, Captain?"

"Here, the Americas, many places about the sea. I can say I've seen the world."

With his men looking on, the prince led me from stem to bow, from larboard to starboard, and everywhere in between. He pointed and puffed out his chest. "Now, Miss Kirwan, let me show you below. Down the ladderway."

My pulse pounded. I gripped my elbow and twisted the ribbons on my smooth half sleeve. "Below? That's where they keep cargo."

"Yes, cannonballs, bread, my sailors and gunports. Nothing else."

His gaze at me wasn't ignorant to my true question. Just 'cause no singing boats were in port today didn't make them not exist. Just 'cause my skin was covered in lace and silk didn't mean the slave songs weren't in my soul.

As if flutes played, his palm waved before me. Then his fingers froze. He waited as if it was an easy thing to follow him.

We'd spent enough time together these past weeks. I was in no more danger from the son of the king than I was his crew.

"Trust me a little more, Miss Kirwan. Down you go."

Remembering I was brave, I clasped the wooden ladder and went below. Soon my boots planted on flooring, more decking.

The prince zipped down and seized my waist. Within the circle of his arms, he held me, smiling in the darkness, the low light.

"Oh, yes, back to our tour. You're in the wardroom bulkhead. To port is the first lieutenant's cabin. Let me show you."

He danced me into a room, one with a hammock tied to each wall and a desk for writing. "See? Much better."

His arms were about me again. The way he touched me, the way I swayed—we didn't need music to share this rhythm. It was too much to feel for a man about to leave. I wriggled from William, scooted under the hammock, and looked out a window hole.

He joined me with his chin on my shoulder. "Will you miss me when I'm gone?"

"Yes. You've made Roseau come to life. Is this the bowels? Is there more?"

The prince spun me. The passion in his eyes made them jet. "I want to look at you."

His cologne water or soap teased of lavender.

His tightening embrace said he wanted more than a kiss.

Wasn't sure what I wanted.

Skittish, I dipped underneath the hammock sliding to the other side, readying for the door. "Where's your next port."

"Barbados."

Fingering the tan canvas and the jute rope that anchored it, I pushed the hammock. It swung from me to him. "People sleep on this? Doesn't look that comfortable. Couldn't you put a bed in here?"

"We could, but then the *Pegasus* wouldn't have enough room for all my men. A hammock provides a certain amount of stability."

He slipped beneath the thing and stood beside me. "A demonstration?"

Thinking he'd climb on I nodded, but his hands went about my waist and he cast me on it.

I bounced as the thing moved. "This would be comfortable, if I were a fish."

He laughed and swung it faster. There was no getting out without tumbling.

"See, very stable. In fact, Miss Kirwan"—he climbed atop and straddled me—"It's cozy enough for two."

His eyes found mine. The rhythm of the rocking danced in my head. He sank toward me. I almost rose to him, with him looking at me, readying to devour me.

"I should be going. You have—"

A young man stepped into the quarters. "Captain, sir? Hmmm. That's my bunk."

"You'll have it back in a moment, Lieutenant. I'm just showing Miss Kirwan a thing or two about a sailor's life."

I hid my face, pulling into his jacket. That must've made it seem worse.

"Lieutenant," the prince said with a chuckle, "I just need to say good-bye to Miss Kirwan."

The fellow covered his eyes, peeking through his fingers as he spun and darted away.

"He's new." The prince hopped down. "He fumbles over titles but has such a nose for gossip."

"I don't think you care much about your princely title, only that you dance better than most men."

Prince William lifted me high then brought me to the floor. His hands remained on my thighs.

I patted his fingers away. "Thank you for the tour."

"Now, Miss Kirwan, don't be like that. You can't blame a man for searching."

I looked up into his eyes and the grin that made him seem boyish and misguided. "I think you brought the wrong woman on board."

"No, I brought the right one. I don't have the time to show her."

"My son and my boat captain will return shortly."

He brushed his lips along my cheek. "I'll need a proper good-bye. See me off with a kiss."

"That sounds like a command."

"I sense you'd rather give orders. That won't do with me."

With my pinkie, I flicked a ribbon adorning his uniform. "Then how will this end, my dear prince?"

His arms wound around me. The medals on his jacket made a tingling noise. "One of us must bend."

"Maybe it's a tie for evenly matched friends."

"Tied to a friend is better. Miss Dorothy, if I can manage port again in Dominica, will you call on me?"

"I must do the seeking? I thought that was princely business."

"Yes, to search for a queen or a princess or a slipper, so I've heard."

"I'm not a shoe, and I am too old to be a princess."

"Well, Queen of Dominica, let this simple sea captain be sent away with the memory of the beauty he left behind."

My fingers clasped his thick lapels. I saw a month of laughs and lightness in his face. No love at all. That was fine by me. I'd be his Dominica kiss.

I took his square chin in my palm. On tiptoes, I claimed his gaze. "Then I can pretend, too."

I kissed him, kissed like a woman sending away a lover, like a woman hungry for affection, like a woman owning her need.

When his hands fingered the edge of my bodice, I pushed away. "Time to go. You must ready your crew."

"Sometimes being a dutiful sailor is dull." He dipped his chin. "I'll be back. Finish what I start. That's a motto to live by."

After climbing back to the top deck, the prince walked me to the wobbly ladder. It didn't take long for Polk and Edward to return. In the safety of the sloop, I waved.

My prince watched from his deck. It made me smile, knowing a prince wanted me and would think of me every time he approached Dominica.

That made me smile bigger.

Polk, sweet Polk grimaced, and I grinned even more.

DOMINICA 1786: A KINDLING

Frances crawled about my feet. She cooed and bumped into the sofa.

"Are you telling me we need more room?"

Mamaí wobbled down the stairs with a pile of blankets.

With one eye on Frances and the other on my mother, I bounced up and grabbed the lot. "You don't need to be carrying such things."

I put the blankets on the sofa. "The next place I lease will have a room for you to work downstairs. A nursery just for Frances. And something for Edward. He's the man of the house, you know. Maybe he needs something that will not tax him, too."

"Such big plans." She patted my arm. "I'm strong. You need to stop fretting over Edward and me."

How could I not? His wheezing was bad again. I almost wanted to consult the Hispaniola neighbors filling Mamaí with stories of healing by their gods or the Obeah doctors of the Caribs for some cure or potion to make him better.

But who could trust a ghost? The priest at my church would need to pray on my boy good.

Picking through my mother's new creations, I studied the patterns she made, the delicate stitches, the weaving flower petals from mudcloth and cotton.

"You keep giving me such fine fabrics to work with, Dolly. I'll keep creating."

My gaze shifted to my table and the letter from Scotland. "I wish you could make a hundred of these a day. We'd be rich."

"I thought we were rich already. You fretting about money?"

"No. Not at all."

She came to me and lifted my chin. "Dolly, what is the matter? What has you fretting?"

I couldn't put it to words, this churning inside. I had received my first letter from Cells, the first in two years just to me.

Frances gurgled and spit and rolled over yawning. I bent and gave her a tickle. She laughed big.

"Never mind me. Look at that, Mamaí. She can be a performer."

I picked up Frances and hummed at my daughter.

Mamaí brushed my daughter's wavy hair, her smooth olive skin. "Thomas is back. He's asked about you."

My fingers balled beneath Frances's pinafore, the sleeveless tunic I fashioned from magazines Mr. King sent. "My sometime solicitor hasn't stepped across my door. We live in the same place for now."

"Maybe he wants to know you're done mooning over a prince. It was all over Roseau that you're Mrs. Prince, stepping out with him everywhere."

"What?"

"The prince is young. He can't quite hold his liquor or his tongue. Talked about his black Doll waiting for him in Dominica. Lizzy and Coxall says it's all over the Caribbean."

My gaze went to Cells's letter. Could that be what it was about? "That's gossip."

"Dolly, are you done with the prince? No man wants to intrude on another's woman."

Mamaí had concerns for the wrong man. Cells was the one who had power over me. He had my Catharina. I bent my head and kissed Frances's spirals. "What consequence could Prince William have to a solicitor?"

"Plenty. Thomas owns boats, boats that transport goods over the seas. The prince could set his guns on him. They can take his goods. It happened to your pa during that long seven-year war."

"Thomas is frightened for his business? Serves him right for leaving."

"Dolly, he's not afraid of no man, but it's not worth the trouble if you want a prince and not a pauper."

Frances yawned. It was time for her nap. "Thomas is no pauper. He does well."

"He doesn't know what you want."

Thomas wasn't the only one.

Charlotte came downstairs. "I'll put my sister down."

I handed my feisty Frances over to my good-natured Charlotte. My pretty, tall daughter had grown up fast in Roseau. "Where's Kitty, girl?"

"Mama, she and Polk took bowls to the market. You and Grandma, go save the man from his ear being talked off."

"Come on, Mamaí. To the Old Market. Then I'm going to get Mr. Bates to help us lease a bigger place."

My mother smiled and I followed her out. "Go for the prince, Dolly. He hasn't abandoned you or lied."

I hadn't thought of Thomas's leaving as abandoning me. It was just what men in mercantilism did, like Pa.

My mind drifted to Cells's unopened letter. Did it have news of Catharina? I remembered her every night in my prayers, every time I kissed Frances and Edward and Charlotte.

Maybe I was stuck in remembering.

We walked in silence until we reached Mamaí's stand.

At her booth, the noon sun left me blinking. I knocked over her wooden sign. I stooped to get it, and my eyes focused on a pair of men's boots.

Fine leather boots that had a jagged edge and a buckle.

European buckles.

"Morning, Miss Doll."

"New boots, Mr. Thomas?"

My sometime wandering solicitor stood in front of Mamaí's stand. "Yes. You like?"

My lips pressed tight. I slipped to the side, setting my ma's sign in place and ignoring the handsome fool in his fine coat, his dark brown hair brushed to a shine. No foul powders.

"I'll see you later, Mamaí."

Then I marched forward. I stomped the cobbles and went in the opposite direction, away from the booth, away from Thomas.

DOMINICA 1786: A KNOLL

I walked a good three miles through a grassy knoll right to the Roseau River. The hem of my white skirt now bore an inch or two of mud.

"Miss Doll, would you mind waiting?"

"I think I've waited enough for you."

"Don't you think you have that wrong? Aren't I waiting for you?"

Arms folded, I kept looking at the rushing water, not at Thomas, who was probably laughing at me.

"You think you might stop. You're getting all wet . . . in murky water, all drenched in sweat. Glistening."

He knew how to tease with his words. I'd always liked that about him, till today. I'd danced with a prince and not succumbed to his courting because of Thomas. Now the prince was gone and my solicitor had returned to Dominica. Knowing Thomas kept his distance laid bare a deep ache. I was a fool, twice over. "Say your business, sir. Then leave me for good."

Thomas whistled the tarn hymn I was foolish enough to teach him.

"Stop singing. The water's too cold to take a swim, not that I'd float in these petticoats."

He inched closer till I felt his breath on my neck.

"I think you'd float just fine. You're full of heat. Heat rises."

"I'm heated." I spun from the silver-blue water to his sea-blue eyes. "I can be hot or cold or flames if I want. I get to. You don't get to tell me what I feel or what I do. I'm not the one that left."

His smile widened, becoming almost a grin, with that lip biting. "So you did miss me."

Rolling my eyes at him wasn't enough. His smile should be slapped away.

I raised my hand, but Thomas caught my fingers and pulled me to his chest. "Well, I missed you, too. Next time I should insist you come with me."

His hold tightened. I was off-balance breathing him, hints of tobacco and sage.

"My business is here, Thomas. My family who needs me is here. I can't just—"

He kissed me. It was hard and fast, making me know that he missed me, that I was special to him.

My feet dangled as he lifted me higher. I locked my arms about his neck to hold on, to not fall. But maybe I had feelings for him—the quiet ones that entrap the heart.

The breeze scented with sweet Bwa Kwaib swirled the waves. They lapped about us and Thomas held me, kissing me like I was his, like he hadn't been away a year.

He eased me to the ground. My boots made a splash.

"I guess you missed me, Doll?"

I stepped away, touching my fire-warmed lips. "No, not at all."

He beamed and hooked his roaming fingers about the cloth buttons of his coat. "Are you sure?"

This time I kissed him, keeping his silly mouth fully on mine. His breath made a throaty purr in my ear. "I see," he said. "I can tell you never thought of me. But I had heard you weren't lonely."

"I hear I'm quite entertaining, Mr. Thomas."

"Makes a man think long and hard if he wants competition. Also makes him kick himself that you blossomed while he was away."

"You fretting about rumors?"

"A little. I'd like to think I'm a prince." He straightened his short-cut waistcoat, another change from Europe, that far world from the islands.

His mouth nipped at my wrist. "I'm a solicitor, a want-to-be merchant, and a part-time sailor. You have ambitions for more. I'm not sure I can give you more."

"You should stick around and see if you are enough."

"Being in one place is hard when you have dreams, but I keep dreaming of you, thinking of you and me. I said you were in my head. Might be in my heart, too. Doll, girl, I missed you so."

"Then you should've seen about me. You should've been man enough to bring me your dreams and patient enough for me to decide if I want them too."

"I'm man enough, make no mistake. I know you're mad. Doll, I have to know if you're finally letting me court you?"

It wasn't as if he gave me a choice. He kissed me before I could answer and sculpted me like Kitty's clay, molding me to him. I just didn't know if I'd become a pot or a bowl or beads.

That didn't seem important, not with his embrace awakening feelings, stirring them to a fever. I shut off my doubts and concentrated on Thomas being here and the river lapping, dancing at our feet.

DOMINICA 1786: A KEY

Thomas stood at the door to a house near the center of Roseau. It was the third place we'd walked to today.

"This has to be the last one," I said. "We've been all over the city."

"Well, it hasn't been unpleasant, Doll. I've tried to keep you entertained."

The man wore his evil grin, his evil and naughty grin.

He'd taken every moment to touch me, to spin a silver web about my soul and slide it into his pockets. Thomas had figured out the things that made my heart tender—him cooing at Frances, him holding her hand helping her walk. I nearly sobbed watching my Edward lean on his shoulder as Thomas read Shakespeare or other English nonsense.

My boy hadn't been feeling too well, and Thomas brought him cheer. There was no need to wait on a mouthy prince when a dedicated solicitor stood at the ready.

Thomas put a key in the lock. It made a heavy clanking sound then he flung the door open. "This has six rooms. Four upstairs bedrooms and two downstairs. There's a parlor and dining room to complete the arrangement."

"A garden for Mamaí. She needs one, she'd be lost without one."

"What do take me for, madame? I'm a *helpin han*, remember. Of course there's one."

He led me past a burgundy sofa and long dining room table to the back door. "A fenced lot will be perfect. Edward can build castles when he's feeling better."

"Frances might want to, too, Thomas. There's money to be

made in lodgings as well as housekeeping. I've been studying King's magazines."

He waggled his finger at me. "No business today. If Frances grows up to be like her mother, she'll build kingdoms."

Thomas sounded proud of me, of how well my business was doing. He was a rare soul. Men didn't seem to care for competition no matter how friendly.

"Let's see more." He closed the back door and walked me down a hall. "This is the first bedroom on this level."

It was a nice room with a large window, but the view was of another town house. "Not too much star counting from here."

"This one should be for your mother." Slow stride, beaming, he went to the end of the hall. "This should be for you."

He bowed and waved me forward.

A magnificent four-poster bed with a canopy draped in white centered the room. Like a virginal bride, it was clean and pure, standing alone, waiting.

Thomas lit candles that sat in sconces in the corners. He opened a window and the hot air of the evening swept in. He leaned on a door that also led to that magnificent garden. "I can enter here when I visit, if we are to be discreet."

He came to me and tugged a scarlet ribbon that clung to his neck. "This key is for this door. I'll keep it near my heart."

I slid my palm up his chest until it rested on his neck, on the ribbon's knot. "Been making plans for us?"

"Yes. You told me I should at the river."

I tugged the key free and put it in my pocket. "No. I told you to tell me about your plans. That's not the same."

"Well, my plans, if you will consider them, are to be with you forever."

"This house is mine to rent, Thomas. Go rent your own."

Though I smiled and showed him teeth and everything, I meant it. I wasn't setting him and me up with a new place but giving my family more room. "This is for the Kirwans, not to make it convenient for you to woo me. Is this it for today?"

Thomas might've cursed under his breath, but that made no difference to me.

He suckled my counting finger like it was a sow's rib bone.

My breath hitched. His antics stopped being funny. His touch had a luxurious feel, like satin to my skin.

"Let me earn that key to you. Doll, we should be together."

"Thomas, stop joking. We . . . We should go back."

"Your mother has things well in hand. Charlotte and Kitty will keep Frances busy for a parasol and some lace. Edward wants to captain my sloop. Worthy bargains for a night with you."

"Stop."

"Doll, what are you afraid of? What's keeping us apart?"

"You're babbling. Thomas, I like this house. When can I sign papers with Mr. Bates? Tomorrow?"

"I have them here." He tugged a rolled parchment from his jacket. "I knew this was for you. I know you. I want to know everything. This is for your family. I want your family. I've always wanted a large one."

The heat in his eyes for me, the sound of love in his voice for my children, warmed my heart, but I had to resist. I moved to the window and studied the carefree Bwa Kwaib, its droopy red petals pointing to the sea. "Men say they want a family. Then things change and they get on boats and leave. It's safer being friends. I can sign the papers—"

He kissed me, shutting up my foolishness.

"I'm Anglican, Dorothy. We can't marry. But you are Mrs. Thomas to me. I love you. Loved you since that first moment you bounced into my arms."

"What? I hadn't said that I love anyone."

"Dorothy, I want you. I'll make whatever promises you need." He caressed my cheeks. "I love you."

"I don't want anything that goes away when adventure comes."

"Adventure is in my soul, and like you, I have things to prove. If I go, I'll be back. I'll woo you all over again. If you felt a tenth of what I do, you know distance and time won't change that."

"Fancy words that still say you'll leave."

"Then what do you want, Doll?"

The shadows of Thomas being a wanderer like Pa, never staying around when I was in need haunted like a death mask.

Or was it Cells haunting me? One silly letter came today, a mate for the one I had burned, and I was back to missing him and Catharina, a girl who would never know my love.

Thomas kissed my neck and slowly undid the ties of my tunic. He exposed my shift and traced the embroidery along my bosom. "Doll, let me be a knight, a knight persuading a queen he'll slay the dragons that keep us apart."

I was lost, not knowing my mind, unable to come up with a reason to resist him.

"Tell me, Doll." His hands were on my shoulders, kneading me like dough, readying to be slid into the hearth. I didn't want to be burnt or formed with a crust so thick love could never warm through.

"Don't be silent on this, Doll. Tell me what you want."

"I have to own these feelings. I haven't been vulnerable to a man, not like this, in a long time."

"Own it," Thomas said, "take it." His hum was in my ear. He planted kisses to my cheek, the hollow of my throat. "Or tell me why we are apart?"

No word escaped my lips. My story was mine, but I couldn't turn from his passion.

Instead, I pushed his jacket to the floor and pressed my mouth to his. He picked me up and carried me to the bed draped in veils, and I readied to christen this house he'd chosen in the way he wanted, the way I needed.

Just him and me and vows of desire.

On sheets that were clean and new.

I let myself love Thomas. I let my whole self be with him and only him.

I was vulnerable, him on top, me sheltered below, him sliding past my fears, penetrating my soul.

Two lush moans, his and mine. He said he loved me, before he broke me.

To the flames, he took me again, swirling molten me, shaping me with whispers, working me with our palms entwined. Light and dark, sun and moon.

Then nothing but stars.

I opened my eyes and focused on him, his smooth chest with tufts of tickling hair, the way we fit, glistening and damp.

I hoped my glass-blown heart was safe in his rugged hands.

DOMINICA 1787: A KEEPING

Thomas sat at the desk in my bedchamber. Well, pretty much our bedchamber.

Like Cells, he was a neat, tidy man except for his stacks. Thomas made piles of his clothes on the floor. His boots lay everywhere. He obviously had never lived in a damp hut or feared trails of ants or creepy-crawlers.

Still, I liked how straight his back was when he sat in a chair, making his notes, writing up documents. Then there was the smell of his fine cigars, nutmeg and cedar. I loved coming home to it.

"Doll, did you like Mr. Garraway?"

The answer was no, but I couldn't say that, could I? Moving to Thomas, I hugged on his shoulders. "Why, do you like him?"

"He's successful. He has connections with merchants in Europe. I do a little work for him, then I'll get my opportunity. My investors and I will be able to transport straight to the Americas as well as all the Leeward Islands."

"I could connect you with Mr. King. He supplies me with goods. I'm sure he can do something for you."

He kissed my wrist. "No, Doll. I have a plan."

"But I could help. It can save you some trouble if the Garraways don't move quick enough."

Thomas drew me into his lap. "I love that you want to help, but I have this well in order."

"But I—"

"Doll. Let me have my plan."

I saw something flicker in his eyes, something I hadn't seen before. He was hurting, frustrated by his lack of success. He never begrudged mine. My business was booming.

I pulled away and folded my arms about my robe. "Sorry your dreams aren't going well."

He lifted from his chair and pattered his bare feet to mine.

"You are my dream. Yes, I need my business to be successful, but don't think for one moment you're not my dream, too."

"Thomas, I don't—"

His kiss was savage, raking over my lips. He hoisted me high, putting my legs about his waist, and carried me to the bed I'd made. Curled about this big man, his thick thighs, I was eager, hungry for him to take my cares away, to make me unsee his troubled spirit.

"I'm in love with you, Doll." His lips curled into a smile. "Have no doubts about me, about what is most important. Perhaps I might plant a seed or two in your thoughts about expanding our family. I want the biggest family. Like thirty children."

"You're joking?"

"Yes, on everything but being with you." He had my robe undone and his lips found my curves. Soon, we were a pile of perspiration, hot and tangled limbs.

I wanted Thomas to be successful, for I knew the lack of it would come between us, as it had with Cells.

Nothing should be between us, nothing at all.

I needed his love. The steadiness of his hands, every tickling touch numbed my fears of losing him. Ambition was a potent mistress.

Slow and steady. Thomas and me. Day became dusk.

Spent, I fell asleep in his embrace, beneath his beating chest.

When I awoke, Thomas wasn't there. He'd returned to his papers.

How long could he serve two masters? I doubted that I and his unfulfilled dreams would ever coexist.

Darkness was all around. I didn't know where I was. Fear had me. It was viscous, clawing at me. I shifted. I fought.

Was it Nicholas?

War drums.

The boat with souls singing to the wind—had I joined them?

"Breathe, Doll, breathe."

Thomas's voice.

"Help me." My voice cracked, broke into stuttered sighs.

His arms wrapped around me and tugged me onto his warm hairy chest.

He shifted a little and lit a candle.

I felt the brightness on my closed lids.

"Doll, it's a nightmare. I have you. I do."

Still couldn't lift my lids. Couldn't take the chance that he wasn't truly there.

"You're safe, Doll. No one will hurt you, not while I'm here."

That was the fear, wasn't it? That the calm and peace we had, our family, would disappear once Thomas stepped aboard his *Mary*.

"Doll, talk to me."

The sound of rain, rare rain, tapped and danced upon the roof. "*Clagarnach* is what my pa called these heavy showers. Our hut leaked sometimes. That brought worms. One-leggers. Mossies, too."

"You're not there, Doll."

"But I could be. There's truth in the rain. It says its thoughts. It cries upon the poor and the wealthy. It can cause a harvest or cut through mountains. It's powerful."

"You want to be rain? Water dries. It goes away."

"We are all rain, Thomas. 'Cause we all go away. Nothing lasts. Maybe I haven't cut through enough mountains."

He hugged me deeper to his breast. His hands soothed my back like I was a child in want of comfort. "You can do anything."

"Can I? There's more soldiers in Roseau. Sometimes they look at me like I don't matter."

"You can't control others. Just me, and I'm willing to be at your service."

His tone sounded light but there was something else there, hidden like a swallow in the throat.

"Sorry, Thomas."

"No. No, woman. If not for times like this and providing you affordable legal services, I wouldn't know you needed me. I want you to need me. I need you to. Those rare occasions when you turn to me, you bold, glorious creature, it lets me know I have your trust."

Still couldn't open my eyes.

Laden with unspent tears, they had to stay shut. This man shared openly his love, but I heard him groaning in his sleep. His own restless dreams demanded his attention. Thomas wanted them as much as I wanted mine. How could I share him with something that would draw him away?

Something had to bend, had to sway.

I couldn't yield. Starting anew was different for women. Why did it feel like time was up, like some hourglass poured out our sand?

Couldn't peek at Thomas, or even out my window to seek my stars.

He tucked one of my curls behind my ear, then decided to yank off my scarf and tugged at the curl papers I'd put in my hair.

"Stop. It takes too long to put it up. Where's my scarf?"

"I have images in my head of you draping me with all your hair loose on my chest. I haven't had you like that."

"You've had me plenty. The old cook in Demerara would call us rabbits."

He stroked the tender skin under my eyes until I looked.

And I knew he saw me, curl papers, scared, and all.

"Then I'm a happy hare. Come here, bunny."

Couldn't fault his logic. Being with him was definitely easier than being chaste and chasing nightmares. I should have more willpower to resist Thomas when I hadn't been diligent in controlling my menses.

Yet he found that spot, that vein along my neck. It was sensitive to his kiss, his teeth. He raked my pulse into a frenzy like rebels' drums.

Maybe the desire for a big family and a babe of his own would keep him from running after Garraway and everyone who'd use up his kind heart.

It seemed only right to give Thomas this dream if it meant he'd be with me, keeping me whole through mine.

DOMINICA 1787: A KINGDOM

I laid my head on the window and looked out at Mamaí's garden. Her Bwa Kwaib flowers bloomed, but the peacock flower, the orange and red petals, caught my gaze. They were pretty even if they carried a dark power.

I was thirty-one. That was a lifetime for some. I wanted this babe, babe number six, until Thomas started traveling.

"Morning, Doll."

He came up behind me and snuggled my neck, that weak spot behind my ear. Three forbidden words burned in my throat, *I'm with child.*

"What has you in such deep thoughts? A new business venture and expansion?"

His fingers slid down my sides heading to my belly, my soon-to-be-expanding belly.

I turned in his embrace and kissed him. This babe should make him choose us over the Garraways. He said he understood me. Then he should know separating was the worst.

Haphazard and maybe crazed, I led him back to the bed we'd shared.

Half undoing my corset, he stopped. "Why do you have to be this delectable when I have to be about business?"

Business.

That word held a sense of doom. "Must you leave now?"

He drew his hand away and sat on the edge of the mattress. "Yes. John Garraway himself is coming. This time with a deal."

When he turned back from tying his cravat, his face had a frown. "Don't look like that."

Like what? Thought I was better at lying with my smile.

He leaned over the mattress and kissed my forehead. "I'll be back in an hour or so, and if you're done with your bookkeeping or training more housekeepers, I promise to remember where we left off. How many do you have now?"

"Twenty-two."

His smile widened as he tugged on his jacket. Happy for me, maybe, but that was his way of reminding me that I worked on my business all the time, that he should be allowed to do so, too, without complaint.

Garraway didn't care about him bedding me and playing father to brown children. He'd say anything to get Thomas doing his bidding.

My head knew the future. My man would be gone. My luck of children with no fathers would continue and he wouldn't be here to help me brave my storms.

The strain of my last birth pulled me into pieces. I feared for me, but what type of woman was I if I held on to Thomas too tightly? "Bye."

"Now, Doll. Don't be like that. You've won enough."

"What?"

"We're here together in Dominica. The lucrative activities are in Grenada. It's a difficulty to my partners to come here to meet."

"And I serve them, on silver with the finest wines. I support you. You're not happy?"

"Doll, it's not a question of happy. It's about my livelihood."

He knew a lot of big words but he was using those singular ones—my: my activities, my partners, my livelihood.

Pulling my knees to the belly that hid *ours* inside, I folded my arms about my legs. My nightgown with tiny embroidered roses draped me, covering toes that had grown cold. "When will you be traveling, Thomas?"

His eyes veiled. He tied his loose locks with a ribbon, making a great show of the knot. "I must leave to go see Garraway at Mr. Bates's."

He grasped the brass door pull. "Doll, I have to try one last time. I can partner with Garraway directly, importing goods from India, the East India Company. It'll be lucrative."

"Mercantilism. That's huckstering for men."

"It's not a competition. I'm going beyond Dominica. There's Jamaica, Barbados, Nevis, Trinidad, even Demerara. Garraway has a plan to trade in these colonies. I can be a part of it."

"I see."

"Do you? This is for us, Doll, for our family. I want to leave something with my name to not only Charlotte and Edward and Frances but to any sons that bear my name. If you don't have any faith in me now, then you never will."

"I do."

"No, you don't. Or you'd see how badly I need to win this."

He clasped the door's edge. "I'll be back tonight. Will you be here waiting for me?"

"Guess you'll have to come and see."

A smirk briefly settled on his face, but he still left.

I lay back among our pillows smelling his sage soap. I needed to gird my strength. If this babe breathed air and I survived, I needed to prepare to be strong and alone.

A carriage slows in front of Kensington. From the parlor window, I watch the horse's legs powering near, the driver with his greatcoat and red cap, the sleek black box.

My heart pounds. I grip the sill, begging it to be *damfo* coming with the day and time of my appointment.

Though I still have to rehearse what to say, I'm ready to see Lord Bathurst. I will practice, for it's the hardest thing to speak of hope and justice when your heart is alone and grieved.

Another glance out the window reveals a carriage. It's small. Only one horse, like Pa's dray, like Cells's carriages in Demerara. I thought my *damfo* would have more.

The last time we met, there were at least four.

The footman holds the door for Henrietta Sala.

My granddaughter has come to visit. With a satin bonnet that points like a ship's bow, tall and pretty, Henny comes through the parlor doors. She wraps her arms about me.

"Grandmama."

She says the endearment pretty, like it's a song.

"Child, come sit. It's good to see you." I wave her to the lovely tray of tea and sweets Miss Smith has left to make my waiting easier.

A blush hits her cheeks, but she walks around the room looking at the shelves, the stylish curtains and paper treatment on the pink walls.

"This place has only become better."

Her back is straight, her chin is high. I see Cells. Well, I should see him. He's as much of Henny's grandpa as I am her grandma.

"You look good, Grandmama. Was the trip unsettling?"

"No. It was fine." I'm afraid to ask why she'd think so. The rumors must be rampant.

I grab her hand, light and dark, soft and wrinkled. "How is Mr. Sala treating you? You two have been married twelve years now."

"Twelve years and many children. I'm a good mother. That's how often it's said."

The edge in her words are biting and admirable. I like a woman who's bold. But Henny is hurting. Like her grandpa, she keeps secrets.

I pour her tea and then my own. "Tell me the truth, Henny."

"My husband's income and the dowry you provided have given us a comfortable house on New Street, around the corner from his mother's school."

"Yes, the Marylebone on Lissom Street. I recall."

"You remember?"

I want to say I know where all my checks are written, but that will make Henny stop talking. She needs to tell me her heart. Then, I can be a rock for her, a safe place to gather and restore her strength. Women need to do that for other women, not torment them for mistakes. "I do remember the school. But are you telling me you are unhappy?"

"I want to sing. Tramezzani and D'Egville of the King's Theatre, they think I have true talent. They want me, little old me to share the stage with them."

"Then why not? Why aren't you following your dream? Singing is why I put you in Marylebone."

"My Augustus thinks I should be at home with the children and give up all my lessons. He used to perform. He doesn't want that life for me."

Henny picks up her teacup, but I hear the echoes of what she doesn't say. That Augustus Sala doesn't want her to have applause. He can't understand her having her own dreams. He does not love her, not as she needs.

My sighing is loud and long. "Henny, I recall so fondly how you loved to exhibit."

She settles her cup. "My husband only talks of his plays. His words, him. He forgets that music drew us together. Now it seems it will draw us apart."

"What a horrible thing for song to do." I sip my tea and wait to see my blood stir in her, that she can't blame others for what she hasn't done for herself.

She unpins her beautiful bonnet and sets it aside. Her dark brown curls hide her delicate ears. Henny looks of money and comfort. Cells would be proud of how she fits into this world.

But that's looks.

Looks won't be deceiving me anymore.

I set my cup down and stretch in my sleek slippers adorned in emerald ribbon. I love green and gold.

"Are you here to ask me to pay for lessons?"

Henny's eyes blink wildly. I thought they'd pop. "No, ma'am. You've done enough. I need help sorting things out, that's all."

"Good." I nod and feel that invisible hand on my purse ease. "You're smart. Surely London has ways for an industrious girl to make money."

"How have you done it? You had a lot of children but you still made your fortune."

"Children never blocked my path, just adjusted it a little. I had help and I figured out the best way for them and me. It wasn't always an easy road."

Henny's light eyes squint and she can't know my meaning. This was best. The past, the missteps, the victories—they are all mine and I wear them like an easy heel or ribbons that slacken from use.

I lean forward, stretching, and spoon a lump of sugar into her cup. "The sweetness of winning, my dear. Don't lose you. Do all for your children, but birth your dreams, too."

As if no one has encouraged her in a long while, Henny grins. Her face becomes joyous and young as she blows bubbles in her tea.

"I always imagined you, girl, performing for kings and queens, singing such tunes. You'll make the papers for the right reasons."

"What if all the trouble is to make something happen that's not meant to be? Augustus was mad when I had a little part. The Duke of Clarence has attended."

"Duke of Clairborne?"

"The Duke of Clarence, Prince William Henry, Grandmama. Your old friend."

I had heard Henny the first time, but I liked the way she arches her voice to say the prince's title. My lips lift like I'm responding to a kiss.

"Then it's true."

"What is true?"

"This woman, she came around this week asking questions, insinuating . . ." Henny scrapes her index fingers at me. "Naughty, Grandmama. You and the prince? Naughty. I thought you knew him because of Mr. King and that evening at Bushy House."

My face feels hot and warm. The memories flow.

Henny stands and paces. Again, I see Cells in her steps, fretting about the governor or the financiers or a prince.

"I lived a life. What did this woman accuse me of?"

"Miss *Van Den Velden* showed me a news clipping from *Rambler Magazine*. Was that you? Were you caught with Prince William Henry? An affair, Grandmama?"

Can she see my thoughts? Oh, how the legend of my daring has grown. "I believe the sketch ran again in the papers, too."

"Grandmama? You—"

A patchwork of images dances between me and Henny. She's sitting too far to whisper my truth. But will this *truth* steal my chance to right the scales for the women of Demerara? No one will listen to anyone made a harlot in the papers. Scandal is no woman's friend.

"Did this woman say why she's chasing ghosts?"

"Grandmama, did you love him?"

"That was a long time ago. Henny, I wonder why it is of such interest now. Who does she intend to tell once her curiosity is satisfied?"

"She didn't say, Grandmama. She tried to pretend she was inquiring for Kensington School, even teased of a job. But I sense she's vicious. She has a personal grievance against you, doesn't she?"

I knot and unknot my scarf, wearing it like the young spirit in me, right across the shoulders above my womanly charms. "A great many things happen when you live long, dearie." Too many to number.

Henny's smart, and I sense she wants to hear someone else's problems to make her troubles seem lighter.

It's dangerous to confide in someone who's rooting for a worse lot than their own.

"Enough of me, Henny. There are more difficulties with Mr. Sala?"

Shrugging, she stood and turned to the window. Tears stream her face. "He drinks too much."

"Men tend to do that, Henny."

"He stays out late gambling."

"Fools tend to do that."

"Grandmama, I think he's been unfaithful."

"Oh." I peer down at my saucy scarlet scarf and slide the knot away, draping it respectfully about my shoulders. "Keep talking, Henny. I'm listening."

"Doesn't Augustus know I have the opportunity to be admired, but I stay home with our children?" She rakes her hands in her hair, mussing the curls. "I don't know what to do."

I knew she was too young to be settling for Sala, Augustus Sala, the first man to pay her attention, but who can tell a fool in haste about love and life.

DOMINICA 1787: A KINDNESS

My Lizzy and her husband stood outside of Mr. Bates's office. The new baby, Jane, wrapped in one of Mamaí's blankets, slept in her arms.

I cradled my largest sack.

"Here, Grama," she said to me.

I set down my heavy bag and took up the precious babe.

Pink fuzzy little creature with eyes of brown and curly black patches on her head. Jane looked like Lizzy when she was a babe.

My daughter and Coxall were much in love, even giggly.

I was happy for her, and this warm little body snuggled in my arms. My stomach swooshed.

"Mama, is there anything wrong? Charlotte's message sounded dire." Lizzy put her hand on mine. "Is something wrong about our paperwork? Is this baby not free?"

"No, child." I offered her little Jane. "This beauty is free as an oriole, a wondrous bird of flight. I need help. It's time for a solicitor to handle my money and investments."

Coxall held his finger for his daughter to catch and hold, maybe forever. "I thought Mr. Thomas does that."

"He's away in Grenada doing his business. This is my money and my investments. I need it controlled by me with instructions I think are right and rightly done."

"Mama, you've dealt with Mr. Bates before. Why are we here?"

I lifted my big sack. "Lizzy can read the documents and make sure what it says matches my intentions."

"Then why did you ask for my husband?"

"To look pretty, Lizzy." I laughed and latched my hand to his arm. "They don't cheat men easily, especially not a white one.

Three signatures are enough for one person to tattle. Coxall, you are important to my process."

"Ma'am, I understand your logic. But how do you know I won't cheat you, being I'm a man and all?"

I adjusted my crisp hat, a sleek pouf with an ebony ribbon. "One.'Cause you come from money. You're used to it. A couple of zeros won't make you change."

Looking up into his amused face, I felt good enough to say the rest. "Two. You love my daughter and this little girl. You're going to make it a point that her mother isn't a victim. You're as good as one of mine, Coxall. Let's put your privileges to work."

My son-in-law nodded and held the door. "Shall we, ladies?"

I walked into the offices of Brayshaw and Bates with poise, leveling my shoulders.

"Mr. Coxall, what brings you all here?"

Mr. Lionel, the clerk who met me at the manumission, didn't look at me. He addressed my son-in-law, as if Lizzy and I weren't there.

With a cough, I directed his eyes. "I came to see Mr. Bates. I need to hire him directly."

The man flipped open a notebook. "What for?"

"I need to set up accounts."

"We don't—"

I took the heavy sack and dumped the gold and silver onto his desk. "This is not all. I have much more."

Mr. Lionel's eyes darted across the room. "Stay here."

The fool took off running and disappeared into a room.

He returned with Mr. Bates. The man looked at the money. Even picked up a sovereign among the glittering doubloons and bit it. Then he and the clerk started counting.

After thirty minutes,

"Miss Kirwan, this is almost five thousand pounds."

"It's four thousand two hundred and five pounds and four shillings."

"You know your shillings." Bates took a handkerchief and wiped at his mouth. "I didn't know you were doing this well."

He saw me now and I didn't mention the bags in my trunk at my town house. "I know you managed Mr. Foden's accounts. He trusted you. I hope I can trust you."

"Yes. Yes, you can. I'll draw up papers. They'll be ready for you tomorrow."

With a shake of my head, I started collecting my coins. "I need it done today. My son-in-law and daughter are busy people. Or should I follow Mr. Thomas and do business in Grenada?"

"No, no, Miss Kirwan." Mr. Bates jerked the clerk by his collar. "Get everyone working on documents for Miss Kirwan now."

Mr. Bates took my arm. "This way, ma'am. You can sit in my office until we have everything done."

"I'll want a receipt, I don't want to be cheated."

His face looked a little green, and his cheeks squished up. "We are a respected firm. We'd never do that."

"That's good."

"And we don't need to count. If you said it's four thousand two hundred and five pounds, then that's what it is."

"And four shillings," Coxall said. "Four thousand two hundred and five pounds and four shillings."

Bates bowed like I was royalty. "Yes, Miss Kirwan. This way."

He took us to his office. This was different from the room with the big table. His desk was fancy, made of polished zebrawood. Big gilded books lined bookcases on either side.

Mr. Lionel ran in with a stack of documents. "Here you go, sir."

"Mr. Bates, are you sure your help is honest?" I squinted at him after cooing at Jane. "Sure, they don't cheat customers?"

"Lionel here is a good man. All my people here are respected."

"Interesting. Mr. Lionel. He looks like a man who cheats. Maybe he has a brother?"

I tossed the other bag from my sack onto the desk. It landed with a squish. "These wouldn't be his, then. That man had a little accident. Accidentally castrated himself 'cause he did wrong to a friend of mine. I'm supposed to, ummm, return his sausages on her behalf."

Mr. Bates dropped his quill. "How is that an accident?"

"I'm not sure. The story's confusing, something about a woman in a brothel." I nodded my head. "Well, here, with my apologies."

"No, ma'am, that won't be necessary." He motioned to his clerk to move my bag of bloody sausages, but the man looked ill and ran from the room.

Coxall moved the bag to the edge of Mr. Bates's desk, then took a handkerchief from his pocket and wiped his palms. "Get Miss Kirwan accounts in London. She'll need ready letters of credit to present whenever she travels."

I remembered Pa trying for letters of credit. He could never get them.

"Those will take a little longer, Mr. Coxall."

I fingered my bag with the sausages.

"But we'll hurry it up." The man began marking up the pages.

"Mr. Bates, I want three witnesses on all my documents just like the manumission paperwork."

"That's not necessary, ma'am."

Coxall leaned forward, like those men in Cells's study when they tried to make a point. He tapped the desk. "My mother-in-law thinks it necessary. Mr. Bates, it must be done."

Mr. Bates nodded and kept writing.

And I couldn't help but smile inside. I'd done this without Thomas. "Last, I need to work on a will."

Lizzy looked at me with fear in her eyes, but I patted her arm. "I have to make sure everyone is protected. The family I fought for needs to survive me. If not, my work is in vain."

She clasped my elbow. "Nothing you've ever done was in vain. Only a fool would question."

Within her strong hold, I felt her strength and her belief in me.

That made my eyes weak. Our Saturday breakfasts had brought us together.

By the time everything was finished, the sausages stank.

But the paperwork was right.

This had to be my finest day, and it was possible because of my family. All my living and fighting wasn't in vain. I had to keep remembering this during the birthing pains and the sadness that followed.

I was right, but this time I hated being right.

Thomas would leave today. He'd be gone for months, not weeks.

I'd hidden my growing belly and pretended to be sickly, to cut him off from my bed.

He frowned at me as he packed his portmanteau. "This is just for a little while."

I nodded and smiled, lying with my lips. "You do what you must."

His sigh sounded like ashes coming down from the cones. "Doll, if the situation were reversed, you'd do the same. Nothing ever stopped you from perfecting your business."

That wasn't true.

I could harlot my housekeepers. I didn't. Some hired out their enslaved to whore because it was big business. Wrong is wrong.

"You're acting like this is forever. I have to do my part to protect my investments. Much is at risk."

"Don't look back, Thomas. Don't blame me for you missing your chance."

He mussed his hair, then slicked it back. "You're making this hard."

"Thomas, how many ways do I have to say go?"

He put on his jade jacket. The silver buttons I stitched jingled. "You could say you love me and you understand. That you'll not make me feel guilty for making my dream happen."

Didn't agree to anything, just gave him his satchel. "Stay safe."

"Don't have faith in me? I'm going to come back as soon as I can. Then you and I will get on the *Mary* and go to Grenada. You'll meet my father."

"I can't leave my family."

"I'm your family, too. When I return, I want you to start acting like it. Believe in me."

I held my arms over my stomach, clasping my elbow like it was chain mail, to keep my baby from upset and my glass heart from chipping more. "Be safe."

He put his hands to his hips. "You stubborn woman."

I wasn't stubborn; I was Pa's word, *bogán*. A spineless creature unable to tell Thomas how much I needed him, how much this baby did.

"Doll, I'll be back a success, and you and I will have that trip. Then you will tell me how proud—"

"I am proud of you now. Don't you know?"

His eyes closed. "I need to be proud of me. You can't be everything, not my heart and the only successful thing in my life."

Thomas needed this. My fears of being alone, of birthing this babe alone, none of that was enough to stop him. He'd gotten me closer to my dreams. I should be woman enough to smile and let him go in peace.

But I didn't move.

He trudged to the bed and took my face in his palms. "Is there a reason you don't want me to go? Say it now."

I couldn't show him what was to come. My gaze soared through him away from the sadness that followed every birth and my new fear of dying, dying alone.

"Doll?"

The words *our baby* and *I love you* were on my tongue, burning like lava. "Thomas, I can't think of a reason to keep you here when you don't want to be."

His gaze lifted to the ceiling. "Fine." He kissed my brow, picked up his portmanteau, and satchel. "I'll be back as soon as I can."

He headed out of the room.

I heard his good-byes to Edward and more promises to Charlotte and Mamaí, even a loud kiss to Frances.

The final slam of the outer door vibrated all the way to me.

Closing my eyes, I whispered my farewell, whispered my hopes he found what he needed.

My stomach retched, and I vomited and vomited again.

On the floor, I loosened my corset and took my first full breath in weeks.

Then I flopped onto my empty bed.

I cried, then lied to my soul. Everything would be fine. I was such a lying *bogán*.

DOMINICA 1788: LOST SOUL

I sat in front of the cradle holding my baby, but inside I felt nothing. Born at the end of the old year, her birth should be a sign, a celebration. Months of carrying her, of talking and encouraging her in the womb left me barren, no more words for her, no song, not even my hymn.

The birth pains were as hard as the rest, but this time I knew I'd die.

Didn't know if that would be a bad thing.

Lizzy and Charlotte could take my place. Charlotte had become an exceptional businesswoman.

I tugged at my empty breasts. Again the milk hadn't come in right. Mamaí hired out for my babe.

I was an utter failure. A bad sow. My hungry baby, Eliza, suckled, clamped on good to my breast, and I could give her nothing.

My mama came into my room. She had a tray, probably more stew.

How can you eat when you can't feed your own child?

"Dolly, feeling better? The birthing fever just broke." She peeked at my little girl. "Eliza is a beautiful little girl. She sleeps good. Look at that head full of hair."

I nodded and crawled back into the bedsheets.

"I'm going to take Eliza to my room, Dolly. You hear me? I want to make sure she's safe."

I knew what she was saying, but she should know I'd hurt myself before my babe. I closed my eyes, nodding like a fool.

It was dark when I opened my eyes again.

But I wasn't alone.

"Thomas?"

"No. Me, Kitty."

She lit a candle.

Her face seemed older. Wide topaz eyes were inches from me. She looked scared. I hadn't seen her like this in a long time.

Yet I hadn't been this scared, frightened of living, since the rebellions.

"You need to get up. You need to go check on your baby."

"Can't you see about her, Kitty?"

"I have, Dolly."

"You should be her mother, Kitty. You can be good to her."

"Dolly, you don't mean that. But who couldn't be good to Eliza? She's perfect. The fattest little cheeks ever."

The birthing sadness had me. I couldn't get out of this hole. I was trapped in the cobbled well in the square.

Kitty pulled me into her arms.

I cried. She cried.

"Sis, watch over Eliza as if she's yours. You protected Lizzy long ago. Do that again for Eliza."

"Dolly, don't die on us. You have to eat. You have to get out of this bed. Mamaí is sad for you. She wants to send for Thomas."

"No."

"He always makes you laugh. He'll be happy to see this baby."

He'll look at me and my lows and steal her away like Cells. This time, I wouldn't blame him. "I'm no good for anyone."

She took the old rosary from my bed table and slipped it in my palm. "You're too hard on you. You always have been too hard."

"Someone should be." I rolled the beads between my fingers. I clutched these during the birth pains to focus, to pray.

"A little food. You need to eat. Drink water?"

No one could understand the darkness that kept calling. If I were quiet, maybe it would slip away. "Just need some time."

"We need you. Your Charlotte needs you."

"What's wrong with Charlotte?"

"At church, she caught the eye of a Fédon."

"The brothers from Grenada? They own a big plantation and transport goods to and from here and Trinidad? Those planters?"

"The same. She likes him, Dolly."

My little girl was in love?

"She needs her mama to help her like you helped Lizzy."

Coxall was all Lizzy's doing, but I did protect her.

My sister jumped into my bed and began brushing dust from my braids. "I'll wash and oil this straw and get you good as new. Maybe Polk can come back and take us to church again. I like Polk."

Kitty probably wasn't talking about Notre Dame du Bon Port. She wanted to go dancing at the mulatto ball. I chuckled at the notion and how it felt cleansing. "My swallow. You bless me, Kitty."

I held on to my sister. Her heartbeat, it was normal and right and true.

I prayed I'd come to myself.

For my family needed me, like I needed them, too.

I bounced Eliza in my arms. Sitting in my bedchamber, I held this little girl. Sleepy tiny eyes with silvered speckles swimming in topaz finally closed. The wet nurse said her suckle was strong.

Looking at my little girl, I felt more love than loss. My sadness had started to break, but it was a battle to get out of the bedclothes.

"Eliza, Mama's going to get better. You'll be proud of me. I have to go do something for your big sister, Charlotte."

What was I going to do without my dear girl running my business, stepping into my sandals to keep things running?

Gently, I placed Eliza in her cradle, tucked her in blankets. "You sleep, little one. I will be good for you again."

Tipping down the hall, I heard Charlotte and Mamaí giggling. Another blanket was being constructed, this one of purple and yellow linen strips. No osnaburg.

My daughter draped a net-like cloth over her head.

"That's like a veil," I said. "Such a beautiful bride you'll make."

Her face bloomed like pink hibiscus. "Thank you, Mama. Glad you're up." She slid her pretend veil to the sofa. The burgundy tapestry of the pillows looked good behind the mesh. "Ready to look at the ledgers?"

"Later. Let's talk of the Fédons. If we agree on things, they are free coloreds and Catholic. Charlotte, you could have a church wedding."

Her blush deepened.

"When will they be here?"

"Any moment, Mama."

Charlotte started to spin. Her cream-colored gown with prints of purple vines about the overdress looked festive.

Mamaí, who didn't seem to like hats, had a turban of rust and gold on her head, just a hint of her thick curls falling by her ears. She was beautiful. Her pink-striped skirt and lemon-yellow tunic were perfect.

Me? I did well enough not to be in a nightgown.

"Kitty picked this up in the Old Market, Mama." She offered me the mesh cloth. "It's *Laghetto* bark. It's a tradition of the West African moors. Mr. Fédon says it's important to be proud of our history."

Mamaí stitched her bits of cloth. "If she's to wear a veil for her wedding clothes, it should be made of fine cotton and lace, not a tree."

My mother didn't see how happy this lace bark made Charlotte.

"Grama, it will make a proper veil," Charlotte said, in a hummingbird-like voice, one battling the senior higher-pitched hen. "I'm proud of our people's heritage. We've overcome the challenges of the spirit."

"Spirits and overcoming, you don't say." Mamaí glanced at me, and then smirked at her pins and needles. "She and this Fédon went for walks while they were supposed to be in church. Chatting about history and things . . . and Obeah too."

Those apple cheeks of Charlotte's were brighter than the blood-red Montserrat maiden berries. "Grama?"

I put my hands on my daughter's shoulder. "Charlotte, I haven't made an agreement with the Fédons. Take care."

Her face pinched up. "Then I shouldn't have written Papa Cells."

"What?"

"I wrote Papa Cells." She lowered her gaze. "I know he's not my father, but he means so much. With Mr. Thomas gone, someone will have to give me away."

Mamaí looked at me, but I didn't know what to say. This was my fault, all this planning and life going on while I couldn't.

Light-headed, I sank onto the sofa.

"Mama, are you feeling poorly?"

"Some tea, Charlotte. That would be nice."

"Yes, Mama. Oh, I forgot." She moved as if she would go to the kitchen but stopped. "Papa Cells sent another letter for you."

I had conveniently burned the last two, but now that Charlotte had told him of Fédon, I had to look at his tidy script.

The letter was bright white parchment, very stark and proper, very much like the man I remembered. "Why don't you tell me what it says?"

"My darling Dolly." Charlotte's face was ablaze.

"Keep reading."

"My darling Dolly, it's good to hear that you are a success in Dominica. Mr. King informed me of how well your business is doing. I am very proud of you."

I groaned at the condescension. Like I needed his approval. I waved my hand. "Continue."

She cleared her throat. "If our dear Charlotte will have a late spring wedding in eighty-nine, I'll be there. I have plans to visit Demerara then and would love to visit you.

"I look forward to seeing you, dearest Dolly. J. Coseveldt Cells."

She offered me the letter. I examined the squiggles and traced my finger over his name. Seeing that man, if I still didn't feel like myself, would be a torture.

So I had to be me again.

Charlotte's eyes looked hopeful. The poor dear held her breath waiting for my agreement.

"Yes." I folded the letter. "Spring is enough time to negotiate a contract. When . . . if *I* start negotiations with the Fédons, you'll write Cells and invite him."

My daughter wrapped her arms about me. "Thank you. Thank you. Thank you. Let me go get your tea."

She skipped to the kitchen.

Mamaí began to chuckle. "The old neighbor's coming for a visit."

"Yes."

"And you have *two* children by him?"

"No birth records say that."

"And stupid Thomas is away?"

"He's not stupid. He's working on his business. That's never stupid."

"Oh, yes it is. Leaving an unhappy, wealthy Dolly alone is stupid. Very stupid."

Mamaí stood and smoothed her sleeves. Then she stretched. "I should go check on Frances. She's napping." She moved a foot or two, but then started to laugh. "Dolly, I'm glad to be here. You can depend on me, and I can depend on you to entertain my soul."

Would he bring Catharina? He didn't mention her in that letter. "Where's Edward?"

"He's feeling good this morning and went to help Kitty and Polk in the Old Market.

"Dolly, I see that head spinning," my mother said. "You're good. The birthing sadness won't last. You don't need any of them."

Frances. Could Cells take her, if he thought me ill?

"You're fretting. Remember, the girls and Edward have a future because of your sacrifices, your strength. If a man can't accept you as you are or not let you be who want to become, you're better off free. You're free, Dolly."

Mamaí talked about someone who wasn't there. "Am I? You had me in the fields, the bad fields of the plantation. Mrs. Ben said you took me and your harvest basket to the sick house. I'm not you, Mamaí. Wish I was."

She took my hands and gave me a hug then a shake. "Push through the darkness and see the light. I know how you feel. No mother who survived enslaved can help it. Dread about our babies—will they live, will they be free, how much will they suffer. That's why the peacock flower is our flower."

My mother kissed my forehead. "The shackles stay on our soul. The dread is passed through the blood. I pray to God it doesn't linger through the generations."

I clutched Mamaí to my bosom. Just an ounce, a bit, of her peace was all I needed.

"Let me go check on the girls. Get them settled before our guests arrive." She held me for a moment longer then went to the upper rooms.

I clutched Cells's letter. I could picture him sitting at his walnut desk writing this. Maybe there was a reason he'd come now. He was a friend before things changed.

The question was would he take one look at me and decide it was best to steal Frances, too.

DOMINICA 1789: LOST ANGER

I sat in my parlor on my new blue sofa having tea with Jean-Joseph Fédon and his older brother, Julien.

Good Catholic boys, free mulattoes from Grenada, they made it a point to attend Notre Dame du Bon Port anytime they came to Roseau.

Beautiful men with rich brown skin. They wore their curly hair full and shiny with a section tied back. Their waistcoat was plain, but the cut of their jacket was short in the front, longer in the back. The shimmer on their brass and silver buttons blinded, definitely well-to-do men. Fashionable planters but with a little mix of pirate in their brash spirits.

Mamaí, with little Frances in tow, came from the kitchen with a tray of refreshments, hot tea and biscuits and was that cassava meal made into bread?

My Charlotte was eager to embrace culture she'd never lived; I waved the trays to the zebrawood table, a gift from Mr. Bates to celebrate Eliza's birth. My housekeeping services increased my coffers and his firm's, too.

My angel napped peaceful and safe. I checked her often. My fear-filled state had started to ease.

Charlotte smiled at the brothers. "My grandmother helped me bake these. I hope they are to your liking."

Jean-Joseph Fédon dimpled big, like his lips would burst if he didn't. "Anything you make, I'm sure is wonderful, Miss Kirwan."

My mother led Frances to seats by the window. Far enough to not be required to be a part of the conversation, but close enough to not miss a word. So Mamaí.

I poured the younger fellow a cup of tea from old Foden's silver pot. "Where do you live in Grenada?"

"My brother and I have farms outside of the capital in Belvedere Estate. That's near the Parish of St. John."

I nodded but I knew nothing of Grenada except that Thomas was from there and he lived near the capital of St. George's.

The older Fédon, Julien, stood at my bookcase. There was tension in his stance, a restlessness in his posture as he poked bindings on my dust-free shelves.

Did he admire Kitty's latest vase, a rose-shaped calabash with ebony women holding hands and dancing? One of her best.

"Books from the British, madame?"

"A little. I have friends in London who generously send me things."

Julien frowned. I felt judged by his onyx eyes.

Jean-Joseph, the younger brother, beamed with a happy rust-colored gaze. The simple gold cross about his neck showed me the strength of his faith or at least the pretense of it.

"Are you devout, Mr. Jean-Joseph?"

"Yes. Our father raised us Catholic. He didn't much have a choice, being French." He said it as if it were a joke, but it wasn't funny, as much as I'd seen planters change religions to better their standings.

He wiped his mouth. "Our father taught us the importance of the sacraments, ma'am."

"Don't say that too loud, brother, we might be among enemies."

A hush fell on the room. Julien's tone sounded bold. Then he chuckled, a harsh throaty noise.

Jean-Joseph frowned in his brother's direction, then set down his cup. "Ma'am, I'd like very much to marry Charlotte. If she'll have me, I'll treasure her. *J'adore* her."

He wiped his sweating palms on his tight indigo breeches. "My brother and I are to return to Grenada at month's end. I'd like Charlotte to come as my wife."

The two would make a handsome couple and could marry in my church, blessed by a priest. There were no laws in our faith to prevent two coloreds from marrying.

Thomas had said he wanted to wed, but his Anglican faith and my Catholic one made it impossible. Then his business intervened, and we didn't have a concubine contract.

Eliza was four months old, and her father didn't know she lived. It had been more than eight months since I'd last seen his face. Just a few short notes sent to Mr. Bates told me he was alive, alive and not here.

All for the best. Thomas was free and so was I.

"Ma'am? Mrs. Kirwan."

"It's Miss Kirwan. A month is too soon. We have relatives who will come in another month. A delay is better. It will allow our solicitors to draw up a proper contract."

His face fell until Charlotte cast him a smile.

"I'll wait for her. Ma'am, may I escort Miss Kirwan for a walk to the market?"

"I heard you two like to do that. Yes. Her aunt Kitty will follow." I called to her and Edward, and they came down. "Looks like you'll have the best guardians. Son, you feeling better?"

"Yes, Mama," Edward said with a salute. If he grew to be healthier, he might have a career in the colored militias.

I glanced again at the frowning brother. "Elder Fédon, will you sit with me while the others enjoy Roseau?"

Kitty shifted her face between the young man and me and shook her head.

Edward, lovely Edward waggled his finger. "Someone's on punishment. He must've done wrong to Mama."

"Out, Edward," I said, biting my cheeks.

Kitty took my son's arm and set off behind the lovebirds.

The door closed.

The competition to see who'd make their complaints known first began with silence.

I was never good at waiting. "Mr. Fédon, what are your objections to the marriage?"

"You think I object, ma'am?"

"Your face is twisted like raisins. Tell me now. Don't waste my time."

"Charlotte is a lovely girl. A free mulatto woman, but has she been in your employ?"

"My employ? My daughter does bookkeeping."

"I mean your employ. Everyone knows Dolly Kirwan hires out the best housekeepers. Housekeepers and prostitutes."

I didn't blink, though I wanted to slap him. "I provide a service. Military men and new colonists need cooks, washerwomen, and housekeeping. I sell furnishings, nothing else."

"Not the fleshly congress? I've heard a number of your women housekeep and work the brothels."

"I take no commission on that business. I don't stop consenting adults. Consenting. You know who I am. You know my fees."

"That's not an answer."

"My daughter has never been a housekeeper. She's not been carnally touched by a man. And is your brother a virgin?"

"What? Of course n—"

"Then this interview is done. He should be pure to be worthy of my Charlotte. Good day, sir."

No man, white or colored, would ever set my standards. That job was for me alone.

DOMINICA 1789: LOST PATIENCE

Panic lit up Julien Fédon's arrogant face, his cheeks twitching, his lips tightening. If he thought he could convict me in my house with twisted beliefs, he was wrong. "Good day, sir."

He popped up from my chair. "*Non. S'il vous plaît ne faites pas ça.* Please, Jean-Joseph truly loves her."

"Let him down easy," I said with a merciless chuckle. "I'll not tolerate false piety. Thank you for showing me what Fédon men are about."

He even looked at Mamaí as if she would help him.

My mama offered a smirk, nothing more. Little Frances tilted her head with her tongue poked out. My four-year-old would learn how fierce I was at protecting my girls.

In this moment, I felt like me. I might roar.

He folded his arms. "I'm surprised you considered this union at all. My brother's not a white man. With the atrocities the *blancs* do, how do you debase yourself in congress with them? Do you enjoy bedding them before or after they taunt you as their N'gga wench."

In a blink, I was on Pa's dray with Nicholas calling me N'girl. He'd done so out of hate and fear of me. This fool called me low in my house.

"Mr. Fédon, are you afraid of white planters?"

"No, but they think us beneath them. I know women like you hitch yourselves to white stars and prostitute your souls to gain a sky of freedom, crowing as if their pasty hides mean status. Hell, you might just be at it for money. What's a few shillings for an honest hour of work?"

"Well, well, Fédon. It's not often I'm called a prostitute to my face."

"Someone needs to enlighten you. White men are not prizes, they're scourges. They rape our women. They steal from our continents then mock our treasures and identity. Why do you wish to deal with the swine and take it to your bed?"

My grip tightened on my cup, but I'd not break my treasure for a fool. "So you're a product of rape, Fédon?"

"Of course not."

"Then one white man thought your mother his equal. Did she feel the same or did she accept your father for his status? Merely marrying him to make you legitimate for inherited money?"

Fédon clasped his hands. The press of his fingers turned pink, then reddish. "My father wed my mother for love. I take it none of your men, your white men, felt the same for you, Miss Kirwan. I'd say that shows poor choices."

"I own my choices, Mr. Fédon, and unlike you I've recovered from being a tarn fool."

"I'm the fool? I think—"

"You're a self-righteous fool. You're a planter who owns slaves. You participate in their same system, the system that steals our ancestry, that forces those with my skin to do anything to gain manumission. Two of us in this room know enslavement—the hardships and terror of being chattel. The desperation to escape from its smothering boot still awakens me. The nightmares choke."

He looked down, but I wanted his eyes on me. I did a fast clap. "I fault no one for doing what they must to survive. Now that I have money, I choose my company. I've always thought of myself as equal to any man, white or Black, never lesser."

I stood with hands to my hips. "My choices are mine, not Charlotte's. She's a treasure to be loved beyond measure. I won't place her where she'll be judged by standards you men can't uphold."

"Standards you can't."

"True. I lived a hard life, full of mistakes. I'm still clawing my way out of some, but this is my daughter. I died that she might live. Now go. Take your tarn butt and go."

Mamaí lifted her head. With Frances on her lap, she clapped. "You heard my gracious daughter, be gone."

Frances slapped her little palms. "Go. Mama say go."

The man went to the door, but he didn't trudge through. "Jean-Joseph is in love. They are truly in love. You'd punish them both because of me?"

I nodded. "Yes. You're the older brother, head of the Fédons. That position demands responsibility. When I paid manumissions for my blood, I became the head of the Kirwans in Dominica. I'll not risk any of them with fools."

"We are not fools, Miss Kirwan."

"Yes, you are if you think I'll let Charlotte be disrespected. You need to protect her as a sister and honor their marriage. Nothing else will do."

He moved in front of me and knelt as if he were a military officer. "I promise, ma'am, to do so. I'll protect Charlotte Kirwan as if she were one of my beloved sisters."

Before I could stop him, he lifted my hand and kissed my knuckles, offering his respect as if I was a queen.

Well, maybe I was. I crowned my head by standing up for me, for raising up my family.

"Forgive me," he said in a strong voice. "On behalf of the Fédons, forgive me."

Headstrong and young were sins to be excused. "Oh, get up." I took my seat and patted the sofa cushion. "Have some tea."

Fédon plopped beside me. "They say you're a fierce negotiator. I should've understood that."

"You're guilty of pride and loving your brother. The latter cancels the debt of the former."

"Miss Kirwan, may I tell my brother you consent to his marriage to your daughter?"

"Let me talk to Charlotte. I'll let you know. I am more in favor of it than not."

I walked him to the door. When I opened it, I saw soldiers walking past.

Again Fédon looked as if he wanted to spit. He took off charging forward, and I prayed he'd not get into trouble.

Frances tugged on my skirt.

"Walk, too, Mama?"

These streets in Roseau I'd traveled often, but my feet felt nailed to the floorboards. "Not today, baby."

Picking up my daughter, I snuggled her face. I'd return to the outside world when I was ready. That day would be soon.

DOMINICA 1789: A WEDDING

The small chapel, Notre Dame du Bon Port, looked good, decorated with tallow candles and white-white anthurium lilies. Very fitting for my darling Charlotte's wedding.

"I'm nervous, Mama."

I came away from the door of the priest's office and smoothed her veil. Though made from bark, the lace looked like silk net. I styled it like the pictures in the magazines Mr. King sent. Each page made me dream of journeying across the sea.

Draped in a light blue gown with silver embroidery, Charlotte turned in circles, making the rich bows trimmed along the folds of silk float. Like butterflies to hibiscus, they covered her from her bosom to hem.

"How do I look, Mama?"

"Like an angel."

Mamaí fastened the veil to Charlotte's hair, braided shining tresses with buckler pins adding height to her curls. Her thick hair looked like an intricate woven basket and smelled of coconut.

"This is for you." I slipped the rosary into my daughter's palm, the leather string of red and gold beads my mama had given me when I fled Montserrat. "Take these with you, so you'll know I and Mamaí are with you too."

My stoic mother's eyes were glossy.

I clasped Charlotte's shaking hand. "Jean-Joseph Fédon loves you. All will be well."

She nodded, tears leaking down her cheeks. "I won't see you much after this."

"Grenada's not too far. I'll visit when you settle."

I held her like she was that babe I bore years ago.

Charlotte hummed our special tune. Mamaí and I joined her.

Rop tú mo baile.

Rop tú mo baile.

Rop tú mo baile.

"This union is sanctioned by my God. Charlotte, my darling daughter. This is good."

A knock at the door made me turn, and my eyes met Cells's hazel ones. "Dolly."

With his lopsided grin, he repeated my name then kissed my fingers.

His short white waistcoat and close-fitting breeches were immaculate. Like the Fédons had worn at our first meeting, his ebony coat was short in the front and long in the back, no pleats, no fancy embroidery. There was more gray in Cells's black hair, but I wasn't sure if that was powder.

Our eyes locked, my anger stirred. Stepping to the side, I waved him to Charlotte.

"Papa Cells." My daughter ran to him and hugged him. He lifted her veil and kissed her brow. "I've missed you so. Missed my Demerara family."

This day was for Charlotte.

The heat in my throat, every angry word I wanted to say I kept to myself. "We should begin. I need to sit by Edward and the rest of my family."

"The priest is here. You take your seat, Dolly. I'll take care of our beautiful girl."

Coming in and claiming everything? Holding my hot breath, I took Charlotte's palm and put it in his. Having to give him anything when he left Catharina in London burned.

I straightened my hat, a bisque straw bonnet with an egret feather, and went out into the church.

The Fédon women and siblings sat at the left. They looked like very proud people arrayed in fine colors of ruby and deep blue.

Lizzy and Coxall and her baby girl sat in the next row.

Polk and Mrs. Randolph had come along with Mr. Bates and his clerks. This might be one of the few times coloreds and whites sat side by side in this church.

It might be one of the last. More and more British had come to Dominica, more warships sat off the coast. The same talk that stopped Catholic worship in Montserrat came more frequently from the politicians and soldiers walking the streets.

It was odd our worship frightened folks, and how I clung to a faith that didn't always see me as fully human or with rights.

God must work in mysterious ways. I headed to Edward. Mamaí joined us as we took seats near Frances and the wet nurse who had Eliza. Kitty smiled at me, but she moved to sit with Polk.

Jean-Joseph Fédon stood with his brother; both wore white breeches and black coats with gold braiding. If they had medals hanging from their chests, I could picture the two as royalty, sort of like my old friend the captain of the *Pegasus*, the prince of England.

A hush smothered the light whispers as Cells led Charlotte to the altar.

The priest said his words.

I held mine in as Coseveldt pledged to give away my daughter.

Then he came and sat beside me. "You've done good, Dolly."

He shook Edward's hand. My son was a good boy; he didn't hiss at Cells.

"I do mean it, Dolly. I'm impressed with you."

Didn't need his approval. I knew I didn't have his respect. "Why didn't you bring Catharina?"

"She's in the middle of schooling."

"She's six, Cells. How much schooling can there be?"

I dug into my reticule for a handkerchief and the fool man gave me his. That scent, his scent, sweet rum was woven into the cloth as were my memories of Demerara. The good ones.

Balling it up, I tossed it to him, then scooted farther away.

He followed, slow and easy, pinning me with his shoulder to the end of the pew.

"Does Catharina know about me, Cells? Do you tell her I ask of her in Charlotte's letters?"

"Dolly, she thinks of you as a godmother."

My breath burned in my nostrils, my throat with words I couldn't utter in church. "When do I see her?"

His lips pressed together. Then he put his hand on mine. "I wanted to ask you later, but I see your eyes. I know you hate me. It's deserved, but I want you to come back with me. I've missed you."

I hadn't thought he'd say that.

I didn't think he'd admit to anything.

I wasn't going to cry.

I wasn't. I wasn't. I was.

He smoothed his cloth and patted my cheek. "I know this is a rush, but leave with me on the *Dolus*. Let me show you my world, mine and Catharina's."

"And then what?"

"Then you can decide if you want to stay."

Cells had thought of this. Plotted out all the pieces like he did with his politicking.

"I have a life here, responsibilities."

"The way we ended was wrong. I was never happier than when I was with you."

"I need time."

He held my hand close to his hip but nudged his head forward. "The ceremony."

Turning back, I saw the groom's gift of a ring. I heard the couple's promises of love and fidelity.

But my tongue tasted bitterness. Cells made a stew of my insides.

"I now pronounce you man and wife. Mr. and Mrs. Fédon."

I did everything but run to my daughter, embracing her and my new son-in-law.

Cells stood right behind me, playing like he'd never left.

Yet he had, and the hurt wouldn't be denied, even if it cost me Catharina.

DOMINICA 1789: A DANCE

My house was filled with people, all eating black cake and drinking rum. The rum was courtesy of Cells for my daughter's wedding celebration.

The chairs I'd borrowed from neighbors left scuff marks against my whitewashed walls.

Mamaí stood beside me, and I leaned my head on her shoulder. "You're good to me. I don't know how I would've done this for Charlotte, or any of the things you've done for Eliza and Frances, without you."

"Dolly, you need time. Your head is clearing. If you need to go away for a bit, you can do that, too. I'm here."

My wise mother had taken a side, Cells.

That tarn politicking man convinced Mamaí he deserved another chance. How could she not be swayed? Cells was classic Cells, attentive, working my friends like he did guests at his old parties. If everyone didn't adore him by the end of the day, it was not because he didn't try.

My poor Charlotte. She beamed in his presence. I'd cut my tongue out before I cursed and told the truth.

Mamaí smoothed my elbow ruffles. The cream linen had flowers and vines printed on it and on cotton voile gathered about the sleeve and round neckline. I used those London magazines to make it. Someday I'd go there, but not with Cells.

Lizzy came and kissed Mamaí's and my cheeks. "I have some news, Mama. I've been holding off telling you, but with Mr. Cells here, I'm sure he can keep you cheered."

"Why don't you tell me? I'll decide how to stay cheered."

"Coxall is building a house in Demerara. We're moving there. He'll manage more of his father's investments."

Both eldest daughters were leaving? "Lizzy, I'm going to miss our Sunday breakfasts."

"I know. And you will visit me. Won't you, Mama?"

Return to Demerara? I looked at her sweet face, smiling at me. "I'm not losing you again, Lizzy."

Coxall came and collected his sobbing wife. "I take it she told you?"

I wiped my wet eyes. "You keep my girl safe."

"Miss Dolly, I will. I love this woman with everything in me."

Between the loving and leaving, I needed air and passed Cells preening like the perfect father.

Julien Fédon looked as if he wanted to toss his glass at him.

I wished he would.

Cells represented everything the Fédon boy hated, Anglican and white.

Funny. Cells was actually neither. Like a color-changing iguana going from cold to heat, he merely blended himself into his surroundings.

Shaking my head, I went out to my porch.

Kitty followed and shut the door with a bang. "What a party, Dolly. With Cells and Polk and Mrs. Randolph, it's like how it used to be."

The sun was setting. Rain was up in the mountains, but not here.

She splayed the ruffles of her striped blue-and-white gown. "Maybe you need to stop having babies. You always get sad because of them."

A little hard to tell my womb to stop when I liked a man's touch. I shrugged. "I keep thinking I'm doing better, Kitty."

The tap of a goblet rang. Like a bell, it vibrated in my ear. "Cells must be giving a toast, Dolly."

Kitty peeked through the window. "You loved him once."

"I was an impressionable girl who needed a hero. I'm my own savior now."

My sister hugged me. "Mine, too. I think we need to go to church tonight."

"We left church."

She wiggled my hips, then clapped a fast rhythm. "No. Your church."

Cells came outside. "What's going on here?"

"Worship songs." Kitty smiled wide and bopped her chin. "I'm going to go check on the babies. Oh, Polk is playing his banjo."

She danced into my parlor.

Cells folded his arms. "Going to tell me about your life here in Dominica?"

"You can see what it is."

"There's some missing things, like why your mother is caring for two beautiful little girls."

"She's a great help."

He reached for me but dropped his palms to his sides. "Frances is beautiful."

I glared at him.

"Eliza is lovely, too, Dolly. Edward is smart. You've done well."

I stepped to the rail and looked out at the street, the passing soldiers. "I did what I had to."

He moved closer, his height towering over me. Something familiar whispered into my empty heart. "You haven't been sitting around waiting for me, but I've pined for you."

My throat became dry. "I . . . ah . . ."

"Let me talk, Dolly. I've left Fanny."

My slapping hand stayed pinned to the rail. "Didn't you try that before?"

"I can't make Fanny happy. We've tried. We're both miserable. There's no peace. I want her better and away from me. I'll stay in Scotland and make sure the divorce is finalized. You come back with me too."

"No. I'm not going to Scotland with you." My fingers pulsed on the rail. I could rip it if only they were stronger. "You need to be faithful to that poor woman. How many years has she been deathly ill? She's put up with enough."

His head dipped and he caressed my chin. "I heard you've been sad. It's all my doing. The way I left. The things unsaid between us."

I always liked his height, how he made me feel secure standing beside him.

"What about Demerara? What if you went by Mrs. Cells there? What if we all return to Demerara and live in the Hermitage? I heard Lizzy's moving to the colony."

He kissed my brow and his arms slid around me. He still knew how I liked to be held. The low circles along the bones of my corset made my spine tingle.

As if a minuet ended, I stepped from him and bowed. "You never fought fair."

"No, I never did." He followed and took my hand, humming and spinning me on my porch.

"I know what I want. I can be ruthless for it. Another chance with you. Let's go back to Demerara, Dolly."

The way he said my name was like he'd already tasted my lips. Like I'd already given in to him, like I was still the young girl who'd loved him hard.

But the woman that I'd become knew the divide between us, the years of punishing myself for failing his love.

It took everything in me to step away, to go through the door of my home like nothing happened.

Charlotte and the Fédons readied to leave. I kissed her and embraced her.

My house finally emptied.

Cells stayed, sitting on my sofa reading to Edward.

I wanted to scream so bad it hurt. Instead, I gathered dishes. "Cells, you should leave. It's been a long day."

He stood and motioned to Edward to go upstairs.

After offering this man a hug, my poor sweet boy did. Had I taught him to accept scraps?

Cells came to me, leaned close to my ear. "Dolly, the *Dolus* leaves for Demerara at the week's end. I want you on it. Just a quick trip, the two of us. We were good friends once, we can be lovers and friends, again. You need me. I see the hurt in your eyes as much as I see what we had."

A thing like that shouldn't be there, not now.

"Dolly, let me take us back to the way things were, the way things should've been. And Catharina, she'll finally have the best, both of us."

"What of her other mother? Won't leaving Fanny hurt my baby?"

He shrugged. "Catharina is resilient. She'll adjust in time."

Then I realized Cells was the same. He didn't care for anything but what he wanted. Today, I was his target, and if I bent then I'd be the same, a broken mirror.

Cells pulled me into his arms, and we fit together like old times, like he hadn't left me. How do you say no to a force bigger than you? You didn't.

You pretended. You lied back and took in everything until you could get away. "I'll think on it, Cells. I'm tired."

I pushed him toward the door. "There's much to consider."

At the threshold, he touched my nose and traced its peak. "Then just dinner, tomorrow."

"I'll think on it."

One last glance at Coseveldt standing in my threshold took me to the beginning. No drums of rebellion, just my pounding pulse. No smoke, just the ashes of what was our love. In Montserrat, I let him into my hut, then my heart. This time I closed the door.

"Tomorrow, Dolly. Dinner. We'll discuss our children. I'll come for you." His voice floated away.

I shook for I wasn't sure if he meant just Catharina.

The one fear I wasn't immune to, he lobbed at me like a cannon-ball. It exploded and deepened the well in my chest.

Kitty came into the room. Then peered out the window. "Mr. Thomas is gone and now Mr. Cells is back."

"They aren't interchangeable."

Kitty shrugged. The poor girl probably didn't understand what I was saying, but maybe they were. They each knew how to hurt me.

"I think you are right, Kitty. We need to go to church."

She tossed a bonnet on my head. "It's Tuesday. Tuesdays are best to worship by the sea."

We headed out the door to the mulatto ball to take communion with a heady rhythm. Music always made everything better. I needed its miracles tonight.

DOMINICA 1789: A FOOL'S STANCE

Heat bathed the packed ballroom.

Kitty and I navigated the crowds.

A fiddler and drummer filled the air with a happy beat that tapped down into my bones.

Men and women twirled, the music taking each for a whirl about the room. The beat pumped life into my chest. Folks came up and asked Kitty and me to dance, but we declined. Hearing the music was enough.

Kitty clapped. "I like church, Dolly."

I brushed one of her fallen braids swelling in the humidity. "You know this is not truly church."

"'Course it is. It heals you. You always come back smiling."

A brawl started in the back of the room.

Men, men in uniform, were punching and breaking things.

I pulled Kitty behind me, like I'd be better at taking a wild punch.

Women near the fight ran out of the drawing room.

Men, the ones not in uniform, began backing away, too. I didn't blame them. British soldiers could run amuck without any penalties. Free Blacks would be jailed if they did the same.

"Kitty, let's go."

My sister had become stiff, like her feet had rooted to the floor.

I put my arm around her. "It's fine, dear. I'm here. You don't need to be here with all this noise."

"No, Dolly. You have to dance. Someone will stop the drunks."

Mr. Lionel, Mr. Bates's clerk, came to us. "Miss Kirwan, I thought that was you."

"Are you having fun?"

My yell seemed to reach his ear, for his smiled broadened. "Yesss.

Much better than going to the brothels. I hear it's s-s-safer for s-s-sausages and such."

His slurring words. The man must've drunk several barrels' worth of wine. He yanked on my sleeve. "Oh. Oh. Miss Kirwan, I hear Mr. Thomas will be back at the end of the week."

He covered his lips. "Oops, I'm not supposed to say. Thomas wants to come back and sweep you into his sloop. Working on a contract to marry you."

Kitty and I guided Mr. Lionel to a chair, for he was very wobbly. Men who counted my money shouldn't be wobbly.

Thomas was returning and wanted to take me away on the *Mary*. Did he think paper would make up for leaving?

Another fight broke out.

The fiddler stopped.

The drummer did too.

A command was yelled.

The crowd of men parted, and in the dust a fellow fell forward. Then he lunged and dropped at my feet. "Sorry, ma'am."

Two men in uniform came and hoisted him upright. He looked at me and pushed free.

"Fellows, this is my doll. This is the woman I told you about, the woman in the sketch. The black beauty, the dame de couleur with my nose and Joan of Arc's hair."

Prince William's flopping arm swatted the air like he'd thought about grabbing me, but was too drunk to do it.

"Stop. You've seen me. Now go with your soldiers but pay for the damages."

"Miss Dorothy, don't go away."

I turned, grabbed Kitty, and started to the door.

"Dorothy, wait. Please. I came to your house but no one lived there."

A hundred eyes were on me. I could feel their whispers. *Miss Kirwan and the prince.*

One person called me Dolly, the doxy for His Royal Highness.

I spun to the miserable man still calling after me. "What do you want, Prince?"

"I came back for you. I want to show you my new boat, the *Andromeda*. I can show you across the sea. Come away with me."

No. No. No. "I have to leave."

I took Kitty's arm, and we ran.

We were halfway home when I stopped midstep. "We left our hats."

"Dolly." Kitty gripped my hand and kept me from turning back. "They'll think you've come back to tease the prince. Remember how everyone mocked your name with his? The Old Market people called you Mrs. Prince for months."

"I didn't do anything. It's not my fault that the drunk man knew my name."

"It will be tomorrow. I took you to have fun and brought us trouble. Maybe you should go with Mr. Cells. Be away from the gossip. Let it die down. You're starting to feel better."

My head spun, then settled. In that moment, finally, I could see clearly.

"I do need to leave, Kitty. Will you help Mamaí take care of my children? Will you make sure our mother doesn't work too hard, but keep our housekeepers working?"

"Of course, Dolly."

"Yes. I need to go and sort things out and come back strong."

I looped my arm with hers, and we ran home. Leaving was the only way to find my way. For the first time in a long time, I knew exactly what to do.

PART FIVE

My Choice

I left myself behind—the pain, the pursuits, even the victories.

THE BOAT 1789: COAST OF DOMINICA

From the quarterdeck of the huge ship, the *Andromeda*, I leaned over the rail, my fingers holding tight to the rough rolled-up weather cloth.

Funny how this felt like osnaburg.

Funny how the past was always a touch away.

William was surprised that I took up his offer. He was curious about me, but this notion was more akin to a lad with a new toy trying to figure out its workings. The prince was in dire need of distraction, and I was desperate to go away.

A perfect arrangement for us.

I'd rather be a mystery than the version of me Cells required. The story of his Dolly, weak, enslaved, terrorized, in need of a hero—only he knew the whole of it. In Demerara, he'd used my past to disqualify me from a future with him and Catharina. Now he'd use Thomas's leaving and my birthing sadness to make *old* me return to him, again spinning himself into a hero.

Never could this happen, not again.

Staying on the *Andromeda* and being a mystery, a toy, even claiming a prince as a plaything was preferred.

"Dorothy."

William stood behind me, warmed by the bright sun, dripping in medals and braiding. "For a woman who loves rhythm, you seem rudderless, even piqued. Is it the choppy waves or has my poor behavior caused your ire?"

The timbre of his voice sent heat to my cheeks. I thought of that awkward dance in his cabin. In front of his wall of windows, he kissed me soundly and hoped his fast and hurried seduction would lead to his bed.

Fast and hurried was never as great as it sounded, thus my retreat to the quarterdeck.

"Ready to go ashore? I can have a boat lowered."

I caught his bloodshot gaze, his red eyes floating in the sea of rum he'd drunk.

"You sure you're well, Prince?"

"I am, and you remain good at avoiding questions. I ask again, do I lower a boat and send you ashore?"

His face was kind, his lips parted, not tight like the sound of his words. Then I realized his voice was trained to offer orders.

"Unless you no longer want to show me the world, I'd like to stay. But you were quite drunk when you asked."

"I made a poor show last night. I apologize. At least I didn't break things like at Miss Polgreen's. My men and I were reckless at her Royal Naval Hotel."

"You got in another fight?"

"Yes, Miss Dorothy, Bridgetown, Barbados, may never be the same."

The setting sun slid closer to the sea, glowing on his brooding form. "Not my finest hour."

He stepped closer, leaving the shroud of dusky light. Looking up into his dark blue-black eyes, I saw questions—about us, about me, about life.

"If I was a painter . . ." His sea-salt-smelling fingers rubbed my cheek. His skin was rough, his touch gentle. "And if my hand was steadier, I'd paint you here. You're lovely."

His gaze drifted to my waist, the lacings of my indigo gown. My ankles showed in my short boots. Indecent, but what decent woman would be here? Whores came for an hour. Courtesans stayed a little longer. What did they call the ones who remained to go across the sea?

Fools?

Brave?

Prince William's steady smile said he approved of my dress, but my stomach tightened. I needed to focus on something other than the obvious—him and me and running away.

"Is your arm still bothering you, sir? Perhaps you should spend less time with drunken men."

"I intend to with proper distractions." He chuckled. "If I entice you to stay, I won't be destroying anything, anytime soon."

He towed me by my laces, pulling me into his strong arms, out in the open, where anyone could see.

Not right.

Not safe for him.

Definitely not for me, on a boat full of British soldiers. They glared at me as if I'd stolen something. Their sneers said I didn't belong.

I patted the prince's chest, my fingers jangling the big brass buttons of his waistcoat. "You said last night you'd show me the world. Not show me to the world."

"It's all the same when you're with me. The voyage to England is a long one. There's only so far to sail before there's a point of no return."

"You're testing me?"

"It's only fair, Dorothy. You're testing me, accepting my offer to come aboard then keeping me at a distance. Let me help you decide. I'm intrigued by you. No need to go to any special lengths to build up the anticipation of my wanting you."

His flirty words made it seem as if it were a small thing to be here, away from my family, all my connections, my power.

Perhaps it was a small sacrifice in his eyes.

"Aren't I here to help you pass the time as you wait for your message, Prince? Then shouldn't I make this moment as interesting as possible? Island girls, sailors think, are mostly for a white man's amusements. I think you're accustomed to being amused."

The rippling of his lips with a hearty laugh made him look so young. "Fishing for compliments of how you're different or how you've captivated my mind?"

My glare should've voiced what I didn't say, that most men didn't care for anything but what they wanted. And that they'll say pretty lies to get it.

It was up to me to believe falsehoods or not.

It didn't matter.

I came for adventure and escaped with the man who returned for me, the white prince who was captivated by black me. William saw me as strong, a challenge. I liked that. "Sir," I said in my sweetest voice, sugary like cane slurry, "I hear a well-placed compliment can clear up confusion and can convince me that you understand that I'm more than different."

He took my palm in his and kissed it. His lips were warm. I'd been his dance partner. I knew that if the rhythm between us became right, it could consume us. "You are more, much more. I must admit I've admired many girls from many colonies. You're the only one I wish to take across the sea. If I have to be patient to figure out your thoughts, I will. It's the key to unlocking all your pleasures. I'm greedy. I want all."

"Being here is my choice. I like that you are gentle and respect me."

His eyes held a shine like his silver buttons. He could be the stars I loved, the ones I always sought from my window.

My fantasy of what this was tangled and knotted with my truth. My frets about my daughters, my mother, my son slipped in and warred with my heart. I'd left them all to be here.

Yet, in William's sidelong look, I remember the dangers of a man wanting me and the joy of wanting them, too. "I'm escaping my life. Heading to England is the way."

"You have means. You could hire passage. You don't have to come away with me."

This was true.

Leaving could be done in many ways. Every man in my life had taught me how. I put my palm flat against the prince's waistcoat. The top button, I coveted. "But still, I'm here."

His hands cradled my face. He tilted my chin. I peered at tall him, at the mischief filling his jet eyes. "Dorothy, you're brave, and I'm lucky."

His laugh sounded lush. I focused on his mouth. Maybe we should kiss again and get it right. The one in his cabin when I first came aboard his *Pegasus* years ago was better.

In all that time, he never forgot me. He'd searched for me by showing a poorly done sketch of him and me and that tarn hammock. "Watch the sunset with me, William."

"As you wish." He put his arms about me, again. His embrace was strong, murmuring of his power. Power that I was never supposed to have or even be near, not in my skin.

This escape was right.

This journey across the sea with a prince seemed right.

I trusted like the fool I was, that if this was a mistake, I'd survive it, like all my others.

THE BOAT 1789: COAST OF TRINIDAD

In the captain's cabin, sunlight, sneaky and bright, showered the room. Squinting, I saw red birds and blue flutter across the wall of windows, seven sets of panes trimmed in fine polished wood.

"The birds, William. They won't break the glass?"

He sat at his desk stretching his hurt arm. Sleeping on the sofa on the opposite wall probably didn't help.

"Don't let the ibis and herons frighten you. They're looking for land to roost. Trinidad's cottonwood trees will give them homes, not the *Andromeda*."

Trinidad? The big boat moved fast. We were far from Dominica but sailing the wrong direction for London.

He wrote something then closed up the book. "Still afraid? You mumbled something like that in your sleep."

I ignored his question, for I didn't remember which nightmare I'd had. There were too many jumbies in my past. I tucked the sheet close to my neck. "Up early? Don't you have leisure time?"

"Leisure time? No. Duty always calls. This morning, it's my letters. Always do them early."

With my hair in curl papers and bundled in a scarf, I didn't feel like stirring. The rocking of the waves might've made for the best sleep I'd had in months.

"Dorothy, we'll be returning to port in Roseau in two days. You could go ashore then."

"But I came to see the other side of the sea."

Pulling on his white stockings, he turned and stared. "Exactly, you have left for a few days and kept me company. That has the makings of an excellent visit."

His voice was calm, pleasant sounding, but my being skittish isn't what he'd planned.

"Perhaps we're only good in short increments." He shoved on his sleek black-heeled shoes. "You can't feign being happy, and I can't take the risk of having a woman here who's not sure she wants to go." He picked up his indigo-blue jacket with flutters of gold on the sleeves, the lapels, and laid it on his lap. "I've told you about me, my duties to the Royal Navy and to my king."

"Your father, that king?"

"Yes." His head dipped, his voice hardened. "Other than your dancing, I know little about you."

"I'm a businesswoman with a large family. Now, I'm on an adventure with a prince."

"You are that, Dorothy, but is this everything? It's a great risk to have you as a guest."

Should I risk letting the son of a king know he kept company with a formerly enslaved woman, a victim of her massa's cruelty? I tugged my blanket closer and focused on the weave, the rich red color like the fruit of the cashew cherry. "Who would bring you trouble?"

His sigh sounded hard. "Everyone has someone to report to."

"Overseers? Let me speak to them and set them straight."

The prince chuckled. "No speaking to my superiors. I've upset a few who objected to my disciplining of officers."

Something in his eyes, a flicker in his gaze, said there was more at stake.

Putting his jacket to the side, he lifted from his chair and slid it with a screech under his rolltop desk. "Dorothy, I've never taken this many risks for anyone. I want you to stay, but you can't be here and be frightened. You're fretting something or someone who isn't here."

His words ripped through me. I was battling the old fears and my doubts about me and worries for my children and my business.

"You're a vibrant lass, just out of place. Maybe born in the wrong place, sort of like me."

"William"—I called his name aloud like a friend, like an equal— "You can't be serious. You have power. Of course you want to be a prince. A prince can do whatever he wants."

"I cannot." Folding his arms, he sat on the edge of his desk. "I have a birthright that makes others do for me, but I have to await my superiors' permission to go home. Is it power if you have to ask?"

"You're saying things to make me not feel so strange. Going away with a prince is not normal."

"Otherworldly, you're not, my dear. The *Andromeda* is not a place for unease unless we're down to one bottle of champagne."

"Champagne?"

His smile reappeared. "Ahh, I do have something with which to tempt you." He leaned over and puts his thumb to my nose. "I want you here, Dorothy, but you need to want it too. I'm not the second prize or third place."

"What are you talking about?"

He offered a light touch to my lips. "Roseau, Dominica, is the next port of call. Think of returning to your life."

"You think I won't choose you?"

"My dear, you've admitted there are other choices. The possibility exists that you'll pick wrongly."

"You're too clever for your own good, William."

"And you're too sweet, too beautiful to be a mere cabinmate. Prove me wrong. Be brave. Stay for the journey and my champagne. Or leave and take my adoration with you."

Big words that surely meant I was a fool. "You're patient. And I feel strange. Do you ever feel crazed?"

His face blanked. He tugged on his jacket like he'd picked a fight with a drunken sailor, then he trudged to the door. "Dominica is the next port. I'll miss you if you leave."

It shut shy of a slam.

Mumbles sounded outside the cabin. Someone watched us. My being here caused William trouble. Why else would those overseers keep him from returning home? Returning to my life might be best for all.

THE BOAT 1789: COAST OF DOMINICA

With my sack in my hand, I stood on deck waiting for William to lower a boat to take me ashore. The buildings of Roseau looked peaceful. The slate-colored thatch roofs of the city were like beads, winding a necklace unto the hills. Clouds moved about the highest peak. Steam rose from Morne Macaque tonight. It might rain.

I should be home rocking baby Eliza, preparing to train new housekeepers. My cooks started their days hours ago, along with my washerwomen. If more British ships came, it would drive demand. I'd be richer.

The chatter of men made me turn.

The prince was at the mizzenmast, the middle post holding the largest white sail. His shoulders slumped, then he snapped to attention. The letter from his overseers hadn't come.

I felt his desperation.

Head lifted, he strolled to me. The veins on his neck bulged within his collar.

I couldn't run from him. I knew why we were drawn together, each of us out of place, maybe a little broken inside. Together we might heal.

He locked his arms to his side. "You've chosen to leave? I thought you would."

In an instant, I dropped my sack. "No. I decided to stay. What's the next port of call?"

His brow lifted, like I'd helped a pirate find treasure. "The next stop will be Jamaica. The governor's a friend. I've promised to throw him a ball."

Men and their politicking. That should be as much fun as digging up yams. "Of course you will. I've never been to Jamaica. Never been that far north."

My friend fastened his palms to the thick rail. "We'll be there a few days then again return to Dominica. I think that's a final test of our compatibility. A last chance to leave me before all opportunities slim to swimming."

He chuckled, but I knew his happy laugh. This was hollow.

"Your letter will be here when we return. It will, William."

His lips hissed, bowing with sadness. "It's not a letter. It's orders. My father's very ill. He may die or worse."

What was worse than death?

Did this man believe in Obeah, the evil that haunted trees? Did jumbies torment the British too? Did death masks like that of Mrs. Ben and Cudjoe and the others that stayed with me live in his shadow?

He picked up my sack. "My father's the king, and I must wait for another to decide if I am to attend his bedside."

"It's odd thinking of you as someone's chattel."

Both thick brows raised, then he turned from me to the sea. "No more of me. You've decided to stay. Tonight, you'll taste champagne. I'll show you the difference between a flat still wine and one properly fermented to exhibit the bubbles."

"Wine with bubbles, sir? Interesting."

"Yes, very. The French owe the British a great deal when it comes to the love of sparkling wine."

"You're always fighting with the French, but you take time to drink their liquor?"

His laugh returned like it floated up from the water's depths. "We are civilized. I can enjoy French vintners and see them in battle the next day. And if I can convince you that champagne is divine, you will dance with me at my ball."

The joy in his voice made me glad I'd decided to stay, but a ball? "Let's enjoy the champagne. That's enough."

"I want to dance, Dorothy. You love to dance too. How could we not be friends?"

We both chuckled, for there were hundreds of reasons why we were never to be friends.

Easing a little closer, I rubbed my sleeve against the wool of his crisp jacket. "You don't need more trouble."

One of his big old arms found its way about my waist. "One minute you're out of sorts. The next, you seem to fancy me. It could confuse a lesser man."

"Good thing you're not one of those."

"Dorothy, I never know how things are between us. I like that." He offered a hug. The scent of soap, good and clean, clung to him. I smelled no wine, no ale. He was sober.

"My dear, why is it we end up here?"

Because my heart needed joy.

Because he returned for me.

This moment wasn't for baring souls. It was light. "You begged me, sir."

"I don't beg, madame. That's obviously not the answer."

He took a wispy lock of my hair, the curl blown straight by the wind, and tucked it about my ear. "The lights of Jamaica are lovely. The natural walks—the flowers and plantings are beautiful."

"William, is London like that?"

"Not exactly, but my grandmother did a great many improvements to a little house in Kensington. The grounds have very fine plantings, mint bushes and fever grasses. The roses and yellow lantanas . . . the vivid yellow reminds me of daffodils."

He rubbed at his mouth like he wished to take back the pretty words. I was glad he said it, glad he could show me his heart. I was tired of trying to figure out lies from love.

"Duty calls. Champagne later."

He gave me my sack, our hands touching for a moment before he left, before I returned to the cabin. I didn't bring a fancy gown for his ball. Without my finest trappings, I didn't think I should be on display in William's world. For the first time in a long time, I wasn't easy in my skin.

THE BOAT 1789: COAST OF JAMAICA

Once past the shores of Montserrat, it took three days for the prince's *Andromeda* to drop anchor in Jamaica. I'd hung the best gown I'd brought, a red-and-blue linen dress. It wasn't enough.

My decision was made. I'd stay below during William's ball. Sipping my glass of Sourire de Reims Rosé, I enjoyed the pink bubbles tapping my nose. The sweetness on my tongue tasted like a mammee apple mixed with cloves.

William slid on his jacket. He looked wonderful in dark, dark blue, and better with white breeches. Splaying my fingers, he took my glass and finished it. "You intend to stay below?"

"I had until you finished my glass."

He tapped a cask. The dull moaning sound meant the vessel was full.

"There's more, Dorothy."

"Yes, but you've taught me that the first pour is best. Since we've broken the seal, the bubbles will fade."

"Then dress and come for new wine. Only the freshest bottles will be served."

His mood was good. The best I'd seen, but I had to disappoint him. The last time I left these walls, I heard the bitter words his men had for me. Calling me a whore hurt, calling me ninny with all the awfulness of my brother Nicholas's tone left me shaking. I hadn't seen such venom in a long time, but I hadn't been this vulnerable, away from my power, my family in years.

I said none of this to William, just smiled at him. "This is your party, sir. Have great fun."

"Dorothy." His face held a little petulant pout then softened. "Come see how a war frigate becomes a peaceful ballroom. When I took possession of this vessel, I gave a ball to honor my father. Now, I toast to his health."

"But you haven't received word."

William's smile disappeared. The tension his party planning had masked returned. "Governor Clarke and his wife will enjoy meeting you."

From his chair, I fingered the cask sitting on his writing blotter. "Some governors aren't good. An old friend of mine had difficulty with the governors of Demerara."

"Some are tolerable. Dominica's governor is a bore. He insulted my good friend Nelson. That man will never be invited on board." Harsh air huffed out of his mouth. "Please reconsider, Dorothy."

"I'll wait for you here. Then you can tell me all. I love your tales."

"Wish you admitted to more. You fascinate me."

After waving him forward with a salute, I filled my glass, a slow pour. The pale liquid danced and sputtered in the crystal.

"Mrs. Clarke, she's quite a character and accomplished. You might get on well with her, but I'll send you a meal."

He headed out. The music of fiddles fluttered inside before the door shut.

William didn't understand. Too many fools waited on deck. With no fancy dress of embroidery and lace, everyone would ask why I was aboard or if I was the prince's slave. I'd had my fill of those looks, every sour face when my black hand was in William's.

His officers went whoring in brothels at every chance. I was sure they'd enjoyed black flesh, but seeing it celebrated in the open was too much for them. Would the other side of the sea be more of the same?

I took up my glass, but the goblet slipped and fell. It shattered.

Heart pounding, I sank to the floor and picked up the chunks. Each bit sparkled a little differently in my palms. Each one could be a bright accomplishment or one of my sharp failings.

No one would know the difference between a victory or a failing, if all the bits stayed hidden.

THE BOAT 1789: THE BALL

The door to William's cabin opened.

Expecting a cabin boy with supper, I rose from the bed.

A woman, older but not old, with thick, curled brown hair swept inside. "You're his mole?"

"What?"

"Or is it his mouse?" Her low neckline and high bodice showed off her bosom, shoving it up for display. The close pearls about her neck drizzled into her dress. She pressed closer and tried to touch my braid, one peeking from my scarlet scarf.

I waggled a finger at her and stepped away. "The party's on deck. Not here."

She put her hands down along her gown of shimmering mango satin. "Don't mean any harm. You are exquisite."

"Excuse me, miss?"

"Kitty Hunter Clarke. Your hair is very fine. Never seen an African or Creole with such hair."

Stepping to the other side of the desk, I put as much distance between us as I could. "My hair is the fault of your fathers, Creole or not."

"A witty Negress. I like that, keep that fire."

"Why are you here, Miss Clarke?"

"I'm the governor's wife. My husband represents Jamaica, but don't mind me. Once I get talking, it's hard to stop. You are pretty, such perfect features and William's wide nose. Just as he described." She clapped like she'd won something. "We must get you dressed. Where are your bags?"

My nervous fingers gripped the edge of the desk. "You need to leave."

"Yes, with you dressed to go up with me." She burrowed into my bag, diving in like an iguana leaping from the roof.

Perhaps I'd had too much champagne, but the sight of the governor's wife rooting through my things made me chuckle.

She stopped digging, her arms folding about her. "You figured me out."

I did the same, crossing mine over my simple tan bodice. "Of course."

"Prince William is such a dear. He truly wants you to come. I thought I could chase you out by being ridiculous. I'm sorry."

No woman outside of my family had ever apologized to me, especially no governor's wife. "Thank you."

It was all I could say and not grin like a fool. "Why did you take up this mission to drive out the prince's mole?"

"I figured the gossips had done their work to make you miss his party. Anyone associated with a man in power becomes the subject of intense conversation."

"You mean hate."

My low words made her cheeks redden. Her eyes drifted as if death masks from her past danced around us. Her chin lowered. "Once I was talked about in such a manner. I want to encourage you. Don't miss life because of loose talk. Come. Lift the prince's spirits."

"Is the situation with his pa bad?"

"Yes. The king may die. Their relationship, it's been strained. The prince is often on the outs. He needs to see him."

Our similarities, William's and mine, continued, each chasing our father's love. When the ship passed Montserrat, I realized I'd given up on mine that last time I saw Pa. I hoped William would make amends with his.

Mrs. Clarke picked up my teacup, half full of champagne. "This is much better in crystal. You'll see the bubbles."

"Not that many bubbles left. The prince said it needed to stay in the barrel fermenting to be best."

I dug into his desk, found a metal tin, poured some champagne, and offered it to Mrs. Clarke. "What does a governor's wife know of gossip?"

"I know it well. I dared to have a passion for a married earl. I was defiant. We loved out of the confines of marriage. Glorious, but my reputation was in tatters."

"Now, you've repented and live a good and holy life helping princes?"

"No. I loved another earl, one who wasn't supposed to be mine either."

Her fresh giggles made me grin. "Today you're a governor's wife?"

"Yes." She sipped from the tin and smacked her lips. "It's been a journey."

This woman sounded educated, looked expensive, but was white as a ghost showing off her bosom. I was educated enough, had some money, but I'd never been showy and definitely was no pale ghost. Jet-rich skin and jewel-bright eyes with thick hips, these were gifts the world lusted for in secret, not on a prince's arm, not in public.

"Despite the gossip, Miss Dorothy, I kept lifting my head, kept showing up, and I definitely kept living."

She finished her champagne. "It's better in a glass." Chuckling to herself as much as with me, she moved to the door. "If I were you, I'd dress. Come up to the ball. Show up. Keep doing it."

The door shut and I looked at the wall of windows. They were framed portraits of the black sky and inky water. A few showed stars. They were faint, but they were there. Stars were always there, even if they were hard to see.

I wasn't a mole. I was a dancer. A dancer should dance, dance while working, dance in church or under the stars. I tore off my scarf and looped my curls with pin bucklers. A freewoman doesn't cover her hair.

Over a simple gown of cream muslin I donned my dress of red

and blue. It was wrinkled, but the heat of the night would fix that. Mouthing a prayer I didn't make William's problems worse, I climbed to the deck.

Garlands of blue hibiscus flowed from polished brass urns positioned every six feet along the massive boat. Fine candles smelling of honey and fire lit tables dressed in white linen. Between the mizzenmast and the main one, a line of people twirled to the fiddlers' fast tempo. Closer to the rear, the stern, servants in silver mantles stood at the ready.

Officers who'd fussed about me being on board were dressed in starched scarlet or jet-colored uniforms. One saluted a painting of a vine and thistle hanging near the bow.

Prince William left his conversation and came to me. With a snap of his fingers a servant arrived and offered a woven crown of golden daffodils and blue lignum. "From my walk in Kingston today. I thought of you."

My hand fell to his arm, but not before I placed his gift on my head.

The sighs, the stunned gasps of women whipping lace fans—I pushed them from my mind and followed my prince to the end of the deck. "You had time to paint? I knew you could."

"I do like a good sketch."

I forgave the smirk on his lips and glanced at his big canvas. "Does it have meaning?"

"Miss Dorothy, the red thistle bush is for the dear Scottish. The red cross and the blue belt is St. George's Cross and Garter."

"What's the squiggle on the blue belt, my most noble prince?"

"*Honi soit qui mal y pense.* It means shame on him who thinks evil of it." He linked his fingers with mine, bare palm to bare palm, no white dancing gloves. "It is a shame to think evil of what is good."

It was. I would stop now.

When he pulled me to his side, I went without resisting.

"Are you hungry, Dorothy? My chef has made white soup, fine

roasted partridges. There's plenty of your favorite champagne. Oh, and I've convinced Mrs. Clarke to accompany us to England, when I finally get my orders. You'll have a companion."

"You think of everything, William."

"Dorothy, I do."

The music and a renewed sense of boldness filled my chest. "Then I choose to dance. I remember you begging."

He laughed as we took our places. William and I danced like the morrow would never come. If not for missing my family, this night would be perfect.

THE BOAT 1789: COAST OF DOMINICA

William returned to his cabin. In his hands, he waved documents.

Sitting at his desk, I crossed my fingers. My heart pounded. "Did the overseers finally give their blessing?"

He walked to me and hovered.

I watched emotions color his eyes, waves of blue and midnight stirring until they were fully jet.

"Yes, Dorothy. They've granted me leave. I can go to my father. I hope I'll arrive in time."

"Don't go making this good news bad."

"You're right." He dove into his trunk and pulled out a bottle.

The calabash-shaped glass, did it have more champagne? We'd had so much at his ball and the days that followed.

"Sourire de Reims Rosé?"

His face frowned, like I'd made his world go away. "It's Rosé de Saignée. It's almost as good. It's different."

"Good but different, William?"

Putting the bottle on the desk, he planted in front of me, my lanky prince. His head bent. He kissed me.

It was surprising and rushed. He was more enthusiastic than I, but he was a little younger than my thirty-three years. He didn't understand the meaning of slow and steady. To show him, I kissed him.

His mouth had a pleasant feel. His arms were strong; they again became demanding.

To make this good, he would need to be tamed. All these fast movements were for dancing in a crowd.

"We should toast," I said. "Let me know what this good but different wine is."

With a few tugs, the cork flew. *Bang*, it hit the wall.

His laughter was full and rich. He filled one glass and then another.

The crystal shone as he handed it to me. "We toast to my orders, my father's health, and to you staying."

He lifted his goblet, but then set it on the desk. "Graceful creature, you've kept me entertained for three weeks. I've blathered. You've smiled."

And said nothing of myself except of my business, nothing of my family or background. Though I felt William was different and his stories of gratitude and friendship with Blacks, like the healer of Jamaica, Cubah Cornwallis, impressed me, I knew the limits of his world.

Or maybe I'd come to understood how things shifted in importance with men.

"What is it that you want, Dorothy? What would make you the happiest?"

If I spoke up now—and told him that I, a woman who'd been enslaved, wanted to build fine things, things that would last and show Blacks could achieve everything—laughter would make the heat in his eyes leave.

Or he'd frown with pity, because his world didn't allow it.

Mine barely did.

We were equals at this moment, and I'd let nothing steal my peace. I rose fully in my power and put hands to his shoulders. "I suppose I'm still figuring things out. This trip is exposing me to many new things."

His brow rose as he captured my waist. "Heaven help the world when you do decide."

He spun me around his desk, dipping me and twirling. Then his lips met the arch of my neck. William nipped my lobe and slid to the hollow of my throat. Then he slipped away returning to his glass.

In his smile lay a dare. I'd have to chase. It's rare for a woman to chase.

Should I?

My gaze lowered to my champagne. I lifted my goblet. "To new and different."

Bubbles floated in the pinkish liquid. It smelled fruity, like a very ripe mango. The taste was good, but I could tell how it would falter if the bubbles were gone.

"It's what they call macerated. The blend of the fruit produces the berry color and offers the strong hints of licorice and strawberry."

"Berry champagne. It's different."

"But you prefer the first, Dorothy?"

The first I loved? The one I thought loved me? Or a kind spirit who made me laugh? "This is good. I'm ready for a challenge. Show me different, William."

He clinked his glass with mine, but his lips skipped the crystal to touch mine.

This kiss was slow and easy, assured with the grace I'd seen when he instructed his men.

With his lithe fingers, he set set down our glasses then eased up my arms. His touch was perfect, urging me to press forward into the unknown.

I allowed his silent commands, his palms stoking the music between us. His pinkies found my laces and untied one after the other, freeing me of my tunic, my corset, everything but desire.

His jacket fell away. The pinned medals chimed as they clanked together piled by our feet. He had me undone down to my shift. There was no way to stay mere friends. We'd danced to lovers.

I curled to him when he picked me up and laid me bare in the bed I'd borrowed. No more separation. This sharing was for us—the comfort of the mattress, the joy of a slow and gentle rhythm.

The son of a king stole my breath, and I gave him my body.

At last, new and different felt right.

THE BOAT 1789: COAST OF ENGLAND

From the quarterdeck of the *Andromeda*, I held on to the rail. The sea and this beautiful city of bricks, Portsmouth, lay ahead. William had commanded the sails, catching each good wind. It only took six weeks to travel from Dominica to England.

Water lapped peacefully on this British shore. At the docks, many ships moored. Drays piled high with timbers roamed everywhere. I could smell the cedar from here.

"Dorothy?" Mrs. Clarke approached. Her hat wrapped in gray ribbons matched her gown. She looked ready to leave. "You've already started the day, so early. The prince is going to make a reefer of you yet."

"Didn't want to miss the sunrise. It was amazing how everything changed. The reddish ball like a cashew cherry appeared from the water."

"Sunrise at sea is lovely but it's too early."

"Not early enough. He's gone." William left the cabin with barely a word.

Mrs. Clarke stood beside me. "He's back to his world. The scoundrel captain goes away, the royal-born prince, third in line to the throne to one of the most powerful nations on the earth, reappears. That world doesn't quite have a place for us."

"Wasn't looking for that. I'd rather visit and discover why every man of significance in my life is drawn here."

"Then you and I should go see this, before we set off to our own."

"Mrs. Clarke—"

"Kitty. Dorothy, call me Kitty."

I'd always done well with the Kittys in my life. Maybe God sent this one to me, an older, wiser, worldly woman, to make up for the sweet one who never aged.

Turning, I looked into this cherub's eyes. "I believe that's why the prince invited you, to show me Portsmouth. He does think of everything."

"Yes, and after that, I take you to London. What troubles could two daring ladies stumble into?"

I went to the cabin and retrieved my sack with my letters of credit, the copy of my manumission, and my coins. There. Now I was prepared for a great deal of trouble.

As the carriage rumbled down the streets, I found myself in awe of this horse-drawn thing. Leather had been stretched and buffed smooth to cover the padded seat. My fingers could disappear in the tufting.

Mrs. Kitty laughed. "Every time I come to Portsmouth, I see new houses and more expansion of the dockyards. Look at that pond, Dorothy. It's for nothing more than cloth sails, to soak and season them to ready them for the ships."

Too busy poking the carriage's cushions, I missed it. "Drays offer transport in Dominica. Nothing is this comfortable."

"You're amused by the simplest things, Dorothy. This doesn't compare to London. So keep your head, miss, and don't spend all your money in one place."

My fist was tight. I knew the value of a shilling and a guilder quite well, but I had to bring pieces of this world back to Dominica.

The coach stopped, and we were handed down. "What is this building, Kitty?"

"This is a warehouse, but not for tools and roofing unless you consider boning for corsets construction material." She adjusted her cream-colored shawl. "We need to get you a coat, a heavy one."

Too excited to feel chilly, I studied this big place, this structure made of limestone. Here wood must only be used for ships.

Waving, I let Kitty proceed me into the warehouse. I stopped at the window glass, admiring a pair of gloves and thick-heeled shoes.

The buckles sparkled. Whether the yellow things would fit or not, I should buy them for the decorations.

"Come along, Dorothy." She gripped my hand. "It's better inside."

She was right.

The fabrics on the shelves were a rainbow, but none as bright in color as my banana-yellow gown.

The inked prints—diamond shapes and scrolling—on the cotton rolls would amaze Mamaí. I pictured my girls wearing these patterns for new gowns.

My lungs stung. It had been more than two months since I last hugged any of them. Eliza and Frances and Edward—did they miss me as much as I missed them?

Or did they hate me for leaving?

Did my children sit at the window waiting for me to return?

I grabbed Mrs. Kitty's arm. "I have to go home. It's time to go."

"Dorothy, you've just made it to these shores. You haven't seen London."

"I need to go, Kitty."

She grasped my shoulders. "Have you given consideration to moving to London and becoming the prince's mistress?"

Not sure my ears were working. "What?"

"Dorothy, it is possible. Every time the prince is out of favor, his pockets are pinched. A wealthy woman could help balance his finances. He will seek one out. Why not you? You could be that woman."

There was a certain appeal in imagining a prince, a man of the world, might need me. But I didn't build my *fhortún* to trap a prince. I didn't leave my life and my family to take up with a man of power who had money issues. Shaking my head like it would fall away, I said no. "Kitty, be serious. He brought me here, but I may never see Prince William again."

"You will. A man who throws a ball on a warship for you will find you. He can't help himself."

Part of me wanted to protest. The decorations and music, all the pomp, was for his pa, the king. But my lover's heart knew. William and I fit together, but deep in my soul I understood the ties between us would be cleaved. Time and circumstances always carried hatchets.

LONDON, ENGLAND 1789: DREAMS

Traveling to London in Kitty's carriage took half a day. We stopped in coaching inns along the way. That was what she called the hotels that hosted rooms with tables and servers and bedchambers upstairs.

Chin lifted, coins readied, I'd grown used to the stares and the false gratitude that a shilling brought.

"You're a foreign princess, Dorothy," Kitty said, wiping gravy from her fingers. Our hearty stew served with beefsteak was magical, and so succulent and tender on the tongue.

We gathered in her carriage and she repeated her princess joke. She kept William to the front of my mind, beyond my fears for his father and my increasing sadness. I missed my family. "Mr. King must send word home when we settle."

"Ah, your voice has returned. You've been very quiet." She thumbed through a magazine.

I hoped it didn't have any more sketches of me and William. His *Andromeda* crew would tell all, like the *Pegasus*'s crew did. No bigger scandal than a prince and a pauper or prostitute. That's how they'd paint me, not as a princess or anyone of means.

"The roads here are better than Jamaica but a rut and divots can ruin a horse." She folded up her book. "Your Mr. King said our accommodations are at the George."

"Do you British ever name anything other than George?"

"We've had a few kings with other names, but William's older brother bears the same." Kitty leaned forward as she rolled her coral necklace between her fingers. "How wealthy are you?"

"I've been lucky."

"Did you know the prince overspends his royal allowance and earns very little captaining the *Andromeda*?"

"He wants my money? Is that what you're saying?"

"No, but it does make you well suited."

"Kitty, please. I don't—"

"Your friend Mr. King could get word to him. It wouldn't be any trouble once William's able—"

"Stop."

"Picture it, Dorothy. The prince could climb the galleried building of the George. The swashbuckler could launch upon your balcony and serenade—"

"Kitty Clarke."

"Sing, dance, lie in bed all day. You can have him if you want him. Think on it, Dorothy."

I didn't fault my friend's enthusiasm, but it made me sad how her talk centered on claiming a man. I understood how she got those two earls. Persistence.

The carriage stopped and we walked into a courtyard. Could this be a castle? She would be bold enough to take me to William.

No guards patrolled, and I doubted they'd let anyone walk up to the throne. I released the breath trapped in my lungs and walked a little easier with my friend.

The beauty of this courtyard struck me.

"Stop for a moment." I caught Kitty's arm and let my eyes feast. More stone sculpted with squiggles and figures dangled above rounded columns supporting the roof. "Marble."

"And limestone. This is the Royal Exchange. The best merchants are inside, Dorothy. I'll introduce you to the mantua-maker of the season.

"The who?"

"A seamstress of the highest regard. And there are milliners."

Hats? Hats like in those magazines. "Then let's go." We stepped deeper into the courtyard. Buildings wrapped three sides of a square. A body could walk under the arch-covered walkway and roam the entire U-shaped length and never get wet.

Kitty dragged me inside.

Tables held gloves and more fabrics, but unlike Portsmouth, servants were everywhere. "Kitty?"

"Those are mantua-makers and tailors, Dorothy. They will adapt anything you like for the perfect fit."

Dressing gowns with deep folds of linen were stitched and draped from hooks. Men with needles and thread stood ready to finish them. This was why Cells and Thomas came back so styled. "This is perfection, Kitty."

"The islands are wonderful, but none compare to London." She bent and looked at a pearl brooch. "You should have jewelry."

My sister's necklace was in my sack. It was very fine, but the luster of these white orbs shone like the moon.

Against the clerk's objections Kitty pinned it to my chest. She fished two guineas out of her purse. "My gift, Dorothy. Get used to these things. The preferred mistress of a prince should have nice things."

This Kitty was pushy. I missed my meek Kitty, my swallow. My sister never pressed this hard, and I didn't think I was the type to be shoved down a path I wasn't sure was mine.

I'd become Kitty Clarke's project. There was no better way to describe it. Milliners and drapers and mantua-makers had me arrayed in fine silks and laces. I turned and glanced at the silhouette I cast on the inn's whitewashed wall. The rooms at the George were big. Mr. King had them save the best for me. His gift for being his successful partner in the West Indies.

That was true, but it was also an indication of the money I'd made him. Men do end up making more. I wondered if I'd have a chance to best that, since my being with the prince proved power and I could be bedmates. Happy ones. Happy ones at sea. William's pa had recovered and except for two nightly strolls in a garden at a big old place called Kensington, I hadn't seen my prince. He loved his walks.

Kitty sipped chamomile tea. My half-drunk cup was blended with Mamaí's herbs. These were for my nerves.

"You look fine, Dorothy. The prince will not be able to leave you again."

Men and leaving were too common for me. I concentrated on the yellowish-white satin gown that was delivered. The color reminded me of the flesh of a Montserratan governor's plum picked too soon. That wasn't me. Or maybe it was . . . This was my time to bloom and to be soft and smooth, sculpted into a Georgian lady of fashion. I twirled again and watched my hem float around my bare ankles. "Kitty, I'm an advertisement in your papers."

She settled in a chair. "When William sees you, he must make you an offer like he'd do any woman here."

My face may have held a smile but my insides twisted, dangling like an iguana about to fall through a roof hole. I sipped my tea. The bitter herbs reminded me of the last time I was a formal concubine to a man who had more power than I. Cells and I didn't last. Why would William and I fare better? "Let's talk of dinner. I'm partial to beefsteak."

"Dorothy, you must consider it."

"The prince and I have a friendship, and I have dreams, Kitty. The things you've shown me, I can take back to Roseau and make a larger fortune."

She frowned with such sourness, I thought we'd swapped teas.

"Dolly, you're in a unique position. I've never seen the prince so taken."

I hid my doubts behind my mother's smile. I didn't know what I wanted. Living in London wasn't my dream, was it? But knowing he needed me and that a prince respected me—that did something to my heart.

Finishing my cup, I smoothed my sleeves, wafting the lace at my cuff. "I do like the finery one buys here."

"Dorothy, you can have all that and more."

"What of my children? I can't be away much longer."

"Bring them. They can be educated here. More mixed-race children are coming for schooling. It could be a new start for everyone."

My head hurt thinking of this. I wrapped my arms about my skull. "No more."

Her giddy grin made me forgive her.

"Shall we dine below, Dorothy?"

Packed with people, the dining room called the Coffee Room would be noisy.

"No. I'd rather send down." I raised my arms, trussed up in silks and satins. "But I should eat very little, if I'm to wear all these gowns your mantua-makers have designed."

"It's good you've brought a fortune with you. A rich mistress or benefactor is an enjoyable thing."

All the clothes and fabrics and silver buttons and shoes I'd purchased for myself and for my family would bankrupt another. It would take at least a quarter to half of a year to earn the four hundred pounds I'd spent.

These gifts stated that I and my family were worth it. We were.

"You're a friend, Kitty. Not sure if you're meant for good or temptation."

"Temptation, my dear, always temptation."

A servant knocked on the door. I lifted from my chair. "Yes."

"I'm looking for a nymph who crossed the sea on the *Andromeda*." The easy masculine voice was William's.

I threw open the door and the prince charged in. He lifted me high in his arms and kissed me before I could say hello.

Kitty's jasmine perfume passed beside me. "Nice to see you, Prince William. Dorothy, I'll be in my room." She left, closing the door with a solid thud.

William eased my feet to the floor then teased my neck, touching the arch he'd learned to tame. "I've missed you."

I stepped away, smoothing my gown of the wrinkles he'd made. "William, how is your father?"

The hands reaching for me dropped to his side. He'd snapped to attention. "Better. The physicians say a full recovery will happen. He's sane. Perfectly sane again."

My breath eased. "My prayers are answered. Hope that you don't mind Catholic ones."

"Not at all. I'm glad—" He took my palm in his. "You think a person is doomed by their lineage?"

"What?"

"Dorothy, do you think a person is destined to be like their parents, their mother and father?"

"My mother's my hero. She did everything for me and my sister. I hope to be a tenth of her."

My voice trailed off, not voicing anything of my pa. He loved us the best he could, but it wasn't enough. Yet, here I was leaving my family, my children, just like he did.

William clasped his arm and rubbed at the wrist. "My father

almost went mad. Many say I'm lost. I'm given to the worst risks. Carrying you here . . . many think I am lost."

The shadows he couldn't outrun tangled with mine. They were too big, too powerful for a young prince and an island woman with unfulfilled dreams. "William." I nudged his chin with my knuckle. "You are strong. You'll best the naysayers."

"You think this, Dorothy?"

"I know so. Remember it when I leave."

"No. You've just arrived. I've been too busy—"

"We've had a lovely time. I'll treasure it." I had to say good-bye first. I wasn't going to be the thing faulted as what ruined him, and he couldn't be the reason I stopped chasing my dreams.

His lips pressed to a line, then he nodded accepting my final truth.

I clasped his shoulders at the blue sash that anchored him. "You have control, William. You're sane. Temper your drink. Limit things to the best champagne, and you'll have no more troubles."

He looked at me, maybe through me. Maybe he saw the pain I tried to hide. I wasn't fine leaving what was between us.

His thumb twisted one of my curls. He drew me close. "I'd hoped to rely upon you as my guide, my muse."

Four months away helped me regain my strength, but I couldn't be a wick for someone else's candle. I was flame. I had to remember that. "You're a survivor, William. So am I."

I slipped beneath his jacket to be next to the soft silk of his waist-coat.

His hold tightened and his mouth sampled the arch of my neck. "You smell of coconut and nutmeg, a hint of sweet sage—a perfect nosegay for me."

He collected me in his arms. "You're not leaving me tonight. I'm not thinking of tomorrow."

I spun in arms that wanted me. This was the dance I was made for, him circling me, stripping away my new silks, satins, and doubts.

Warming each other in the slow allemande we'd agreed upon, a prince of England and an island queen found the perfect embrace.

One moment we were upright, kissing like fools, the next the world went topsy-turvy. The humming of our bodies—the giving and receiving of love—was in my ears, drilling into my heart, tying our souls in an everlasting knot.

I sheltered in his arms. He buried himself in my embrace. I was his safe harbor. He was mine too.

In my heart, I'd keep this peace. William was woven into the fabric of my lids. Tomorrow and every day forward, I'd forever see him in those moments of weakness, knowing his love was the path not chosen.

DOMINICA 1789: MY RETURN

I'd returned from my six-month journey to the other side of the sea refreshed and a little scared. How would my family react? Would they trust me again?

Sitting on my sofa in my town house, I watched Eliza toddle around the room, walking with her head up. I had missed her first steps. She'd just turned one and was so much bigger.

Frances sat at my feet. My four-year-old was mad at me. So was my sister Kitty. She hadn't come down. Didn't look at her presents. Only Mamaí and Edward were in good spirits.

My son sat next to me, reading me the notes from Mr. Bates. Bates kept collecting fees on my behalf. All my contracts were in place.

One could say my absence was unnoticed.

Not sure how to accept that other than to praise Mamaí. She kept everything good.

"Papa Cells visited us a lot while you were gone."

"What?"

"Yes, Mama."

"Edward, how do you feel about that?"

"It was nice, like at the Hermitage, Mama. He wants me to write him."

My sweet boy feared I wouldn't let him have a piece of his father. I hugged him, pulled him tight in my arms. "Of course you can. I want you to."

I took a bundle and placed it in his lap. "This is for you."

His grip was tentative, like it would be taken away.

Clasping his fingers, I caught his gaze. "You didn't think I'd come back?"

He nodded. "People don't sometimes."

My heart broke. "The next time I see the world or go anywhere, I'll take you with me, all of you. No more splitting up."

My son's smile blossomed. It radiated as he opened the wrapped parcel, tearing away the cloth and paper stuffing to expose a black tricorn, a low one like Cells's exploring hat. My son tossed it on his head, hugged my neck, then jumped up and down.

Again, I held him. I'd never seen him this happy, and if looking like his father and wearing this hat gave him this much joy, then that was fine.

Eliza bumped into my knee. I scooped her up and put her in my lap, then turned to Frances. "Come on, Frances, forgive me."

She poked out her lips. She held out her defiant chin, that cleft showing. Maybe Cells taking more interest in Edward might be beneficial for all the girls.

Well, that was a better way to think of it than him wreaking havoc on my family.

"Mama," Edward said, "Charlotte sent a letter."

My girl. Married to the love of her life.

Edward's happy face turned sad. His eyes squinted. "Mama, she's in trouble. She wants her papers before she's tossed in jail."

"What!" I took up the squiggles and saw danger. "I have to get to her. I have to—"

Edward frowned and Frances's expression turned so sour I thought she'd gotten into Mamaí's teas.

"I meant we're all going. All of us are going to Grenada to make sure Charlotte is safe. All of us."

My young children gathered about me. I hugged them with my heart, but my stomach stewed. My Charlotte was in danger and it had to be those Fédons' fault.

The cool air, the light north wind from the bay, chased sleep from my eyes. I had to get ahead of the rain. I patted the horse I'd leased and climbed into the dray, ready to head for the hills to Belvedere Estates. The arrangements for this visit to Grenada were made quickly. Mr. Bates contracted lodging for me and took a longer lease than I wanted. His judgment might prove right. Being near Charlotte for more than a month would ensure she wasn't without support. It would also give me time to convince her to return to Roseau if these Fédons couldn't protect her.

A tall fellow pointed at me. He stood on the other side of the thin street, near a building no taller than a coconut tree. Grenada's architecture was so different than Dominica's.

"Miss Dolly, that *is* you."

Caught. And by one of Joseph Thomas's loud business associates, John Garraway. Resisting the urge to flee, I pasted on Mamaí's distant smile. "Yes."

"Miss Dolly." He waved his chewed-up straw.

"Yes, Mr. Garraway."

"I'd heard some talk about you being in Grenada. Here for a visit?"

"Business, sir. How are you?"

"Business, you say." He tugged on his sagging jacket. "Thomas said you were an enterprising woman. Does he know you are here?"

Well, the man wasn't living in Thomas's pockets or he'd know Thomas and I ended more than a year ago.

"I'm in a hurry, Mr. Garraway. An appointment. Do take care."

He tipped his hat, and I took up the reins.

Then his fingers fastened to the side of the dray. "Well, Miss

Dolly, I hope you have a good day. Hope your business lasts longer. Thomas will be back soon. I know he'll want to see you."

My smile fell away. "You have a good day, Mr. Garraway."

Snapping my wrist, I forced my horse to move. It took two hours of empty trail before I simmered down. The quiet of the forest blanketed me. Ferns offered a canopy. Moss and dried mud carpeted everything.

Rising slowly, the dray climbed the next hill. The air here was thinner and sweet. Red beak-shaped flowers lined the road, but so did large sugar plantations, on the left and right.

Like I sat in Pa's dray and tried my hardest not to see the terror, I was there again and couldn't *not* see the misery.

I missed none of it. The sight of half-naked souls toiling in woods famous for chiggers made my stomach rip into pieces. I stared down at my fisted hands. I couldn't look up again until there were no more plantations, till the right side had become good again.

At the top of the mountain trail I scanned the valley below.

Plowed fields.

Endless parcels of land sectioned with cane sprouted to the sun.

Then I saw black and brown men in shoes and straw hats that looked like thatched roofs. This was Belvedere Estates, Charlotte's new home.

My heart fell and slammed into my gut. *Holy Father, let the coloreds not be as bad as the whites. Let whips not be used. Let punishments have no teeth.*

If not for Charlotte, I'd turn around and pretend I didn't see this, how free colored fell into the ways of owning folks just like the whites.

Hitching with hiccups, I held my breath and counted.

Then I let myself forget. Like I had in Montserrat, I stopped seeing the fields. I focused my strength on Charlotte and the house with green shutters.

My daughter must've seen me. She came running at top speed. As soon as I climbed down, her arms locked about me.

"I'm here, baby. I'm here."

How long we stood draped in the other's embrace, I wasn't sure. But I knew this was where I was needed, not London.

"Mama, the *whites* here. They're hateful. They keep trying to tear us down. They'll enslave us."

I pulled away a little but put my palms to her chin. "What have the *whites* done?"

She clasped her palms about her high-waisted cotton gown. "They are demanding papers of all free coloreds. If you can't prove your manumission or birthright in time, the governor will sell you."

Charlotte had grown up as Cells's, the daughter of a rich rum maker. She'd worshiped and danced with whites. What had happened to make my child fear them?

"Explain, girl."

"They put many of the coloreds' wives in jail. Mary Rose, Julien's wife, she was a week away from being sold."

I pulled my daughter against me. The pounding in my chest must speak for me. I'd let no one, no one white or colored hurt her. "I have a copy of your papers. You're safe."

"Miss Dolly, good to see you." Charlotte's husband came out onto the porch; clinging to his billowing linen sleeve was a young woman in a bright gold tunic and plantain-green pull skirt. I loved her fine hair plaited and pinned under her crown, a turban of red and palm green.

"Miss Dolly," Jean-Joseph said, "this is my sister-in-law, Julien's wife, Rose. Mary Rose Fédon."

Offering Charlotte a handkerchief, I nodded at the woman and extended my arm.

She gripped it. "Pleased to meet you, Miss Kirwan."

"Good to meet you, Rose. It's Dolly."

Her eyes were bright and her chin raised and noble. Hard to believe this woman had been jailed for weeks and survived. My poor sister had been changed forever in a day.

"Yes, ma'am." She turned back to Jean-Joseph. "You don't have to walk me back."

"No, Rose. My brother wouldn't want any Fédon women unprotected, not now."

Colored wives being jailed? My pulse jittered. A few minutes alone with Charlotte would tell me if I needed to give up my new lease and steal my daughter away from Grenada.

GRENADA 1789: MY DECISION

Charlotte seated me in the comfortable sea-blue parlor of her home. She set a tray of guava leaf tea and sliced mammee apples on the small bamboo table by my chair. These apples were the sweetest, silkiest things I'd ever tasted, better than what I remembered from Montserrat.

She opened her papers and mouthed the word *manumit.*

Her face eased; the tight grip on my heart did, too.

"Tell me now before your husband returns. Fédon . . . he good to you?"

My girl blinked with her fine dark eyes, a blush settled onto her cheeks. "Yes. Why would you think not?"

The outer door banged. My son-in-law popped his head inside. His brown skin held more of a tan than I recalled. He must be hands-on with his fields. Perhaps he was a "good" planter if that truly was a thing.

"Ma'am," he said to me, but his gaze locked on Charlotte.

He went to her, the approach like a dance, slow, intense, then whirled her around like he hadn't seen her in ages.

My fears about their marriage all but disappeared. "Why was your sister-in-law targeted, Fédon?"

Jean-Joseph sat in the chair beside me. "My brother and I are not silent. We want the right to participate in the governing body. It's not permitted because we're colored and Catholic."

"Mama, we had to do another wedding, an Anglican service for the council to accept our marriage."

This made no sense. Two weddings? Having to carry papers? "Why?"

"How do you explain a system that's prejudiced against our

worship? And I don't need to say much about skin, do I, Miss Kirwan?"

He didn't.

In London, Black and white freely worked the docks and the fields together. Many colored souls had jobs in Town and in the shops Mrs. Kitty and I visited.

Yet it was not hard to see the sneers, the fluttering of fans my dark flesh caused until my coins silenced them. Would there ever be a place where nothing but talents and love mattered?

Jean-Joseph heaved a heavy breath. "Because Julien had started to organize the Catholics, Rose was targeted. They'll hurt our women if we do not stay lower than them. What better way to strike terror than to attack our hearts?"

He unclenched his hand and closed his eyes for a moment. "If not for Dr. Hay, Rose would have been sold into slavery. She's a proud Carib. Never been a slave."

The natural pink of Charlotte's apple cheeks paled. "Mama, I don't know how I'd survive being locked in a jail. Poor Rose."

I stared at her. I hadn't told her of the evils of what had been done to me or Kitty or the souls lost to boilers and the sick house of Pa's plantation, none of the evil of the left side of his land. I'd stopped my mind from seeing it. I refused to speak of the horrors. I'd cleaned the sick house floor so often. Couldn't smell peppermint without thinking of death.

Maybe I should've explained more, told more of my story.

Instead, I whispered dreams. I showed her stars, not the bits of broken glass behind my smile.

Now she might be too fragile to listen.

Jean-Joseph stood, slapped his palms to his tan breeches. "No more sadness in my house. Let me tell you of Belvedere's harvests."

The man smiled and began rattling off numbers of acres and seedlings. His conversation was easy. Seemed to me that Charlotte and this plantation were Fédon's dream.

"Miss Dolly, you saw the fields. What did you think?"

"The fields. Seem . . . seem big. You'll have a good haul of cane."

"Julien will build our own boiler. Then we can process our sugar ourselves. We'll be self-sufficient. This will keep my wife safe. She can depend on me."

I nodded, hoping it would be this way, but I doubted if any man truly knew what it meant for a woman to depend upon them.

My decision was fixed. I'd stay in Grenada and make it safe. Charlotte would see Kirwan women could survive anything.

GRENADA 1789: MY RIGHTS

From the high point of Blaize Street, I could peer down at the horse-shoe bay and scan the coconut-colored sand that led to the black stone walkway of the promontory. This made Grenada seem old and settled.

Maybe that was why it was so hard here, they were all stuck in old thinking.

White planters and white merchants of the city didn't respect anything that wasn't pale, British, Anglican, or male.

I lost on all accounts. I was wonderfully colored, happily Catholic, and very much a woman.

The roar of the sea called to me. In Roseau, I could go to the water or walk beside the river in comfort.

Not here.

Sometimes I wasn't sure if I'd make it to the sea. If not for Charlotte needing to be with her husband, I'd take everyone to London and begin anew.

I'd made the wrong choice, but I'd have to live with it. Mrs. Kitty Clarke wrote me that my prince had found another Dorothy to love, a Miss Dorothea Bland, an Irish songstress.

That was the thing about choices, they haunted like death masks. Forcing a smile, I entered my new shop.

Mamaí came from the storeroom, arms full, looking me up and down. "You're in deep thought."

She would know a false smile, wouldn't she? I took pots from her hands. "Thinking of Roseau."

"Dolly, I never asked what happened on your adventure."

"Saw wonderful things. Stores with big glass windows, full of the goods I'd only ever seen in newsprint or dreams. I want more tables. I want . . . door."

A face pressed into the opening, one I'd hoped to see later when I was more settled.

Joseph Thomas.

Turning my back wouldn't make him go away, wouldn't make me unsee him.

"Doll, may I come in?" He stared at me, but I didn't move.

Mamaí ushered him inside. "We're not open yet, but come in, Mr. Thomas."

He crossed my threshold. His hair was a little shorter but still full enough for it to be caught by a ribbon. He rolled a wide-brimmed tricorn in his palms. Same dusty boots. "Doll Kirwan, you look good."

With a nod, I moved to my shelving where Mamaí's blankets hung. "How can we help you?"

He bit his lip and shuffled in his jacket and pulled out papers. "I came to offer free legal work."

"Mr. Bates handles all my documents. I don't need you."

He held out the paper. "You need this. I do too."

If this was the contract he'd been preparing that Mr. Lionel mentioned, the man was a fool. "Don't embarrass yourself. You need to leave."

"My daughter needs her papers. Grenada can be a dangerous place without paperwork showing you've been manumitted or born free."

Mamaí dashed toward our stockroom. "You two . . . talk."

She disappeared.

A breath released from Thomas as if my mother's antic proved him right, that we shared a child. He gave me the paper. The squiggles had my name and his and Eliza's. "What is it? I'm not selling you my daughter. Definitely not giving her to you."

He gripped his open shirt collar. "Doll, I need to protect her and you. I want to see her."

Rolling up the papers, I moved to the door that should have glass and flung it open. "I'll have my solicitor review this. You can go."

With a nod, he started to leave but stopped. "I never meant to hurt you. I never meant us to part for good, but I had to chase my dream. Think about letting me see Eliza. Her father's a fool, but one who loves her. Think on it, Doll."

Joseph Thomas walked out of my door, but this time he'd be back. In Grenada, maybe everywhere, Thomas had rights, rights that might exceed mine. I wouldn't have another child taken, not like Catharina.

Mamaí came out of the stockroom. In her hands was one of Kitty's masterpieces. A clay vessel that she'd fashioned like a green calabash, smooth and shiny and ripe.

"My sister has such talent."

"She does. Kitty's chosen a safe and beautiful world, or maybe it's chosen her. You and I, Dolly, we live in the true world, one with consequences." Mamaí took the papers from my fist. "Making peace can sometimes soften consequences."

Or make them worse.

Didn't know what the lesser evil was, pushing Thomas away 'cause I hated him or keeping him close because I feared he'd take our child.

GRENADA 1790: MY STORE

Edward and I stood outside of my shop as men carried barrels from my storeroom and set them on my dray.

"Mama," he said. "I'm checking the list."

"Good, my boy. Use those fingers."

My son looked dapper in pants of emerald green and a matching coat. I took extra effort to dress him well. I had to make sure that no one mistook my boy for someone to bother. Helping Governor Samuel with his party should further make sure that everyone knew this was my Edward, and we were no threat.

My fears for him had increased. My girls and Kitty stayed inside, but ten-year-old Edward wanted to be the man of the house.

"Good job, son."

He smiled and flipped his paper, counting the tablecloths the governor's secretary ordered to celebrate his second appointment to the position.

"Mama, I can go with Mr. Polk to deliver these goods. Simmons Street is not that far."

It wasn't.

Simmons was known as Government Street because the courts and councils gathered there. It was only a few blocks away. My son, my only son, had been doing better, not as sickly. Today was one of the first since moving to Grenada that he awoke with no wheezing.

"Can I, Mama? I want to make sure they don't cheat you."

I clasped his shoulder. "Promise not to overdo things? Then yes, my little man. We're almost done."

He coughed and smiled. Then I realized he'd been holding it for a chance to go. With a hug, I let him know he didn't have to pretend. I wouldn't stunt his dreams. "Tell Polk I said to drive slow and careful with you."

Cells sent Polk to keep an eye on us. He'd been sending books and gifts to Edward and my little girls every two months.

I should send him thanks, but I let Charlotte's be enough. The man rarely did anything without something in it for him. I had to keep remembering this, especially when Edward wore his black tricorn.

Sunshine bathed the street. My half sleeves even in cotton would stick to me. I glanced at my shop. The whitewashed brick building with its jet fish-scale-tiled roof was something to be proud of.

"Miss Dorothy."

That voice. I hadn't heard it since London. I spun to see my friend, Mrs. Kitty Clarke.

Arrayed in pink and white like the monkey apple flower, this fancy woman wrapped me in a big embrace. "When my husband said he'd visit your governor, I had to see you."

"Come into my shop. I'm honored you stopped by."

With a smile that only a kitten slurping milk could share, Mrs. Kitty wandered inside. Her expression went blank as she circled.

Her nose crested high as she poked decanters. Nothing gave her away. I hated and loved that about her.

"Happy with your choice, Dorothy?"

Wasn't going to answer that heart question, instead I pointed to my shelves. "You can see I took back ideas from London. Now please, look and spend money."

She laughed, and I savored an easier breath.

"This shop is magnificent. The china, even the Wedgwood, could be from a shop on Bond Street."

Clapping my hands, I almost danced, but that would be undignified. "When they said other governors and their wives were coming, I hoped to see you. Hoped you'd stop by and offer your approval."

"We talked about waiting for approval."

"Fine, then I'm waiting for your money."

Kitty pointed to a china teapot. "I will take that and the linen with the purple trim. It will look wonderful in our new home. We'll be leaving Jamaica soon."

"Back to England?"

"Canada. Clarke continues to be promoted. It's my duty to support him."

Waving his checklist, Edward ran to me. "Mama, Grandma says the governor has sent a note for more champagne. Do we extend credit to him? No money came."

"You must, Dorothy," my friend said. "A party without bubbly champagne is a dull one."

She winked at me and I dipped my chin to her, then turned to Edward. "We'll invoice him. Put the bottles in the dray, but make sure that his secretary signs the invoice for the addition." I counted up her items. "That will be six pounds and four shillings. I'll have these crated and taken to the governor's."

She fished into her bag, a silky, satin thing.

When I saw the clipping crinkle and spill onto her glove, I felt my cheeks heat.

That was one of those sketches the prince used to find me in Dominica.

"Where did you get it?"

"A friend in London sends me the oddities from home. It was in a magazine, then reprinted in a newspaper. This predates our boat ball. Sort of looks like you."

"Might be with our mutual friend."

Kitty's gaze was warm and frank, but she said nothing about another chance with the prince or my choice to leave. She wasn't one to judge other women's decisions, even if I wanted her to say she understood.

Looking for approval was rotten business.

"Here." I shoved an invoice to her hand. "Please print your name up top."

She did and offered the invoice back, but in the exchange the old sketch dropped to the floor. A boot fell upon it.

A shaggy, dusty leather boot.

Thomas bent and picked up the paper. "I presume this is yours."

Mrs. Clarke adjusted the feather in her bonnet. "Seems you have business, Dorothy." She gave me a hug and took the paper from Thomas. "I should make this into a miniature to remember you."

Thomas's face reddened and her smile widened. "Keep in touch, Miss Dorothy. Promise?"

"Promise," I said and waved good-bye.

"It's true? You went with him?" His puffy cheeks glowed. "You left our daughter for him. Do you hate me that much?"

"It's none of your business what I did. I went away and came back, the same as you've always done. The same as all men do."

He rubbed the scruff of his neck. "If you don't want my baby, give her to me. All I ever wanted was—"

"No. You think you want a family? You want your *fhortún,* your dreams. Don't pretend differently."

"That's what you want too."

"I'll have it all, Thomas. I went away for me, but I returned for my family. Can you say the same?"

"You don't think I would've come back? If I'd known—"

"We're no second prize." I moved to a shelf and straightened the display of bowls, the red and green ones Kitty sculpted. The dainty bottle with the lips and curves of a singer was one of her best.

When I turned, Thomas remained, frozen like the ice I'd sampled in London.

"Sir, what can I help you with? My shop has very fine goods. We can supply your household with servants, too."

Thomas stepped closer. "You and Prince William. Are you still in love with him?"

"None of your business. If there's nothing to purchase—"

"Do you still care for him? For me?"

"Does it matter?"

"It does, for the prince is not here. I am."

Taking a cloth from my pocket, I dusted a shelf. No green dust, no specks. "He's in London. His whereabouts are well known."

Thomas swore under his breath, and for a moment I felt powerful. "I wasn't the one who forgot us. The bloated belly and swollen feet and the sadness so thick I was blinded by it—that was mine, mine alone."

"Doll, I'm sorry."

"I'm not. A prince of the world chose me, and I chose him. Now I'm in Grenada for Charlotte."

"You don't leave much for a man. Do you, Doll? No room for him being wanted or missed. Or him wanting and missing you."

"Thomas, you made a choice."

"Let me see my daughter. I'll love her and cherish her. Be the best father."

Edward came into the shop. "Mama, all is ready. I checked and checked—Mr. Thomas!"

My son ran to him and Thomas scooped up my boy.

"You've come back," Edward said, gulping air.

Thomas set him down easy. "Yes. Grenada's home for me."

"Edward, go with Polk for the deliveries. Don't forget to get the paperwork signed."

"Yes, Mama. Mr. Thomas, you stop by the house. Grandma, Kitty, and Eliza would love to see you."

"I want to, son."

I willed my face not to respond, not to steal the joy Edward had from seeing this man. When my boy ran off to the cloakroom to join Polk, I waggled my finger at Thomas. "Don't come without a proper invitation."

"But you will let me in? There's hope."

He turned and powered through the door.

I let him go knowing I'd have to let Thomas visit to keep him from using his legal skills to steal Eliza.

GRENADA 1790: MY FAMILY

Mamaí sat beside me on the sofa, as I sat on the floor of my town house holding out my arms to Eliza. I loved the way her chubby little face lit up when she made it to me. I scooped her up and held her close.

She didn't hold it against me, leaving; Frances did.

The spunky four-year-old took more than a month to warm up to me again. Last night, sleeping in my big bed as we looked out my window at stars, she told me how much she had missed me. And that she liked me happy.

"Lizzy sent word through Polk." Mamaí stitched the ruffle hem on her newest creation. "She and Coxall had another baby, a boy. That's three children for their little family."

My heart smiled. "That's wonderful. Is she healthy and fine?"

"Yes, your daughter is good." She put down her needle. "Dolly, Eliza should be baptized. We can do it at the end of service, while we still get use of the church."

The Catholic oppression was getting worse. "I know. The government keeps making new rules. I have favor with the governor. We have to trust that protects us."

My sister came into the room. She leaned on the door's frame. "I miss outdoor church like in Montserrat or your dancing one in Roseau."

The woods of Grenada had more bugs than anywhere. It was no wonder everyone flocked to my store for ointments. The old ways that Mamaí knew, passed down by her mother's mother from Africa, were by far the best. The nut oil of the cashew cherries healed lesions. The crushed-up seeds of the fleshy custard apple killed lice.

Kitty sat beside me and put her arms about me. "I saw Mr. Thomas the other day."

Mamaí didn't look up from her blue threads.

"Yes. I see him and all the other captains. Business is booming among the settlers. Soon we'll have as many housekeepers as I did in Roseau. You should make more bowls." I touch the necklace she made me. "And more of these."

"No, that was special for you." She kissed my cheek. At least she'd forgiven my leaving.

Mamaí glanced at me over her stitches. "A baby needs a name to be baptized. Tell her, Kitty."

She pulled her knees up to her chin. "Thomas asked about Eliza. He wants to see her. Seems her pa should."

Kitty's smile was sweet and true and picked my heart clean of looking for excuses.

"Did I ever tell you two I miss your pa sometimes?" Mamaí's hummingbird voice blasted like a loud horn.

Wordless, Kitty and I spun to our mother.

"I do. Especially when you both are restless. That reminds me of him."

"You want Pa back?" My tone sounded squeaky. I swallowed and tried again. "I could get Mr. Bates to reach out to him. But, Mamaí, you're not old. If you want—"

"Girl, that's not what I miss. But late at night, there are times I wish he were here."

It was the most she'd ever said to us about caring for Pa. I had questions, but this was her truth to say.

Mine was that I'd been testing Thomas's newfound devotion to prove he wasn't going anywhere.

The past few weeks, he showed up in the evenings to walk me home.

"Thomas is Anglican," Kitty said in a sad hushed tone. "He gets to worship inside without threats. He gets to walk around outside without papers."

The harassment of us free coloreds kept tightening. A cousin to Charlotte's husband was arrested and jailed for two weeks until she could prove her status. They kept targeting colored women to humble them and their men.

"You know he and Edward are boating again." Mamaí nodded. "Your own son is sneaking around on you."

"Edward? Is that what's getting him worked up? That can't be good for his health."

"Daughter, please, that boy is smiling more than I've ever seen. More than a letter ever did."

Cells kept writing our son, but Mamaí was right.

Kitty took Eliza from me. "Edward smiles a lot with Thomas. Naptime for you, little girl. Frances will be up soon." With my youngest hugging her neck, my sister left the room.

She was a good second mother to my children.

"He's back for weeks. No whoring around for him or you. And he walks you home every night."

I offered Mamaí a frown. "He was always good when he was here."

Having said my barb, I walked onto the small porch. Night had fallen. The stars above seemed to do a great deal of signaling, like the lanterns that guided boats to port.

Maybe I should listen to the stars and give a little to Thomas. What would it cost me, if I offered Joseph Thomas a bit of my life?

GRENADA 1790: MY BUSINESS

The busy morning in the shop succumbed to afternoon slumber. I found myself yawning as I dusted an upper shelf. The bell on the door made a merry jingle. I turned with my ready smile. "Good . . . afternoon."

Thomas stood there, hat against his chest, hair combed and parted to the side. "Miss Doll."

His voice was low, not sultry. He put his hat to his chest. "Miss Doll, I have come to be a patron today. Housekeeping services."

"Housekeeping?"

"Yes, you remember I was never very good at picking up after myself."

"This is true."

"Well, everyone raves over your girls. The navy men can't get enough."

Pulling out my dust rag, I brushed at my clean counter. "The commanders of the reefers love good services."

"I've heard." His eyes became distant for a moment. Then he moved closer. His gait was slow, like it pained him to move. "I wish they'd take their boats and go away. They threaten to enact a blockade at any moment. That would hurt your business, would definitely impact mine."

I went to my ledger book trying to think of which girl would be perfect. Probably someone old on the verge of stopping work to live in the hillside would be ideal.

"Make it a good girl, one with good hands." He picked up one of my palms. "Strong but soft, given to tenderness, even when it's not deserved."

I drew my fingers away. "Flirt. What happened to you?"

"Exploring the woods by Black Bay Beach. The black sands are silky. The woods they back into are thick."

"Sounds lovely."

"It is but for the bugs."

He followed me to the shelves, wincing with each step. The man was in pain and since my dear family kept up with his whereabouts, I knew it wasn't the clap or other whoring diseases.

"Thomas, how soon would you need a housekeeper?"

"As soon as possible. The discomfort grows knowing I can't help myself."

"I see. The girl I have in mind—"

"I want you . . . to arrange things as soon as possible. Won't be able to walk you home tonight. Please leave soon and be safe."

He took out a sovereign and left it on the counter, close to my ledger book. The fool knew it was too much, but that was to impress me or to tell me how much he suffered.

I felt sorry for Thomas. This was as close to begging as he'd come. He was prideful.

He went to the door. "I stay off Grand Etang Road, Number 12. Thank you, Doll. I love you . . . for doing this."

His words were a whisper, but I'd heard them as if he'd shouted. He still loved me.

The man played dirty, trying to twist up those old feelings in my chest. It hadn't been too steady lately, so it was easy to do.

Now he'd gotten his backside fouled up. Chiggers could tear up a man's skin worse than anything, anything next to lashes.

Charlotte came into the shop. "Was that Mr. Thomas?"

"Yes, I believe it was."

"Has he returned to stay?"

"You know I don't know the mind of any man, especially not that one." I closed up my ledger books. "How is your Mr. Fédon?"

"Wonderful. He's wonderful. I love him so."

Her voice trailed off and then vanished.

"What's the matter, Charlotte?"

"Jean-Joseph and his brother keep getting worked up over perceived slights. They hate the British. Sometimes I think they'll take up arms."

She sighed and shook. "I wish we'd be away from here sometimes."

I held my daughter. "I remember being scared to sleep sometimes in Demerara."

My pretty brown girl quivered in my arms. "Papa Cells would never let anything happen to you. He still writes asking about you."

Groan. Sighing inside, I shook my head. "Child, you have to believe you're safe. Fretting over things you can't control will never sit well."

"Papa Cells writes the same thing."

My head was atop Charlotte's thick crown of braids. She didn't see me roll my eyes. "He's right about that. Jean-Joseph Fédon has the passions of any young man, but he'll get to be older and wiser. His love for you will keep him safe."

She nodded but held on to me like I was a comforting blanket.

Jean-Joseph came in, handsome in his onyx waistcoat. "Miss Kirwan, how are you today?"

"Just fine since I've seen my girl."

"Well, the dray is full of supplies. I think we'll head on before the storm brews."

"You're not predicting bad weather?"

"No, ma'am, not a rainstorm. All these cyclone soldiers crawling all over the place like they own it. They think they have rights to our women. Never."

I picked up my ladder. "They have rights to the ones who wish it, the ones who've been paid a fee."

Jean-Joseph trotted over and took it. "Just not right. Where do you want this?"

"The storeroom. Thank you, young man. Then come have your say."

Charlotte put her hands to his buttons. "No. Let's go. Bye, Mama."

I clasped her arm. "Let him speak. Mr. Fédon?"

"While I appreciate the things you've been able to accomplish, Miss Dolly, they shouldn't have our women, and you shouldn't provide them a means to get them."

I tugged off my apron. "Then that would be stupid."

"That would be principled."

"Again, stupid. You think that my not providing safe opportunities for my housekeepers will keep men from wanting them? I make sure my girls are paid to clean and cook in safety. If more is offered, it's the woman's choice. No one's forcing anyone."

"Ma'am, I mean no disrespect, but it's distasteful." He shook his head. His close curly hair bounced. "There are other ways to win and to earn money."

"Fédon, that's what freedom is. The ability to do what we please to earn our bread. It surely must extend to women too."

He looped Charlotte's arm. "There are other ways. You'll see."

The fellow was bullheaded and honest. Expecting him to also be fair was a lot for a man.

Admiring his forthright stance and how well and in love they looked, I smiled at Charlotte and Jean-Joseph. "I look forward to you making other ways for women, Mr. Fédon."

Charlotte kissed my cheek and dragged her husband out of my shop. They crossed in the path of soldiers probably heading for entertainment near the shore.

My daughter snuggled closer to Fédon and kept him moving. There were enough soldiers with guns to make trouble. A hotheaded young man needed to take care.

I locked the door and prepared to walk home alone. Tomorrow, if I wanted an escort, I'd need to go fix another stubborn man.

GRENADA 1790: MY MAN

With a basket of tools, sheets, jars of cure-alls, and a little rum to chase away the pain, I made my way up to Grand Etang Road. The man had the nerve to lease far enough away that I had more than enough time to talk myself out of going.

But I didn't.

The plain building of wood construction made me miss England.

Thomas's door was open, and I stepped inside.

Right in front of a small sofa and table sat a pile of clothes on the floor. Typical of him.

Putting my basket down, I passed his clothes, then turned and scooped up his jacket. It smelled of sea salt, cigar, and man.

I always liked that.

Tapping loudly in my sandals to stir him if he was awake, I walked deeper inside.

It seemed empty and sparse. No paintings, no books, nothing on his desk.

It was well past supper, he should be about. Had he taken to bed? Maybe he'd become ill.

My frustration dissipated a little more.

Then I heard a whisper, a hot laugh, a high-pitched voice.

Sweet, fiery jealousy swept inside. I had to remind myself that I hadn't kept myself lonely waiting for him. There was no reason to be mad.

But I came to remove chiggers and talk of our child.

The front door opened. In came Thomas and a pretty young thing Lizzy's age at his side.

"Oh! Miss Doll," he said, "this is Miss Lemont. She's here for the housekeeping services. I didn't think you'd take me on as a client. I'm in poor shape."

Was my stare at Thomas enough to burn a hole clean through him? "I wasn't, either, being shorthanded. Thought I'd see to it, but—"

The young woman started backing up. "Miss Dolly, I didn't know this was your man."

"Mine . . . mmm no." I glanced at the beaming Thomas. "Miss Lemont, when I thought about those dripping sores and the pus . . . He needs to be cleaned before the infection sets in."

I walked to the miss and shoved my basket, making sure to expose the pliers. "Here, you get those out of him right away. And try to keep your hands clean. It's awful."

She pushed the basket back. "No, Miss Dolly. I was looking into the position, but it seems you have it."

The young thing was quite nimble. She rounded Thomas and fled out the door.

He shut it, his head shaking. "Was that necessary, Doll? You could've just said the position was filled. It is filled? It's hard to get good help. And I like to be handled properly."

"Take off your pants and let's get to this."

"Love a forceful woman." Like I'd asked him to dance, he stepped to me. His gaze wrapped about me, but his fingers locked upon his waistband.

Then he kicked off one dusty boot and then the next.

Belt strings went over my head as his breeches dropped.

"Follow this way." He led me to his bedchamber, with his thick bowed legs lumbering until he flopped facedown into his pillow. "I should've known you wouldn't let me suffer."

"Stay quiet. You haven't won anything."

The bed rocked as I climbed next to his pale behind pointing up. "You're here. Means I have a chance to fix things."

"Hush."

"I found something, well, someone, for you."

I tugged my basket closer and began rummaging for the ointments. "I need you to stop talking. I have to concentrate."

"But this is important. I found your grandmother. I came back to Roseau to tell you, then your mother said you'd gone away."

Mamaí knew her mother was being located and said nothing?

"I found her, Doll, to prove to you I was serious about building our family. It was stupid to think you'd wait."

I hit his leg. "I need to concentrate. I don't need you saying these things when I'm about to dig a chigger from your arse."

"I'm an arse. I checked with her master last week. He's still amenable to sell her. Your grandmother, Sally, is here in Grenada. We can have her freed and with us."

The lump in my throat grew heavier. "Please, I have to fix you up. When I left for London, I was done with you. I didn't think about us. There was no us."

"Doll, I thought of you every day, but everything I did failed. I was lucky to get out with my investments. I came back to Grenada to bury my father. An only son burying an only son. No more Thomases."

"I'm sorry. I truly am. Now quiet. You've got at least two chiggers."

It took longer than I wanted, but he did indeed have two burrowed into the fat of his taut buttocks. With a needle and pliers, I worked and got one out, then the other. The man didn't whimper until I poured rum into each of the wounds. Then I put on Mamaí's cashew cherry oil.

That burned.

He winced. "That hurts, but rub me and make it better. Be a *helpin han*, Doll."

"You keep yourself clean and out of the woods, you'll have no problems. But you are warm with a little fever."

With a yelp, he rolled over. The man wasn't shy.

I tossed sheets on him.

"Just a fever? Don't you have something in that basket for it? And goodness, that stings. Stay and talk to me about Eliza. How big is she? I want to see her."

"Come tomorrow for dinner. You can spend time with your daughter."

"Thank you. I won't hurt her. I love her. I've loved her since I heard she exists." His hands settled on my hips.

This was never good, me straddling Thomas with his fingers trying to find skin.

As fast as I could, I swung my leg and slipped off the mattress. "I came to fix you up, that's all."

He kissed my wrist. "I'm mediocre at shipping, at mercantilism, at everything important. I'm a very ordinary businessman."

"Your free legal services are superb."

"Doll, I'd love to offer my services and my heart."

With a shrug, I tried to leave but he kept holding my hand. "You don't care I went with a prince to see the world, that there are sketches of me and him and a hammock?"

Thomas eased up and kissed me. He kept at it until I kissed him back.

"Don't care. He's a sea away. I'm right here. And I want to be a father to Eliza, and Frances. Plus poor Edward is still outnumbered. I need to be your lover and friend. Not particular about which you choose first."

No. We'd done this before. I'd trusted and failed. "You need the sea. I understand its call now. The prince—"

"I love you, Doll. That never stopped, not for one minute. It never will."

I had stopped loving him. I'd pushed him out of my head when the birthing sadness made it hard to love myself. With my hand latched to his, I stared at his dusty feet, the arch of his toes. "It's late. I should go."

He followed me to his main room, clutching the falling linen. "I don't want anyone caring for me that's not you."

"Well, I don't hate you anymore."

He bent and kissed my cheek. "That's enough."

"Go back to bed. Meet me at the store tomorrow to walk me home and meet Eliza."

"Our daughter." He closed his eyes. "Put me to bed. You remember how."

"What?"

"Or I'll follow you home just like this."

He would be ridiculous. I pushed him back to his bedchamber and made him lie down. "Keep yourself covered and cleaned. I'll send a girl to keep you tidy, but if you need hands-on help, you call for me, Thomas."

"I'm asking now. Infection may have set in. Could make this fever bad. I don't want to be alone."

Fevers were dangerous, and I had waited too long to treat him because of my stubbornness.

"Don't leave, Doll. It's dark. The streets aren't safe."

His sea-blue eyes held concern and much more. "I won't ruin things this time, Doll. You can trust me."

It was dark, and I'd made everyone promise to not travel the streets at night. "I guess I'm stuck here."

He patted the mattress. "Here's your spot."

Thomas's arm tucked about my lap. "Thank you, I didn't want to die alone."

"Now I know you're joking." His hold was firm and tight just like I remembered, like I liked.

"Doll, I've been dying knowing I lost my Kirwan family."

"Thomas, please."

He snuggled his head on my lap. "And I'll be good. Unless you don't want me to. Should be plenty of ways to pass the time and break this fever."

"Thomas."

"Fine. At week's end, if my end is better, we'll ride out to Mount Qua Qua. There's a plantation up there where Sally is."

Despite my doubts, a man claiming to be devoted to you, trying to free your grandma, needed a path to get to you. I'd show him the way to be friends again. We were better at that than lovers.

'Course, with his hands clasped to my hips, snoring into my thigh, I wasn't clear where this path stopped.

Armed with a bill of sale that Thomas had crafted, he and I set off to Mount Qua Qua. This was the way to get to Belvedere Estates. If I'd studied those plantations instead of averting my eyes, would I have seen my grandmother?

"This Runyan, he owned Sally and sold off my mother?"

"Yes, ma'am."

Thomas rolled his hips and sat in a new position on the cushion I brought him. Wasn't anything like those padded carriages in England, but it should help.

His fever did linger and he spent time at my town house until Mamaí's teas finally broke it. The man still looked to be in pain.

"You didn't need to come, Thomas. I could handle this."

"This is not exactly for my comfort. I'm not letting you out of my sight, traveling my Grenada. This is my island, and we're headed to people who won't recognize an enterprising woman, 'specially one like you."

He was being Thomas, not saying the obvious. That my grandmother's owners were the worst type of planters—rapists, thieves, murderers—all under the legal system of enslavement.

We weren't even there and my stomach knotted.

"Doll, you're looking a little green. You feeling well? Edward didn't look good this morning, either."

"You keep driving. My grandma is enslaved, and I have the means to free her. No dawdling 'cause I'm feeling poorly."

He waved his hat at his face. "You're a strong stubborn woman."

"And that's wrong?"

"No. It's one of the things I love about you."

From the side of my eye, I saw his chuckles. His smile was full and lovely, but I looked away to the thick growth of ferns hugging the muddy trail. Tall scraggly pines and thick bamboo made canopies of shade. It was cooler here, not humid like it was near the shore. I was glad for the warmth of my shawl and kept praying that the rain would keep.

Thomas shifted. "This could've waited another week so I could do it alone."

I hated I had to let men, white men, British men, do my bidding, but it offered me better pricing and kept the cheating low.

This made me realize how much more I had to do to make sure Edward and my girls had their chances to shine.

The air smelled like horrid mint. A delicate mist shrouded the top of the mountain. "At least it will only get cooler."

Thomas tightened the reins and made my horse go faster. We moved with a bit of speed. "We could sit a spell at the crater lake if you need to rest. Heard it's romantic."

"Sir, if you say one more thing about stopping, I don't know what I'll do."

He slowed the carriage to a crawl.

"What? Woman, what exactly are you going to do? I have the reins. I'm driving this beast, Doll."

"I'm going to stare at you and wish you fall off the dray."

"Not happening. And if I did fall. I'd still catch up and make you slow down."

He started to laugh. "Maybe you are feeling better. You've threatened to kick me out of your life again. That's particularly cruel when I have plans to give you a few more of my children."

"What, Thomas? We're not together. How can you even think such a thing?"

"'Cause you've been kissing on me when you check on me."

"No."

"But you've been thinking on it. I think about you constantly. And it's time we do something about it. Something legally binding. You will know I'm with you, and I'll know where to come home to. You will too."

My heart raced, for I had kissed him a little and checked on him a lot. "Fevers are bad."

"I love you, Dorothy. Marry me."

He took my hand and slowed the dray more.

The smoky crater lake, Grand Etang Lake, sat calmly to my right.

"Don't say no, not without hearing me or thinking about it, or letting me have my way with you once."

"Can we talk about this foolishness later? I need to save my strength for the negotiations. My grandma Sally's freedom is more important than your jokes."

"Fine." He made the dray move a little faster.

At least Thomas was listening. But a week of us getting along, of him visiting and playing with Eliza and Frances and promising to fish with Edward, didn't make us one big family.

After passing the lake, we drew closer to a plantation.

Silk cottonwood trees rimmed the land. That white bark was unmistakable. Sugarcane fields, high emerald stalks, grew everywhere with brown dots holding up the rows.

A little closer, the distant dots became men, black and brown. Sable women followed behind picking up the cutting.

Half dressed or poorly dressed in these woods of chiggers was cruel. An overseer on horseback shouted and whipped at them.

The angry shouts.

A low mournful song hummed from the enslaved. The moaning kept them in rhythm. The tune meshed with ones stuck in my head from the slave boats, *yo-yo-yo*, and my memories from Pa's plantation, the left side, the bad side.

The mint.

The peppermint.

The familiar feeling of death swept over me, ripping at my skin.

That moaning was stronger. There was no escaping it. No not-seeing it, not today.

* * *

In my mind's eye, I was little again with more osnaburg than others because my pa, a white planter, claimed me. From those first days of helping Mamaí at the sick house, I learned not to see the bad. I always looked to the right, never the left.

Whipping was on the left. Stocks and the sick house were on the left. Mamaí would make me help her aid the sick, the ones raped so bad they bled for days. I wiped up the blood, cleaning with peppermint water.

On the left . . .

Pick and sing.

Bleed and sing.

Die and sing.

. . . on the left.

If I saw the evil and accepted this as my future, it would eat away my dreams like acid, burn them to nothingness.

The dray stopped. "Doll, can you hear me?"

"My pa was massa, Thomas. All the pain was done in his name. He never stopped the doings on the left side. Never once did he acknowledge the pain. Overseers weren't dismissed for cruelty or killings. Thomas, I'm as bad as Pa. I looked away to the right. I always look away."

"Doll. You're not him."

"The jumbies and death masks say I am."

Thomas gripped my hand. "I don't see anything."

"I didn't want to see it either. If I saw it, then I couldn't dream anymore. I'd have to take my place in the fields with the people born to hurt then die."

"Doll, you're here with me. You're safe."

"I can't die in those fields, Thomas."

"I'm not letting you go. Never. You're scaring me, woman. We just need to complete the deal. Let me do this. You sit here."

How could I when my blood ran in these fields?

At the main house of Runyan's plantation, we stopped. Thomas left the dray as I scrambled down.

"Doll?"

"I have to do this."

He nodded and led me to the main house. It was no owl house, no stilt leg supporting it. Floods weren't their worries. Broken shutters, busted steps—there was plenty. I paused on a tread not sure it would hold.

"Hurricane damage," Thomas said. "The killer of 1780. Ten years and still not fixed. Runyan's hurting for money."

A ragged old man in a perfect straw hat sat on the porch. "What can I do fer ya?"

"Mr. Runyan," Thomas said. "I've come about buying Sally. I've been in contact with you through Mr. Bates."

"Oh, yes. Ya want to buy old Sally."

He looked over me to Thomas, sneering like I was some dog at his side. "Ya've been sending papers?"

Thomas stepped in front of me. "Yes, I just need you to sign."

My head was mixed up. I clung to Thomas's coat like a coward.

Mr. Runyan covered his eyes like the sun weighed down on him and that perfect hat—no gaps in the weave, no raw edges or holes from bugs, nothing from toiling under the sun.

"Sally was good for me back in the day, but she's old. What use is she to ya?"

"I represent a party who has interest in reuniting her to family."

"I suppose she does have family." Runyan spit tobacco near my boots.

Thomas took the contract from me.

Runyan's gaze on me felt dirty. "Who's that? Yar good luck piece?"

"I'd say so." Thomas gave him the papers. "We agreed on thirty-five pounds."

"That was what I said, but now I'm a thinkin' Sally awful popular."

No.

He couldn't change now.

I folded my arms. "Look, you made a deal."

He laughed and rocked in his chair. "Can't you keep your wench in line?"

"I'm no one's wench. I'm—"

"She should be, being small and round." Runyan leered and rocked. "Pity's she's black as tar."

Thomas groaned and made eyes at me. "Runyan, let's finalize this offer."

With a hand to my hip, I found my courage. "Reduce the amount, Thomas. That's what I'm saying."

Thomas craned his neck to the ragged roof. "Miss Doll represents the entity interested in the transaction. She's made you a very good offer. Take the thirty-five pounds, Runyan, or the amount will go to twenty-five pounds."

"They let the coloreds do that? Well, the way these *ninnies*, the chin-up ones, are in Belvedere Estates, they must let 'em all do it."

He didn't say ninny, said that other word. He might as well had finished with N'girl.

The tension in Thomas's grip tightened. He was going to strike this old man. "Apologize, Runyan."

"For what? Those free ones don't know their place. They need to be quiet and sit back and be grateful for what they have."

Sit back and take it? Noooo. "This man needs to sign today . . . or no deal."

Runyan's eyes went wide. He took his hat and fanned his balding gray head. "Ya bluff. Now, I'm in no hurry. Sally's old, but she still has some looks. They bred her to be pretty. Not white enough but definitely not coal dust like your doll."

My mouth went dry. "The deal is done. Let's go, Mr. Thomas."

Thomas grasped my arm. "Not even the twenty-five. You sure?"

"This fool has no need of the money." I leaned closer to the old man. "And it's clear he may not have many more days. Mr. Thomas can take up this deal with your heirs. Rats like you always raise greedy rats."

Runyan stood up from his chair. "Wait. Don't let her talk to me like that."

"I can talk to you anyway I want. My chin's up." I stormed off the porch.

Thomas put the papers into his jacket and descended the shoddy steps. "You know what you doing, Miss Kirwan?"

I couldn't answer, but scrambled atop the dray, right into the driver's seat. I grabbed the reins before Thomas had a full grip on his seat and had the thing moving. We had to get away.

A mile or two in silence didn't stop my shaking. The steam of the crater lake made my face wet. Then I realized it was already wet.

Thomas took the reins and made the dray stop. He sat there with his hand on mine, listening to me sob.

"I should've listened to you, Thomas. I couldn't let him win."

"The old coot," he said, "he was just trying to stroke another five pounds."

"Runyan could kill her tonight or hurt my grandma bad, but my pride got in the way. I let her be enslaved another hour 'cause I couldn't let the old massa win. I'm horrible and shamed."

He pulled me against his shoulder. My wet face burrowed into his neck, ducking into the folds of his linen shirt.

"Thomas, I poked at my brother. I couldn't let him win. It's my fault he hurt me and Kitty. My fault. I just couldn't sit and take it."

"That fool's actions aren't your fault." He swept me deeper to his chest. His hands knocked off my bonnet and sank into my curls. "And don't you ever take abuse or dim your light because of a fool. You're remarkable. The rest of us are trying to catch up."

"You need to hurry. And I can't fail my family again."

"Let yourself be caught sometimes. Let someone else help. I'll get that old buzzard to free your grandmother."

Thomas was being sweet, and I was a crying fool.

Shifting in his seat, Thomas took up the reins and guided us slow and easy back to St. George's.

When he leaped out of the dray, he came to my side. I slid into his arms and let him hold me. "I want to be caught."

His embrace tightened. "I'm home, finally home. I'll get Sally freed."

"Thomas, I told Mamaí I had a surprise for her. What do I tell her now?"

He dimpled. "Let me take care of this, too."

He looped his fingers with mine and led me up the steps to my house.

Mamaí and Kitty, and the children, were in the parlor. "Hey, everyone, Doll has finally agreed to marry me. We're finally going to be together. We're all going to be a family."

My mother jumped up from the sofa and kissed Thomas's cheek. "That's the surprise? How wonderful."

"I wore her down, you see. I need her. She'll be my Mrs. Thomas."

Kitty and my little girls gathered around me. Edward hugged Thomas's legs.

I was furious. We hadn't agreed to anything. Then Frances climbed into his arms and hugged his neck. "Papa. I get one now."

Mamaí hugged me and left her hand on my stomach. "Babies need fathers, Doll. Ones who'll claim 'em and keep 'em safe. Then no one can take them away."

Her whisper chilled. She wasn't talking about Frances or Eliza, was she? If my family wasn't crowding and crowing, I'd start crying all over again.

GRENADA 1790: MY CHURCH

I let Thomas take me on a one-day sailing trip to Dominica, and we ended up puttering about in the sea for three. It gave him plenty of time to prance about the deck of his *Mary*, listing his passionate reasons why he and I should be "us" again.

The boat docked, he tied up the sail against the blue painted mast, and helped me out. "Let's walk a little before we head to Mr. Bates."

We wandered into the Old Market where we had had our first long chat. The cobbled well was still there, still alone, still deep.

"Come on, Doll."

Hand in hand, Thomas took me to Mr. Bates's office.

Mr. Lionel stood up to greet us. "Good to see you, Miss Dolly." He led us to a room. "Your housekeepers are still being productive. We are collecting fees. Your fortune grows."

I offered him a smile, but not much else.

Mr. Bates waved us to seats. He was a little thinner with the same brass spectacles, but thicker lenses. "This contract keeps your assets intact and in your control, Miss Kirwan. If Thomas were to outlive you, he'd get a share along with your natural children. Is that what you want, Thomas?"

The solicitor was at least consistent.

"Yes, Miss Kirwan has worked hard to provide for her family, not for an able-bodied male. I intend to be old and gray with her, but I shall not live beyond my usefulness."

"Miss Kirwan, are you fine with this paperwork? I've made sure all the protections are in place for you and your heirs."

I looked at the paper, the jumble of words. I knew what my name was and Thomas's.

Should I just trust that the legal papers said the truth I wanted? No. "Where are the other witnesses? I always do big documents in three to make sure it says what I want it to say."

"Yes, ma'am," Mr. Bates said. "My clerks will head in now."

One by one, they entered, read me the papers, then left.

By the third one, I could probably recite it by heart.

Thomas smiled, not upset that I had doubts.

He knew me.

He didn't take offense, but he should be offended. I had a secret that this union would cover.

Mr. Bates again turned the documents in my direction. "Ready to sign now?"

Maybe. "Not yet."

Thomas tossed his arms behind his head. "Mr. Bates, can you give us a moment?"

When the door closed, he leaned near. "You scared of commitment, Doll? The obligation to live in harmony too much?"

Maybe. "No."

He put his hand on my chair. "Then what is it?"

"These papers say I have to depend on you. And you me. That sounds like a lot."

Thomas sat back, a thoughtful look swept across his face, sorrow. It stole his smile. "This protects your assets in the unfortunate circumstances of death. My cousins or business partners can claim nothing."

"So you'll still be dealing with them?"

"A man has to have time to dabble. But responsible dabbling. This protects you from that but not from me. I intend to haunt you. I'm never letting you go this time, ever."

"A jumbie? You sound pretty confident for a dead man."

"Well, I'm not dead yet. Maybe if you commit to me, I'll pass away from shock."

"Then I shouldn't sign. We should go dance by the docks. We've never danced, Thomas. Never."

"Is that the way to get to you, Doll?"

It took everything not to touch my barely flat stomach. "It's worked before."

He kissed my palm. "I know, and my rhythm is off. I'm going to learn."

Looking into his eyes, so blue and clear, I had to confess. "Thomas, I'm with—"

"With me, Doll. And I'm with you. And all your children become mine. Any one of them born after we wed is legally mine. Remember me? The man who wants the big family."

I raised my eyebrows. Somehow, he knew I had William's babe in my belly and was willing to make that child a Thomas. Mamaí and Kitty did do the laundry. They were friendly to Thomas. They must have told him. How else would he know?

"Doll, I'll be there whenever you're sad. No more being alone for either of us."

Fear of the birthing sadness was enough to say yes, but my lips weren't moving.

Thomas sat on the desk in front of me. "This is my way of letting the world know you're mine. If it keeps a prince or a scoundrel or two from Demerara away, that's fine with me."

"You're not going to regret hitching yourself to a Catholic? If Grenada continues to harshen, you wouldn't have to lie. You could go on just fine."

"I'm not fine without you, Doll. I don't know how else to prove myself."

His easy humor started to slip. He didn't understand that it wasn't him or his love that I doubted. It was me. I slid the paper and held it to the light coming from the window. "A contract, like Lizzy and Coxall. Why does this paper make me feel like chattel?"

"It's not a bill of sale. This isn't about the past. No one but you and me. We're building together. I know you have dreams, woman. I'm ready to help them come true."

"If you were to wake up one day and think you should be at sea, making deals for your sloop, I don't want this paper to stop you."

"Doll, I made up my mind when I saw you in your shop. I watched how happy you were stocking shelves. I want you happy. I love you. I know you love me, even if you don't say it. This time we do it right, but we start right."

What do you do when a force bigger than you comes against your fears?

You believe, let him in, and hope for forever. Still a fool, I picked up the quill and signed the paper. "There. Now you can officially call me Mrs. Thomas."

He elbowed the door, and Mr. Bates and Lionel seemed to fall into the room. "This is done, gentlemen. I'm escorting Mrs. Thomas to the Old Market."

We walked in the dusky light through the quieting cobble square. We missed the well for he led me down an alley to Notre Dame du Bon Port Church.

I clutched the iron gate. "Charlotte's wedding was beautiful here."

"Won't be missing any other family celebrations." He pushed open the gate. "Mrs. Thomas, let's commit a bit of heresy and marry properly with a ceremony before God."

"But it's not legal. The Holy Father hasn't—"

"Well, he should sanction it. Maybe he will someday. Our love is as honest and pure as any, even if it's a Catholic and Anglican uniting."

My fingers laced with his, and we stepped through the courtyard and into the chapel.

At the back of the church, Edward, Kitty, and Polk sat. My son and sons-in-law and all my girls were there, too.

But Jean-Joseph Fédon didn't look happy, and he separated himself from the jovial Coxalls.

I put them all out of my head when Mamaí gave me flowers. They were lovely—scarlet sabineas, pink and red hibiscus, but she laced them with the red and yellow bulbs of the peacock flower.

It was a little late for that wicked flower. My tea had failed to control anything.

This child would memorialize my choices. I'd build a world where this babe would be a prince or princess.

Mamaí sat by an old woman who had Frances and Eliza.

Then I realized that the stranger with silver hair and a weathered face scorched by the sun looked like my mother.

Thomas leaned down. "Yes, Miss Sally is free. Seems Mr. Runyan had a chance to think on it." My husband's voice vibrated on my ear. "We settled on twenty-five pounds but that I'd pay the manumission fee."

"I'll pay you back, Thomas."

"Consider it your gift." He grasped my hand. "Ready?"

His friend, the drinking minister from Lizzy's ceremony, was at the nave under a crucifix of the Lord. This service felt truer than the papers, and should last longer than my prior concubinage.

I sniffed the vanilla sweetness of my flowers. They were a thing of beauty and pain. Pure happiness couldn't exist without sacrifice. I understood that now. Though I had a man who loved me and was committed to me, somehow I knew I wasn't done paying.

I waddled down to the shore and held up my hands. "This is it."

Kitty chased behind me. "Slow down, Dolly. Thomas doesn't want you to fall."

"Can't slow down, sis. I have to show you this."

"Dirt?"

"No, this. This plot of ground. I own the land. This is where I'll build a hotel. I might even add a musical church."

Her face brightened. She clapped. "You bought it? But there's nothing here. Does Thomas know they cheated you out of a building?"

With a shake of my head, I smoothed my thick middle. Thomas knew what he wanted to know, that I'd birthed one son, Josephy, then a daughter, Ann. In seven months, I'd soon give him another baby. "Kitty, I'm going to bring the elegance from across the sea here to Grenada. My hotel will be a work of art."

"Why can't you be happy with the store and the housekeeping services? Why more?" My sister looked down at her sandals that had beach sand. "Why do you have to keep pushing? Josephy was early. And we almost lost you with the last babe."

"Ann is fine. She breathes. She's growing."

My sister clasped my stomach. "Don't take on anything until this baby is here. You're not strong, sometimes."

"The sadness is not as bad." I lied and lifted her chin. "And Thomas and you make everything good. I recovered much faster."

Kitty balled her fists and jumped around in the wet sand. "I'm not good. I don't want to lose you. I'm scared. Can't you be easy?"

"No. Kitty, I'm going to put a hotel here. I'm going to construct something big and wonderful. And all the coins from the navy men visiting will be ours. Edward will run this for me when he grows up. I have to make sure he and Josephy have businesses. That's how my princes will survive."

The local council had made more rules that showed how they hated the colored planters. I needed my sons to have businesses that were not sugarcane estates. That was safe money. "When Frances grows up, she'll run the store on Blaize. She's already good with numbers for a six-year-old. Exceptional."

She grabbed me. "I'm scared, Dolly."

"Kitty, I learned so much in England. I know what it takes to get the top coins. Why let men get wealthy when that wealth could be ours?"

"Aren't we doing fine? Do we need more?"

We were, but I wanted more. "Yes. My connections through Coxall and King can supply me the finest goods. Thomas has brought some of the Garraways, the good solvent ones, into my network. I can't stop now because I'm a woman, a woman with child."

Kitty tugged at her puffy sleeves made stiff with cording. I had the overdress of red linen designed for her because the silky fabric made her smile. She loved bright colors.

Then I remembered Kitty still danced with the old, the time before everything changed, when it was her and me against all the jumbies, all the evils. To soothe her, I took her palm in mine and hummed the old for her, our old hymn.

Rop tú mo baile.

Rop tú—

"Don't die, Dolly. Don't go away."

"Kitty, I'm going to be fine, but Thomas and Mamaí will care for you if I'm sick. You promise to keep this baby safe."

"Yes, Dolly. I will."

I turned my back to my land. My sister needed me more than trying to build. This dirt, this plot of land, was still mine. It would have a hotel, Mrs. Dorothy's hotel, the finest offerings in the Caribbean, fit for a prince.

Or a wonderful solicitor.

Thomas and Edward, Frances, and Eliza were out on the *Mary*. The blue pole of the sloop bobbled out in the water. I wanted to wave, but he was too far to see.

His businesses struggled, but the man was the best father to all my children, even going to Belvedere Estates to check on my Charlotte.

Life was cruel. She was barren, and I was a fertile sow.

"After this baby, can you be done, Dolly?"

I loved my children. I loved making children but not the darkness and struggle bringing them into this world.

I offered Kitty another hug. "Let's go see what Sally has cooked."

Our mouths watered. My grandma was silent most of the time, but she could cook anything from hens to breadfruit stews. "Maybe she made oattie bread."

"Mmmm." Kitty licked her lips. "Oh, that's good with cream."

My sister quickened her steps. "Come on, but talk to Thomas. No more babies."

Her pretty voice was hard and definitive like that was all it took, just saying it out loud.

With a shrug, I patted her arm. Joseph Thomas wouldn't understand. All he wanted was children. They were his pride.

After this one, I'd resort to Mamaí's garden again. For I wanted my dreams, my family, and Thomas. Everyone would have to understand.

GRENADA 1792: MY SONS

Little Harry had a strong cry and a bigger appetite, more than I could offer. When he was done with me, I passed him to Kitty and she took him to the wet nurse.

My eyes shut until I heard Thomas's laugh.

Blinking, I saw him in our bedchamber, a happy room with sunny yellow paint.

"There's your mama, Josephy. She's looking tired and scrumptious."

"Mama." My boy held Thomas's hand and walked beside him. His little steps were unsure, but getting better. Being born early didn't seem to hurt him too much. In another year, we might not notice at all.

Thomas picked the wiggler up and sat on our four-poster bed, then leaned in and kissed me.

It wasn't the chaste offerings he'd done the past month since birthing Josephy's little brother.

This was hunger.

This was the beginnings of the dance that would flood my womb with another baby.

No more. Nine was enough. At thirty-six, it should be.

Josephy pulled at my braids. They slipped through his tiny fingers.

"How we doing, Mrs. Thomas?"

Propping up against the pillows, I snuggled Josephy, loved his dark, midnight eyes. "How's the hotel going? Did you get the laborers started?"

Putting sloppy kisses on top of my squirming Josephy's head, Thomas took the two-year-old to the door. "Miss Kitty."

My sister came and poked her head in. "Yes, Thomas."

"This one's ready for you. I think you said oat porridge and a bath."

She winked at me. "Come, Josephy."

My son waved. "Bye, Mama."

Thomas leaned against the door. His white shirt beamed from beneath his slim emerald waistcoat. He came to me, scooping me into his arms. "You're beautiful. Maybe I can get you something."

His lips nibbled his way down my throat. Like a habit, my arms reached for his shoulders.

Then I pulled my hands away. "I asked about the workers."

"The government is getting stricter. They've asked me to hold off on construction for a while. Samuel Williams is acting governor again. I think it will be better when the permanent person is in place."

"Thomas, I own that land outright. How can they stop me from doing what I want?"

"Not many can, Doll. But the governing council can do pretty much what they want. They think you're building a brothel."

"No. It's a hotel, where important guests can stay."

Thomas's face blanked. He wiped his mouth, but I saw the change.

"What is it?"

"Nothing that matters. Doll, you're doing well. We're doing well. We don't need to cause problems."

I grabbed his arm. "Thomas, what is it?"

He looked down at his boots, those old dusty boots with the buckle he wouldn't toss away. "Doll, the council is in charge. We don't need to call attention to us."

His strong voice had a sound of something I'd never heard from him, fear.

"What happened?"

"They stopped Edward last week."

I felt my eyes widen. "My boy, is he well? Edward!"

"Yes." Thomas pulled me back against him. "They had him cowering, about to put him in jail until I came along. Pure intimidation."

"You should've told me. He's my son. I could've done something. Don't they know who he belongs to?"

His arms stiffened. "Edward is ours. I claim him now too. Doll, I don't need them targeting you or him or any of our family, especially not our sons."

"You think boys are more prone to harassment? They'll go after them all, boys and girls. I've been laid up too long."

"It's confinement. It's necessary for a woman to have a safe birth."

"Well, I don't need more births. Those men need to know who they're dealing with."

He put his hands to my face. "You're filling with fear, hysterical nervousness. I told you. I protected Edward. We just have to be more careful."

"No. I'm going to fix this."

Thomas released me and bounced up from the mattress. "It's hard to talk to you like this."

"Send Mamaí to me. Have her bring her tea. Tell her whatever she needs to strengthen me, put it in the pot. I'm not going to be confined again. I have to be strong to fix this. They came after Edward."

"You don't need tea or poison in your body to keep you from being pregnant again, Doll. There's better ways."

He stormed out of the room.

Thomas was angry, but I wouldn't soften. My children were under attack. That was more important than anything, even his anger.

The opening of the hotel was ablaze. The front parlors were packed. It seemed all of Grenada had come to celebrate. Even the new governor, Ninian Home, had said he'd stop by.

But I wasn't there.

In my town house on Blaize Street, I sat still with my insides cutting to pieces. I prayed for healing, waiting by Edward's bedside.

Dr. Hay put his fingers to the side of my son's throat. Then he put an ear to his floundering nightshirt. The man stood upright and shook his head. "Any moment. I'll send up Father Mardel."

Thomas clutched the doctor's hand. "Thank you for what you've done. Let Mardel wait. Tell the priest we're not ready."

Priest Mardel had been coming to the house, holding church in my parlor for our neighbors. We needed secret meetings since the government seized the church.

I hated Grenada for that. Now it was stealing my Edward.

The doctor nodded. "Sorry, Thomas, Mrs. Thomas."

He left and closed the door. It was a quiet final, world-shattering thud.

"Why did you thank him, Thomas? He didn't fix Edward."

"Doll." Thomas clasped my shoulders.

No man could make my boy breathe right when bulam fever fell upon him. But God. God on high should stretch his finger to my twelve-year-old son, touch his temple, and save his life.

"Everyone tried," Thomas said softly and knelt at my side. "Even Sally and your mother. Nothing. His body is weak. He's always been a little weak. That chest of his won't fight for air."

"You're giving up? You always give up too soon."

The tremor in his cheek made me see how pale Thomas was. Nothing to Edward's fine brown skin.

"You're in pain, Doll. I'm going to ignore that."

"Haven't you done enough of that?" Thomas stayed in a bedroom down the hall or on his boat most days. He was never gone long enough for the children to think anything was wrong or for me to think he'd deserted us.

But he was gone from me, from our bed.

I'd lost him somehow, even though he was close enough for me to reach.

Boots tapping, he stood. "I think you should walk around. Get blood flowing in your limbs."

His palm lighted again on my shoulder, then disappeared.

I swallowed hard. "Maybe he'll wake up. When he was small, Cells . . . his doctor was able to get him to breathe again."

Thomas's sigh was long. "You know I want him to get better."

"You do your ritual. Get your prayer books, and I'll do my sacraments. Somehow, God will hear, Thomas. He'll save Edward."

"Doll, you heard Dr. Hay. He's been treating him the past two years. He knows. Feel his wrist. There's barely a pulse."

"Hush. Edward can hear you. Edward, you have to get up. Mama's hotel, the one you helped me with, it opens today."

"Doll."

"Did Hay try everything, Thomas? Did he? Or did he see a brown face, a small brown face, and do just enough to collect a coin?"

"Don't think like that. Woman, you can't. You've never thought—"

"I just never said. There's a difference." I picked up Edward's wrist and blew on it. It wouldn't take my heat. "You told me not to keep pushing. I didn't listen, I built my hotel. Maybe the council members got to Hay."

"Hay's a good man. He truly wants to save lives. Charlotte's sister-in-law says he's good."

Rose Fédon? "Harry or Josephy, one of them needs to be a doctor. Maybe one of Lizzy's will know medicine. Then we'll know that coloreds will have the best care. I'll know someone cared."

"Don't do this, Doll. Don't let skin separate us now."

"It will just be one more thing, Thomas."

He took a handkerchief from his pocket, a big linen square and mopped his face. "My blood surely should be in Edward's veins. He's my boy."

Thomas leaned over the footboard of the bed then gripped the walnut posts. "Edward would want you to keep your strength. Maybe get up and check on baby Harry."

"The wet nurse and Kitty have him. Mamaí is taking care of Ann. Grama Sally has the rest of the babes. Frances and Eliza will take this hard. Charlotte, too."

"You're right. He's still fighting. He's strong and stubborn like you."

"It's my fault. I let him work too hard these last few months."

Thomas moved to the window and acted as if he didn't hear me. I guess I'd become too good at pushing him away.

He pulled back the curtain. "I can see the hotel from here. It's a sight, the lines to get in. You'll make a great deal of money tonight."

This time I said nothing.

If Thomas thought money would distract me, he was wrong. My boy had all of me. I'd watch his chest until it stopped moving.

Mopping my son's forehead, I saw Lizzy's pout in his drawn face, Charlotte's lashes.

"I count another ten boats coming up from the harbor. More guests. More money."

"Get away from the window. If you must busy yourself, go down and get another candle. Let's make this room bright. Edward hates the dark. I told him to be brave. I haven't been brave. I faltered so many times."

"Doll, you're tearing yourself up. Please."

I shot him a look that hit him like a wet rag.

Like soursop fruit picked too soon, I dripped in bitterness. "Is this the cost for me surviving my twelfth birthday, that he wouldn't celebrate his?"

"Quiet, woman. You're spewing pain."

"It's all I have."

"You have more than that." He wiped at his eyes. "Edward's drifting to peace. Let's be civil and send him off knowing his family is going to be well."

Edward coughed. His eyes didn't open. His wheezing shattered my chest.

"Our boy loved helping." Thomas's voice broke into bits. Then he pulled his hands together again. "Checklists. He loved those checklists. He loved making deliveries with me. I never left him alone to do them, not since that first bit of trouble."

I didn't know that. I thought Thomas sulked on his boat. Edward did those deliveries every day until he got sick.

"We used to stop and watch the construction, Doll. He loved the hotel, every beam, every wall."

"The dust from sanding and painting walls to make things perfect. It's what's done him in. My choice for this hotel made him ill. I'm guilty."

I pulled free of my shawl. It felt tight like a snake coiling about me. "Everything I've done was for my children to live better lives and to keep living better lives. Now this."

"Even London?"

"What?"

"You left your family to get over me. You left Edward, too."

"Jealousy now? Did you think I built the hotel for the prince to return? That was low for you."

"You're still keeping up with him. I saw the letter."

"I received a note from Mrs. Clarke, my friend. The wife of the former governor of Jamaica. She's moved back to London. She loves to send gossip. When I go to London again, I'm going to see her."

"Good, you two will chat of the prince."

"Mad now, Thomas? My boy is dying."

He gritted his teeth, his rare temper flaring. "Our boy. Ours. Someone whose loss we share. You won't be selfish in this. My love for Edward is true."

"I'm not selfish. If I were a man, I'd be admired."

"I am a man, and though you claim the hotel as yours, everyone helped. When you were laid up having our babies, I made sure your orders were carried out. I was here for you, not off dancing in London or on a frigate. And though my face isn't brown, I understand."

I couldn't believe him, spewing this nonsense. "I know you helped, but I can't be fair right now, not when Edward's tipping into the grave."

Tears blinded me. "Go sulk on your boat. Or let it take you away. I've been waiting for that."

He threw open the door like he'd pull it off the hinges, but he stopped and came back inside. "Push me away when the next crisis comes. I'm losing my son. I'm not going anywhere."

Thomas combed at his hair, thick and dark, beginning to show threads of silver. "I'll not be run off. I'll support you like I have. Maybe you'll see that one day."

He sat on the other side of the bed. "You told me to be good to your mama even when it was hard. I'll do that for you, my boy."

He kissed Edward's cheek.

We both held our son's hands, but I didn't know how to say sorry, not with all the tears lodging and sticking in my windpipe. What good was all my building if I outlived my children?

GRENADA 1795: THE WAR

I stared at Mamaí and Frances, the backs of their capes, red and brown, flapping as they headed out of my store. They were holding hands. Tall brave Frances. Stoic Mamaí. I wish my daughter had read us better news.

My London solicitor had gotten Mr. Webster to agree to terms, but all the paperwork wasn't done. It would be many more months before my mother's first daughter, Ella, would be freed.

Mamaí's stoic face looked broken, but only for a moment. She veiled her pain and went out into the street.

I hurt for Mamaí. Ella was my Catharina. One daughter sold off by my mother's pa, the other one given away by a weak mother.

Though I had Charlotte send Cells a message for Catharina on her birthday, that didn't make up for not knowing her. I only missed one note. The year Edward died.

Three years gone.

Catharina never knew him, her blood brother, never saw his smile or his love of checklists and making deliveries. I found every one of his lists in the desk in his room. His checkmarks were crisp.

I closed the shop door and rearranged a shelf of silverware.

Charlotte would come today. Hopefully, she'd read another tale about Catharina at a ball. I knew what a British one was like.

My daughter was safer in Cells's world. My colored one was under attack.

The council began stealing from the free coloreds with taxes and fines and license fees. I understood better why Cells was desperate to cling to his place in society.

My eyes drifted again to Blaize Street. By now, Mamaí and Frances should only be a few blocks from home.

I'd wait for Charlotte and balance my ledger, but the sense that something was going to happen, that a jumbie was around the bend, never left.

Checking the pocket watch Thomas gave me showed another hour had passed. His gift was a subtle hint for me to mind the time and come home.

My daughter and son-in-law should be here by now, and I could see her pregnant belly. Finally, my girl would have a baby.

Boom. Boom. Boom.

The beating on my door made my heart explode.

"Doll! Doll, let me in."

"Thomas?"

My throat closed up as I ran and let him in.

He swept me up into his arms. "It's bad, Doll."

I felt him shaking. I shook even more.

The scent of him—cigars in his coat, ale on his lips, filled me, soaked into my skin. Part of me did not want to move. I wanted his arms, all his power.

Hadn't been in them much. I wept at how much I'd missed him. We lived as strangers in our house.

He broke free and paced. "I'm sorry, Doll."

"Tell me what has happened."

Thomas took my wet leaking face into his hands. "Charlotte. Her husband and his brother have started a war."

"A war?"

"A full rebellion, fighting is everywhere. They coordinated attacks all over Grenada. All the colored planters, all the slaves, even some of the Catholics have come together. It's all-out war, Doll. One led by the Fédons."

"The governor and the governing council caused this, Thomas. They've been hurting the coloreds and the Catholics. You can't keep stepping on our necks. Something was bound to snap."

He towed me back into his arms. "We need to pray the Fédons are smart enough to win."

My Charlotte was in trouble.

Hot-blooded men had started a war that could get my daughter killed.

Fighting burned all Grenada. Gunfire raged. Even now cannons sounded close. I couldn't sleep and paced in Edward's room. How could I close my eyes with no word about Charlotte, her safety, and the baby?

Tarn Fédons. I hated the restrictions, the taxes, but a rebellion couldn't be the answer.

I didn't know what to say to the children this week. So I said nothing and loved on them more. On the sofa, with the older ones on the floor, the younger ones huddled around me and we listened to ten-year-old Frances and seven-year-old Eliza read. Five-year-old Josephy and Ann, and three-year-old Harry clapped with delight before I sent them to bed.

Mamaí and Grama Sally stayed downstairs working on a blanket together. The old woman was silent and giving me and Thomas the oddest looks, saying in Twi how did I find the one good blanca man.

He was good, but we weren't united.

The house was quiet now. Soon the sun would rise.

Thomas came into Edward's room holding a candle. "I heard noises."

"Couldn't sleep."

"I thought Harry was out of bed again. He's a roamer."

He turned to leave, but I didn't want to be alone. "Don't go."

Setting his candle on the desk, he fingered our son's papers. "His checklists. Goodness, I miss him. He was an excellent sailor."

Thomas's sigh sounded tired. He folded his arms across his nightshirt, a long flowing cotton thing that went past his ankles. He could be a priest wearing a white alb, just needing the rope cincture about his waist. "If you're not well, Doll, I could send word to Hay to come visit."

Didn't want no doctor. Just Thomas, for things to be right for us again.

"You're a good man, the best pa. Frances's voice sounds strong making out words. Thank you, Thomas, for getting her books."

"She's my family."

"Frances claimed you as her pa. Almost from the beginning."

His gaze burned with truth, his endless love. "I never cared who their fathers are. I just loved them."

My throat thickened, and I needed to confess. "I never told you that Edward had a sister."

"You don't talk about a great many things unless it's eating you alive."

"This is. Catharina's her name. When I was low after birthing her, her pa convinced me he'd do a better job of raising her. He took her away to London and I haven't seen her since."

He crossed to me but kept his hands to his side. "Keep speaking. I'm listening."

"I was afraid you'd do the same with Eliza or any of our children. I can't think right, not when I'm low." I sniffed and pushed back tears. "I never meant to say hateful things to you. It's just . . . I'm terrified of my weaknesses being used against me."

"Well, it doesn't help that you're married to a fool."

"No, that doesn't help. But it's the best thing for me."

He came the final two feet and rubbed my tired shoulder. His love came through that soft touch. It wrapped me up and added steel to my spine.

"How could the Fédons do this, Thomas? The British will kill them. Give a planter a reason to kill a colored, and they will."

"Rumor has it the Fédons have been plotting this for years, since Rose was jailed. Dr. Hay signed her Certificate of Freedom that kept her from being sold."

"I guess Hay is not bad."

Thomas tugged me by the sash of my pink robe. "You should go to sleep."

The look in his gaze didn't say sleep. It said restless, and rabbits, and another baby by dawn. His love for me was coming back. He wasn't guarding it. He trusted me not to be careless with it.

I wouldn't. Not again. "We missed you for story time. It took you a long time to come home."

"Testing routes to leave," he said, his voice low and solid. "We need to be prepared."

"Leave?"

He sat on the desktop. "Doll, you've been lucky and have made many friends in Grenada, but the government likes to target free colored women. They want to humiliate them for the wealth women like you've earned. They're sending messages to men like me, too, the ones who don't care a whit about race. They want us to know we've no power, either. If the Fédons don't win, Charlotte will be killed. All our children are targets because of our connections to the leaders of the rebellion."

There was no way to breathe after harsh words like that, but I made myself suck in air.

"They'll kill Charlotte? She's to have a baby. No, Thomas."

"We need to be prepared to leave it all behind and go."

I tugged on my lacy sleeves. They needed to be fairy wings to fly me above Mount Qua Qua and swing low to Belvedere Estates to scoop up my girl.

"Doll, our family's not safe. And we're not, not with Charlotte with the rebels."

"I hate what has happened to us here. But starting over, Thomas, is frightening."

He reached for me and pulled me near. "We can start over. You can conquer anything, Doll. Anywhere we go, you will be blessed."

"Maybe you are a priest. My hymns are rubbing off on you."

"Think on it. Pack something for the children if we have to escape on the *Mary*."

I didn't want to start over. I needed to wring those fool Fédons' necks. "Rebellions come and go. I've lived through two or three

already. Maybe the governor will wise up and pull back these restrictions for peace."

"There's no going back, not when both sides have guns."

My mother talked to me about guns and numbers long ago in our
hut in Montserrat. Never thought I'd fear the consequences of those
with my skin having more weapons.

"Doll, the Fédons and all the freed slaves make a sizable force.
They're winning right now, but more British forces will come. You
remember your friend's ship, the *Pegasus*? It might return to establish
order."

It was the *Andromeda*, none of what the news clipping said. But
that was an old fight, not what I wanted tonight. I took his hand and
held it close to my chest. "I miss us."

Thomas offered me a small smile, one that made his cheeks seem
fuller, not lean from lack of sleep.

The pounding of hooves sounded below.

He moved to the window. In a blink, I was at his side hoping that
soldiers weren't at our door.

Two men on horseback, both in deep blue frock coats trimmed
in white ribbon traveled up Blaize Street. The rising sun struck the
gold braiding shining from their shoulders. They sped past.

"That's Nogues and Philip," Thomas said. "They must be coming with a message. They're heading toward the government buildings on Simmons."

Charles Nogues and Joachim Philip were bold men of color,
known to be hotheads and combative like Julien Fédon.

"They must have a message from the rebels. I know it's not surrender. Lord help us, Doll."

I held on to Thomas, old soul Thomas, rock-solid Thomas.

He returned my embrace with one of his own, strong and tight. I
needed him. "Family is the most important thing."

Good. He'd understand if I had to leave *us* to save Charlotte.

GRENADA 1795: THE WINDOW

My gray skirts flounced at my heels as I went upstairs to Edward's room.

It remained empty, though someday Josephy or Harry might want it as theirs.

Sally had cleaned. The linens and bedframe smelled of soap and orange oil polish.

His window, a fine glass window of nine panes, called to me. The smoke in the sky was almost the color of my gown. Everything was on fire.

Several times a day and even at night, I searched the sky from here. A month of heavy fighting had scorched the earth. The stranglehold the rebels had on Grenada kept growing. Reports said they held over forty important men hostage, including Governor Home.

Why should my hotel be spared? It lay in ashes by the shore.

"Dolly?" Mamaí came into the room, her arms loaded with linens. "Come away from the window."

There was no turning away from the ashes. It burned bright and hot and white against the blond beach sand.

"It's a funny thing, how fast it all comes down, Mamaí."

She came to my side. "Don't torture yourself."

"Torture? It took months to build with bricks and oak and stone. Many hours and meetings, time I could have spent with Edward. Now they are both gone."

I leaned forward and put my forehead on the whitewashed wall. It felt cool, but I was hot, my insides sick.

"The rebels have control except for St. George's. Not sure, Mamaí. Not sure which side burned my hotel."

She rubbed my arm as if to bolster me, adding crinkles to my straight cotton sleeves. "No need to choose a side, Dolly." She touched my cheek. "Charlotte's fine. We'd have heard something if she weren't."

"You think so?"

My mother nodded and closed up the curtains. "She's safe where she is. Jean-Joseph will let nothing happen to her."

She planted herself in front of the window, blocking me from viewing the ashes of my dream.

"Charlotte's going to be fine, Dolly. And you will lead us to the next building or whatever it is you think up. My faithful girl, my brave one, you will."

Linens flying, I pulled my mother close, holding her to memorize the softness of her bosom, the sound of her strong heart. "I love you."

"Love you." Mamaí smiled, and we folded the sheets. She thought she brought me comfort over my hotel, but she stoked the flame in me. My decision was firm.

Rushing into the hall, I almost stumbled in my satin slippers. "Thomas?" I was lost. He wasn't in our bedroom or the parlor. I crossed into the room we used for the children's schooling. Tutors I'd found through the priest would come in secret to make my beautiful brown children readers.

My husband's voice settled upon me before I saw him. He sat on the floor with Eliza and Frances at his feet, him reading that naughty Tom Thumb.

The boys, Josephy and Harry, and my baby girl, no longer a baby, Ann, were hugging on their pa, gathered around him.

My husband was the best of men. Why was it hard for me to see that he was happiest with family? Of course he craved more children. Yet he had become content with what we had.

I'd never been content with what was before me, always pushed for more.

"Ah, Mama's here," he said.

I settled down beside him and scooped up Ann. "Eliza, your pa has read enough. He'll be hoarse. You read, then Frances, you next. You did well last time."

Thomas smiled wide, probably noting, like me, every small thing about the children—how they were growing, the things that made them unique—Frances loved numbers and ledgers, Ann sewed only bright-colored fabrics, Josephy took over Mamaí's garden, Eliza studied spices, and Harry tried hard to read legal papers.

The pit of my stomach knotted then unraveled into a thousand threads. In that moment, I knew if I were gone, Thomas would make sure they each kept on pursuing the things they loved.

The girls were bubbly. "Another story. Another," they said in unison. Eliza's voice was light like Kitty's, another swallow in flight. Frances interrupted. Her tone was lower, and she mimicked Thomas's dramatic pauses, his silly expressions. "Something with pirates, perhaps."

Kitty and Mamaí came inside. My mother clanged her stew spoon. "Supper. Grama Sally has made coconut stew. It has cod, salt pork, and breadfruit."

They gathered our brood and herded them down the hall. Thomas helped me up. "You must join us for story time more often. Perhaps tomorrow. I'm very good with pirate stories."

He waggled his brows and turned to the door.

But I clutched his jacket, hard with a jerk.

This man of mine pivoted. I held tight to his silver buttons and towed him toward me. He willingly came.

The knock of his boots on the floor lulled my heart to a faster beat.

His kiss pressed me against the wall. He tasted good. Coffee? Hints of caramelized plantains.

"I love you, Doll, even when you make me spitting mad."

"I'm beginning to notice." I slipped beneath his jacket. He found the boning under my shift.

He snuck me to our chambers, like it was a secret to love.

The door barely closed, and we kissed like fools, like rabbits.

Hungry, we loved like nothing had happened, like time and fear hadn't poisoned the air.

We danced. It wasn't quite the minuet, but the rhythm was easy, slow.

My body arched to his and his hands were willing to hold me, to caress me until I shivered.

'Cause I did shake as I feasted on his love.

I knew what I must do.

This dance must be the best, possibly our last. I had to go save my Charlotte or die trying.

The house was quiet. Thomas had left for his boat. This was the perfect time to act. I pulled my dark claret-colored cape over my head and snuck down the rear stairs. I waited in the moonlight for the soldiers to pass. Curfew had been imposed in St. George's.

Peering up at the stars, I wished it had a map to beam down and point to where my Charlotte was.

"Don't go, Dolly."

The voice was pitchy. "My true swallow."

My sister stood in the doorway. "No, Dolly, don't go to the store."

My breathing returned to normal. Kitty thought I was heading to work. That was an easier lie than the truth. "Go back inside. Protect the children for me. You can do that."

"I always will, but who's going to protect you? You've been so sad. I've heard you crying about Charlotte."

Maybe she did know I was heading through the rebel lines and government strongholds to get to Belvedere Estates. "Kitty—"

"I remember how you wept at the Hermitage and every night after Charlotte was born. Worse than how you cried after you bore Lizzy and all those people died. Don't leave sad."

Her whimpers cut through me; I was surprised she hadn't blocked those memories. "Kitty, I'll be all right. Mamaí's here for you. Thomas too."

She hugged me, tight, like how she held me when Cells put her in my arms in the carriage after he redeemed her from Montserrat's Marketplace.

"Swallow, my pretty swallow, I have to do what's right. That means I can't be safe. I have to take risks. Understand?"

It felt like forever, a good forever, in her embrace. "Dolly, don't be long. Come home as quick as you can. Then we can play . . . like all was well."

"Yes." I kissed her brow. "Go on now. Go help Mamaí."

When she turned and closed the door, I went down the street. Staying in the shadows, I approached the mews. My horse and dray were ready.

I was ready, confident I could get to my little hummingbird.

Taking out a coin, I put it in the stableboy's hand.

The fellow nodded.

He might suspect I was about to do something crazy, but my money made him look the other way.

Hopping into place, I picked up the reins.

Then I put them onto my lap.

Thomas, angry-lipped Thomas, stood at the entry between me and Blaize Street.

Thomas didn't say anything as he stepped aboard the dray. I scooted over and gave him the reins. If he was going to fuss, I'd just drop him back at the house.

My heart drummed. The horse's hooves pounded.

The dray didn't stop at our home.

The stars hanging above the harbor came closer.

The smell of salt and sea washed over my nose, but my gaze counted the soldiers in the streets. Some waved. They knew my deliveries.

Thomas pushed his hat back, exposing more of his worried brow. "Did you know all the routes to Mount Qua Qua or anything near the Belvedere Estates are blocked? The council's militia and a few British soldiers are manning them."

"I could've gotten through."

"They've lost colleagues to the carnage. Fédon, free slaves, Maroons from the hills, even the old French have killed and rampaged the plantations. They aren't letting you through."

"I'm Doll Thomas. I sell goods to most of them."

"Some know you. Some respect you. But on these trails, you look like a wealthy colored target. If one side doesn't kill you, the other will."

"I could do it."

"Woman, you are capable of anything but good sense."

I grabbed his arm. "My child's out there. I have to try. If I fail, I know you'll take care of our children, our family."

"Is that why you ruthlessly seduced me? Two nights straight."

"Yes, all part of my master plan to have another of your babes while I fight the British and the Fédons."

He chuckled as he stopped the dray by the dock and handed off my horse to his friend Garraway.

"You're going to do this, Thomas?" his friend asked as he unhooked the horse from the reins.

"Yes," Thomas said. "We have to go get our eldest, Charlotte."

We? No. My plan was for him to be with the children.

"Be careful," Garraway said. "The fighting's been heavy tonight. The rebels killed their hostages, including the governor."

"Governor Home?" My voice was a squeak. Cudjoe and his jumbies must be swinging in the trees, triumphant. There was no going backward when the coloreds killed whites, especially white men in power.

Thomas cursed under his breath. "That's forty men; Dr. Hay was a prisoner. You sure?"

"Yeah." Garraway gave Thomas a lantern. "Everything you wanted is ready by the *Mary.*"

What was ready? What were these men planning?

Thomas started down the beach and I charged after him. "Wait."

He didn't. I had to catch him. "You've been planning to do this for a while?"

"Yes, Doll."

With a sigh, he parked in front of me. "If I told you to stay and let me do this, you wouldn't."

"No." I grabbed his arm and forced him to stop. He spun, kicking up grains of white sand. They caught hints of moonlight and shimmered like fireflies about our boots.

"Thomas, unless you can pretend to be French, you'll be killed at Belvedere Estates. We have to do this together."

"It's not like I could stop you." He waved me toward a small sailboat. The *Mary*, his sloop, was anchored next to it. Carved and hewn from a gommier tree trunk, the thing looked majestic on the water, bobbing in the waves. It was sleek and small. This thing would be hard to detect.

"More soldiers have arrived. More vessels are patrolling to form a blockade of Grenada. Our son-in-law and his kin have most of the island, but it's an island. They'll soon get cut off. Now is the time to try to get Charlotte."

"If we get her, Thomas, gather up our family and let's get out of Grenada."

He put me in the boat then pushed it from the dock and started paddling. Thomas dimmed the lantern, but not before I saw guns in the bottom of the boat, the long ones called flintlocks. He was ready for war.

I prayed that God hid the stars until we struck land. I didn't want Thomas to use those weapons. One of us had to make it back to our family.

The current felt choppy, shifting the boat like a leaf on a rushing stream.

Thomas stretched and adjusted his paddling. "Tracking the smuggling routes has come in handy. We'll land north of Grenada. Our way will be straight to Mount Qua Qua. Belvedere is over the hills."

I put my palm to his jacket. "You know when we land you won't be able to go with me."

He kept moving the paddles, up and down, pushing.

"I said you know you won't be able to go with me, Thomas."

The groan leaving him, the rush ushering from his nostrils, made me release his coat.

"I've been doing reconnaissance. The rebels are five miles from the beach. Then over the mountain. I think that's where the Fédons have set up their headquarters."

"I can do it alone. And if I fail, I'll know the children will have you."

He clasped my arm. "I knew you were going to do this without me. I've accepted that with you and me. I'm your *helpin han*, here to help you get where you need to go, to lift you, so you can grab all your dreams. When will you know this?"

I put my lips to his knuckles. "If I never said I love you, Joseph Thomas, don't think I don't. Just too stupid to mention it."

"I know. I'm stupid, too, very stupid. Always when it comes to you."

He picked up his rowing. If we both lived through this night, I'd have to remember to tell my husband how my world wouldn't be the same without him.

Thomas lit the lantern and gave it to me. "Go up the beach. Head straight up."

One touch of his fingers curving on my wrist—almost not wanting to let go but mostly supporting me, steadying me on the shore—told me everything there was between us—the love, the fear, the pride. "Hurry back, Doll."

Turning away took everything in me, but I had to get my child.

With the lantern held high, I followed the trail. It was me and the darkness, walking together stumbling, trudging over pebbles and branches.

Funny.

I'd spent what felt like a lifetime not seeing, not looking at things that hurt me or left me without hope. Now I struggled to keep my vision.

If I hummed, would Charlotte hear?

Hiding in my cloak, my hand slipping in and out of the slits formed of the napped broadcloth, I edged up Mount Qua Qua.

Then I heard singing.

Pushing through the ferns, I saw men crowding around a fire. Father Mardel stood, leading them in a prayer. He wasn't in priestly robes, but a black tunic with braiding, black breeches, and boots. The man was well connected in St. George's and other parishes throughout Grenada.

Now I understood how the Fédons had recruited and organized the rebellion.

Sitting around the flames were free colored people like the Nogues, but also men who looked as if they'd come straight from the fields. That said a great deal about the relationship of my son-in-law's kinship with the enslaved, for massa and his chattel to join forces.

But I hadn't come to evaluate their plans. I came for Charlotte. Hoping no fool would shoot, I stepped out of the clearing, waving my lantern. "I come for Charlotte Fédon."

Men ran toward me, bringing with them the smells of gunpowder and shed blood.

"Charlotte Fédon. She's my daughter. Charlotte Fédon."

I said her name over and over.

A woman came from a tent. "That's my sister's mother," she said. "Let her alone."

The men did, but this lone woman marched toward. Wonderful, braids shining in the moonlight, Rose Fédon strode to me like a general.

But her skirts bore dark stains, stains that weren't mud.

My heart clenched.

Selfishly, I held my breath, held the hope in my chest that blood was from the battle.

She clasped my lantern and lowered it. I wanted to resist. I wanted to be blind to the truth—that I'd come too late, that I'd wavered too long to be of help to my girl.

"Come this way, Miss Dolly."

Heart in my mouth, I followed. At the entrance to a cave, she stopped. "The priest, Mardel, calls this a sepulcher. It's the resting place of a hero."

I couldn't breathe. My eyes glazed over.

Rose held me up. "Go in, Miss Dolly. She needs you."

Her face was blank, but in her eyes, I saw peace. How did she have that with death so near?

My footfalls echoed, drumming as I moved into the cave. The place smelled of dampness. The shroud of misty fog that surrounded Mount Qua Qua drove into my throat. I couldn't let it flood my lungs, drown me like a rushing ghaut.

Then I saw Charlotte. She was prostrate over a pair of feet.

Jean-Joseph's.

He lay still. His chest was covered in white cloth that had soaked through. Dark red. His gentle face, brown turning gray, mouth open, eyes turned back—I added this mask to the collection in my head.

"Charlotte."

She didn't look my way. My girl had his cross in her palm along with my mother's rosary, the ones Mamaí had given me when I left Montserrat, the ones I'd given Charlotte when she married.

"Stay back."

"It's Mama, Charlotte." The closer I came, the more her weeping gnawed into my gut. My hand slipped to her shoulder. I wanted to draw her up in my arms like she were a babe. "Charlotte, I've come for you."

She didn't move. She mumbled to the Holy Father to save Jean-Joseph . . . and her babe.

The baby? No! Charlotte's baby. No.

Blinded in my tears, I crouched beside her. We prayed, prayed like it would change the stains on her skirt, prayed like time would turn back, prayed that she and Jean-Joseph had no cares.

Prayed like God would hear the tears of a Black mama and care.

The Holy Father hadn't quite looked away. My girl still lived.

"Home, Charlotte. Let's get you home."

"Home is here, with my husband."

"No, with me, your brothers and sisters, Thomas."

"How can I honor Jean-Joseph, Mama? I lost our baby. Nothing of him will survive this day. He's gone, and the one thing that I could've had to keep him alive, I let go."

Nine children had filled my womb, had breathed air, had sent me crashing into despair, but nothing, nothing, nothing cut this deep.

I pulled my girl into my arms. "You're his legacy, Charlotte. He wanted women respected, free from harassment. He's a patriot. He died for true freedom."

She leaned on me. "Don't know what to do, Mama."

"Come with me now. We'll make our way together."

She pulled at her tunic like her skin itched. "You think Jean-Joseph wouldn't mind, if I go rest?"

"He'd want you to, Charlotte."

Rising together, I offered my strength and wrapped my cloak about her. We headed out of the cave.

Rose lifted Charlotte's chin. "Julien understands. Go with God."

Like a priest, she smeared ash in the shape of a cross on my daughter's brow. Part of me wanted a blessing too. We still had to make it back to Thomas and sneak into St. George's.

The price on Charlotte's head had to be great. She was a Fédon woman, the wife of a revolutionary.

Dr. Hay was sitting on a log by the fire. He nibbled off a plate of salt pork and plantains. Our eyes locked.

The last time I saw him, I was filled with hate. I needed someone to blame for Edward's death, but he was innocent. "Rose, can Dr. Hay go with us, too? I'll make sure he's no trouble."

"He'll be freed soon. I give you my word. Now go. Dawn brings new fighting."

"Thank you, Mrs. Thomas." Dr. Hay started forking plantains

into his mouth. "Your mother has a cure-all for shock. Ask her to give it to your daughter."

Mamaí probably did. Sally too.

Keeping Charlotte close to my side, we headed down Mount Qua Qua. We needed to leave Grenada. This place meant death, and I was done losing.

Mamaí walked me to the docks. The sun was high, the waves calm on the deep blue water. The breeze couldn't separate us. My fingers were locked with hers.

My heart wasn't right. "I don't want us to split up. I promised—"

"It has to be done, Dolly. You're only going for a month or two this time."

Holding her a little longer, I looked over her shoulder at my poor Charlotte sitting alone in the *Mary*. Running away was hard.

"Kitty's mad at me. She doesn't want me to leave. She's fearful."

"I'll be with her. She's my daughter. You take care of yours."

Mamaí's voice wasn't harsh. The hummingbird was sweet in her rebuke, but I'd never be comfortable with my swallow being sad or hurting. The safe world Kitty built couldn't be unraveled because of Grenada. It couldn't.

"Thomas is coming. He must have the paperwork."

My husband couldn't get the approvals for all of us to quit the colony, only a few. The excuse of a quick trip for business would have to be our lie.

My mother's face had her treasured smile, small and perfect. "Dolly, it's for the best. Kitty and I will keep the girls safe."

"Polk says that Captain Owen lives in Bridgetown, Barbados. He was a good friend once. He could vouch for our story and make Charlotte a Foden, not a Fédon."

Her smile dropped away. If it fell to the ground, someone would step on it as if it were a millipede, the two-leggers in her garden. "You're going to trust the man who never checked on his child?"

Owen knew the truth. Frances was not his. It might be folly, but I was desperate. Hiding Charlotte in a world needing paperwork for coloreds . . . to quit a colony, to walk, to breathe. Making Charlotte a Foden was our only hope.

"Frances will keep the accounts with the housekeeping. There's more invoices to come."

Thomas pulled the dray near, the horse trotting across the shore, flinging sand against the high-walled wagon.

My numbers girl, Frances, sat alongside him, with the boys, Josephy and Harry, fidgeting and bouncing about the dray's flat back. The closer they came, the more her guilty smile grew. That meant Thomas had let her hold the reins again. Beautiful girl. Olive brown, nose beginning to sharpen, shadowing a perfect oval face with a tiny cleft in her chin that a quill tickled when she counted and adjusted ledger entries.

Mamaí released my arm. "Go on now. We'll be fine."

Thomas gave Frances a kiss and defiantly gave her the reins as he tipped his hat to me. Then he went to the rear and collected Josephy and Harry. They swung from his arms like climbing iguanas.

"Doll, I have the paperwork. We can leave for Barbados. Charlotte Foden is ready to travel."

He eased the boys to the ground. "Get in the *Mary*, fellows."

They scrambled into the sloop, sitting next to Charlotte. My husband turned and helped Mamaí up into the dray.

I went to Frances's side. "I trust you to manage things and be a help to my mother, especially with Ann and Eliza."

She saluted me. "Of course, Mama. Ann already follows me around, mimicking my ways."

"Girl, give your proud ma a kiss."

She offered a toothy smile, then bent and put her lips to my cheek. "Proud of you. Take care of dear Charlotte."

Her eyes locked with mine. Not sure if she understood all that was at stake, but this old soul would manage well in my absence. Without even pretending to let Mamaí drive, she started the dray back into St. George's.

"Garraway will watch out for them until we return." Thomas's voice sounded confident. Wished I was as certain.

With a sigh, I let him help me into the *Mary*. I sank next to Charlotte. Her widow's weave of indigo and black was the only thing I could get her to wear, once I coaxed her from the bloodied clothes.

My grieving child wanted everyone to know the truth, that her warrior and baby had died.

"Sit down, boys. We are about to cast off." Thomas's command made them freeze in midair. Harry and Josephy settled close to the tiller.

I'd never seen the boys grin more.

Yet between them I saw a death mask, a shadow of Edward. Goodness, how he loved sailing with Thomas.

Charlotte probably saw one too. Her gaze stayed pinned on Mount Qua Qua.

Thomas untied the thick jute holding the *Mary*. He stopped before undoing the knot and stood up straight. Like he'd become a shield, he stepped in front of the soldiers rushing toward us. Scarlet uniforms filled the deck. These men had their long guns drawn. We were at the mercy of the colonial government.

One soldier slogged into the *Mary*'s hatch. Others searched the deck, hitting along the hull as if looking for a secret passage.

Heart pounding, I stood in the breeze. It swirled my knotted scarf as I looked at the waters. Though I could swim and draw the British soldier's fire, I couldn't save my children from bullets.

"Stay put, Doll. No one move another inch." Thomas marched to the soldier with the most medals pinned to his jacket. "What's the meaning of this?"

His voice sounded calm but indignant—a trait men in silver buttons, important men, excelled in.

"Sir, we need to make sure you're not transporting contraband." The fellow barked more orders and gave his men permission to rip open our portmanteaus. I feared they'd take my manumission papers and burn them.

One fellow looked long at my daughter, then at me.

Thomas hopped into the boat and caught my arm. This possessive move told them we were his, his family.

He stepped again to the man examining papers. "Must we be delayed further?" His tone sounded affronted, not like he'd offered them documents sporting lies. "Your men have searched every inch of my ship. Let us be on our way."

This man, an officer by the braiding on his jacket, slipped his finger over the pages, creasing and flipping Thomas's handiwork. "Some rebels have escaped to Trinidad."

"None here. We're on our way to Barbados."

A soldier came from below. "No stowaways or guns, sir."

The look on Thomas's face, his cheeky smile—the man was too smart. He'd prepared for the worst.

One soldier peered at Charlotte, making flirty eyes at her, but she offered him nothing. My daughter was a stone, quiet and still.

It was good to be rigid like a rock. If she could feel the hate they had for the rebels, for the Fédons, she might do something rash.

"Your papers are in order." The officer pushed the documents to Thomas, and all the soldiers trudged off the boat. "Have a pleasant trip."

They moved away and boarded another boat.

"You're leaving here without weapons, Thomas?"

His smile was broad. "I have secrets, too, you know."

He untied the *Mary*, angled the sail, and started us moving. "Josephy, secure the boom. Grab the line. Ed . . . Harry, help me tie off the sail."

Thomas looked at me and I put his gaze into my heart.

The wind pushed us into the open sea. Big ships like William's *Andromeda* were at a distance but they could easily overtake us.

"Josephy? You ready for adventure, son?" Thomas put the boy's palm to the tiller.

"Yes, Papa." He was a proper little reefer.

Young Harry plopped at my feet. His little body had shivers, but he was trying to be brave.

Charlotte's gaze remained on Grenada. The view was better now. The steam of crater lake could be seen, swirling the rebel stronghold.

"You think the Fédons will win, Mama? You think Julien and Rose will lead our people to victory?"

"Maybe."

Couldn't tell her the truth. Once the British frigates brought more troops and hit the ground with all their numbers and guns, the rebel coloreds and Catholics would be slaughtered.

BARBADOS 1795: THE WINE

Bridgetown. I wanted to like it. This could've been a place to escape to and rebuild when we could retrieve our family from Grenada.

Barbados itself was beautiful, a jewel of an island with the whitest sand beaches I'd ever seen. The emerald hills were sculpted with houses that seemed settled and calm.

That was at a distance.

Up close, we slept under thin netting to keep the mossies, the blood-biting bugs, from giving us dinga fever. Dinga made the bones and joints ache. Folding up my net reminded me of Charlotte's wedding veil.

My poor daughter.

She didn't rise from her pillows. Sobbing in her sleep had robbed her of energy.

Pushing off her netting, I stroked her hair and plaited a fresh braid. It shifted to the side, but her thick curls were soft. The humidity in the air had her tresses and mine feathering. This moist heat, how it made everything sticky, was something to get used to. "I'm going out for a little."

"That . . . that's good." Her voice was so wet, so sorrowful.

"Charlotte, why don't you eat? Let me get you something."

With the handed-down rosary and Jean-Joseph's cross tight in her fist, she shook her head. "Later."

"I'm leaving now."

She didn't respond.

I offered a kiss and covered her. I didn't know if getting her back to Grenada with a new name would help. Leaving Charlotte gave me little comfort, even if the cook I'd hired would stay and watch her. I pushed out the door onto James Street and headed to the docks.

Going this way, then that, I lost my bearings and stumbled upon a pink stone building with round corners. The shape I hadn't noticed as we'd passed it last night, but the singing coming from inside caught my ear.

The tongue was foreign, but it sounded like a hymn. Was nice to hear a public crying out to God. And in such a building—shuttered windows basking in the light, arched frames pointing up, all housed in coral limestone—it looked hopeful on this bright Saturday morn.

The rebellion had stopped Priest Mardel's house meetings. The priest began those when the Grenada council seized the Catholic churches. That had to be the sign to leave a place, when men made laws to take from those who were different.

The hot sweaty air reminded me I couldn't stand around. I had to keep working my plan and find Owen. Someone at the harbor should know the boisterous fellow.

I turned down Swan Street and passed vendors and hucksters. Plantations and cane fields stood on both sides of my path. The enslaved here were barely clothed. Many were barefoot.

My heart broke for them. The memories, the regrets, the death masks, all the things I couldn't change often came to my eyes. How do I stop thinking about these things?

Swiping damp locks from my face, I stepped onto the harbor. The heat made my arms sticky, even with sheer sleeves. The bay churned with sloops and smaller sailboats, but I couldn't find Thomas's *Mary*. That blue pole holding its main sail had disappeared, but he'd probably taken the boys to deeper water to catch bright green dolphinfish.

"Miss Dolly!"

That shout? Polk?

Cupping my eyes, I looked out and saw my friend. My heart leapt. I hadn't seen that bald head since the rebellion started. Kitty missed her *damfo*.

Polk was in Barbados. He'd know how to find Owen.

His craft, the *Dolus*, came closer, the water parting at the sloop's bow. But he wasn't alone.

A man with a black hat and white jacket and a smile for days came up on the deck and waved.

I sat on the patio of a modest house, the ancestral home of John Coseveldt Cells. Just off Tudor Street, he had a view of the sea, no plantations.

"Dolly, admiring my garden?"

Of course I was. I needed something to distract myself from the unwelcome news that Owen was rotting in an English prison for smuggling. "It's lovely."

Ginger shoots fanned jade leaves as it coiled itself into long spirals. Palm fronds and tall grasses lined walkways that traversed the garden. In the corners were the yellow and red plants that framed my womanhood, the peacock flower.

I pointed to it, the harbinger of choice and hate. "Why do you grow those?"

"That, the plant with the red petals?" He picked up his cup of tea. "It's called the Pride of Barbados."

"Pride?" I thought of it as a remedy or preventative for shame. Maybe that was pride, to think one might be able to control consequences.

"You're not eating, Dolly?"

"I'm not here for a meal. When will the British release Captain Owen?"

He picked at the cheese that was on the table before us. "You want him again? Thought your ambitions were higher." Cells wiped his hands on a napkin. "How many children did he leave you with?"

"No more than you wanted."

His frown deepened. That tarn cleft taunted me, made me think of my Edward.

"Our son forgave me. We'd gotten to better terms, better for a long time."

"My boy's heart was so big."

He offered me his handkerchief, a smooth white linen. That soft scent of sweet rum brought it all back and I wept.

"I'm sorry, Dolly. I'll always be sorry."

Cells reached for me, but I jerked away. "Tell me," he said, "what you'll do now, being in Barbados hunting for Frances's father. Perhaps I can help. A substitute father?"

His hazel eyes burned. He wanted me to confess that Frances was his, but some secrets were grave bound. I folded his linen cloth. "I need Owen for Charlotte. He needs to vouch for her and claim she's Mr. Foden's daughter. If the British authorities suspect she was the wife of one of the Fédon leaders, she'll be taken into custody and hanged. Jean-Joseph was lesser known, less showy than his brother. My Thomas was able to get her paperwork to quit the colony for a few weeks. I'm not sure how long the ruse will last."

"You're reaching for all your old lovers? Still, a solicitor is a low bar. What of that prince of England?"

I'd never seen Cells this jealous. Very dangerous state for a man given to reason and plotting. "Thomas is my husband."

My voice held even, not a bit of celebration, but my wide smile danced.

His smirk disappeared. He slunk back inside.

It was irresistible to see him bothered by my marriage. My unease lowered, and I followed him into the drawing room. It was grand, with empty bookcases on each side of a large mahogany table. None of the books I'd seen in Montserrat or the Hermitage.

My brooding Cells swiped his finger along a shelf. "The housekeeper needs to dust and keep this place free of moisture. That stops the green dust."

"Mildew. I was such an ignorant girl when we met."

"You had a lot of living to do, but no one kept dust or green dust away better. You've learned a lot and changed."

Compliments from him were dangerous. That was how his campaigning started. I went to the garden door and thought of fleeing. The lush fernlike leaves of the Pride of Barbados weren't enough to hide me.

"It's a shame I'm free and you aren't. Are you, Dolly?"

"Does Fanny know this?"

Cells was behind me, hovering. "Probably. God rest my late wife's soul."

I swallowed. My jest must sound callous. "Sorry."

His sigh burned my neck. "She went in peace. Catharina and her sister and I were with her."

Sister? Coseveldt had another child?

"Let me answer the questions you won't ask. Louisa is three. My wife and I, after all these years, had a daughter."

I closed my eyes. "Do you care for Catharina as much as you did before you had a legitimate daughter?"

"You know I do. Catharina and Louisa were well loved by their mother. They are both at the Hermitage in Mrs. Randolph's charge."

My heart went wobbly thinking of her being back in that house. "Is Catharina happy in Demerara?"

He clutched my arm. "Our daughter is mourning. The loss of her mother has made her unhappy, even rebellious, but she'll settle down."

"She's lost the woman she's called mother and you've taken her away from everything she knew. I can understand why she'd be miserable."

"You could know her. She would've called you Mother by now if you'd returned with me after Charlotte's wedding. But you had a prince to keep company."

It would be like Cells to make Catharina's sadness my fault. I pushed him away. "Don't make your failings with her my doing."

He moved and dropped into a dining table chair. "Forgive me, Dolly. That's not what I meant. I failed you. I've done so many things wrong. I want us to be friends. For Catharina's sake, we need to be."

Was I capable of forgiving this man who made me question my worth? Staring into his eyes, the face it took forever not to hope for, I didn't think it possible.

"You came for Owen, thinking he could vouch for Charlotte. Dolly, the minute things get difficult, he won't be around. Questioning from officials would be too much. That's why he's jailed. We can't risk Charlotte's safety."

He was trying too hard with all this reasoning, but his voice was soft, drawing me to him. I went the opposite direction.

"Dolly, I have an idea to save our Charlotte."

At the door, I stopped short of seizing the door latch. "Cells, tell me what you're plotting."

"I'll take Charlotte with me to Demerara. I'll get her established in the colony as Charlotte Foden. You know I can look authorities in the eye and not reveal a thing."

Trusting Cells to do something that had no benefit to himself? I shook my head. "I know you can lie and not blink, but this is my daughter."

"The child I helped bring into this world. Who danced in the halls of my Hermitage like she was my daughter. The child who never wanted for anything until we parted. Can you doubt I'd do this for her?"

In that moment, I couldn't. Nothing he said was untrue. Hadn't I always felt he loved her like she loved her *Papa Cells*?

"What's in this for you, Coseveldt? What's the benefit to you?"

"Nothing. It's a risk, one that could ruin me. If I falter, it could take away all the credibility I've built."

"Then why?"

"Why do what's right, Dolly? Because maybe it will show you I've changed. That you can trust me once again."

He slipped from the chair, strode to me with that confident walk, and put my hand in his. The strength in his palms, his fingers remained. He was older, with salt-and-pepper hair. Lines etched his face. Tiny crinkles set about his well-groomed mustache. He still looked good, well preserved to my aging eyes.

Together, we clutched the latch. "Bring Charlotte to me tomorrow and the next for dinner. We can determine if she will carry on this deception."

"Because you'll be at risk?"

"Yes. I'm willing to do so, but I have to know she is as committed to this as you are. Your determination has to be hers. Then she will succeed at all costs."

Ignoring his backhanded praise, I had to admit that Charlotte was fragile. I didn't know if she'd go with Cells to Demerara, but I needed to try. "I'll get her to come. I know she'll want to see you."

"I'll have Polk take you back and pick the two of you up tomorrow evening at six."

Fingers still entwined, we slid the latch. Flinging free, I shot through the door. "Have Polk hurry. I've been gone too long from her."

For Charlotte's safety, there was no other choice than trusting Cells. I had to figure out how I would deal with owing him. And how I'd tell Thomas.

BARBADOS 1795: THE WAY

I sipped red wine, a claret cupped in fine crystal. This was the second dinner Charlotte and I had with Cells. It was different being his guest and now his equal.

He waved off a server, one fully dressed with shoes. I didn't ask her status. I was glad this older woman with silver hair curling beneath her red-and-blue-patterned scarf looked healthy.

"Dolly, you keep staring at my bookshelves."

"I spent a fair amount of time cleaning them. Can't help looking at how empty they are."

"The humidity is bad in Bridgetown. I've ruined more than one special treasure here. Mildew is everywhere. My books stay in cedar trunks."

His gaze at me burned, like he knew my thoughts, but I abandoned his gaze and concentrated on the feast of roasted partridge over dandelion greens. The oattie nut bread, the texture of it, always tasted of happiness.

Yet I could barely lift my knife. How could I eat when Thomas and I had had words? Well, I said a lot of them and he listened as I tried to convince him and my soul of this arrangement with my old love.

Cells, the easygoing man, had Charlotte talking in more than one sentence. She smiled when he mentioned the Hermitage.

"You and your brother loved roaming the halls. I miss that." Cells offered a thoughtful look and lifted his glass. "A toast to Edward."

Part of me wanted to toss my goblet at him and watch the burgundy-colored liquid stain his rich-man-white white jacket. "What type of toast? Will it be a light one?"

Cells bit his lip, then said, "It will be my deepest regret to not have been a better man to my son and to you, all of you."

Charlotte pushed away from the table. "At least you two had a son to bicker about."

"Sit, Charlotte. Your mother and I are making peace. It's hard sometimes with a sea of misunderstanding separating us."

My daughter clasped the back of the chair. Then she smoothed the full skirt of her widow's weave and retook her seat.

"Hmmm." He thumbed those lips of his. "Charlotte, your mother and I think that you should quit the colony of Grenada and move to the Hermitage."

"Quit?"

"Yes," he said, "we should all gather in Demerara. It's ready for business. It's finally growing, now that it's firmly under English control. The French and Dutch are never to claim it again."

"How good, Cells? You're finally right. Only a few years off."

Charlotte stabbed a cut of boiled yam with her fork. "This is peacemaking?"

"It is," I said. "It's how we navigate things. Tweaking his nose, reminding him how we survived without him."

The instant I said it, I regretted it. "Sorry."

His smile returned, for he knew I was still hurt by his leaving, his taking Catharina.

"This will help make amends. Yes, Dolly and all the Kirwan-Thomas brood should come to Demerara. We could be one large family. Never had that."

If he'd chosen me, I wasn't sure if I'd have as many children. And Cells didn't love like Thomas did. I wouldn't want my heart broken again and again because my babes didn't fit into Cells's white world.

He left his end of the table and came to ours and waved a servant to refill my drink. "Dolly, there's a great demand for services in Demerara, but you're probably waiting for the rebellion to end to reap British contracts. I hear you're still collecting on your contracts in Dominica. Always my enterprising Dolly."

"We weren't all born to run rum plantations."

That took his smirk.

Charlotte dropped her fork. It made a hollow clang on her bone china plate. "You two couldn't make it two minutes. No matter how you put it, for there to be new business with the British, the Fédons must lose. I need to return to Grenada and fight with Rose and Julien."

"Charlotte, you can't say those names in public. They link you to the rebellion. You could be killed."

"Maybe I should be. Maybe I should die and be with Jean-Joseph. He must think I'm a coward. A coward like you two pretending you hate each other, when you are the same." She pushed back from her chair. "I need to leave."

My daughter bolted across the polished floorboards. I bounced up and caught her, putting my arms about her, holding her up. "Charlotte, we squabble, but we both love you. We both want the best. That's why you're returning to Demerara."

She stayed in my embrace for a moment then ran toward the door.

"Stop, Charlotte." Cells's voice vibrated, loud and strong.

She dropped her hands to her sides. The air went out of her. "Yes, Papa Cells."

"I'll have someone escort you upstairs to a bedchamber to refresh yourself. I'll make peace with your mama while you rest."

She swiped at her eyes and nodded. The look on her face was that of a little girl lost.

I wish I knew the words, the herbs, the way to make it all better. Then I realized her *Papa Cells* could.

With a flick of his wrist, Cells pointed to a server who escorted my daughter out of the room. Then he said, "Everyone, please leave us."

All the fellows in onyx mantles that had lined the wall disappeared.

"She's grieving very hard, Dolly." He moved to the glass doors that led to his garden. "She's not you, Dolly. No one is as strong as you. We must convince her to come live at the Hermitage. Catharina and Louisa will love her."

He opened the double doors and let humid air inside. The smell, the citrus and perfumes of flowers, overtook the meal's.

Cells walked toward me. His hair wasn't powdered. The gray and black locks had a tinge of blue in the candle's light.

Handsome in his short cream waistcoat with silver buttons that glimmered, he stopped inches from me. The heat made his hazel eyes quite green. "How did I let us get here? To this place where you hate me. Where we can't act in one accord."

"Cells . . ."

Like he'd shed a mask, his trademark smirk ripped away. "This is my fault. I never should've left you. I should've been more direct in my intentions in eighty-nine. I should've been the one to take you to see the world, no one else."

"Nothing you could've said that day would have changed my mind."

"Maybe you didn't know what a blackguard Prince William is. His womanizing in the Caribbean is legendary. His support of the old ways . . . he's full throated about it. He wants the British to drive every rebellion into the sea."

William wasn't that way but defending him to Cells would show him I was bothered by his opinion. "I suppose I'm too liberal then."

"No, Dolly. You see what you want. That's why you loved me. You saw only the good, not the selfish bastard I am."

The heat, the kiss of heavy air, the longing in his voice—all dampened my face, my bodice. His admission made it hard to breathe.

He rubbed his face. His cheeks looked very red. "Is there nothing I can say to convince you to come back with me?"

"There is noth—"

"I love you. I love Dolly, always did."

Cells caught my hand and spun me to the wordless dance that

had always been ours. "I couldn't say it before, not with all my secrets. But you know everything, except how I burn for you. How
every moment away from your light is a torture. I've been in the
dark too long."

I was in his arms, half turned against his chest. The satin of my
sleeves bunched, catching on his buttons.

His breath singed my neck. "I'm free of the vows I said to God. I
know you hate me, but I feel the passion in your skin. It's still there
for me, for us."

"I should go to Charlotte."

"Dolly, I let you get away once. Not again."

"Release me. I'm walking out of here."

"Even though you still love me?"

"Were you always this conceited?"

"Probably. Only you and Fanny complained."

I slipped away. "I'm happy now. I'm with Thomas. Be the man I
always wanted. Be my hero. Save my daughter."

"Can't I save you, too?"

It took everything to not fall prey to the memories, the good ones
we'd shared. "You took Catharina from me because you were convinced I couldn't care for her the best. This time I'm admitting I
can't take care of Charlotte. I need you to."

He closed his eyes for a moment.

It was enough to escape to the bookcase before the rhythm of his
heart claimed mine.

"I love Charlotte, Dolly. I'll keep her safe."

I offered him a smile and headed to the door. He moved faster
and held it open. "If friendship is all that is available, I'll take that
for now, but the bond between us will never break. It will grow
stronger when you realize as I do that we should be together—"

With my palm, I cupped his mouth. I couldn't hear his lies or his
truths. "Take care of my girls, Cells."

He kissed my fingers. "With my life, Dolly. With my life."

Breathing heavy, like I'd succumbed to his campaigning, I walked out of the drawing room to Charlotte's cries.

I wanted to offer a last hug, but I couldn't.

She'd only go to Demerara if she had no choice.

I mumbled good-bye and ran, hoping that me leaving Cells was the best for Charlotte . . . and my soul.

GRENADA 1795: THE WIN

A distant cannon sounded from the hills. Mount Qua Qua must be under direct attack. How long could the rebels hold on?

Trying to get comfortable in my bed was hard. St. George's was still safe but business was cut in half. My shop stayed closed most days. The blockades kept goods from flowing. Grenada was never going to be the same again.

"Doll, the noise is far away. Go back to sleep."

Thomas sat at his desk working on wills for his clients. He turned in his chair. "You all right?"

"I don't know."

"Stop fretting about Charlotte. You made the right decision leaving her with Cells."

"What makes you think I'm thinking about that?"

"It's all you've talked about since you've been back. That and the store."

"What should I be talking about?"

"Well, you could talk about me and the boys. We were lonely and had to do a lot fishing while you and Charlotte spent time with *Papa Cells*. I hear he's an engaging host."

Thomas's voice was a mixture of tension, humor, and good old jealousy, but I'd ignore it. "A party won't save my girl."

He put down his papers. His boots, dusty and smelling of sea salt, knocked as he came and sat on the bed. "Charlotte is fine, Doll."

"Mamaí says the lieutenant governor locked up more rebels while we were away. They were hanged. It's an awful thing to see a man strung up. Awful."

"Charlotte is safe."

"I know Cells will protect her, but she has to lie about Jean-Joseph, the love of her life."

"Well, thank goodness you'll never have to do that. I'm right here."

He sent those boots flying then lay in the pillows and took me with him. "I do owe Cells, Doll. If the fool knew what he had when you worshiped the ground he walked on, I wouldn't have you now. Same thing with that prince."

"You're trying to make me laugh again."

With a kiss to my forehead, he snuggled me to his shoulder. "You might make me crazy, but there's no one for me but you, woman. Keep dreaming good dreams. I want to see how many stars you catch."

"Thomas, I do believe that you know how to love me right."

He looped the strings of my nightgown about his thumb. "Might need to practice." He tugged the satin loose. "A great deal of practice."

No man in my life, none had supported me, not like Thomas. He wasn't threatened by my dreams or my past. I should assure him of my heart and say to him the three words he said easily.

Instead, I gave Thomas words he craved. The ones that made him happiest. "No more tea."

"What?"

"Put another babe in this old womb if you can, sir."

In the small light of the candle, I saw his lips lift and crest. "That mission sounds like it will require a lot of practice. You sure, Doll? Babies are hard on you."

"You're here to keep me well. I have no fear."

I dropped my sleeves and waited for his touch. I wanted to be consumed by Thomas, wrapped so deeply in his love that there wasn't me without him. Then I wouldn't hear the cannons or the guns or any sad memories in my soul. Wouldn't ever think of the other paths I could've taken, not while in Thomas's easy arms.

They moved me to where he could be with me, where he could

edge up my hem and caress my thigh. He was neither fast, nor wild, with his kisses. He'd studied me. He knew me, and I knew him.

I threaded my arms about his neck as Thomas hummed, singing my name. "I didn't actually fret too much about Cells. You kept coming home to me each night."

"Smug."

"No, just patient. I win, Doll."

"Win what?"

"Being the man who gets to hold you when you're scared."

I wasn't scared . . . much.

But it was foolish to argue when he was spinning me to that moment where our breaths became raspy, our hearts labored with the same rhythm. Maybe I didn't need wild and strong when this rhythm, this steady love, could last. Thomas had me arching to him, aching for his fingers.

If this womb could work one more time, I knew Thomas would be beside me loving me through the darkness.

GRENADA 1797: THE WHISPER

Frances read Cells's letter to me at the breakfast table. He mentioned that all was well and that in public Charlotte had kept up a brave front and said nothing when Demeraran colonists celebrated the failed Fédon rebellion.

A year had passed since the British ended that war. Mary Rose and Julien were killed or imprisoned, while I birthed another daughter. Dorothy Christina, my Crissy, came out screaming. I never doubted she'd live but nothing stopped my torturing myself about everything, especially not being with Charlotte.

Cells's squiggles assured me that no one outside of the Hermitage suspected a thing. Our Foden-Fédon ruse had taken hold. Yet he failed to mention anything of Catharina other than her good health. I went down the hall wringing my hands, wondering about his games or if he plotted to provoke an earlier visit from me.

No one could leave Grenada yet. The government hadn't eased restrictions. Now my sparrow was sick.

Outside Kitty's bedchamber, my worked-up mind blackened to nothing, drifting into the Obeah shadows and all the death masks I bore. Her bone-rattling cough ran through me sharp and pricking like a knife to my spine.

Nothing worked, no doctors, no teas, no liniments, no prayers.

I slipped down the wall, drowning in my own sobs.

Sally kicked my foot. "Why you out here?"

"Umm . . . I don't know."

Her head lifted to another of Kitty's barking coughs. "I thought your man told you not to 'cause he didn't want that baby sick."

Little Crissy slept good, all through the night now. The birthing sadness robbed me but Thomas poured his love into me, but Kitty . . . She needed strength, much more than me.

Not fair.

All those years ago in Mamaí's hut, looking out the window, those stars were ours. Not just mine. Our dreams. Ours . . . Kitty and me . . . us.

I lifted wet eyes to Sally. "No. My husband wouldn't do that."

Her chin nodded, her silver head and long braid shining like a halo in the dim sconce's light. "Well, he's the only good blanca I know. You're good too. Don't let *her* leave alone."

The stoic woman pointed to the bedroom door and walked away.

My *her*, my heart, my swallow, my sister, my first friend.

I stood, smoothed my wrinkled indigo sleeves down to my wrists, and went into her room.

It was hot inside and smelled of lemony tamarind, more of the old cures for bad lungs.

Mamaí mopped Kitty's sweaty brow.

"May I sit with you?" My voice was a whisper, choppy and tear-filled.

"Look, Kitty. Dolly's here and might have news of Polk."

Kitty looked weak, pale with drawn-in cheeks. Black vomit spattered the cloth my mother used to wipe Sis's lips.

"Swallow, may I sit beside you?"

"Dolly? You've come to play?"

"Yes." I ran and put my ear to her fevered chest. "I'm sorry."

"Stay with me until I sleep, Dolly. The dark frightens me sometimes. It's scary."

Climbing onto the mattress, I let her snuggle against my side, my knee, like before, like in our hut. "You beat the shadows. We won. Let's hope to see stars tonight. I'll wait here with you."

She sniffled. I did too.

"Dolly, tell Polk . . . he's . . . my good friend. You, too."

"Save your strength." My mother's calm voice was wet. Her

hair had fully turned white at her temples. The rest was brown and curled beneath her head wrap.

Kitty stretched her fingers to Mamaí and settled deeper against my thigh. "I died in the stocks at the Marketplace, Dolly. But you gave me my life again."

I clutched her fingers, tracing each knuckle. "There's more life for us. More dreams. Get better."

"Keep dreaming, Dolly. Keep—"

Her coughing became a whisper, but it echoed and lingered until it vanished like smoke.

And I stayed with my swallow, holding her hand, memorizing her face until I was sure her spirit flew. She was forever free.

GRENADA 1799: THE WORST

In Edward's old room, I held baby Elizabeth, my new grandniece. Yawning like her, I wanted to head to bed. I'd trained two new housekeepers last night. "Business is good, little girl."

My contracts were almost to fifty, the level I had before the rebellion. In another month things would be calm enough to visit Demerara.

It was time. Catharina needed to meet her true mother. Little Elizabeth Penner was motherless, the granddaughter of the aunt I never knew. Negotiations for Mamaí's eldest daughter, Ella. The sister I never knew had finally come to live with us and brought this little bundle.

Elizabeth's golden brown eyes were wide and searching. "Can you see the freedom here? Can you feel it?"

She yawned and grabbed at me like Catharina. Cells's evasive talk about our girl wouldn't stop me anymore. There was something he and even Charlotte weren't saying, as if I was too weak to endure the news. Kitty's death and lingering birthing sadness stole so much of me, but I was ready again for the world. I had to finish our dreams.

Elizabeth suckled her thumb.

"Save that for counting, little one." I settled her in her cradle, the one used by all my children since Demerara. "I'm going to be your special friend, like my Mrs. Ben was to me. I promise."

When the babe finally slept, I crept down to the parlor. Frances and Ann were passing a book of poems Thomas had gotten for them.

Blam.

Something fell.

I peeked into the kitchen. Eliza and Sally were laughing at the sack of flour that fell from the table. They were usually a stoic pair.

"You want to help, Mama?" Eliza asked in her chipper voice.

"No. I'll wait to be amazed at what you two cook."

They went back to measuring and stirring, and I turned to the open door that led to Mamaí's garden.

Harry and Josephy weeded and cleaned up the rows between the callaloo and yams. I knew they hoped to do their chores early. If Thomas felt up to it, they'd go fishing on the *Mary*. Mamaí and Ella were out there, too, drinking tea.

Ella was nice, but my heart still wanted Kitty, still grieved seeing her latest art.

Mamaí came inside and passed me in the hall. She touched my cheek. "You feeling poorly, too?"

How should I feel? Dread stayed stuck in my throat. "I think I want to be away from Grenada."

She gripped my hand. "You ran away once to see the other side of the sea. You can't be thinking of that now."

"No. That's not this season, but someday, I'll take you all."

The pressure of her touch increased for a moment. "Don't run. See that your family needs your strength. See it, Dolly, see it now, before it's gone. Before he's gone."

My eyes locked onto the secrets in her beautiful wizened eyes.

Him.

Thomas.

I ran to him, to the room we put the wee children for learning. Thomas was on the floor perched against the wall. One trembling puffy hand stretched out to baby number ten. Dorothy Christina, my Crissy, wobbled and swayed with a book on her head, but she made it to him before the thing with its gilded spine toppled onto his leg.

Thomas reached out, held her close. "Such poise my darling. A society woman in the making. I'm proud of you. You'll rule the world like your mother."

Mamaí came inside. "Crissy, time for you to eat."

The child offered a frown with her bright pink lips. "I'm coming, Grama." She put the book on her head again and pranced to the door.

"This way, oh queen," Mamaí said.

The two hobbled out, but my eyes stayed on Thomas. I finally saw, finally allowed myself to see how pale his skin, how thick his ankles were, like his heart wasn't pumping blood good. At fifty-eight, for a white man, one not working the fields, he was too young to be sick.

"Help me up, Dorothy."

I lent him my arm, my strength, and I held him.

The feel of Thomas was different. His embrace had no strength. The thick sound of his chest was like Edward's.

No. Why, Holy Father? Why?

He kissed my cheek, with his finger he swiped at my tears. "Get my boys, woman. I need to sail with them."

"No, you need to be in bed. We can fight—"

"This is one fight you can't win. Get them."

Stubborn fool.

Thomas knew me better than any, and I knew him. I rushed from the room and did as he asked. This time I wouldn't stop what he wanted.

The sea stirred different shades of blue and green. The sun was high and bright reflecting on the *Mary*'s white sails. The trademark blue-painted post of the mainsail looked proud.

Josephy steered. Harry adjusted some lines then stood by his side. Frances, Eliza, and Ann gathered at Thomas's bare feet. I couldn't get his boots on. His feet were too swollen. I put them at his side.

His breathing was hard. He clutched his chest and gave a pained look.

The boys grinned.

They didn't know this was good-bye, but Frances and Ann, my sensitive souls, did. Frances more so. Her world was Thomas and books. She could be a solicitor if not for the profession being for men alone.

Thomas sighed long. "Josephy, take the boat in now."

"Pa! Just one more time."

"No." Thomas winced. "No, my boy."

"Mind your father." I said each word slowly. They inched out of my trembling lips. "Then you all go on back to Mamaí. She and Sally and Crissy are waiting on the shore."

My sons caught my weak eyes. They nodded. The tiller turned. The sail moved.

The *Mary* made it to shore. Thomas had his eyes closed. "I love you all. Mind and support your mother. She's not done dreaming."

Spittle leaked from his mouth, but he blinked heavily then looked to the sky. The children kissed his cheeks and touched him then they went to Mamaí. Frances ran back and hugged him one more time.

"Go on, my love," he said, but I undid the rope. We caught the next big wind, and I steered away.

"Now why'd you do that, Doll? I pictured just sitting here at the dock in my boat, watching you and the family walk away. You ruined it."

"I'm a lousy first mate." I snuggled against him and pulled his cold face into my bosom. "Not letting you be alone in this. You're going to go from my arms."

"Well, you do have nice arms. Leave me out here in the *Mary*. Let my partners get the insurance money when the waves destroy her. It's the least I could do for Garraway et al."

That was my man. Always thinking and doing for others. "How long have you known?"

"Since Dr. Hay told me."

That was six weeks ago. Six weeks, I could've told him how much he meant to me, how much he touched everything in my life and made it good. "You sure he's not fixed you like Edward?"

"Doll."

"I know. I just want to laugh, anything to not think about you not being here."

"I told you I was going to haunt you, woman."

I settled a blanket on us, hoping its warmth would push back into his limbs. Trying not to sob, I held on to Thomas. He was my air. "I love you. I don't know when I learned to trust us again, but I can say it now."

"I knew. There are no words for what's between us."

He nuzzled my cheek, then slipped his chin into the crook of my neck. "Listen, there's paperwork in my desk for you and the children to leave here. I don't know if it's safe to remain. The government could again impose new restrictions. With me gone . . . Don't let the family we built be destroyed."

"I'm going to try."

"I want to die in the sea. Then I'd kiss you every time you crossed the waters."

Thomas, beautiful Joseph Thomas, was the one man who loved me and my dreams together at the same time. I didn't have to choose.

"Starting over is hard. Where would I go? How do I even say the words without you?"

"I wrote to Coxall. His name and influence can secure your leaving here and joining the British Colony of Demerara."

Lizzy and Charlotte and even Catharina were there.

"It's the perfect place. And I know there's a man there who'll protect you."

Cells? I didn't need anyone Thomas. "No."

"Promise me when you see the world again. Take our family."

"You can tell me all this. I should tell you not to die."

He laughed and wheezed. His hand settled on my thigh, ruffling one of Mamaí's old jump skirts, this one with red and gold prints of palm fronds.

"No petticoat, my queen?"

"No, and not a queen."

"Maybe the island for you is England. You know people there. There are other queens there. You wouldn't be lonely."

"Don't be setting up my next bedmate. It's not funny. Can't think of ever replacing you."

"Where was all this ego-building talk when I could take advantage of such praise?"

"We have a lot of children birthed between us. You took plenty. And you gave plenty."

"All of them, any one you bore, all Thomases in my heart, Doll."

He smiled at me, one that seared wounds in my soul. "Get off the boat, woman. Don't let our last memory be of me dying. None of that death mask talk."

"I'll stay till the end, then I can take you with me."

An hour or so passed. He was silent looking off at the distance. "Not afraid anymore. You . . . the family . . . fine—"

His head tipped forward and rested against mine. I kissed him as his ghost went to sleep.

Like he loved me one last time, I felt his magnificent spirit surge deep inside me, rattling and filling the deep empty spaces in my chest.

When the shades of evening started to fall and all the warmth had left Thomas, I slipped away, stripped off my short boots and stood on the edge of the *Mary*. Feet flat on the waxed deck, I took a final glance of my short boots next to his dusty ones, then dove headfirst into the choppy waters.

PART SIX

The legacy

The truest threat to freedom is a bunch of old men.

DEMERARA 1800: THE RETURN

Dawn broke through the dark sky. The sun rose casting orange and red light across the bow. I couldn't sleep in the cramped sloop's hatch with Josephy's snore. Neither could Crissy.

She stood beside me on the boat deck, but I had a tight hold on her arm. The curious four-year-old would fidget and launch over the side if I took my eyes off her.

It was sort of sweet, to think of my youngest having no cares. I'd secured a *fhortún* of twenty-two thousand pounds. I wanted more, wanted to be able to set my boys' future with not only the finest education across the sea, but their professions. Crissy and Eliza would continue to have the best tutors, like Ann and Frances.

At fifteen, Frances was the head of the family that stayed in Grenada. She convinced Ann, Mamaí, Sally, and Ella, along with my grandniece, to stay in that colony. That girl was so persuasive, I relented.

She meant to keep expanding there as I'd done when I retained my business in Dominica. My Thomas network would include the two islands and now Demerara.

Splitting up the family that Thomas and I built was horrid, but Frances's dreams, her arguments, were too strong for a heart missing my husband and my Charlotte. The hope to finally know Catharina pushed me forward.

"Mama. Look at the water. I want to touch it. Papa loved it. It's green like turtles."

"It is green, like young snapping ones or the big frogs we called mountain chickens in Montserrat."

"Big frogs. Grrr. How awful. I like the water. Not frogs."

Filling my nose with the sweet clean air, I, too, marveled at how the water had changed from the dark blues of Grenada to the sky blues in Trinidad to pale green the farther south we traveled. Soon it would change from green to white and brown as we approached the Demerari River that my boat captain said the British now called the Demerara River.

Odd picky change, but I supposed it was important what the main waterway was called.

Eliza came from below. Yawning, she gripped the side. "Mama, you and Aunt Kitty used to live here?"

"Yes. When we were young." In silence, I bowed my head—praying, grieving, missing my swallow.

Noises drummed below. Heavy earth-shaking footsteps sounded. My boys.

Josephy and Harry had awakened and crawled from the cabin. They wrestled for a spot along the deck.

"Boys. Stop that," I said.

They did, waggling fingers and whispering to continue their battle tomorrow.

Josephy had his father's build—I could see him captaining a wheel—but Harry, my Harry, had Thomas's smile.

"I see land, Mama." Harry started jumping and skipping.

"The rooftops aren't as pretty as in Grenada, but some are taller," Eliza said, leaning more over the side.

I tugged on her tunic and made her come back. "Neither you nor Crissy are going into the sea."

Josephy took Eliza's hand. "Is Demerara the same, Mama?"

"I don't know. It's been years."

The first time I approached this colony, Kitty and I crouched low in Cells's *Dolus* waiting for Polk to say it was safe.

Running from Nicholas, enslaved, carrying only a sack of clothes and scarves for our hair was how we set foot on the dock thirty years ago. At forty-four, I would walk onto the soil a freewoman, a woman in a bright yellow hat in the company of her free children.

My captain, John Gloster Garraway, a nicely tanned young man, the son of Thomas's partner, navigated the sloop as if he were born behind the steering tiller. I noted how settled he was, how he took after his calm mulatto mother, Franny, not his risk-taking father.

"Just a few more minutes, Mrs. Thomas," Garraway called out.

Like he'd done it a hundred times, he steered to the westward side of the Essequiba River to avoid sandbars, guiding the sloop to the mouth of the Demerara. I couldn't wait to step my boots on the red mud of the colony.

The captain and my boys unloaded our portmanteaus, big brown leather trunks, and stacked them on the dock.

The heat baked my face as it did that first day. I loved the dry heat. Half the books Thomas had bought, I'd brought. The dryness meant they'd not suffer the green dust.

"Mrs. Dolly!"

I adjusted my hat and turned.

Lizzy and Coxall. They ran to us waving and shouting.

I hugged each one.

"Mama, we're happy you've come."

"You two look good."

A little thicker, but still handsome with a head of dark hair, Coxall beamed with pride. "Is that Joseph Jr. and Harry? I'll help them gather your things. We have a dray to take you to our house."

"Thank you," I said, half watching them, half watching Crissy.

Eliza came near, her fingers clasping my youngest's wrist. "Look. Charlotte has come, too."

That was all it took for Eliza to leave my youngest and run past me and Lizzy to get to her other older sister.

There was no stopping her. I caught Crissy's wrist and watched Eliza cling to Charlotte's waist. Soon they both stood in front of me, but my second born remained draped in black, all but her hat, a white confection with a feather.

"I've missed you," I said with a whisper of a voice. I gripped my daughter, then reached out and grabbed Lizzy, too. Now, I had the first two girls of my heart and my last. Then I dragged in Eliza; she couldn't miss any of my love.

"Ma'am."

A young man had called to me. The nerve of him thinking I'd release children to greet him.

Hmmmph. That almost-important cough.

"Miss Dolly?"

The fool wasn't going away. I looked to the left. "Yes."

"I don't know if you remember me."

I wiped my eyes with my handkerchief, then squinted at the well-dressed fellow in a wide-collared coat and knee breeches.

"It's D.P. Simon, ma'am."

I glanced at him again as he stood behind my Charlotte. It was him. Amazing, the boy who was in love with her all those years ago.

But Charlotte was dressed in widow's black, five years since the loss of Jean-Joseph.

"D.P. Simon. It is you." Before I made a foolish comment about him and Charlotte, a young woman, a short one, looped her arm about his.

She was stylish in a linen print round gown. A matching bonnet covered her jet black hair and shadowed the small cleft in her chin.

"Miss Dolly, this is my wife, Catharina, your daughter."

I didn't know what to react to first. My daughter? His wife?

Catharina, now seventeen years of age, the child I hadn't seen since her birth was here.

I didn't move. I stared at her. I was happy and confused. Simon had been a decent boy, a good neighbor. But wasn't he twice her age?

"Newlyweds? Congrat—"

They looked at each other like a secret or conspiracy passed between them.

Catharina tightened her hold on D.P. "No, Mama Kirwan—"

"Mama Thomas." I was gentle in my correction. Who knows

what Cells had said, but at least he told her the truth. I was the one to give birth to her.

She smiled, her pert mouth forming a pout. "Sorry. Mama Thomas, if that is what you wish to be called. Simon and I have been together for five years. We have a daughter. Henrietta."

His voice became squeaky. "She's four. You must meet her."

Did my face look numb? It surely had to with my child knowing a man since she was twelve or thirteen. Had I passed the curse of growing up too fast to Catharina?

She launched into my arms. "Oh, Mama Thomas, I'm pleased to meet you."

I held her, I think. My head ached a little too much to know. I blinked a few times, thinking of how best to kill this *Nicholas-type* man who preyed upon my young daughter.

Yet another man had to die before D.P. Simon. John Coseveldt Cells. He wasn't on the dock. Where was he?

Oh, Holy Father, let at least Coxall and Lizzy's house be well. There was too much to fix in Charlotte's and Catharina's lives. I'd returned to Demerara none too soon.

I sat on the rear patio of Lizzy and Coxall's house. No stilts like Pa's owl house but sprawling in size. Coxall did well, expanding his father's business for shipping goods throughout the Caribbean. That would come in handy for the store and the hotel I had dreamed up in my head.

Plenty of servants, plenty of head-scarfed maids fluttered. These fine servants dressed in baize and cotton fabrics with strips of silk kente of yellows and red. I didn't ask their status, free or enslaved. I wasn't ready to poke into their business, not with Catharina weighing on my mind.

Charlotte sat beside me, Lizzy across in a chair.

My eldest filled my cup from her shiny silver tea service. The filigree on the pot reminded me of Mr. Foden's. "Eliza's found our books, Mama," Lizzy said. "She's in a corner reading."

The dryness of Demerara kept paper from mildewing; I would need to build shelves for Eliza in our new house and import as many books as I could. "She loves to read, Lizzy. Thank you again for your hospitality."

Harry and Josephy ran past rolling barrel hoops with Lizzy's brood. Crissy gave chase but her little chubby legs couldn't keep up.

This was peace, but I'd come for the storm. "Tell me now, why Cells allowed Catharina to marry this young."

"Don't be mad at Papa Cells," Charlotte said. "He had to travel back to Europe. Some holdings needed his attention. He left Catharina in my charge. She hated being here, hated finding out . . ."

"Finding out she was my daughter. Finding out that she was Black because of her true mother."

I hadn't realized how it would sound saying it aloud or how my heart hurt. My first daughter born of love hated me, while my two born of violence were proud of me. How was this right?

Charlotte gripped my hand. "I failed her. I was too caught up in my own misery to notice how she misbehaved."

"This can't be your fault, dear. You never—"

"It is, Mama. D.P. came over to visit me, but Catharina loved him instantly. Or wanted his attention, instantly. She's a force to be reckoned with. Very persuasive."

A flash in my head of that little baby grabbing the world with both arms fell upon me. "Of course she'd be." Catharina was Cells's daughter as much as mine. "But a man, a grown one, should know better than to deal with a child. Twelve is a child."

"D.P. was a widower. His wife and child had died of cholera a year earlier. He resisted Catharina's flirtation, but she made him laugh. The man loves her very much now."

Lizzy sipped from her cup then set it down. "Five years married, he's completely devoted to her, but he spends too much money to keep her happy. Our sister is very used to getting what she wants."

That was Cells, persuasive and powerful. Might even be a bit of me.

"I tried to convince her to be cautious, but she didn't heed. Even taunting me like I'd never loved. Papa Cells chose not to tell her of Jean-Joseph. He didn't trust she'd be discreet."

The girl I'd longed to love sounded horrible. I dropped two cubes of sugar into my tea. "Is there no good in Catharina?"

The following silence was damning.

"She apologized later, Mama. Our sister doesn't take kindly to anyone questioning her plans."

Lizzy picked up the teapot like it was a stew pot with one hand on the handle the other palm flat on its belly.

The distraction was good. There was something I could teach her after all these years.

"Catharina uses you to guilt Cells." Lizzy's eyes sparkled like bits of glass. "I tried to show her how wrong that was. She didn't listen."

My heart swelled. We'd come far, Lizzy and I. Getting to be with her all over again was a treasure.

"When Papa Cells returned, he was so angry. He didn't write up a marriage contract. He left and hasn't been back."

"No contract? She and D.P. could've married. They are both mixed race."

"It did not matter. D.P. is a Sephardic Jew. He won't convert to Anglican. That's the one thing he hasn't done for Catharina. She's a proud Anglican."

Anglican? Raised in Europe, what was I to expect with Cells's shifting faith? Sitting back, watching the children play, lurching from side to side on the lawn chasing barrel hoops. Everything should be as easy as this.

I picked up the pot, holding it strong with my wrist. Then I showed her and Charlotte a proper pour. Not a drop spilled. "I learned this at the Hermitage, then again in London."

A servant came to Lizzy carrying a folded paper. The squiggles seemed tight like Prince William's. The paper was fancy like his, too.

"Oh," Charlotte said, "a note from the Simons."

Nodding to the servant, Lizzy took it and popped the wax seal. "Mama. You've been asked to dinner tomorrow by Catharina and D.P."

Charlotte sipped her tea. "I'll come, too. When Catharina gets fussy, I can help."

It hurt that my daughter with Cells was spoiled. Could I have fixed that if I'd fought harder to keep her?

Lizzy poured another cup, but this time correctly, arching her wrist. A glance at her and the lovely brood on the lawn and I decided I hadn't done badly.

"I'll go to Chance Hall alone and face what I must. Lizzy came to understand my choices. Maybe Catharina will too."

No matter what had happened, all my children would have the love and strength they were due. That was my vow. I lumped it on my pile of unfinished dreams.

* * *

Chance Hall was a magnificent estate, one built of stone and wood, not just boards. My sandals pattered on the stone tile floor of the entry.

Such a big house but scarcely any servants. Lizzy's smaller house had more.

Looking for people, I stopped at a room that had a tile floor. A square or two in the center had been removed. The spot held white sand like that of Barbados. Above this hung four brass chandeliers, each shiny and polished.

The windows of this room were arched like the ones I saw on the pink building, the Barbados temple.

"Twenty-four candles, ma'am, can be suspended above." D.P. Simon stood at my side, tall and thin with dimples and long sideburns. Well dressed in a tan satin waistcoat topping a linen shirt, he looked more a man of business than a planter. "This room mirrors a temple in Bridgetown, the Nidhe Israel Synagogue."

"In Barbados, I'd heard singing one Friday night but didn't see the temple clearly until the next morning. Is it a pink building with rounded corners?"

"Yes. You know it?"

I answered with a nod. "Must be special, since this is such a good room for sun. It would make an excellent parlor."

"It's for my faith, ma'am. Many of my community come and worship here. When the Dutch controlled, they were good to us, but the British are harsh. We have to hide. I hope the oppression never gets so bad we must be expelled like my forefathers from Spain."

"Expelled? Is that like running away?"

He chuckled. "A little, only you're forced to go."

His God didn't need the woods to meet him but a nice room with outdoor sand. "Simon, I know about hiding and faith. English rule is everywhere. They're powerful."

"It's hard, ma'am. I've made a point to practice my faith even in business." He stared at me. "I don't do like the rest, their slaveholdings. I don't do as well as the rest."

"You must hold to what you believe."

"I wish Catharina understood. I'll give her anything, but not my faith. My ancestors are in my bones. I wait for her to go to town with her sister for the zeved habat. On the first Shabbat when I knew she'd be away, the men of my faith blessed Henrietta. I hate hiding."

He was still the sweet young man I'd known, but him and my daughter? "For a righteous man, you've come under some dark influences."

"I didn't know! She seemed sophisticated . . . worldly." He blushed. "She told me she was older and I believed her until it was too late. My fault, but Catharina mesmerizes me. She took a broken grieving man and gave him hope. I asked Mr. Cells's forgiveness. He never gave it, but at least he didn't shoot me."

"Don't get too comfortable. You don't know what's in my reticule. Now that you know she's mine, not white but a mix, do you feel cheated?"

"Never. Aren't we all a mix of something?" The tension in his face eased. "She's beautiful and spirited. I envy Catharina sometimes, knowing what she wants. Since we aren't promised our days, maybe her ways are best."

The grief in his tone fell on me. I wasn't happy but I understood a little better. "Take me to your family, Simon."

We walked down a long hall. Pictures of family, of men and women, hung on the wall like in Cells's Hermitage. At the end, surrounded in gold framing, was a sole woman, a portrait of Catharina.

I put my palm on Simon's. "Wait for a moment."

The set in her deep hazel-green eyes looked brave, even regal. The light cleft of her chin, noble. "Lovely, Simon."

As if he'd relearned to breathe, he smiled, a toothy out-of-kilter one, then led me to a parlor.

In a silvery gown that looked like the painting, Catharina lounged on a pale green sofa in a grand room with milk-white walls. Her dress reached the floor even with the lace tucked up about her ankles.

That was Scotland's influence. Maybe even London's.

"Mama Thomas, you are here. My chef has prepared fine treats."

The low table separating us held gold platters of little round brown cakes that smelled of ginger and molasses.

Elegant treats.

Catharina wanted to impress me. I oohed and ahhed to show appreciation. "You needn't have gone to such lengths."

"It's no trouble. My father said you were used to such and have dined with royalty."

"Cells tends to run on."

Her nose, with my pa's hook, wrinkled. The movement shifted shadows upon her chin. "He always tells me the truth. Almost always."

The tension in her voice couldn't be masked. How had she grappled with the *truth*, the Black mama she didn't know, the white one she did?

Did one just blurt out sorry?

Sorry I let you go?

Sorry you're not white?

Sorry you don't know the struggle and beauty of Black—of being and living it?

Her smile returned. "Papa says you've become quite well off with your business. The hat on your head alone with all those feathers is very expensive. Looks like something from Will Clarke's on Wigmore Street in London."

It could be.

Thomas King still supplied my needs for bonnets.

D.P. bent down and made faces at his daughter, reminding me of Thomas with Frances, Eliza, even Ann. "This is Henrietta, Mrs. Dolly. Our first."

"I'm four, ma'am." The voice was bright, even polished, for a child. "Papa calls me Henny."

Catching D.P.'s eye, I saw the same pride when my pa called me Dolly. I almost . . . wept. Never saw him again, not after Dominica. Heard he died in his beloved Ireland years ago. Never made a go of Montserrat, the left and right sides of the plantation were gone.

Funny how simple things bring the past back. Patting my damp cheek, I cleared my throat. "Call me Grandmother, if that's fine with you, Simon, Catharina."

My daughter's frown had grown but she nodded. "I guess I wondered why I felt different sometimes. Now I know. You're my mother, the one who bore me."

Her tone sounded like an indictment. It was soft, but it pierced like I'd stepped on slivers of glass.

"Papa said it was his doing that he took me away, but I'm sure you had your reasons for letting me go." Her tight words pulsed with anger. I felt myself bleed onto the floor. The strongest peppermint oil wouldn't cleanse the carpet.

To explain that I was enslaved and weak with birthing sadness didn't make much sense given that I stood in front of her in my lovely hat and expensive silk gown with silver buttons down my front. Instead, I moved around the room with more oohs and ahhs. "You keep a fine house."

The stiffness in her cheeks eased a little. Catharina arose and scooped up the pretty little girl in the yellow dress. Paper-white skin with her curly hair tied up with a pink ribbon, they could walk those streets of London. They'd pass for white like not a drop of my shed blood was in them.

The haunted look in Catharina's gaze told me she wished there was none.

I ached from her pain. I only breathed again when she put Henrietta into my arms. "I hope we become the best of friends, all of us."

My daughter moved to D.P. and straightened her husband's cravat. "To start, let my husband help with your business dealings. He's better than Coxall."

Triumphant and grinning, she linked her hand with D.P.'s as if she'd won something, except there wasn't a competition.

Focusing on this little one, I kept my mouth shut, for Catharina was a child who went to bed in London looking for answers as much as stars. Despite the past, I needed to help the little girl in her, in Henny and me, to see we could win just as we were.

DEMERARA 1802: THE ROUTE

Another no. Another fair offer for a vacant piece of property had been rejected by a planter who had no plans to develop it himself.

Thomas King stood at my side near the plot of land I'd picked by the shore. "I hate to keep giving you bad news, first from London, now this. I'm sorry, Miss Dolly."

A breeze stirred the beach, lifting the creamy grains and tossing them. Loss and losing whirled, digging deeper into my chest. This had to stop. I needed to win again.

"Fullarton looks to be entertaining Miss Charlotte. And you thought she'd be bored."

King possessed a large sense of humor, but I was pleased that his local merchant, John Fullarton, caught my daughter's eye. They walked down the beach. She shimmered in the sun in a lovely gown of light yellow and green. My girl smiled again.

"Beach property in Demerara is very expensive. Close to the equator, hurricanes are rare. Things built here last."

"That's why I wanted it." I gripped my arms, holding in my grieving breath. "I wanted to start building a hotel before the rainy season."

King wiped his brass-rimmed spectacles. They'd gotten thicker over the years. "Have you thought about land closer to the capital? Stabroek is lovely and not far from where you live."

"That area has mills and government buildings, not travelers, not frigates."

"Mrs. Dolly, the landowner is being particular."

I stared at him as if my glance could burst his lenses. "I'm not trying to open up a brothel."

He lifted his hands. "I know. I know."

"And I want to be called Mrs. Thomas." Almost three years had passed since my husband died. I needed to hear his name said aloud, not just in dreams. Then maybe I'd feel his encouragement again.

Lowering my lids, I relaxed my lonely stiff shoulders. "It's important what you're called and what you answer to."

King chucked a rock into the sea. "Mrs. Thomas it is."

His little boy, my godson William, ran up and down the shore gathering seashells. That little fellow was wild, not minding the heat.

Watching someone without a care lifted my spirits. Yet how could I build a hotel to honor my stars if no one would sell to me?

I wanted to build here. Here where I could imagine Edward and Thomas in his beloved *Mary* sailing to me. Frances sent me a piece of that blue post of the mainsail that washed up on shore. I put it with my other treasures in my closet near my hats. "Mr. King, I have the money. How do we do this?"

"Maybe you need to be patient a little longer, Mrs. Thomas. That is, if you want here."

Wait? Never. I saw how the British planters made D.P.'s business hard. Because of their distrust of his faith, good ole Anglicans and some Catholics limited his opportunities, charged him more for everything. They'd bankrupt him.

Not me. I wanted my way at a fair price.

Shaking my fists, I jangled my reticule. The *ting-tang* sound of my coin purse made a rhythm that should make the Demerara planters take notice. "King, I pay three times more than any to lease rooms off America Street. My housekeeping services are run out of my parlor. I want a shop again. I want to be the source of artisans' goods for this colony. That's how my businesses operate in Dominica and Grenada."

He shook his head, then his bald head offered his blank banker's look. "You're doing some business here. That's good."

"Folks don't need to see how I live. It gives them ideas. Are you telling me to give up?"

"Not you, Mrs. Thomas." He pulled his hands together, not in a prayer, but like he plotted something wonderful. "Perhaps we should be more strategic. Look for allies."

"Strategic? That sounds sneaky or costly. I don't want men dipping into my money."

King shrugged. "Men weren't what I had in mind. Follow me. Fullarton, watch my boy."

The fellow nodded, but with Charlotte's arm entwined with the merchant's, I wondered if either would pay attention to little William.

Mr. King took a route close to the shore to one of the existing hotels. The water lapped the sand, pushing shells and jade flotsam. That feeling of moving sideways against the water pressed.

I trusted that the financier who found ways to evade the British blockades had a plan. He'd been a friend and partner through the years. It meant something for him to make me godmother to his son. A reformed slaver now investor from London wouldn't lead me astray, not when I had helped him find his path.

When we stopped at a brothel, I began to question my judgment. "Why are we here, King? I didn't think you were the type—"

"No. No." He tugged on his jacket lapels. "I'm a reformed man now, but I want you to meet some people who might help. I've arranged for you to have lunch with the Entertainment Society."

He opened the door. "Go on inside. Listen with an open mind. They may have a different approach for us to take."

It took every inch of my willpower to put my boots inside this place, a brothel like the one I'd danced and whored at upon first coming to Demerara.

"Everyone needs a little nuncheon," he said from the doorway. "I won't be joining you. Send for me if you have a new strategy. I'll make sure Fullarton returns Miss Charlotte home."

Farther down the hall, a servant, a young boy in a turban and a blue jacket and matching breeches, waved me to a room.

At the threshold, I viewed a group of women in marvelous hats, free colored and Black women. And they'd saved a seat for me.

DEMERARA 1802: THE RIVALS

A white tablecloth with the corners starched and squared lay before me. With the looks these women passed each other, I could've been right back at Pa's cistern. The gossips in Montserrat looked down on me because of my dark skin.

A fashionable woman holding a glass of wine extended her free hand to me. "Miss Dolly Kirwan, please join us."

"Mrs. Dorothy Thomas—is my name."

The head woman, a lovely brown-skinned lady, pointed to the open chair. "But you have family here. They claim you as Kirwan."

Full raked back, the chair was spindled but had strong-looking legs—it would hold me, even if I fidgeted. I sat and tried hard not to let the feet squeak on the bare floor. "It's Thomas. Ladies, you invited me."

"Consider us the welcoming committee of Demerara. Some call us the Entertainment Society. I'm Rebecca Ritchie. This is Elizabeth Ross and Mary Ostrehan Brett."

This head woman seemed younger than me and wore her hair in pinned curls like I had long ago. Miss Ross was older, olive in complexion with dark topaz eyes. She dressed well and wore a dazzling sea-blue turban covering her fine graying hair.

Miss Brett, I'd seen in Stabroek. Another freewoman, very light in coloring like Catharina and Lizzy.

Silent, not paying attention to anything but the lace shawl that hung about her shoulders, she seemed annoyed to be here.

Freewomen, all lighter than me. Funny. No matter how old you were, there was something about rejection that slipped past everything and etched hate on your insides.

After a sip of the flat champagne, I put down my goblet. "We now know each other's names. Now what?"

Miss Ritchie wiped at crumbs settling into the embroidered satin of her bodice. Her lean fingers tapped the sides of her crystal. "I'm very curious about you. You're trying to set up businesses here in the colony?"

"I'm already in business. I want to expand but keep running into trouble."

Miss Ross giggled, shimmying her smooth silk jacket with its innocent ribbon bow tied about her sly neck. Then she sobered.

My troubles must have been done on purpose. Trying not to stab the fruit, I picked at sliced mangoes and yellow governor's plums on the platter near me. "Tell me, what would make my path easier?"

After clearing her throat, Miss Ross said, "Demerara is like Jamaica and Barbados. We have enough hotels to cater to sailors. They pay for entertainment. We don't need anyone else in that line of work."

The math of competition was not hard to understand, but they didn't know me, didn't know my strength or the size of my dreams. These were the cistern women, merely clothed in better fabrics. "I'm not trying to build a brothel. I'm building a legacy, a luxury hotel, fine enough for a prince. More visitors, important ones, will come. That's the business I want."

Miss Ritchie's brow furrowed. "I don't understand."

I adjusted the brim of my fine bisque bonnet, delaying just a bit to whet their appetite. "I've seen the boom in Roseau and St. George's. I understand what visitors need. They will spend money and tell their friends."

"No mulatto balls for you?"

"I'm more interested in accommodations than entertainment."

Miss Ross shook her head and frowned like she'd bitten three lemons. "Is that a no?"

"I make my money huckstering the finest goods and offering the finest housekeeping, all on par of what is expected in England. I do not peddle flesh, but I know flesh gets peddled."

Convincing people with their minds made up against me was useless. I took a sip from my glass. The flat champagne puckered my lips. Prince William would never approve. Barely any bubbles kissed the glass. "Remind me to get you better champagne the next time we talk."

"A bribe? How fun." Miss Ritchie laughed.

Then I did too. My problems weren't solved, but I'd found my humor.

Miss Ross refilled her plate with mangoes. "Mrs. Thomas, I know you've met with resistance. The sooner you become established, the better. We need the men in government to see us freewomen as a part of the community, not as threats or exotic fantasies they can't speak about to their European mamas. Demerara can't become Grenada, where they use laws to terrorize us."

No, it couldn't. "The abuses against the free coloreds led to rebellion. I've seen enough of those. I'll do anything in my power to prevent that. And I assume you want to help me since you sent for me, unless this champagne is punishment for dreamers."

"It's good champagne." The previously silent Miss Brett sounded angered, her tone firm and blunt. "You don't know of what you speak."

"If this were Sourire de Reims Rosé and left long enough in the barrel before bottling, it would have bubbles, lots of bubbles. You'd smell the berries before you drank. Champagne is a celebration of music and the tongue. You're poorly served, Miss Brett."

Sopping up her grins, the laughing Miss Ross popped bread in her mouth. "I like her, Rebecca. Mary, let's give her a chance."

"Sourire de Reims Rosé? Kitty Hunter Clarke said she'd met a Negress on a royal boat off the coast of Jamaica. You wouldn't know—"

"Mrs. Clarke was a good woman. She lived a life of shame and beauty. But I only saw the beauty."

Today on the beach, Mr. King had told me of Kitty's passing. How could I explain the simple joy of receiving letters from her?

I wasn't about to get teary-eyed in front of strangers or rivals or whoever these women would be to me. Instead, I toasted memories.

Lifting my goblet high, I watched the fine crystal sparkle in the light. "To Kitty Clarke."

Miss Ritchie clinked hers with mine. "I can't wait to see what you think is better than this."

"So, ladies, have I suffered through this glass for naught, or did I pass your test?"

Miss Ritchie's smile pursed. "Not a test per se."

I stabbed my last piece of the tart plum. "Friends, foes, or friendly rivals?"

"Not quite rivals or foes," she said. "That leaves friends, I think. I think we'll grow to be good friends."

The stewing Miss Brett patted her fingers on a crisp white napkin. "You should look at the Werk-en-Rust area for land. Most of the area was an old cemetery. It's close to the Demerara River, the main waterway. It can have as much traffic as the Ritchie Royal Hotel."

Miss Ritchie put down her glass. "Bite your tongue."

"I'll look into that area. Thank you."

The ladies chattered among themselves, the latest gossip and politics of the colony. I sat observing them, marveling at the width and depth of their talk.

Except for Kitty Clarke and my family, I hadn't seen many friendly women who knew smart things. I had to admire women helping women. It felt right.

"What's wrong, Mrs. Thomas? Besides this champagne."

"All my life, I've been singled out as that one woman, that one different from the rest. Now I'm sitting with women, good powerful women. And you want to help me. That's different. I like this kind of different."

Miss Brett smiled. "My mother's my hero, but even she had never seen something like this till Demerara."

"To the Entertainment Society." Miss Ross raised her glass.

I gladly drank the bubbleless champagne, but my heart saw this and memorized their faces, the sound of their bold voices. I hoped this fellowship of smart women could outwit the men trying to stop me.

DEMERARA 1804: THE RULE

Sitting in the back of the dray with Charlotte, I watched Josephy drive up the trail. My fourteen-year-old lanky son took us to see farming land. I liked parcels in town, far out here meant a plantation.

Josephy completed schooling in Scotland at the Inverness Royal Academy. He came back excited about farming and spent months searching for the right plot. I fretted for him. Laborers for his dreams to make the land successful wouldn't magically appear. I couldn't get any for the parcels I bought in Werk-en-Rust.

The dray passed the wharf area. On the platform were half-naked men, barely in breeches. From the smell of mushrooms in the air, it meant their black skin had been shined with palm oil. The bugs, everything from chiggers to biting forty-leg centipedes, would be drawn by that scent.

"Mama?" Charlotte grabbed my hand. "Are you well?"

"Yes."

"But you're shivering."

"Nothing. It's nothing. I turned my neck the wrong way. I shouldn't look to the left."

With my eyes closed, I wished I had no soul like the rest of the planters, the enslavers of men. They'd use this labor to build. Not me, only free—free whites, free coloreds, or free Blacks.

My son turned his head, and I beheld a glorious grin. "Mama, wait until you see this acreage."

Our carriage headed down a dusty road. Cottonwoods, cedars, and palms lined our way.

"I've learned a lot from you," he said. "We head to Mahaica. It's perfect and only an hour away from Stabroek."

Soon, we parked in a clearing, a flat area with emerald bushes. Josephy jumped on his seat and threw both his arms high. "We're here. This land is for us."

He scrambled down and secured the dray. "Mama, sis. Let me show you where we will grow cane and coffee."

Charlotte walked forward cupping her eyes. "Lots of good cedar. Good hardwoods for building."

I kept my face even. I didn't want to give either too much hope if this wasn't a good investment.

"Look," he said as he walked into a small path cut between cedars, "it's nice acreage. No swamp. No mosquitoes."

Charlotte adjusted her blue bonnet and pressed forward. "Harry and Eliza can't get sick anymore. The wet season had them both coughing."

Never been as scared for my children as when I heard a rumble in their chest. "No bugs or illness is good."

My son towered over me. "Is this too much exertion? I know you haven't been sleeping."

I hadn't. Still not used to sleeping alone. Still not used to remembering what was gone. "I'm fine, son. Let's see what's beyond the trees."

The crash of waves, the sound called my name. I dashed forward.

"Mama, wait." Charlotte's warning wouldn't stop me. I had to see if these forty-eight-year-old ears lied.

At the top of the hill, the smell of salty air met my cheeks like a sloppy wet kiss. On this plateau, I could see everything—the sea, distant ships, peace.

The shade of trees offered a respite from the dry hot air. My sleeves stuck to me. A bead of sweat curled from my ear down my long neck. "This land, this is wonderful. I'll buy it, Josephy."

He grabbed his sister and started to dance. Just needed Polk's fiddle and this would be the sweetest place. If I couldn't have the shore in Stabroek, then I'd have it here. "Get the paperwork, Josephy."

"Mama, we should call it Roseau where you and Pa fell in love."

My son, the man with the tender heart. "No, that doesn't fit." I tapped my nose, then tapped his and Charlotte's. "A friend talked of how his pa loved outdoor spaces. I saw it once, walked it at midnight. Let's call it Kensington. This could be our Kensington Plantation."

Charlotte nodded. "Kensington sounds good, but can we afford this? I know you've been fretting over Catharina and Mr. Simon's finances."

Their situation had become dire. They were going to lose Chance Hall. I didn't know what to do. I was helpless watching planters—many of Cells's friends, some I'd served long ago at the Hermitage, some employed my housekeepers—call their notes and charge Simon so much interest.

I sucked in the hot air then sighed. "You let me and her father figure out what to do about Catharina, but this, my darling boy, my daring girl, is going to be ours."

I'd push back my plans for my hotel if I had to. It wasn't the money but the labor that slowed things. That and the planter men.

My son dashed down the hill. "I'm putting my feet in the water."

Charlotte didn't budge. "You sure you want me to help?"

"My girls are every bit as smart as my boys. And you, my Charlotte, know how to run an estate. Jean-Joseph use to brag on you. You can do it."

She looked down, like this good earth might open and swallow her. "Would Jean-Joseph be proud of me, knowing I've taken up with a white man? He hated them."

"He hated the evil they did, but Fédon loved you. He'd want you happy. I've seen how Fullarton treats you." I lifted her chin. "Like a jewel, a precious star."

"He's good to me. I'm a good wife, but we have no children. Maybe my barrenness is judgment."

I pulled her to me. "Don't you go doubting yourself. Babies don't make your worth. Having them adds to your happiness."

"Easy for you to say, Mama. You've ten children."

It wasn't easy for me. I couldn't tell her how I regretted some moments, how the birthing sadness stole my joy.

I hummed our hymn. *Rop tú mo baile.*

I sang away my sorrows and kept at it until she sang too.

The woods have always been good to me. It was my first church.

"Charlotte, if you never have a babe, birth something here in this land. Then be like my sister Kitty, the best auntie. That's honorable and decent."

She kissed my cheek. "Then maybe you should move forward. Papa Cells will be back for good in a few weeks. He never forgot you. He never remarried."

Before she started repeating the platitudes I'd offered to free Charlotte of her mourning robes, I waved to my son. "Josephy! Put your boots on. Let's head back."

He nodded and plopped down, tugging on his dusty boots.

"Mama," Charlotte said in her sweetest swallowlike voice, "Mr. Thomas has been gone almost six years. Papa Cells is coming back. He's waited long enough, don't you think?"

Josephy took his sister's arm and headed toward the dray.

I looked back at the sea. I was in love with my departed Thomas.

Nine years was a long time since I last saw Cells, but there was nothing to fear with him coming back, nothing at all. I charged down the hill knowing I still couldn't lie to myself even when I wanted.

My carriage stops on Lambeth Road at the Marine Society Office. Official buildings in London are hewn in fortified stone, very different from the wood government buildings of Demerara.

Seems to me Lieutenant Governor Murray would have time to build such great works if he weren't oppressing his vulnerable citizens. What good colonist wouldn't pay a fair tax to build lasting things?

A footman in a scarlet mantle helps me down. I glide to the pavement like I've taken a step on the ballroom floor. Part of me wishes this footman was Polk. My, how he'd love these streets.

Today isn't about dancing, it's about escape. Well, maybe those are two sides of the same coin.

I nod to the footman. "I'll send for you when I'm done."

"Very good, ma'am."

The fellow has perfected the disaffected smile. The awkwardness of being ordered around by a woman like me affects all men, until I tip them with a shilling. Money teaches respect quickly.

Sailing through the doors, I enjoy the scent of orange oil wafting in the air. Mr. King keeps a tidy office.

Before I announce myself, William King rushes from his office. He sweeps my old hand into his young strong one. He's his father's son, diligent with spectacles, honest. That's how I'll remember Thomas King.

"Please, Mrs. Dorothy, head this way."

The son tucks my arm into the crook of his. I'm proud of his success. I'm proud of how the Kings have grown my investments.

The door closes, and he has his palms out. "Give me. I know you have a sack of goodies."

I should tap those fingers with my fan, but I reach into my bag for two jars of preserved golden ginger, spicy and sweet, and another filled with tangy red guava jelly.

His round face lights up and he digs his fingers into the ginger before I can stop him. "Elizabeth is going to love these."

"That is if you leave any, greedy boy." I ease into the chair, all my nerves hidden in a smile. "How's Elizabeth?"

"She's well. She's been an aid to my mother. Father's passing hit us hard."

"Elizabeth's a sweet, diligent girl. I'm glad I introduced you."

"Me too." My godson is happy. His joyous blue eyes warm me. It always amazes me how the son of a slave transporter fell in love with a woman freed from slavery.

"Your pa turned out to be good."

William looks over his spectacles. "You gave him a way back, you know. He was tormented over what he'd done in his quest for riches."

"The chase will do that. No one is immune to poor choices."

"Well, transport is now illegal. With the talk of abolition heating up Parliament, I'm sure we'll see the end of legal slavery in our lifetime."

At sixty-eight, I truly wish it happens during my days.

William sits at a desk that's tall and wide, surely built by his family's fortune, but the son leads a charity organization for homeless boys. He taps the blotter on his desk. "My father took pride being the governor of the Foundling Hospital. He said it almost rivaled assisting you."

He scoops another ginger treat. His mouth puckers from the sweet fire. "You're not here to reminisce."

"You're King's son. I need advice. If I wish to sell all in Demerara, how long will it take? How much is at risk if I do?"

He scratches his chin. "The estates, the farming lands, everything? It's quite a lot of property. You sure you're looking to liquidate quickly?"

"If that means to sell fast at the best price, yes."

"Selling fast never gets the best price, but you know this." He eyes the jelly. "I need a crust of bread."

"Oattie bread?"

He nods and dumps two pieces of ginger in his mouth.

They burn his tongue. I remember how the treat always did. William's a man who likes pain and pleasure. His loving marriage to a colored woman cut him from many social circles, his work with abolition from others.

"You're sure you want to sell now, Mrs. Dorothy? I know Demerara has been chaotic. Perhaps wait a little longer."

"King, if I make this drastic change, I'll need your assistance and discretion."

"As always. Would you move to London or Glasgow or another of your islands?"

"Not sure. There are many places dear to me."

His eyes have a glow. Does he know this isn't my first time thinking of living in London?

He scoops up an additional piece of fiery ginger. "Is there a certain gentleman of the world you might be running away with? You have a great deal of spirit."

"If I do this, I'm not running to no man. More likely I'm running from them."

With his chin nodding, he adjusts his spectacles. "To make one of the bravest women I know flee, it must be a lot of men."

I wouldn't say it all now, not until my dear *damfo* told me meeting with Lord Bathurst was impossible.

"I'll look into things, Mrs. Dorothy."

"Thank you. You were your pa's joy, you and your siblings. Take comfort in that."

He walks me to the big area with clerks and desks. "I do. As Elizabeth reminds me, what happened cannot be erased. A pot of good now doesn't wipe away yesterday's stains. Sounds like something you'd say, Mrs. Dorothy."

"It does, doesn't it? Smart girl. Busy with your mother, she must not have time for anything else?"

"You know she does. Can't stop the woman and her projects if I tried." He kisses my cheek. "Elizabeth wouldn't want these men chasing you off. I'll let her know you're in town and to visit."

"Good. But do let her finish her project first."

"Oh, that's a given with my dear wife." William turns to one of his clerks. "Send for Mrs. Thomas's carriage. It should be in the King's Mews."

"That sounds royal unless it's one of your ventures."

"No, it's in honor of the new king."

"Yes, one of those Georges, George IV."

After a final hug, he leaves and I sit and wait. From the window, I see someone who looks familiar.

Tall, reddish-gray hair.

I close my eyes and wish I could unsee him, the likeness of him.

The man passing by the glass could be Nicholas Kirwan. His tyranny made me run to save my life. The Demerara Council is making me fear for my livelihood.

Breathe in. Breathe out. Breathe in. Out. The fellow passes. Old Mr. King told me Nicholas died in a bar fight in 1788. Someone finished Kitty's scar. His evil was gone.

Bathurst must stop the evil of the Demerara Council.

My *damfo* will gain this meeting. I believe she can.

I close my eyes. I'm Doll the dancer. She needs to live again in my head. She always has hope. She knows how to win.

DEMERARA 1805: THE ROBERTSONS

The sun set as my Eliza held Gilbert Robertson's hand in the living room parlor on America Street. Her high-waisted gown of muslin, with deep pleats that formed a train of beige and pink stripes, made my dumpling look taller, every inch a princess.

Eliza was a good girl. She deserved the world.

The cloudless day was perfect for their ceremony, which included signing of the concubine contract and a blessing from a minister, an Anglican one like Mr. Robertson.

"Mama, I'm happy." Eliza's eyes widened at the figure for her dowry, one thousand pounds. My housekeeping businesses boomed. Frances kept my services in Grenada and Dominica growing. A hundred and ten clients now in total between the islands. For Demerara, I was up to forty. Pity my land projects, my hotel and plantation, weren't thriving.

"Mama? You seemed distracted."

Blinking, I hugged her, a big bear hug like I was Thomas. "Your pa would be pleased at your smile."

Over her shoulder, I looked at my Demerara family—Charlotte and Fullarton; Lizzy, Coxall, and their brood; my sons; and Crissy gathered for this union. My heart thought of our loved ones in Grenada. "Your sisters, Frances and Ann, send you their love. I know everyone in St. George's does."

Only Catharina hadn't come or sent well wishes.

The Simon finances were worse.

And I'd said no again. No more pocket money. No more coming just to get money.

I hadn't seen her in a month. Money was all that tied us together.

My Harry picked up his fiddle. "I think there should be dancing."

He zipped a tune, almost as good as Polk.

Couples danced, and the younger children played in the place meant for Mamaí's garden.

I wished Kitty was here. Eliza was the child we shared, the one her goodness and mercy poured into when I had none.

"Mama, don't cry." She wiped my face. "You need to dance."

Charlotte's laugh drew me. She conversed with Lizzy. Charlotte's hand shifted from her flat belly to her hip.

"Eliza, you let your sister be a special aunt to your children."

"Mama, I might not have them right away."

"Oh, you will, child. Put those birthing hips to good use." The way Gilbert Robertson looked at my girl, I knew he'd prove me right. With Eliza's vigor for life and her seventeen years, she had time, a lot of it.

Robertson, the sandy-blond man, put a finger to her chin. "I told you, Eliza. I'd find a way to get you hired out to me. I'm glad it's for the rest of my life."

She gave him a small smile while her cheeks turned cherry red.

The fellow was besotted. I did my best to keep 'em apart until he begged to commit.

There were too many men like Cells coming to Demerara who had families across the seas. They wanted a housekeeper to clean and a harlot for their beds. Nothing wrong with the former or the latter if the woman chose and was protected when the fellow sailed back home.

My girls were special.

They were free. They wouldn't settle for anything less than a fully committed partner. We called it husband, official with papers. The men in charge only called our contracts common-law marriages when they wanted our assets.

Crissy and Lizzy's Dorothea talked in whispers. They weren't outside with the others. They were growing up fast, with shapes that said easy loving. Girls needed schooling before thinking of men.

My good friend Rebecca arrived carrying a bundle.

I kissed her cheek. "Glad you could come."

"Wanted to help you celebrate and to tell you my bricklayer would be available next week."

Hiring out laborers from other merchants and friends was costly and slow. It was all I could do. I handed Rebecca a proper glass of Rosé de Saignée. "It's not my favorite but look at the bubbles."

Rebecca took a sip, then another. "You shall now be in charge of any beverage service for the Entertainment Society."

I picked up a goblet and clinked my drink to hers, but my mouth became dry. Catharina and Cells stood at my door.

Charlotte, my peacemaker, went to Cells and her sister and drew them into my rooms.

"Dolly," he said. More gray in his salt-and-peppered hair, but his hazel eyes seemed lively, vibrant.

"Hello, Cells."

His mouth twitched. His gaze met mine, but Charlotte had his arm and led him to Eliza.

I watched him hug the bride, another common-law, Catholic-Anglican coupling.

Josephy pounded his chest. "To my sister, Eliza. We wish her great joy."

In the next song, I heard Thomas's words trying to tell me not to be alone, but I wasn't. He was in my head and in the joy and character of the children we raised.

After two glasses of champagne and well-wishers coming and going, Cells parked beside me, touching my arm beneath the cuff of my short sleeve. He looked good in his onyx tailcoat.

"You've done well, Dorothy. Another fine girl."

His part was a little deeper, but he still had thick hair, nothing receding. He'd gained a little weight in his face, making him look strong.

I was no spring chicken. I wasn't thin, not that I ever was after Catharina. Blessed with curves and pluck, I'd developed into a grown woman who needed no compliments on what was my duty. "Excuse me. Have to say good-bye."

"Of course. That's our pattern. Unless we are finally in the same place."

My mouth opened, but I quickly sidestepped him and went to

Eliza and Robertson. I walked them down the stairs and stayed until they left in his carriage.

Eliza waved. She looked happy. My heart was full.

Wiping my eyes, I lingered watching them head down America Street.

"Mama."

Catharina's voice.

I turned. She stood on the bottom step. "Eliza looks very happy. And Mr. Robertson, too."

"Yes. I'm glad you came to see your sister."

"You offered Eliza a dowry? A thousand or two thousand pounds?"

"That's your sister's business, Catharina."

"You didn't offer something like that for me."

"I wasn't informed of you *marrying* until I came to Demerara, five years too late. You're going on ten years of wedded bliss, far too late for a contract. With Simon's finances you could be attacked to his debts."

She smirked for a moment. "The word is *attached*. But I see your point."

"Do you, Catharina?"

She took my goblet from my fingers and sipped. "This is good and expensive. I think I deserve more consideration since you left me to pursue your dreams. Dreams that allowed you to afford such fancy champagne."

"Did Cells tell you that was my reason?"

"No, but look at you and how well the children you raised are doing. I've missed everything. Can't you see how I'm suffering?"

"Catharina, it's been five years of you using my guilt to get your way. No more. I even bought you a pew in a church in a faith I don't share." I kissed her brow. "Go on back upstairs and enjoy your brothers and sisters. Forget that you again tried to ask for money."

"Don't you care how I cried? How I always felt different? How when my baby sister was born and I was forgotten."

"Catharina."

"Don't you know how I wanted a large family to love me? Papa was always away and sulking when he was there. He missed Mama treating me different than her own flesh. Did you fight for me at all?"

It became hard to swallow again. I took my glass back. I wanted to shatter it, for my heart broke hearing her pain. "I wanted you with me, but your pa wouldn't allow it. He had a better life planned for you. I begged him to let you stay, but a woman has no rights when going against a man over property or children. Cells claimed you. He had power over me. There wasn't a tarn thing I could do to stop him taking you from my cradle."

"You're smart and wily, Mama Kirwan. You could've done something. You could've convinced him."

My child's use of Kirwan was as good as a slur from her pert lips implying my union was nothing. Had to remind myself that this was her pain talking, mouthing off to me.

"Catharina, you're smart. You have to take some responsibility for how your life has turned out."

"Things would've been much better if I knew you, but you didn't want me because my father didn't want you."

Maybe I could've fought harder. I relived those days so many times, but it was done. Nothing could change the past and this young woman standing in front of me didn't know her worth.

I reached for her hand. "Catharina, I named you after my dearest friend Foden's estate. I heard the name Catharina and it sounded so grand. I wanted you to be everything, to be grand. That's in your power now."

"How, when you won't help me? How, Mama?"

I regretted that I had had no power to keep her and hated that she didn't know how I fretted and cried for her and thought of her in my prayers at mass. Still did. I rubbed at my brow, wishing I had drunk more to numb the guilt that would always bubble inside over losing her. "Nothing can change the fact that I gave you up."

"Then help me now. Two thousand pounds could help us now."

"On top of the thousands I've already given you? No. Catharina, it's not enough to pay all your debts. You and Simon should sell Chance Hall and start over. I'll help you begin again. I've done it several times."

"No, Mama. We deserve a grand house. That's owed to us. We've suffered too much."

"The world doesn't give you what you deserve."

Her tears stopped and she shook with such violence. "It should. I've been cheated."

"You have." I reached for and held her to get her to settle, to let her feel the love in my soul, but she needed to listen. "You've lived with privileges none of my children have. No one knew you were my daughter. You never lived with people hating you for being born of a Black mother. In Demerara, Cells is well regarded. You chose to leave your father's protection and marry young. When are you going to take responsibility, even a spoonful?"

She broke from my arms, head wobbling. "No. We can't sell Chance Hall."

"Catharina, you have a daughter. You can't raise her to be strong without taking charge of your life."

She wiped at her eyes like she'd clawed them free. "It's your fault. It's your blood. You."

"My fault that you married at twelve? That your husband overspent? That he's bankrupt? That he didn't figure out how many people were against him and his faith before it was too late? I bear mistakes, but none of those are mine. They aren't your pa's, either."

Her face sharpened as her brow arched up. "You still want him?"

"What?"

"I can get him back for you. Papa said you loved him."

"I did when I was young and dumb."

Head thrown back, she crossed her arms. "It's never dumb to be lost in love."

"Yes, it is. You have to love yourself more than a moment, 'cause moments pass."

Catharina balled her fists at me. "That's not what my father said. I trust him."

"I've lived some things and thought I was ready to make every decision, but I was stupid just like you."

"I'm not stupid. D.P. loves me. He's dedicated to me."

"Then honor him. Don't come here playing little-girl games. Catharina, you're a woman, a married woman. Act like it. Henny's watching. Your daughter will pick up everything bad."

"No, she won't, 'cause I'll keep her from you. You have to be the cause of my failing."

I clutched my goblet tight about the stem. I thought it would break. "You need to go."

"You don't like the truth, Mama?"

"If you owned the part of me that's in you, you'd be with your husband and you'd figure out how to cut expenses, and not pressure him for trinkets to show off to people that hate him."

"That's not true. I'm good to him."

"Go home, little girl. Come back when you have your house in order. The next time, you bring Henny and any other children you may have. They need to know a woman who builds, not one who tears things down."

Catharina's face burned fiery red. "You know nothing." She pushed past me out the door and jumped into a carriage. She grabbed the reins and started it moving.

I let her go because I did know her. I was her. I prayed she'd come to herself, to grow and be what Henny and D.P. needed.

Of course with their carriage gone, I'd have to get Cells out of my house.

DEMERARA 1806: THE ROADBLOCK

Wednesday meant a trip to Kensington Plantation to check on Josephy. I leaned on the fence watching my hardworking young man. I needed a distraction. Crissy and I had just left Eliza. She lost her baby girl three weeks ago. The child had been doing well, then she wouldn't wake up. My Eliza was broken, and I had nothing to say to make it better.

Nothing.

It was hard seeing my bubbly child filled with sorrow, but I'd keep coming even if it was to sit beside her. She needed to know that the sun would rise, stars would shine, and her mother was there for her in the midst of the birthing sadness.

Josephy waved. "Mama, come look at this."

Walking through the plantings, I pulled at the leaves sheathing the stalks. The musty fragrance, the scent of virgin cane wafted. Green and healthy, with no white grubs or brown furry borers. This was good. "Josephy, you've succeeded."

"It's the rich ground, Mama. I wish I had more fields turned."

Wiping dirt from my palms, I went to the dray and climbed up next to Crissy. "This is something to be proud of. Maybe I should start calling you Thomas Jr."

He leaned on the fence. "Josephy is fine. Papa called me that." He put a long blade of grass in his teeth. His curly, curly hair had matted. The boy wasn't fussy like Harry, who hated to be untidy.

"Mama, next year I'm starting on the house out here."

"Dreams," Crissy said. "That's his."

My son laughed. "Tell Charlotte she was right. The irrigation for this section ran easier just like she said."

It was good to hear that from my boy, that he valued his sister.

That's what siblings should do. "You're lucky Charlotte has time now that she's running my store."

In addition to helping with my other businesses, Charlotte split her time helping Catharina with her new baby and the Kensington. My children supporting each other warmed my insides.

"Tell my sister I need her advice planning the next field. This one will be coffee as soon as we hire more workers." His face fell, joy flowing out of his frown. "Mama, I'm not asking you for more. You've done enough, but I wish we had more to hire out. Have you thought of buying—"

No slaves. "No, Josephy, I hadn't."

"The planters are withholding laborers on purpose. I heard that if they think we accepted their ways, things would be easier. That's what Mr. Cells said. I don't think he's wrong."

That tarn man had started warming up to Josephy and Harry. Now my eldest boy was preaching Cells's ways. Cells, the Hermitage's owner, a Demerara slave owner, a busybody who always tried to curry favor with men in power. "I know of coloreds who did the same and the white planter still made their way hard. In Grenada, that led to rebellion."

Josephy looked down. I shouldn't have scolded him for Cells's meddling. "Son, I'm sorry. I'm proud of all you've done."

He lifted his chin. A small smirk shone beneath his flat nose. "I guess I'm just going to marry and start having children or wait for all my nephews and nieces to come help."

Head shaking, I laughed. "No, you take your time and choose a wife wisely. I'll get us more workers, Josephy. You'll see."

"Thank you, Mama." He picked up his scythe and started cutting the brush.

I blew him a kiss and started the dray moving.

"Looks like bamboo in that field," Crissy said.

"It's filled with gold, my dear. Better than anything."

Her young face wrinkled with serious lines forming on her brow.

"Better than gold? Then maybe you need to do something to get Josephy help."

Her brown, almost black eyes were wide, innocent.

But mine weren't.

I knew the evil answer. I didn't tell my children about much of my life in Montserrat when I was part of the evil. Maybe I needed a reminder.

"Let's head back." I whipped the reins and started to town.

Crissy slipped her arm about mine, snuggling closer on the seat. "Mama, you hire out people to huckster for the store and for house-keeping. Can't you get some workers in exchange? Someone good on a plow? A bricklayer? A mason?"

I hired out women to be top-notch housekeepers, but I knew many were paid for sexual favors. I ignored the wrong. My distinction of respectability seemed hollow, hollow like bamboo.

"There's lots to consider, Crissy."

She shrugged and drifted back into her safe ten-year-old world.

"Mama, what about Mr. Cells? He comes to the house a lot. Charlotte says he has a big plantation, lots of workers."

No. No. No. He came around only to convince me I needed him. He made it seem as if he only visited to offer his opinion on Catharina and Simon. The man refused to do more for our daughter and wanted me to abide by the same. He hated that I'd paid to enroll Henny at Kensington School in London without consulting him.

Thomas King found a perfect place that would take free colored girls. The tuition and passage were costly, but Henny had to be better than me, better than Catharina. I was glad that my daughter didn't stop me from knowing that sweet girl.

"You're not going away again? You were gone almost three months."

"Harry started at Inverness Royal Academy. He'll do fine just like Josephy. And I had to check on Kensington House, to make sure it remains a good place. You'll be going to school there, too, when you are older."

Crissy's eyes grew big and sparkled like stars. "I get to be on a boat again! Wait till I tell Dorothea." Crissy was close to Lizzy's girls like my Ann and Frances in Grenada.

Frances's latest note told us that Sally had passed and that my darling Ann was expecting. Those dang Garraways were itching for a connection to my family, especially with Thomas gone. Her courtship was fast and unexpected. At least John Gloster Garraway was the best of the lot.

Ann was happy. I sent her the shiniest silver tea service I owned, Mr. Foden's set. It always meant so much to me.

"Mamaí, your grama, may come to visit next year. May even bring Aunt Ella and little Elizabeth."

"They all could come sooner if you weren't distracted by figuring out where to get workers."

This was true. I oversaw every step of my hotel's construction. With building stretching on for years not weeks, all my time was consumed. Whipping the leather strap against my palm, I made up my mind to reach for a solution. Cells. "Maybe I should talk to the owner of the Hermitage about hiring out his *workers.*"

"It shouldn't be hard, Mama. He likes you."

"What are you talking about, child?"

"He stares too much, like you're a roasted goose. I don't like it. Doesn't he know you're with my pa forever?"

Her tone was bold like an overseer's.

"Crissy, you want me to grow old alone?"

"I'm not leaving you."

"You will for school."

"I won't leave you here with a hungry man. Not for my mama."

Cells? He wasn't bad, but he wasn't good, either.

"Mama, you're thinking about him? What about my papa? Don't you still love him?"

My baby was just three when Thomas died. He was the best pa.

"You didn't answer, Mama. Charlotte was right. You like him too."

"I'll never forget your father. He was the best of me. I have a business to run. I may have to make some choices and ask favors to keep working on my dreams."

Crissy pulled away a little and stuck out her lip. "I don't like him."

If she knew Cells and my history . . . well, she'd still not like him.

Seeing him in town, at meetings, even by the shore, had become easier. When the fancy invitation to a ball he'd host on Friday at his Hermitage arrived, I was a little surprised.

Yet, the ask should've been expected.

When Demerara's governor used my business for his housekeeping, I knew it would be a sign of legitimacy to Cells.

He liked to be among the influencers. I was on my way to being one.

Charlotte had sent my refusal. Maybe I'd been too rash. If I could hire out Cells's workers . . . his artisans could finish my hotel this year. Then any free laborers could be hired for Kensington Plantation.

Then I'd owe Cells. What was in it for him? His price would be costly. Too costly.

"Maybe we should do something that's not business. Where shall we go this afternoon?"

Her face brightened with dimples showing. "Let's drive on Robb Street and look at the fashionable houses. I like when we do that."

Crissy was my dreaming child. She needed a bedchamber with a window pointing east to see the best stars. "It's Wednesday. We'll drive by our lot out at Werk-en-Rust and then on to the marketplace. Then to the fancy houses."

All Crissy's dimples bloomed. She was a garden of lotus flowers with her pink jacket.

Yet my sweetheart wouldn't be happy for long, not when she saw the bodies of women and men that looked like us, glistening and naked in the sun, awaiting purchase.

DEMERARA 1806: THE RHYTHM

I parked in the grass near a long stretch of sand along the river. The Demerara was smooth and calm today even with her waters filled with vessels.

On the left, the left side I tried never to see, were the flat-bottomed boats. It was Wednesday, auction day. Those vessels were filled with huddled masses of black and brown limbs.

I wasn't close enough to see their eyes, but I imagined them to be like Kitty's the day of her auction—bloodshot, bulging with fear, but dry from shedding too many tears.

When we lived at the Hermitage, my sister and I never came here. We never went anywhere on Wednesdays. I refused to see these boats when I walked to Foden's Anna Catharina. I couldn't believe I was here now.

Crissy tugged on my sleeve. "Mama, what is this? What are they doing to those people? Why are we here?"

Why were we?

'Cause I was too pigheaded to tell my children born free or almost free about the horrors of my pa's plantation, the killing system that the planters condoned.

'Cause I didn't want to ask Cells for help. Though he'd figure out a way to lie and make it feel like the truth, I couldn't be indebted. That was worse than selling my soul.

Adjusting the brim of my hat, I climbed down. "Stay here, child. Don't leave the dray."

Fear rolled in my gut, swaying me like a drunk as I crossed to the docks. Twenty feet from the first slave boat, the foul smell of palm oil and sweat and fear clogged my throat.

Crowded. The field, the boats. Some whites picnicked like it was entertainment.

An old man poked an enslaved girl in her shoulder with a cane like he prodded a sow. He came down and stood in the grass beside me. "Look, runaways gathered too. Just joking. You look too wealthy for that."

"Did you have to do that, poke her?"

"I'll do what I want with my money." His gaze swept over me like I was slathered in oil. "No ninny is goin' tell me how to buy *ninnies*. That's what I get for being civil."

I heard his words, but he didn't say *ninnies*. That was my head again, making the slights feel less like stabs. Hadn't heard that name said to my face in years. The money I had, the money I tried to protect, had kept the ugly away.

Being here was ugly.

Owning people was worse than ugly.

I tried to think I'd be better than these white men and women. I'd clothe my enslaved people. No one would fear rape. I'd get them blankets and big provision grounds to grow the food, all they wanted. I'd teach them how to save for their manumissions.

A hundred lies filled my chest, all to convince me I was better than these louts poking and cursing as they bought men and women.

Once I bid, I'd never go away from this decision. A little bad was still bad. A good owner was still an owner.

"Woman, you going to bid? I want to make sure to drive up the price. You look like you can afford to lose money."

No.

I wasn't one of them. Couldn't become one of *those* planters.

"You gone, dumb woman?"

From the old fool, I ran. In a blink, I was at the dray.

Crissy had stayed put. "Mama, what is it?"

"They think they're buying slaves, child, but they're not. They're buying stolen dreams. These planters accept that they can't make do any other way. I can't be one of them."

But I was them once. When I had Cells buy Kitty for me, that made me one.

Run to Cells. Run to him now.

I settled into the dray.

"You're going to buy a dream?"

"No. I'm going to get an agent. I thought he might be here."

Head down, Crissy became quiet. Maybe she accepted my lie or counted this as grown-folk business.

Come Friday, I'd secure an agent, someone to handle what I had no stomach for. One man had already proved to be perfect for the job.

My horses slowed then stopped outside of the Hermitage. My driver bounced out and helped me down. My gown of plantain yellow with a gauzy overdress the color of the creamy white flesh of mammee apples fluttered as I walked.

Moving slowly up the stairs, I tried to think of how to ask, then what to ask, and more importantly what I was willing to pay. With Cells, there had to be something in the deal for his benefit.

The music and heat hit me as soon as I entered the hall. Years ago, the Hermitage parties hosted fiddles and flutes. This tune was strange. I'd have to peer into the drawing room to find out.

Past his study, I lingered at the portraits. If I'd not pinned my turban perfectly to show off my curls, big sleek spirals, I'd doff my pale yellow hat to the lone female. I'd come to this house a servant and returned looking the part of a conqueror. The aunt must approve.

Then I caught sight of a new painting. In a thick gilded frame was the massa of the Hermitage. John Coseveldt Cells in the power and strength of his youth, clad in his favorite whites—white embroidered jacket, big cravat, waistcoat and breeches, even white leather shoes.

In a moment, I was young, in my jet maidin' outfit setting the table, looking at all the things I'd never beheld. Then I became his Bilhah enjoying private suppers in his study, listening to Charlotte and Edward dash through the halls.

The memories brought a flush to my fifty-year-old cheeks.

Time to find the original massa before I was a sweaty fool. I stepped into the dining room and walked to the threshold of the drawing room.

All the doors and windows were wide open. A tiny breeze sauntered through, warm and spiced with heady lotus lilies and peppery fever grass.

A young woman exhibited on a boxy-looking thing that made the music.

Polk, good old Polk, in a starched black mantle, came into the dining room. He bore a silver tray. "Mrs. Dorothy, I thought Mr. Cells said you weren't coming."

"Changed my mind." I put my hand on his arm. "Good to see you."

He lowered his tray of crystal goblets filled with claret. "Here. One of his finest wines. You're a guest." Polk shook his bald head and made a *uh-uh-uh* sound. "Oh, if Mrs. Randolph could see you now, she'd bust something. The woman went to live with her children three years ago, but she'd love to see you in your glory."

I finished one glass then took another of the fruity wine and looked at my reflection in the shiny crystal. Full-figured, thick thighs swathed in silk, ebony skin polished with coconut oil, bright light eyes filled with hope, and no silver yet in my curls—broken pieces, reworked by time and fire, clean up good.

"Join the guests in the drawing room, Mrs. Dolly. Massa is having his daughters play the new pianoforte."

Daughters? I sailed through the threshold. Catharina sat at the chestnut box too. She'd been shadowed from my view. My heart swelled with pride as I saw her making music.

My Catharina, now twenty-three, looked calm and assured

exhibiting. My palms became slick, hoping for her. A young brunette sat with Catharina, must be Cells's other daughter. He stood near, tapping the top of the pianoforte.

Seeing him there supporting both girls made me feel good.

Then he saw me, his smile widening. I returned to the dining room and put my goblet down and wished my heart would settle.

When I looked up, Cells was at the door. His grin spread to his hazel eyes. This look of approval was for me, me alone.

Clapping broke our shared glance.

He put my palm to his arm and led me inside. "Everyone is dancing. My daughters will continue to indulge."

Cells had never done that at any of his parties, touch me or place my arm on his. These events were scripted. Music and exhibition, dinner, then dance, but no us, just them and this world of finery and flattering talk.

The girls played again.

Catharina beamed in my direction, then bent her head to the big music box.

"If everyone is to dance, that would mean us, too, Mrs. Thomas. It's two-four time. I'm sure it wasn't the popular dance the last time you were in London, in eighty-nine."

"The last time, Cells, was last year. In 1805, I'm sure I'd heard of a country dance."

The surprise in his face, the hint of pink in his cheeks made me chuckle. The all-knowing man didn't realize that I kept going across the sea even without a prince.

"We should join them, Dolly. I did ask everyone to dance."

The rhythm came to me. It prickled my skin.

Cells drew me to the center, close to where his guests danced. We clapped hands and exchanged sides in rhythm to the song. Expert that he was, he'd kept us moving until we were a part of the line. The parade of turbans and headpieces—pinks and yellows and golds, with feathers and without—bowed in front of their partners. The crowd of planters and politicians and wives swayed and hopped and spun.

As I mimicked what everyone else did, I studied faces and the lack of ones. D.P. Simon wasn't here, neither were any of the women who'd helped me. I was the only free person of color with an invite.

That hit me hard.

These people, these planters and politicians and maybe wives, too, were the folks I battled to hire free laborers. The men gaily dancing without a care plotted and made things difficult. They had no problem hiring my housekeepers or buying my huckstered goods, but growing cane or running an exquisite hotel or having dreams of being more was wrong to them. They'd smile in my face and ruin me like they had D.P.

No more twirling or giving away my cares to the rhythm. I let go of Cells. "Excuse me. I need some air."

Head held high, I moved to the closest garden door and escaped.

I had only four more paces, then I'd be at my carriage and away from this party, away from the Hermitage. The torches lining the path exposed hibiscus bushes and the cannonball trees I loved.

"Mama?" came a voice behind me.

Shuddering, stopping, I turned. "Yes, Catharina."

Dressed in a light blue gown with white satin gloves, she clasped her hands as if she were nervous. "I'm glad you came tonight, Mama Thomas."

"I'm glad too. You play beautifully."

She shook her head. "I'm grateful. I finally saw you and my father together. Now I believe him when he said I was created in love."

Catharina came to me. With tentative arms, she embraced me.

My eyes were wet. "I may not have made all the right decisions, but know I loved you the moment you moved in my stomach. I wanted nothing but goodness for you. I still want that." I touched her face, drawing a finger down her nose, landing in that wonderful cleft in her chin. "It's Friday, Catharina. Simon is home worshiping. Go see him, support him. There are forces against him because of his beliefs and probably because he married you. Having me as one of your mothers will do that."

She locked her arms tighter about me.

If coming to the Hermitage was for this, then I was full. I'd figure out how to fight for my building tomorrow.

"Do you still love my father?"

Her question echoed against my chest, vibrating deep. There were things I missed, would always miss when Cells was my friend. "I did long ago."

"Don't go." John Coseveldt Cells appeared on the porch. He

clasped the rail with his solid hands. "Dolly, dinner hasn't been served."

"I need to leave, Cells."

Catharina clasped my arm. "Oh, stay for a little longer. I'll play again."

"Dear girl," he said to her, "go entertain our guests. I think your mother came to talk to me."

Our daughter's gaze swiveled between us. "I think I'll leave early, Father. Good evening." She went back toward the house.

"She's me, Cells, wanting Pa and Mamaí to reunite." I touched my brow, smearing beads of sweat. "Coming was a bad idea."

Cells trotted to me. "You came to talk, Dolly. Come inside." He clasped my hand like he always did, strong and gentle, and led me straight to his study.

The door shut. Music seeped through his wall of books. "So what is it that you've come to say?"

"Where's the small talk, Cells?" I moved from him to the shelves. "Show me a new book in your collection." I swiped my gloved fingers along the surface. "No green dust."

"Small talk is what you want?" He stood beside me, the click of his dancing heels announcing him as much as the rush of my heart.

He tilted his head and looked at me the way he did, the way he always did in here, even when I didn't understand.

"Not much has changed since Barbados, except we both are widowed. You have Catharina in your life. My vain attempts at giving her the world can't be held against me."

One hand went to the shelf above me, the other to my right, and he leaned in. If I moved an inch, I would feel his white silk waistcoat, the silver threading on the buttonholes.

"I've been respectful, Dolly. I let you grieve. I let you come back to Demerara on your own. I've even kept my distance while you settled. Have I been punished enough? What will you hold against me that's not your beating heart?"

His head dipped to my parted lips. He kissed me softly.

I didn't jerk away. It had been too long since I'd been desired.

He pulled back a little, then he dove in and kissed me like he always did with everything.

Wild, pressing against me, he swept me against his dustless bookcases, and I let him.

He ruined me again, with a touch that said I was all he'd ever wanted. With his lips on mine, I panted and dove my fingers into his shorter cropped hair, that curled about his ears.

When he became more insistent on searching the pleats of my gown, fingering the low cut of my bodice, I remembered myself and stepped to his side. "I didn't come for this."

"But you're here, Dolly. It's time to get us right. Come back to me."

He caressed my face again and he devoured my mouth and my will to resist.

But I had to.

His passions were bigger than mine, but this time I couldn't give in or look away or surrender. I clutched his hands and backed up. "I'm not returning to you, but I need your help."

Breathing hard, he moved to his desk. "Same thing, Dolly."

"That's your terms? Well, at least I know how being indebted is a benefit to you."

"From what I remember, we benefited each other." He sat, his fingers latching on to the edge of the desk. "Tell me what you want?"

"Without any conditions, let me hire out your men skilled at building. I have a hotel that barely has its foundation. My son is desperate to grow his plantation. He needs help too."

"Ah, the Kensington. A nice touch to remember the prince. His favorite palace?"

"His grandmother's, actually."

Flames erupted in Cells's squinting eyes. His lips thinned. "That's funny, Dolly. Polk says Joseph Thomas Jr. was born in eighty-nine."

Early in ninety, but I wouldn't correct him. "His birthday has passed if you are so concerned."

Cells laughed. "Twenty-one-year-old Frances, does she ever ask about Captain Owen?"

"You're jealous of a prince and a sea captain? How awful for you."

"How could I not be when we share the same taste in women?"

If he thought that a slight, he was wrong. "The prince didn't mind sharing a boat with me. My black skin was beautiful to him. My dancing, too. Men with true power aren't threatened by me at all."

A twitch went across Cells's cheek. "Such aspirations, Dolly, to be a royal concubine. Perhaps the idea came from all the fairy tales I read Charlotte and Edward."

I wasn't sure how low a jealous Cells would strike and wasn't waiting around to find out. "Thank you for the invitation. Good evening."

He blocked my path. "I turned my world upside down to come to you in eighty-nine. I'd separated from Fanny, embarrassed her with all her society. I'd filed the paperwork for divorce in her native Scotland myself. I had it all planned and you hadn't the decency to tell me that you didn't love me anymore. I had to see a sketch of you and the prince in heat."

"Cells, that was a long time ago. Don't—"

"I knew you were ambitious"—he rubbed his neck, pushing at his thin cravat—"but to bed a man who considers you a dame de couleur, his nickname for island whores, that's unfortunate."

"William wouldn't. He'd never—"

"William, is it? He blamed them for his ills when he toured the West Indies."

Cells sounded angry and entitled, but he wasn't entitled to me.

"Massa, you expected I'd be waiting for you? Was I to put my dreams on the shelf waiting for when it was convenient for you to love me?"

He rubbed at his mouth. "I'm selfish, Dolly. Always have been. But I've never loved anyone but you. The lies that were given to me to uphold made my life hard. I was desperate to keep them, to keep my position. Then I met you and from the beginning you were this light with big, bold dreams. Who wouldn't be drawn to that?"

"Then why do you wonder about the prince?" I meant it as a joke, but Cells's face became bright pink from ear to ear.

"Is Frances mine? Does Josephy rightly belong to that damned prince who made love to you and then gave speeches in Parliament about how the enslaved wanted to be enslaved? Happy Negroes, he calls us."

"Us? Feeling a might free with your words given your party guests are next door. Cells, what are you talking about?"

He started to chuckle. "You're better than me, Dolly."

"I thought we'd established this before eighty-nine."

"You're better than me at keeping up all the pretenses. How many secrets are in your head? How many men have been drawn into your light until they are too blind to see themselves burning?"

"That sounds very bitter. I didn't know I was more powerful than you."

"Dolly, I hurt you, and now you'll never give yourself fully to anyone. That heart in you is hard. You'll never risk anything for love. Did Thomas just accept that, like he accepted Josephy?"

Cells had made me the master of his fate, of Thomas's and the prince's. It was awful for him to believe that I was cold when I simply found a way to survive. My strong will kept me sane and whole and protected. "You've saved these lies for me all these years. I don't know what to say."

He ran a hand through his hair. "You could answer my questions."

"What's in it for me, Cells? Dolly, the evil temptress of men, it makes you sound so weak."

Cells's smirk returned. "Or it exposes you as an opportunist. Many island women latch on to the planters to better themselves."

"Then I would've latched on to Foden, the only man who was a true friend."

Cells raised his palm as if to argue my point, but he slapped it against his side. "I was a friend. You know that. You've come for my help, but don't want me. Fine. Give me the truth."

"Will this truth give you comfort because you won't have to reject Frances for not being as pale as Catharina?"

"I want the truth. You want my laborers, you tell me. Or be content with huckstering and housekeeping. I've heard of your difficulties finding labor."

I sighed, the frustration churning in my gut. "Why did I expect help from you? You're one of them, an old man set in his thinking. You're like the fools who eat at your table, laugh at your jokes, and make you so careful—their opinions matter more than your own blood. Those old men are making sure our daughter's family suffers. And you're letting them. Well, you always wanted to be one of them, an old white man."

"Catharina chose her path. It's not what I wanted for her."

"And you let her suffer. Your friends who dance on your polished floors persecute Simon because of his faith. Simon is punished because his principles won't change. But that was never your problem, changing."

The look in Cells's eyes. The hazel had become icy. He wasn't going to lift a finger to help. He'd have no problems closing his fist to the woman who got away.

Then I'd be the vision of who he thought I was. A dame de couleur, the harlot.

I went to Cells and put my arms about his neck.

"Dolly, what?"

Like I'd done with Catharina, I hushed him, putting my finger to his nose, his lips. Chased shadows in the cleft of his chin. "Shhhh."

"I'm sorry, Dolly. We . . . I can fix things. If we could—"

One kiss to his right cheek. One to his left.

Then I put my lips to his and enjoyed his husky breaths. He murmured sorries, whispers of love, and a moan to start again.

It was good.

It felt right.

But this was my good-bye the only way he'd understand. I finished this kiss and went to the door.

Chin up, turban in place crowning my curls, I left Cells and didn't look back.

My driver saw me on the steps. He pulled my carriage in front, and I climbed inside. "Home as fast as you can."

I knew what I had to do. I had to beat the old men at their game and do things that sickened me. On Wednesday, I'd take a purse full of coins, and stash clothes and food and blankets in my dray to cover the nakedness of the men and women I purchased.

Those dreamers would be safe with me. I'd teach them how to make their way in this world and how to dream again. I wouldn't make their path to manumission hard.

These were the vows I said as I prepared to sell my soul. If I had to be a full member of the planter class, the slaveholding class, I'd be a better massa than them all.

GLASGOW, SCOTLAND 1810: THE TRAVEL

Glasgow had the best air, fresh and cold. I stepped off the boat with nineteen guests, nineteen pieces of my heart in all—each of Ann's and Eliza's children, Catharina's older ones, and all Lizzy's children and her children's children came with me, as well as Charlotte, Crissy, my grandniece Elizabeth, and my son Harry.

The seven-week passage was easy. The children laughed at the heavier clothes—my girls' scarlet capes, my boys' long greatcoats of brown wool—until we hit the chilly air.

Josephy wouldn't leave the estate. Even the temptation of seeing the actual Kensington Palace in London didn't tempt him. I intended to see William this time. Perhaps it was for the best that Josephy didn't come.

Charlotte came down the ramp with Lizzy's youngest, Anna, in her arms. Both sets of topaz eyes beamed. "Thank you, Mama," she said, "and I must thank Papa Cells too. If he hadn't encouraged me, I would have missed this." She hugged her niece.

"The man knows you deserve to see what stars look like over here."

Charlotte giggled. "This is exciting."

I knew she had a dream, Lizzy's Anna in her arms. Hopefully, this visit could encourage Charlotte to grab new ones, ones that would be solely hers, not her husband's or a want of a baby.

"Oh, Papa Cells wants to do better. He's trying."

Maybe he was.

As if our argument had shook something loose in him, Cells fended off Simon's creditors as long as he could, but Chance Hall was sold off. Before we left, I gave my son-in-law a calabash for his special sand. Then he could carry his worship anywhere.

"Oh, Mama. Papa Cells gave me a note for you. I'll read it to you when we get settled."

"A note? Yes, save it for London."

"Yes, Mama. Come on, Anna." Charlotte swaddled the fidgeting girl and walked down the gangplank.

I covered up with my heavy shawl, counting my family as they left the sloop for the dock. "Can you keep up, Elizabeth?"

"Yes, ma'am, Aunt Dorothy."

Little Elizabeth Penner wasn't little anymore, but a lanky twelve-year-old. I made her cape black to honor the passing of my sister Ella. Frances said Mamaí grieved hard. I thought of my Edward and how hard it was to outlive your child.

Eighteen-year-old Harry took my arm. Big like his pa, he'd become my protector. "My schooling at the Inverness Royal Academy was good, Mama. I enjoyed it, but I'm anxious to see London."

"When I filed the papers to quit the colony for our trip, you can't imagine such noise they made. Me bringing nineteen, not just one or two."

"Pa would be proud. He always wanted this."

That was true. *Godspeed, Thomas darling.* Part of the sea we'd passed through had to be stirred by his hand.

Harry's chin lifted. My boy was brilliant. He'd use his book learning to become a solicitor. Like Thomas, he made it his job to review my transactions.

Harry must've read my thoughts. He bent and kissed my cheek. "No fretting."

"Just thinking of your pa. He wanted all of you to see the world. I wanted us to own it. We were a perfect match."

William King, my godson, waved at us from the dock. He'd grown tall, just like my Harry, but his frame was stocky like his father's.

"Mrs. Thomas, ma'am," he said, giving me a hug. "Father sends his regrets, but he'll meet us in London. Then when all is done, I will return with you to Demerara."

"You're coming back with us?"

"Yes, ma'am. It's been too long since I've been. Father is giving me more responsibilities. I wish to be half the man he is."

Harry took the hands of two of my Coxall grandsons. "Come along, gentlemen. Let's make sure our portmanteaus and trunks are transferred to Mr. King's carriage."

"I hope more than one, godson. We are a large and merry party with sharp elbows. We need room."

William made a grand show of counting each. He was very much his father's son, all the good pieces, the humor and loyalty.

Mr. Thomas King liked to say he turned over a new leaf in his life when we partnered. For my part in that, I was pleased. "William, you and your father will love to see my hotels."

"Hotels?"

"Well, the one at Werk-en-rust is done and booming, but the new house in Cumingsburg, I may turn that into one, too."

"But wasn't it for your particular use? It sounded perfect for you to slow down and enjoy life."

"I'll never slow down, never unless I'm ready for the ground. The house I'm building on Robb Street will be the grandest of all." My bedroom and that of Crissy's will face east, the direction of the most stars in Demerara's sky.

"Mama," Crissy said and slipped in between us, batting her eyes a hundred times at William. "I don't think I should be going away to school, yet. I should return to Demerara and be of more help to you before I settle down with my own household."

Not even subtle. She added more lash batting.

Where was this sense of desperation coming from? Crissy was pretty and smart. I wished she and Elizabeth would bond. They were close enough in age. Maybe some good sense would rub off on one and the joy of living to the other.

Oh, dear.

Crissy grinned again at my godson. No boys or men for her yet. She was fourteen and to be enrolled in Kensington House. With an education, she could rule the world or at least run the one I'd built.

William patted her arm away like the good boy he was. "Oh, Dorothy Christina, you have many years before you need to be thinking that way."

Humor stirred in my heart but I dared not let it spill. Crissy had a daring streak in her. She'd lived on Catharina's tales of compromises and intrigues from her time in London. My Crissy would be bold enough to try to ensnare a prince. I needed her on her best behavior when we met mine in London.

Prince William. So many years since eighty-nine. So many changes. I'd become a bigger success but at the cost of compromising and ceding to things I never thought I would.

"Mama?" Crissy tugged my arm. "What's that faraway look?"

"Oh. I was thinking of Kensington. Kensington House for young ladies. You'll be trained in languages and accounting in addition to math and reading. And Henny's there."

"Your mother's right." William took my hand. "Her endowment will keep it going."

Endowment was fancy talk for investment. I had more money than anyone could count. The risks I took, the bit of my principles and soul I sold, had beaten the men of Demerara.

They couldn't stop my rise. I gave penance with endowments to schools for free coloreds, but I could not deny that I had become what I hated: a slaver to best other slavers.

Dark faces, like mine, passed us to work on the ships in port. Freemen. Each of my enslaved could gain their liberty. Each of mine knew the amount to save for their manumission, forty pounds. I set the path and made sure each was trained. The world was changing. Abolition couldn't be that far off, not the way white and Black kept mixing.

Crissy slowed her steps behind a redcoat soldier who tipped his hat.

Henny and Crissy were close in Demerara. I wished Henny wanted to stay at Kensington House. She'd convinced me to look into Marylebone School. Marylebone was a place that excelled in music studies. Henny's voice had turned into one of an angel. Kensington House had no dedicated music teacher. I hoped this visit would change Henny's mind and keep my girls together at Kensington.

My daughter lingered behind waving her fan at another man in a scarlet uniform.

"Crissy, come on."

She offered me a pout but obeyed.

Wished she had more sense.

"William, do we visit Inverness Royal Academy today? I have two Coxalls and a Robertson to enroll."

"No, today we get you all settled. Tomorrow, the academy."

Harry beamed and tugged on his chocolate lapels. "The boys will love it. King George III gave it a royal charter. You will see, Mama. It is a wonderful place for learning."

My life was to be firmly rooted in King George III's influence, from towns with his namesake, to his son the prince, and to taking my money to educate my blood.

Prince William, I'd see him at a public dinner. No mole in the shadows this trip. My wealth ensured it. Hundreds of housekeeper contracts, the best artisans, and my land had made me one of the richest women in Demerara.

When I saw him, the prince, what would touch my heart first—the memories of what we shared or his "happy Negro" talk? Cells wasn't just jealous about my affair with the son of a king, he'd been truthful. The prince had changed and made pro-slavery speeches that could be voiced by the worst planters.

How do you speak truth to His Majesty's son when your hands were also soiled?

The words would come to me. They always did, wise or not.

LONDON, ENGLAND 1810: THE BALLROOM

Our carriage slowly entered Bushy Park. It was dusk. The fading sunlight kissed the jade grass that lined the graveled trail. William loved walks. I could see why he chose a place outside of crowded London.

We passed Kensington Palace on the way here. The daffodils were in bloom by the fence. My cheeks surely flushed thinking of a midnight walk on the arms of a sailor who kissed me after he placed a single yellow flower in my loosed hair.

The house came into view but not before I saw paths lined with daffodils. My pulse raced and I pushed from the window.

"Mama." Crissy's voice was a whisper. "You're fidgeting. You'll tear that fan the way you are jostling it."

My hand had the lace thing vibrating. I stuffed it into my reticule and tugged up my slipping satin gloves. I wished Charlotte had come. She had a calming way about her. She remained at my leased house with the rest of the grands and my son. As I dressed, she read me Cells's letter.

It was filled with more sorries. This time those words penned by Coseveldt felt sincere. Then she read to me the note he sent after I left his party, when I had intended never to see him again.

He'd included a clipping of Prince William's 1799 speech to Parliament. Ten years from our voyage on the *Andromeda*, our romance in London that changed my world, the prince accepted the *happy Negro* talk of the planters.

How could the prince forget our affair of equals? Why did his liberal mind close?

Maybe he did go mad as he'd feared.

I'd know tonight.

The carriage stopped on the south side of Bushy House.

It was breathtaking. All brick. Fourteen windows on this face. Prince William's residence was large. Not since the Nidhe Temple in Barbados had I seen curved walls. Bushy House bore rounded sections that curled and fanned out on either side of the main building like swallows' wings.

The similarities—this had to be a sign.

A footman handed me out of the carriage. My fingers were sweaty even with the chill in the air. The lack of heat did nothing to make my gloves stick less to my palms. My eyes trailed to the green-gray slate tiles of the roof. Stacked tightly together, they looked like Roseau's reeded housetops. Another mirror? So much of my life's journey was reflected here.

When I saw Mr. and Mrs. King coming, I whispered to the Holy Father to give me strength and those right words to change my prince's mind on his politics.

"Shall we, ladies," King said, and we followed him to the doors on the left, the left that had always meant trouble.

At the entrance, servants took my heavy shawl and the capes of my girls—Crissy, Elizabeth Penner, and my granddaughters, Henny and Dorothea. Dorothea was my namesake among Lizzy's daughters.

Inside, my eyes went to the ceilings. Like the wings outside, they were curved above. The trim was the whitest I'd ever seen. Hanging, floating in the air were chandeliers of beeswax candles.

The scent of the dripping wax possessed the fragrance of vanilla. I thought of Simon's chandeliers. They were sold off. He and Catharina and their family moved into my hotel at Werk-en-Rust. My heart was heavy for them. I hoped Cells comforted each one as they settled. *Holy Father, let all be well and for Simon to have brought his sand.*

Dorothea linked her gloved hand to my arm. "Grama, you stopped. Is this protocol, like the curtsy?"

"No, dear, just a rest."

Her grasp remained strong, the hold was as if she needed to pick me up from a faint. I wiggled a little and freed myself.

"Mama, this is no town house. It's a grand mansion." Crissy's tone sounded polished, but her eyes were as big as guineas. The child had seen nothing yet. My old friend knew how to give a party.

Quiet, brown-skinned Elizabeth smoothed the pale blue silk of her sleeves. More modestly dressed than the others, she wore her gloves pulled up so as not to show her elbows. I had silver ribbon woven under her bodice and the round neckline. The fullness of the dress had hints of embroidered pink and blue roses. She was a fresh garden right after the rainy season, the best time for flowers to grow.

The fabrics for Crissy and Henny I'd chosen to add warmth to their fair skin. My Crissy looked stunning in a gold-colored dress that floated to her ankles, exposing matching satin slippers. Henny wrapped herself in light orange silk with box pleats down her back forming a train. She'd gained some hips. If she danced, I hoped the shapeliness added to her poise.

Dorothea wore blush pink, which drew out the red tones of her olive skin. Her short sleeves were puffed and stiffened with muslin. The delicate embroidery that took a week to complete displayed like a coat of arms down her bodice. I hoped the vines and blooms meant strength.

It gave my heart joy watching them be fitted and measured and treated like princesses. The milliners and haberdashers and mantua-makers coming to and from my leased residence had only seen such a sight back in eighty-nine. My girls, my colored girls, were able to witness money trumping race in a flourish of ribbons and bows.

Mr. Thomas King took my hand and his wife's, then led us down the polished wood floor to the drawing room. The old man was dapper in his black tailcoat and pantaloons. In a way, the old dress had returned with the length of men's jacket fronts again cutting across the hips.

His wife in blue and Mechlin lace dressed her silver hair more naturally with pinned curls and tea roses, no powder. I was glad to see those flakes lose favor.

A man in a cranberry red mantle stepped forward. "Mr. and Mrs. King and Mrs. Thomas."

All the important *S*'s said aloud.

We entered the ballroom.

Silence swept through the crowd.

The drumming of my heart, the fluttering of our slippers, and the swaying fans pricked my ear.

People pointed, but we moved about the floor with our shoulders level, our heads high.

I warned the girls to expect such stares, even leers. Though fashions changed—the cut of a coat, the drape of a dress, the style and length of curled hair—the heart of most was the same, stuck in the old ways.

Seeing colored girls led by me, a woman with beautiful jet skin invited to the prince's ballroom, must be shocking, causing such stirs.

Music and conversation started again.

"Ladies, let me go see who else has arrived." The Kings left us at the rear of the room.

I took my fan out and waved it, but I looked through the lace at my young women, free, intelligent, with their lives ahead of them. May they forever be enriched by this moment.

This visit across the sea, this dinner with royalty should let them know nothing could stop their rise.

The smell of sweet sage wafted. My breath caught at the sight of the large glittering chandelier. Cut glass, broken and shaped into long straight calabashes hung on the wrought-iron fixture below a ring of candles. The light shone on us, on colored girls readying to greet a prince.

LONDON, ENGLAND 1810: THE TEMPLE

I saw him, my old love, enter Bushy House's ballroom. The man in cranberry announced Prince William as His Royal Highness, the Duke of Clarence.

His swagger had aged. His hair was full white, but he still held command as if he stood at the helm of a frigate.

"This way, ladies." Mr. King walked us to the center of the room, right under the sparkle of the chandelier.

"Miss Kirwan," the prince said.

"Yes, Your Highness."

I pushed at my skirt, a white silk that made waves about my ankles, and took a deep bow, then I rose.

"It's Mrs. Thomas now. A lot of changes have happened since we last met."

Prince William's gaze fell on me and perhaps the twinkle of gold braiding stitched to my bodice, a special reminder of his military uniform and our time together.

The man needed to remember that season or he'd never listen, never change.

"This is Mr. King and his wife," I said.

They curtsied and bowed.

William acknowledged them and then half turned to the woman who joined us. "And this is Mrs. Dorothea Bland."

His Dorothea. His other Dorothy.

I looked at the woman who might've been me. She was a pretty woman with dark hair and eyes. Her smile was small, almost happy. I wondered if I'd stayed in London, would William and I be together? Would I have guided him to the right side of things, like the support of abolition?

Mr. King didn't bow to Miss Bland. His chin barely dipped. He explained earlier that Miss Bland was not William's duchess.

Still, I nodded, good and deep. As one concubine wife to another—I must give my due. "Pleased to meet you, ma'am."

Her mouth opened and pressed into a deep circle. "The duke talks of the dames de couleur he met through his travels." Miss Bland offered me a sly wink then hid behind her lacy fan. "Such fun talk."

The prince's cheeks darkened. For a moment I sensed tension growing in his face, the slight flaring of the nostrils we shared. "Mrs. Thomas," he said, "introduce me to your fine daughters."

It was sweet he thought me young enough to have borne all these girls. "This is my daughter Dorothy Christina, my grandniece Elizabeth, and my granddaughters Henrietta and Dorothea."

I waved them forward, and as we'd practiced, they dipped like hummingbirds nipping nectar, graceful and precise.

Miss Bland motioned to a young lady. "The duke and I have ten children, the FitzClarences. Augusta is one of our daughters. Augusta FitzClarence, these are the Thomas girls."

The young woman lowered her chin. She was the image of her mother with William's dark eyes.

With pleasantries exchanged, I caught the prince's gaze roaming about the room.

It saddened me that he was still searching.

He glanced toward an exit. The outside glowed with torches. "Are you fond of the weather, Mrs. Thomas? I remember you thinking it cold in London."

"I like the cold now. It offers brisk conversations."

He placed my hand on his arm.

Our steps left a wake of open mouths and hot whispers, but we took a turn about the crowded ballroom together.

We kept going and slipped out the doors to his lawn.

Like we had long ago in the gardens of Kensington we walked. Silent and steady with my hand clutching his forearm, we moved away from Bushy House.

"Dorothy," he said in a voice a little louder than the breeze, "I'm informed that you've made quite a success of yourself. I hear that you're one of the wealthiest women in all the colonies. Your choice to go back to your life was the correct one."

His compliment teased my nervous smile. "Thank you. I heard your father is ill again. I'm sorry."

"The king won't recover this time." He patted my arm. "Let's stroll a little more. I'm partial to the exercise. I remember that you liked to walk too."

"With the right partner." I went with him, stride for stride. We headed to a structure with a dome-shaped roof. Massive stone columns supported it.

"Dorothy," he said, pointing, "this is a temple I set up to honor my late friend Lord Nelson. I once had the foremast from his ship the *Victory* set here."

"A temple? You worship God in the outdoors? Don't Anglicans demand buildings?"

He chuckled. "The other wing of Bushy House, opposite the ballroom, holds my chapel. This structure, these columns are special, a memorial to a just man." William's blue-black eyes seemed far away, but then they drifted to me, wrapping about me like my embroidered shift.

The strains of a banjo or violin touched my ear. Before I knew it, William had laced his fingers with mine. We danced, danced like we had during our secret walks at Kensington.

But I wasn't here to remember that love. I broke from him and let my palm flutter to my hip, to my fine lace and silver threads. "I must tell you something."

His smile disappeared. His breaths, heavy and long, eased. "Mr. King said that you needed to speak to me."

"I had to ask for forgiveness."

"Dorothy, I hated that you left me, but that was hundreds of years ago."

"Leaving was right, but you asked about my life again and again. William, I refused to tell you of my past. I was wrong."

He put his hands behind his back and stepped into the temple. "I grow peach trees here. I farm a little. My children play and run past my windows with fruit in baskets. It is good to see. I don't look back to what was."

Josephy loved to work the soil. My boy must've inherited this from Mamaí and the prince. Into the temple, I moved to William's side. I had to tell him. I had to try. "I showed you a mask of how I wanted to be seen. It wasn't true."

"Women always get worked up over little things. What you said or didn't say is of no consequence now—"

"I never said a word of my enslavement and its evil, how I nearly died or the deaths I witnessed. I hid the truth deeply within me. It only leaked in nightmares."

With his pinkie, he wiped a tear from my cheek. "Was it that bad? Look at you. Successful, still beautiful, still with eyes of fire and sunshine."

"By not saying or sharing my story, I let you think enslavement was tolerable. It's not. It's murderous. I fought every day hoping to be freed."

He touched my shoulders. "Your situation is different. I spent time in the West Indies. I saw slaves singing and dancing in the field. It couldn't all be horrible. You're the exception—"

"Broken glass still sparkles when the light hits it. It might even look like diamonds or chandeliers' jewels. It's still ruined and in need of repair. Time will fix it, if you live free."

I took the copy of his speech from my reticule and pushed it into his hand. "Your words to Parliament. You said the Negroes were happy with enslavement. Chattel doesn't sing of joy. Sorrow is their song."

He fingered the papers. "The slaves I saw were happy and cared for."

"Did they have shoes?"

"What? Some. Maybe."

"Do you leave the Bushy House barefoot, without a shirt, waist-coat, cravat, knits, or jacket?"

He squinted at me. "No."

"You know the harsh conditions of the islands, the bugs. Massas hate spending on shoes for stolen people. Why must you whip and lash their flesh if they are full of joy? If enslavement creates love, why are women raped who say no to sexual congress?"

"You saw horrors, I'm sorry for that. Mr. King says you own slaves too. Are you bad?"

"Yes, I am. I own people. I needed labor. The planters bankrupt anyone who doesn't conform. I'm not proud of this, but I figured if I own them, I'd make sure they were safe, had shoes, and paths to freedom."

"So you have benefited from enslavement?"

"Until you men in power make it illegal, I'll do what I can to keep as many away from the planters who have no heart."

He folded his speech. "This was said in 1799. It's old. The transport of slaves that I supported is now illegal."

"The whole system must be made illegal. You have ten children? Would you give any to enslavement if a planter said they'd make them happy?"

William pivoted and stepped from his temple. "No. Of course not."

I stepped into his path as if we again danced the minuet. "If we had a son, a beautiful boy who looked like you and me, who loved the earth and growing things, whose dark eyes shone with the miracle of the harvest . . . you'd want me to give our babe to one of the happy planters you met on your walks?"

His gaze pierced my heart. I'd given him this truth, just didn't say Josephy's name.

The silence between us grew. It danced me back to the *Andromeda* when William was my distraction, and I was his. My heart wanted to paint a different sunset for us if I'd stayed with him. We would've had more evenings with those gorgeous orange and cherry skies that slipped into the sea.

But I left and built dreams. William stayed and grew older, more a man of his times.

The shake of his head was slow. He bit his lip. "I spoke out against the Abolition of the Slave Trade Act, but it passed in 1807. Transport is no more. What I said no longer matters."

"If I'd told you how I clawed my way out of enslavement, the nightmares I'd seen and survived, then you surely would've understood and tempered your endorsement. Ten years of fewer slave boats. So many would never have known enslavement."

"You flatter yourself, madame, but I was confident in my positions and those of my friends."

My soul whimpered. I lost the hope that I might've countered the planters' lies, but I was always good at seeing what I wanted.

"Dorothy, you rose above whatever happened." He raked his hand through his thinning hair. "You look no worse for wear. I suspect you're of different stock. I've never met a woman like you. Let's not quarrel."

"I survived, William. That only means I was lucky."

He glanced over my head toward Bushy House. "Dinner will start soon. Plenty of champagne. Tell me how to make amends? You helped me at a difficult time."

"Your planter friends keep finding ways to inflict new harms. You have influence, William. Your brother will be king. Others in Parliament can be swayed by you. Tell my truth. Support abolition of any kind."

He offered a quick nod, too quick. I wasn't an equal anymore or even an amusement.

I'd failed. I was another of his damned dames of couleur. Not telling my truth when it might've mattered will haunt me. It was another death mask for my collection.

A gentleman came from Bushy House. "Your Grace, there you are. You are needed to lead us to dinner."

"I must go, Mrs. Thomas. I'm glad we chatted. I'll think on this."

He and his friend left and headed to the ballroom.

Moving to his temple, I sent up prayers. I needed strength to keep my chin up, to collect my girls. Slow walking, off tempo to the tinkles of the pianoforte, I held my breath and went inside. Crissy and Henny danced—perfect rhythm, perfect steps with partners, one in uniform, one in black and white. Dorothea and Elizabeth chatted near the door with the prince's daughter.

My heart beamed looking at my girls, so pretty in the flicker of the candles' light. In the eyes of everyone, I hoped they noticed how their warm skin and mine glittered in the sparkle of the chandelier.

Broken glass can be fused and reshaped. Heat can make jagged edges smoother, stronger, ready for service or whatever the artisan wished.

Tonight, I'll tell these young women my story. They'll hear me, take my words, and work them into their souls. They'll know all my truth, that we weren't just lucky, but beauties and dreamers and survivors, most of all.

DEMERARA 1813: TROUBLE

"Mama," Charlotte said, holding me, "Frances says that Crissy is safe with them."

My heart started beating again. "She was supposed to come straight here."

"The blockades. The Americans and the British are fighting again. The British have frigates patrolling. They want to make sure the war that began in 1812 doesn't spread to the colonies."

"Grama, I love your hats." Little Anna ran back into my big closet. My new house on Robb Street provided infinite places to hide.

I sat on the edge of my four-poster bed draped in ivory linen and fine lace curtains almost as smooth as mossie netting.

I picked up Frances's letter. Her squiggles were always neat. I made out words like *love*. Mama. Crissy. I scrunched it up and pulled it to my chest. "Why do the Americans have to pick a fight now? They already won their freedom in seventy-six."

"Papa Cells says it's a bunch of nothing about restricting trade. My Mr. Fullarton, however, says the Americans are tired of their soldiers being impressed into the Royal Navy. It's almost the same as enslavement. The British soldiers abduct the Americans and force them to labor on frigates."

"Oh? They stop the transport of Africans and now they enslave Americans."

"Mama, you own slaves. Papa Cells owns slaves. How is it different? Is it different? You told me what you lived through, but you own scores of people who aren't free."

"I can't stop enslavement. I can rail against it and protest it, but it doesn't stop these cruel planters from buying slaves. Between me and the Entertainment Society, we women have more than enough money to buy every enslaved person in Demerara to keep them from abuse. Any time I can buy a woman or a girl, I do. I know I've saved her."

"Wish the world would change, Mama."

I patted my mattress for her to sit. I put an arm about her.

Anna ran out with one of my poufs, one Thomas had bought me in the first few weeks of my being free. I took it from her and fingered the white satin.

"I wish it would, too. Miss Rebecca and I buy the enslaved when a plantation goes under. It's all we can do until men change laws."

Anna popped out and modeled another hat; this one was black with a white banding. Her little gown of blue twirled when she spun. I think the hat helped her keep her balance.

I thought of my youngest. "Crissy hated being away. Miss Smith, the headmistress, said she was doing well."

"It's far, Mama. Across the sea is far."

"Well, now she'll be in Grenada. I worried about your sister, Ann, marrying Garraway, but they seem to be doing well. Maybe between her, Mamaí, and Frances, the three of them can speak some sense into Crissy. Then when the blockades are done, she'll come here and stay in that bedroom I made for her. Elizabeth loves hers. The war prevented her from enrolling at Kensington House."

Charlotte nodded her head. "She has tutors like I did. I didn't turn out badly."

"You are the best. And my Elizabeth is brilliant. She's already figuring out ways to improve our inventory accounting."

She straightened another of my hats on Anna. This one was straw with a wide brim decorated with rust-colored flowers made of silk and crowned with orange, white, and blue feathers. My favorite hat.

Beaming, she hugged her niece. "All your daughters and sons and grands are smart."

"If ever you want one, I made a bedroom for you, too. This is my dream home. Wait until I'm finished with the cistern to decorate my yard."

Her finger splayed my curls, which had started to silver. "Papa Cells will be here tonight."

"As will Rebecca Ritchie and the entire Entertainment Society. Your papa Cells won't know what to do with himself."

She offered me a sly eye, but I was unmoved. "He'll do fine, even if I ignore him."

"Mama." My daughter looked at me like I was lying about not caring what that man did. Or who enjoyed his humor.

Well, I was lying.

There would always be a thing between Cells and me, and as much as I only wanted it to be our shared daughters and grands, I knew there was more, just wasn't ready to admit it.

In my formal dining room with white trim and molding and rose-painted walls, my godson William King pushed away from my large oval table and lifted his glass.

He waited for my server to place a fresh platter of yams in the center near a shiny candelabra that Cells gave to me as a gift for my new house.

"Ma'am, Mrs. Thomas, I need to ask you a question."

I started to pick up my glass of bubbling Sourire de Reims Rosé. "Young King, you have the floor."

"I know I was quite upset getting marooned in Demerara because of the blockades, but there are hidden blessings."

"You sound very serious," I said and fingered my glass.

Cells looked particularly guilty in his indigo-blue waistcoat and black tailcoat and ridiculously wide cravat. He knew something.

"Mrs. Thomas, I'd like your permission." He let out a long sigh. "I wish to marry Elizabeth. May I have her hand?"

I fell back against the stiles of my mahogany chair.

Didn't see that coming.

Rebecca, who'd moved closer to Robb Street to sup at my table, giggled and emptied her goblet. "I knew it. Charlotte, did you know?"

My daughter shook her head.

I believed her. Lying wasn't for her, and anything that wasn't Kensington Plantation or our store or her nieces, she didn't much notice. Her husband didn't occupy her time. They weren't happy. Maybe she should use that bedroom I made for her.

The door to the dining room swung open and in came Josephy. He looked tired but he'd had the decency to go up to his room and freshen up. The boy had put on a clean shirt and breeches. "Did I miss it?"

William looked his way with his eyes stretched wide. "I'm asking now."

"Oh." Josephy took a seat next to Cells and began filling his plate with crusty pigeon pie, salted cod, yams and garlic, then dove into the compote of baked mangos. He waved as he started eating. "Continue, sir."

My son's antic made my shy Elizabeth Penner, my beloved grand-niece, my little *damfo*, cover her face. A blush turned her brown cheeks the color of my pink champagne. When she first came to live with me after losing Ella and Sally, I took her on walks along the shore and told her that good things would be in her life. All the losses she'd endured would never stop her. We promised to be special friends, my *damfo*.

If this was to be, I'd be happy.

My son gobbled and drank the champagne Cells poured him. "Come on, King, tell my mother how much you love Elizabeth and would die without her."

My godson coughed. "You just did."

I smothered a laugh. Both Elizabeth and William were reserved. I didn't see this working.

Then he knelt and took her hand. "What he said." He bent his head and kissed my niece's hand like she was pie and yams and champagne.

Her face was cherry red. "Yes."

I'd come to love Elizabeth's presence in my house, loved the way she was a critical thinker.

Thomas King and I had been close all these years. He'd helped my business grow. Now the son of a former slave trader was going to marry the daughter of a former slave.

Cells, who kept barging his way to my table, stood. "To the happy young couple. I've known your father, William, a long time, and Elizabeth, I've grown to know you these past three years. You're bright and sweet, and King is damn lucky."

William rose and brought her hand to his chest. Elizabeth grinned. "We say tarn, Uncle Cells."

Could I smirk at tarn and fume at Elizabeth's endearment of uncle? Cells and I weren't married. I could barely stand him, though I saw him two or three times a week, once with Charlotte, then again with Catharina and Simon. Then he'd show up with one of my vendors or when Lieutenant Governor Codd managed an invitation.

I tapped my knife on my glass. "Before this goes any further, I have a few questions."

Keeping Elizabeth's fingers, William finally looked at me. "Yes, ma'am."

"What does your father think? He's liberal and changed, but England is still England, unless you intend to stay in Demerara. Mixing of races in London—"

"Is not novel. Many planters are sending their daughters for education. Many are marrying there. We won't be the only ones. We're ready to take the challenge. A love like ours can't be denied."

Cells glanced at me. "He's right. Tarn right."

"We"—William looked to Elizabeth—"we'll live mostly in London, but we'll visit here as often as possible. Working on investments for my father between here and Trinidad had me frustrated. Then the simplest conversations with this one intrigued me. I think I loved her when she lent me a stick of charcoal. It was the best borrow."

"Sir, you actually still owe me. My aunt sells them in her store for three shillings."

He took a ring from his pocket. "Perhaps this will settle my debt."

The band of gold looked old and set with a small diamond. Thomas King did approve. That had to come by post. Letters were the only things getting through the British navy.

Rebecca signaled one of my servers. "I think we need another bottle of Sourire de Reims Rosé."

"This was the last, Rebecca. Nasty blockade. We will have to settle for Rosé de Saignée. It's just as good."

Cells looked amused.

Josephy, too.

I finished my glass. I did like my table full. My house on Robb Street should always be like this. Then I grew sad, for it wouldn't. The children and grandchildren would keep growing up and leaving. I'd enjoy them for as long as I could, even if I had to share with Cells.

I sat by Josephy's bed.

He was pained. The yellow fever hit him hard. They called it that here, but I knew this was bulam, black vomit and all.

"Mama." He coughed. "You need to go. Can't get you sick."

"Nonsense, boy." I mopped his brow, trying to keep his spirits up. His poor lungs kept working hard, too hard.

Like the Fédons, Josephy never asked of an enslaved man anything he would not do himself. They were workers to him. He treated them like humans, and he could not avoid the diseases that befell them too. Many were gathered outside this big house he'd built at Kensington Plantation.

His eyes had changed from beautiful and dark, to bluish brown to red and then full yellow.

Now, they remained closed.

"Josephy, no. You need to get up. We need to talk about the fields."

"Mama, Charlotte can do it. She's a good one. Eliza's husband too. Robertson was mighty helpful last year for harvest. Don't fret, Mama."

My eyes leaked badly. I didn't know how to make it stop. Charlotte thought she might be with child. I'd sent her home to protect her. I'd lived a good life. If I went now, they just needed to lay me out with my best hat.

At sixty, I wasn't ready to go.

At twenty-six, neither was my son.

"The doctor's outside. I could get him."

"No, Ma."

"What about something to drink?"

He nodded.

I held a glass to his lips. He took one swallow, then pushed the glass away.

My shaking fingers barely set it on the nightstand.

"Mama, I see Papa's boat coming for me."

"No. No. Don't take him, Thomas. Don't."

"You gave me the best father, you know. You chose right for me."

Did he know?

Josephy was a brilliant young man, a prince among them. "The doctor said something about the bad air. I'll open a window."

He held my hand. "Just sit with me."

"Kensington needs you. You love this place."

His eyes opened, just slits. "I did it, Ma. My dream. I did. This house . . . All the fields. Papa, see. Even Aunt Kitty sees—" He fell back.

"Josephy. Josephy!!!"

The door opened. The doctor I hired from town ran in and waved under my son's nose. Then he put his ear to Josephy's chest. "He's gone, Mrs. Thomas."

"No. He's just asleep. He's going to wake up and get out of this bed. He's just asleep. Asleep like Thomas, Edward, like Edward."

"Mrs. Thomas."

I fell on Josephy, wrinkling his nightshirt, trying to feel a rhythm, any rhythm.

I heard nothing, not even a short small breath.

"Mrs. Thomas, we have to deal with his body. He's still contagious. You need to get out. You can't get sick too."

"Come on, Dolly. The doctor said to leave. You have to listen to someone sometimes."

"Cells?"

I turned my wet face to him.

He was in all black except his cravat.

"You dressed for the grave, Cells?"

"Charlotte sent for me, Dolly. Is Joseph Thomas Jr. gone?"

"Yes," the doctor said. "Take her out of here, Mr. Cells."

Cells's arms grabbed my shoulders. He made me stand and walk out of the house and onto the porch.

With his arms about me, he called to Smithy, my cooper. "Mr. Thomas has died. We must mourn him. Tell everyone."

Smithy took off his hat and covered his jacket over his chest. "Sorry, Mrs. Thomas. I just started savin'. Massa wanted to see me free."

"You keep at things. You will be." My voice was mostly gone. I leaned against the post supporting the deep porch.

"I'm taking you home." Cells tugged me to his carriage. "We are going to drive real slow."

"Cells."

"And you're not going to be Mrs. Dorothy Kirwan Thomas. You're Dolly, the girl who could be weak to her old friend, Coseveldt."

"I don't know who she is anymore. Maybe she's asleep, too."

"She's there beneath all the heavy armor. She's there, and I believe in her."

He held me tight. I breathed him, citrus and rum, but someone needed to do the breathing and the thinking. "He was such a good boy."

"All your sons are good men, Dolly. You raised them to be fine men, regardless of their fathers."

I buried myself in Cells. The well, the bottomless well in my chest, broke like a flood, all my tears cut ghauts and ruts into my soul. What was the use of building a legacy if the ones who deserved the fruit never lived long enough for the harvest?

Polk guided his sloop close to the docks of St. George's, Grenada. "Mrs. Dolly, you need to stay calm."

I surely looked at that bald head like it should roll. How could Crissy do this?

Before I could fuss, soulful Polk smiled big. "Kitty used to skip down to the docks to greet me. She was some kind of special."

How could I stay angry at a big old bear who loved my lost sister almost as much as I did?

I gave him a hug and climbed onto the dock. "I promise not to kill or go to jail. Come back for me in a week."

"Yes, Mrs. Dolly."

Dressed in mourning black, I sweated as I walked up Blaize Street toward my old dwelling house. Frances and Ann met me halfway. I hugged and kissed on them. "We are so sorry about Josephy."

Swatting at tears for them, for my lost sons, I caught my breath. "I wished you'd all seen each other one last time, but tell me of Crissy."

"Mama, Robert Garraway has left her. She's delicate now. You can't fuss—"

I cut my eyes at Ann so hard, I must have sliced her throat. Her husband's brother had done this. He'd ruined my youngest.

Frances pulled her palms together. She needed to pray that there was enough mercy for everyone. "I trusted you all to protect your sister."

"Mama, we tried to stop her. She even signed a contract with him thinking it was marriage paperwork."

"A concubine contract? Didn't she come to you with it? Frances, you use Mr. Bates's firm for all my business here. Did they look at it?"

"Not until we discovered them, and she claimed they were married."

"Are they?"

"No." Ann's head shook so hard, it might fall off. "My brother-in-law used her innocence up. I'm sorry, Mama. If he returns to England before she becomes twenty-one, this *marriage* is null and void."

Crissy was just twenty. That man had a whole year to escape. "She gave away her virtue on a promise to marry?"

"Yes, but sis thought she was married, and she loves Robert Garraway."

I threaded my fingers together to keep from fisting my hands. "Where is Garraway now?"

Frances stepped back and shrugged. "He disappeared."

"Why? Why is he gone now? Knowing I was coming, did that make him hide?"

Ann looked at Frances, and she returned the same blank look.

Then I started running. My sandals pounded the pavement. I had to reach my house to see what else could be wrong.

I knew she was flirty, but chancing her future on a promise? Love doesn't make contracts with "leave you" clauses.

With Ann and Frances panting behind me, I leaped the stairs, then jumped through the door.

Mamaí sat next to Crissy.

My daughter appeared alive and breathing, but her back was to me.

My mother came to me. She threw her arms about me and held me. Her grip was still tight, her hair was short and full white. Her wrinkles and dimples had merged, but she was a blessed sight.

"The peacock flower tea is in the silver pot. Crissy wanted it. Now she won't drink." She kissed my forehead then left the room.

My head spun.

Pregnant.

And Crissy wanted to miscarry.

I rounded the couch and my baby sat with her hand on her stomach, one that barely showed.

Ten minutes flew by as I glared at the tea service I gave Ann, Mr. Foden's prized gift. The filigree on the sides was too pretty to house liquid death, not the way he loved life.

"I'm sorry, Mama."

My voice left. Our Thomas's blood was in her veins, in this child, one of choice, not rape. The tea that controlled the menses of enslaved women wasn't meant for this.

Sitting next to her, I held my breath. I wanted to yell, to rage, but one glance at her apple face said she'd already called herself that and fool and harlot—probably every evil name.

Instead, I laced my arms about her. "I love you, Crissy. Your father and I, we loved each other. You were the baby I gave him to finish his dream of a big family."

"Sorry, Mama." Her voice was a wet whisper. "I thought a baby would bind us together, not make him run."

"You wanted this baby when you thought Garraway wanted you? Don't drink then. This tea is for hate, not for love."

I pushed the cold cup away. "I'll love and support you. But think it through. Don't do this as punishment. Garraway doesn't matter."

"I wanted this baby and his love. Mama, is it wrong to want both?"

"Listen. You're strong. You come from a line of strong women. We will help you, but you need to be thinking right. Thomas's blood is precious."

"What if I have this baby and Robert never comes back? I'll always be tied to him."

"You'll be tied to the memory of love, nothing more. I'll make sure this baby knows the best kind of love."

Crissy sobbed. "You won't hate me?"

The girl feared my condemnation more than anything. I had to stop sulking over the dreams I wanted for Crissy and replace them with new ones. I rubbed her back. "You'll come back with me. I have a room—"

"No, I have to stay. We'll come to you as two or three if Robert returns."

I wanted to wring his neck, but it sounded like Crissy had that frantic type of love. Catharina and Crissy, had they inherited this desperation from me?

"Crissy, I didn't get things right with your pa until our second chance. Maybe when this baby is born, you and Garraway will have that second chance too."

"Mama, I can't do this without you."

Almost smothering her in my embrace, I held and rocked this grown child of mine.

"I built a room for you in Demerara. It has a big window to view the stars. I can put a cradle in there, too.

She started blubbering, and I called to Ann and Francis. "I know you two are at the door. Come in."

The door creaked open and in they trotted.

"Come sit. I have a story to tell you all. I need to tell you about your blood, how strong you all are. You are made from iron and sacrifice."

My girls listened to all the horrible tales, the sick house, Nicholas, everything including the loves of my life, the plantation owner, the solicitor, and a prince. I ended with my greatest loves, my children and me. Somewhere on my journey, I started to love me.

I won't ever stop.

My girls needed to love themselves, too, and to believe they were worthy of their dreams.

DEMERARA 1819: TRIBULATIONS

I whirled around and around in the large dining room of my Cumingsburg's hotel. The heavenly scent of coq au vin filled the air. That was what my French chef, Louis Le Plat, named this dish of old tough roosters stewed tender in claret with yams and onions. His Provençal fish stew of lobster and scallops and mussels had such a silky taste in the mouth. Once Lord Combermere, the new governor of Barbados, tasted it, he would believe he'd died and gone to heaven.

He surely would croak knowing colored girls had made his week in Demerara a success. This would be a win for the Entertainment Society.

Mrs. Ostrehan Brett's assembly rooms held a festive tea. Rebecca's Royal Hotel hosted a subscription ball with the finest crystal I'd ever seen. Tonight, my dinner would be the crowning jewel.

Every table in my ballroom held a starched white cloth and a perfect vase, ones my sister Kitty made. Shiny clay vessels of red and purple painted with happy dancing women made me feel her presence. I lifted my glass and offered her a toast.

I wobbled and fastened my hand to the back of a chair. The fine spindles shone with sweet orange oil. I swayed. I was in a fog like Mount Qua Qua's.

This night was important. I, Dorothy Kirwan Thomas, was implored by Demerara's lieutenant governor John Murray to organize this week. It was sort of funny, Irish Murray picking me. My Irish Montserratian roots felt particularly proud. I lifted my half-empty glass for a *béaláiste*. "Well done, Dolly."

Toasting alone seemed hollow, but I'd been by myself a long time.

Harry came from my cellar with a notepad. The checklist in his palms almost made me weep.

"Mama, we have plenty of champagne. Plenty of Sourire de Reims Rosé."

"Lord Combermere is part of that British world of princes and kings. He'll appreciate my selection."

I'd sent a barrel to Bushy House as a wedding present. Prince William married a princess. He'd gone through a series of wealthy mistresses after he and Miss Bland parted. The papers mocked him badly about how empty his pockets were. It was good he'd found someone to marry, someone nice so he wouldn't have to dance alone.

"Harry, you are a dear. Will your widow friend be coming tonight?"

"Mama, I have no time for friends and to be choosy."

At twenty-seven and a man, this was true.

Plucking my glass, the low ding sounded like a black curassow's call. In my window open to the stars, the bird sang its love songs. "Here's to time."

"Mama, are you well?"

"Go check on your grandma and your sisters. They've all come from Grenada for tonight's festivities."

Polk's son went and got them. My old friend himself was in my kitchen helping Chef Plat, eating what the fiddler called extras— things that Polk judged would go to waste.

My son held my hand. "Tonight is going to go well. Don't be nervous." He kissed my cheek and went out of my ballroom.

Tonight would go well.

I put my glass on the stand the servers would use for empties. I truly had no worries. My Charlotte had everyone in order. Eliza, too, but she'd be with Polk in the kitchen. Catharina wouldn't be coming. She was with child again and wanted nothing more than to sit on her sofa with Simon massaging her feet. They still lived at Werk-en-Rust.

They didn't have much, but their love had been made stronger. It appeared that she was right about them. For this, I was glad.

My simple gray frock and headscarf wouldn't do. The pale green gown with beading at the bodice and hem hung in my room. The matching turban when placed on my silver curls would make me a viscountess or princess. No, an island queen, for this silk crown had the colors of Montserrat, Dominica, and Grenada, their sea-green and coral pinks about the banding.

Walking from the ballroom, I saw Cells crouching at the lion's cage. The young cat had a shaggy mane but Kitty's topaz eyes. The white-chested animal with streaks of tan and brown in his coat growled at Cells.

"Good cat."

Cells stood up, slowly. "You trained the beast well, Dolly. You've done so well. Beyond my expectations."

He walked toward me with his swagger. For an old man in his seventies, he looked good. Fully gray, even in his mustache, he'd aged well.

My lips smacked and I covered a giggle. "If I weren't fretful that either he or I would break a hip, we'd be in the hall rolling in passion on the purple silk tapestry."

He blinked at me and then coughed. "Dolly, you know you said that out loud."

Oops. "Must be the champagne. Forget what I said."

He stopped in front of me. "That's a little hard. Once a thing is said, it's truly hard to ignore."

"No, we can ignore it. That's how we work, how we've learned to live."

The musicians I'd hired started to play—a flute, a fiddle, and drums. The rhythm took my breath as Cells touched me. With his palm at my waist, I was transported to the time he taught me to dance. "This is not the allemande."

The man was still tall, still able to crowd me. His arms had strength. He pulled me to his chest, spinning us. "It's called the waltz. Maybe you and I had to wait until the dance was right."

He kissed me.

I backed him against the wall with my hands along his shoulders.

The smell of the fresh paper treatment hung above the molding filled my nose as much as his bay rum cologne.

Cells held me, my face burrowing into his cravat. His lips again fell on my brow. "If I'd known that a little champagne was all it took to get to you, I'd have ordered barrels years ago. What is this brew?"

"Sourire de Reims Rosé is what I love. But this is Rosé de Saignée. You taste the berries and the grapes. It stays longer on the tongue."

"Let me taste the blend again." He kissed me deeper this time.

My heart pounded and knocked against his ribs.

Maybe Coseveldt wasn't that old and maybe I wasn't either. And maybe I'd been a fool to think that I could be alone forever.

"Tarn it. I'm Crissy."

"What?"

"I haven't told you yet. Fool girl has run off with another man, Major Gordon, to Scotland."

"Sorry, Dolly. I know you've tried."

"Oh, kiss me, Cells, before my head clears. Before I start fretting about that girl or this dinner, or any stupid reason that I put between us."

With his wicked smile, he did. His hands warmed places I thought dead, and I reached for a man who'd always been there at the right time, in spite of our worst selves.

"This isn't what the leaders of Demerara and Barbados need to see, two ready-to-be-naked bodies entwined next to my lion."

"Marry me, Dorothy."

"No."

I put my arms about his neck and kissed him quiet.

"Marry me, Dorothy."

"Will you stop talking if I agree?"

"Yes, after you say yes."

I was drunk and crazy and tired of running. "Maybe."

"Close enough."

His lips pressed against mine made them curl. He tried to lift me, but that groan said his back would give out. That wouldn't do for either of us.

Clasping his jacket, I led him down the hall. "This way."

"I should be good and say you have a very important dinner, but I was only ever good when I was with you."

A scream loud and earth shattering seared my soul.

Cells ran to it, tugging me with him.

Down the hall, I saw my mother screaming. Charlotte looked like she'd pass out.

"What has happened, Mamaí?"

"L-Lizz-y and Co-Coxall." Charlotte's voice shook and cried.

That rhythm. The stuttered breath, the way a person could barely breathe, barely say a word when the worst came.

Cells took the paper from Charlotte. "They drowned. Their ship went down. I'm sorry, Dolly."

My strength disappeared when he confirmed disaster.

I couldn't breathe.

I couldn't lift my head and sank to the floor with Mamaí. Lizzy was both our babies. We sobbed like fools.

Cells had his hands on my back. "I'll send word to Lieutenant Governor Murray. I'll let him know tonight is canceled."

"No." I pulled away and found the strength to stand. "No.

Charlotte wiped her eyes. "Mama, it is for the best."

"No."

They didn't seem to hear me. "Nooooo!" I shouted. "I will wear my hat and force a smile."

My mother nodded and put on her classic smile. "I'll be ready, too."

Charlotte cried and ran down the hall.

"I'm going to dress." I stumbled forward.

Cells followed. "You can't possibly go through with this, Dolly. No one expects you to do this. You're human. Take a moment to grieve."

"Grief doesn't let you choose. It comes for you. This evening has to go on. It's bigger than me, Cells. It's bigger. Colored girls don't get second chances to shine. You have to take the moments when they come."

"Then I'll be with you. But I think—"

"I said what I'm going to do." I left him and went to my room.

"Dolly, we can have supper. You and I, we can grieve. Dolly?"

I closed and locked the door.

Then I fell against it and let my tears flow. I had to get them all out, or I wouldn't get through this dinner with dry eyes. Then I'd have to tell my namesake, Dorothea, and all my grands here or away in school that their parents were never coming back from across the sea.

The heavy knock on my door had to be Cells, but I couldn't move. No one would see me again until dinner. Then I would be dressed and proudly wear Mamaí's smile and my turban.

Rop tú mo baile. Rop tú mo baile.

That was Cells singing my hymn through the door. I sang, too, then stood and washed my face. The world of governors, of princes, even Cells would only see strong Dorothy Thomas, not Dolly who'd again become broken glass.

DEMERARA 1822: CHASING

Cells paced in my parlor. "The British government is going to keep pushing until a rebellion happens here. Shortsighted fools."

"What are you talking about? We're supposed to be thinking of another baby gift for Charlotte."

My darling girl had birthed Mary Fullarton two years earlier and now Sarah King Fullarton rested upstairs in my house on Robb Street.

Nothing was better than seeing those pink bundles laid in a polished cedar crib.

Maybe it took her man coming and going to renew their love. "Cells, we need to think of Charlotte. She has her dream. Two little babies of her own."

He pushed at his high cravat like it made his neck sweat. It was a thick linen. Perhaps it did.

"I'm excited for Charlotte. I love those little girls, but a rebellion could endanger her, the children, all of us."

"What?"

He paced now, back and forth. "They're sending missionaries like Wray, and now this Reverend Smith is spreading talk about freedom of the spirit. That's nothing but abolition."

"Abolition is needed. It should be done."

"The planters here in Demerara, of which you are one, don't want this. There will be insurrection. The damages from the civil unrest will be staggering."

"Abolition must happen. The fear of freedom being stolen must end."

"Dolly, you own more slaves than anyone. You've passed the

numbers I ever kept at the Hermitage years ago. Do you know how much you've paid? How much money you will lose?"

"If I don't own them, someone cruel will. The hunger for black flesh is too great here." I shot him a wink. "You should know."

He went pink in his cheeks. Though we enjoyed each other's company again, the man never knew how to walk away from an argument. "Dolly, you're a slave owner, but you've been listening to the missionary's drivel? Has William King been sending you Wilberforce's pamphlets?"

Yes, he had. He and Elizabeth quietly supported the cause. Those two knew right from wrong. They were a quiet force for good.

"Cells, I do all the things Lord Bathurst, the secretary of war and the colonies, wants. I adhere to his fancy Amelioration Laws— I allow my enslaved to go to church on Sundays. I've always given them off on Saturdays and Wednesday nights. I pay wages and give them plenty of clothing and shelter. No families are separated, they get big provision grounds. And, never, ever, ever have I allowed flogging. Stocks for a thief once, but that was as much as I could tolerate."

"Yes, you run your plantation and businesses with fairness."

I squinted at him. "All that makes me is a good slaver. None of that replaces freedom. Abolition should happen."

He pulled his hands together around his hat, a boxed beaver pelt dyed black. "Dolly, the planters are too strong. They control the council and the militias. People will die. If tensions are allowed to fester, the people you've been good to will die."

"Everyone needs to be brave. I've been called to be strong all my life. Others should be too. You see how Coxall's brothers cheated Lizzy's children, their freeborn children? No one of color is safe if slavery still exists."

"Dolly, I won't be able to protect you. There's talk about you and Miss Ritchie, all the women of the Entertainment Society. People fear the power you have with your money. They are pushing me to make you aware." He shrugged. "They actually think I might have some influence, but only because they don't know you as I do."

Every man in that council had dined at my table. Now they were pulling on Cells's coattails to quiet me. That was an awful position for him to be in when he had divided loyalties.

Mine were clear. I'd push for as much change as I could as long as there was strength in my hand.

I put my fingers against his lapels. Part of me wanted to curl my palms about the dark revers and not let go.

But I had to let go. I'd choose for him.

"I'm no better than the others, the good planter folk, except my story, my life, is written in my skin. The world has to change. I'll send a collection to Pastor Smith." I bit my lip. "Holy Father, forgive me sending tithes to Anglicans."

"That only stokes rebellion. Why don't we go away? We can take all the grands like you did before."

"How do we protect my grands from your daughter Louisa? Her children will say they should have Kensington Plantation?"

"They'd never do that."

"It's money, Cells. If whites can cheat mix-raced heirs out of their inheritance, they'll find a way to do it to mine. Look what the Coxalls did. I'm paying for each of my grand's education. Until the world changes, the white side will squeeze mine."

My dreams weren't done. No sitting on porches waiting to become ghosts. That was the problem now. Loving while you're old meant sooner or later one of us would get sick and put on a death mask. I didn't want that. Couldn't stand to have any more in my head.

"Cells, I'm going away. You'll have to argue with me about this in a few months."

"You're leaving and you didn't say anything?"

"Little Emma, Crissy's daughter, is ready for Kensington House. Then I'll head to Glasgow."

His face reddened. "You're going after Crissy? The daughter who keeps dishonoring you. She frittered away every cent you've ever given her."

"Yes, I'm going to Crissy in Scotland. I have to see if she's being treated well. I may not approve of what she's done, but I can still see about her."

"You just overcame a fever. Dolly, might I remind you that bulam killed two sons and your sister. You're not invincible."

"I have to go. If you still want to argue, you'll have to wait until I return."

He backed away from my sofa. "This Major Gordon is almost husband number three."

"You're adorable when you are mad, but don't go getting that heart racing too fast."

"Then I should come with you. We could marry in Scotland."

"No. This trip is for Emma and Crissy. Harry will come with me. He's all the protector I need."

"I'm just to dither waiting for you? I feel like a kept man without much keeping. You trot me out for special occasions. Here's John C. Cells who's Dorothy Thomas's dinner guest, her dance partner upon occasion."

"I don't invite you to everything. Charlotte does. Coseveldt, you need a woman who'll make you her priority, one with fewer hats. My children are my priority. All I want is a friend who shows up, shares a little supper, and surprises me."

He took off his lenses and wiped them with a handkerchief. "I thought every woman wanted to be cherished."

"They do until they can't stomach the terms of the contract. I've learned to cherish me."

His smirk returned. "Then I want to be cherished. Let me be one of *yours*. I want some of that famous Dolly Thomas attention. Chase me about."

Now I released a laugh. "At least you finally have owned what you want."

"What are you talking about, Dolly?"

"You want me to chase you like I did all those years ago. I won't follow you around, pine for you, or put your needs first."

"Is that wrong when two people love each other? To want to be together, to grow old, well, older together. Maybe I want to leave my hat next to yours, just once in that fancy closet with the tissue paper and shelves."

I drew him close and kissed him, long and with all the passion I could muster.

"And I want to remember us young and wild, not waiting for the other to get sick and die."

My hand trailed his cheek, my fingers tracing his frowning lines, the mustache that was trimmed and silky silver. "I saw your face when I was sick. I don't want that image of us to be the one that's left."

"You remember the good about us? I can't tell sometimes."

"Always, Cells."

"Woman, I know you love me. I know you'd rather spit than say it. I need you to bend just a little."

He wasn't listening, and I was tired of explaining, tired of the sadness in his hazel eyes. "You are free to go—"

"Stop it." He clapped his fingers and folded them to a prayer. Then he closed his eyes. "Travel safely, Dolly Thomas. Godspeed."

With his black hat popped onto his head, he went out the door.

"Coseveldt."

I whispered his name as if it was the last time I'd ever say it.

Saying good-bye to him always hurt, but this was for the best. I had a boat to catch, children and grands to make secure.

DEMERARA 1823: CAPITULATION

I stepped off the sloop onto the dock and a bustling afternoon at the Demerara River. Tired to my bones, I waited for my things to be gathered, the crates and packages and presents I bought in Europe. Traveling across the sea and back had been uneventful. The gentle waters had stirred, changing their colors as I sailed to install my granddaughter, Emma, at Kensington House and to see about her mother, Crissy, in Glasgow.

A dray pulled close.

For a moment, I thought it was Polk or even Cells.

It wasn't.

No, it was better, Rebecca Ritchie. Neat as a pin, wearing a straw bonnet crowned with white lotus flowers on the brim, she waved. "Hello, stranger. Back from traveling the world?"

"For now." I laughed and cocked my favorite confection, my woven hat with orange flowers and all the peacock feathers. It was too fine for boat travel, but I'd changed my outfit when I saw the brown waters of the Demerara.

Well, part of me did think my other old friends might show, Polk with his grin, Cells with his black beaver-skinned top hat. They'd seen me off and welcomed me back to Demerara more times than I could count, but not the last. Cells hadn't returned to my house on Robb Street after our last parting.

Rebecca bounced down and hugged me tightly. "Have your servants fill my dray. I'll take you home."

Signaling to one, I had them load my things and my mammee apples from my stop in Grenada to visit with Mamaí, Frances, Ann, and all her brood. These custardy fruits looked good. The dishes they would make. Frances had our businesses doing well.

The tensions between British colonists and French settlers continued, but the island was peaceful.

The only successful slave rebellion in the Caribbean was Haiti, back in 1804, eight years after the slaughtered end to the Fédons' gambit.

No one wanted war. Everyone yearned for freedom, but not the bloodshed, the hard work, or the fair governing to keep it.

"Look at you. The sea agrees with you."

The blue and orange feathers of my hat wiggled as she twirled me around. My skirt belled. The pleating beneath my bosom of the striped mango silk billowed.

"And you have your apples. You visited Grenada. How is the family?"

A groan churned from my soul and fled my mouth. "Ann's husband, John Gloster Garraway, was left in the lurch when his brother, the scoundrel who ruined Crissy, ran up debts."

Rebecca pointed to hurry the men securing crates and bundles in her dray. "Oh, no. That Robert is nothing but trouble."

"Was trouble. He's nothing but dead. But John Gloster had to sell the Garraway estates."

I felt for them. John Gloster and Ann were doing better now that he focused on working for the courts. "Rebecca, it brings to my mind my legacy, the fortune I've amassed. Nothing I and my children built should be consumed by one of my girl's husbands. I'll speak to King and my London solicitors. There has to be something I can do to prevent theft after my death."

"Don't talk death, but theft is a harsh way to put a husband's privileges. A white's man debt should be his, not siphoned off our hard-earned money. Lord knows we suffered a hell of a lot more to earn it."

John Gloster wasn't white. He needed two more generations of separation from Black blood to count as Creole white. Nonetheless, Thomas's old friend Garraway made sure his boys claimed influence like they were as pure as London's bright snow.

Yet, knowing D.P. Simon's plight with his creditors and British planters, part of me wondered if the causes of John Gloster's problem had as much to do with his mixed-blood as his reckless brother's debts.

Rebecca climbed up into the dray, ready to drive. "Dorothy, come on up and let's get you home. Robb Street is positively boring without you."

Hiking up my skirt, I took my seat and clutched the sides. Rebecca drove fast, too fast.

"How is life on the other side of the sea, Dorothy?"

The dray lunged forward and I slipped against the wood back. "Watch my hat."

"Sorry, dear."

She eased up a little on the reins, but I braced and clutched the brim of my straw confection. "Europe was unchanged, still building with bricks and bustling. London was the same, even with its new king, George IV. Another George."

My friend slowed her beast. The clicking of hooves now paced with my easing pulse. "Did you see your prince again? Have wild fun with champagne?"

"No, Rebecca."

She laughed and so did I. William had married in 1818 to a German princess. London was all abuzz about his happiness. It didn't surprise me. As he'd been with each of his *Dorothys*, in their respective times, he was singularly devoted to this woman. Mr. King said he was happy and now lived within his means.

It was good William kept trying for his happiness. He wasn't a coward about it.

"Dorothy, you tired?" Rebecca slowed the dray, as if a more leisurely motion would restore me. It would take more than an easy gait to jar me from the safe path I was now on.

Looking at the road, the houses with shutters and large-paned windows. "More construction in the growing colony. Always changing."

With a sigh, Rebecca pressed a hand to her chest, rumpling her flower-printed shawl. "You've delayed enough. Tell me the worst about Crissy."

Clicking my tongue so loudly the horse whinnied, I slapped my thigh. "It's awful. I sat at her table and her fool lover, Major Gordon, made polite threats of abandoning my daughter if I didn't give him ten thousand pounds. Then he had the nerve to make loving, silly eyes at their new baby, Huntly."

"Ten thousand pounds, Dorothy? My goodness."

"Yes. And she's worth it, but you don't settle for a man to love you for money, especially not my money."

The dray hit a rut, and I clamped my fingers again to my hat. "Easy."

"Sorry," Rebecca said. "You couldn't convince her to return?"

I shook my head. "She's desperate for him. Crissy doesn't see he's no good. I don't know if she ever will."

The dray stopped in front of my house, my lovely two-story home with bright windows to see the best stars. My daughter and Huntly should be here. "I want my chef back."

"But Mr. Le Plat's sauces are divine." My friend stared at me with her easy smile, the one that spread when she read bad news. "You know Cells has sold everything and moved to Barbados."

"What? Everything. The Hermitage too?"

"Yes. Sold it to his other daughter and her husband six months ago."

Louisa got it, not that Catharina and D.P. could afford such a fine estate. They still lived in my Hotel Werk-en-Rust. I waved to my servants to start unloading and to make my windows looked lived in, but Rebecca's soft brown eyes stayed on me.

She must've seen my lips curling to a frown, and my eyes, the ones Coseveldt first noticed, felt a little glassy. "I suppose he listened to me after all."

"Funny how they do that at the wrong time." Rebecca's voice sounded low and wise, whispering sorrows of her own misadventures with her soldier or her sweet daughter Martha Ann's turbulent loves.

When I climbed down and smoothed the wrinkles from my hips, I leaned back on the sidewall. "Get the Entertainment Society together for a meal on Sunday. I have presents for each of you."

When all my things were out of the dray and into my house, Rebecca took up the reins. "You've been missed, my friend. The ladies and I will inform you of all Demerara's politics. Lieutenant Governor Murray keeps tightening restrictions on the enslaved. He's encouraging planters to take away their going to church."

Why do they always go after worship? "Is Murray afraid they'll learn about freedom by listening to the priests? That they'll demand what they already want?"

"It's the missionaries he's fretting over. He thinks they are plotting rebellions."

With a shake of my head, I threw up my hands. "No priest is Cudjoe. They help people find peace."

Then I thought of Father Mardel, the third in command with the Fédons. My stomach tightened then dropped. Priests could rally revolution against the planters and the governing council.

Rebecca nodded. "I hope you are right. Glad you've come home."

Waving at her, I realized I was back in time to use my influence to stop fools on both sides from violence. Once I became reacquainted with my stores, my hotels, my hucksters and housekeepers, I'd jump into the local politics, hold court in my parlor, and set things right.

Then at month's end, I'd go see about Kensington Plantation and see firsthand how Eliza and Charlotte were running it and if there was any discontentment in our provision grounds. Just because I was liberal that didn't make my land immune.

DEMERARA 1823: CAUGHT

Back three months, now this?

Under attack on my own land.

No. This was not happening.

With my shoulder I pressed on the cellar door of the big house at Kensington Plantation. It had been barred from the outside. "Let me out, Smithy!"

"For your protection, Mrs. Dolly. For your protection. The rebellion isn't meant to hurt you, but we have to be free."

Smithy was my cooper, the best cask and barrel maker in Demerara. He was well on his way to purchasing his freedom. "Smithy!"

The man barged in on Eliza and me having tea in the parlor. He shoved us down into the cellar.

"Smithy, you let us out."

"The king, the British king, Miss Dolly. He's made us free. He sent orders to the lieutenant governor, but that man won't free the slaves."

Murray, that fool. If that was true, then he'd caused this rebellion. "Smithy, I'll find out what has happened. Let me out of here. You know I'll deal with you fairly."

"I know, Mrs. Dolly. I couldn't rest if something happened to you. Your son, Mr. Thomas, is looking down from heaven and would want you safe. Stay here till this is over."

Drums pounded.

Shouting, running. The smell of soot.

"Smithy." I beat my palm against the door. "Is my house on fire?"

"No. Now stay. I have to go."

Seemed my cooper was a leader in the rebellion. "Smithy, you're too kind to be Cudjoe!"

Forehead sweating, Eliza pulled at her pale-yellow sleeves. The muslin stuck to her.

"Mama, I'm scared."

I pulled this girl, this wife, the mother of four, this business-woman, into my arms. "Smithy is a good man. We have to believe that. We're going to be fine. Look around the cellar. Make note of what we have."

"Will this be as bloody as Grenada?"

Her voice was smaller, a mere breathy plea. She was eight during that rebellion. Charlotte. How was she handling this? Fullarton was gone again, and she and her babies were at Robb Street.

Holy Father, keep them safe.

Eliza shivered. She didn't do well with fear, never had.

"Don't fret. Some rebellions are only a few days. Kitty and I lived through many in Montserrat."

The great St. Patrick's Day Massacre in Montserrat was one day of terror. Many coloreds died. How many would die in Demerara because that fool Murray tightened his fists on the enslaved? If King George IV, Prince William's brother, freed the slaves, Murray shouldn't stop it.

"Let's look around, Eliza, for tools like a hatchet."

With a nod, she searched on shelves, while I studied the door hinges.

"Found some rope, Mama. Some barrels and maybe a scythe."

I took the tool from her hands. Rust stained the sharp blade; I saw Kitty protecting my baby Lizzy. Then I pictured Josephy leaning on it, clearing his fields. "Show me the barrels."

She led me to three. A tap on one gave a warped hum. They were full.

"Well, we might have something to drink, but champagne should be bottled properly to keep the bubbles. Once we open it, we'd have to drink it all. Hmmm. Would that be bad?"

"Mama, you make jokes. I don't want to die."

"That's not happening." I took the scythe and rammed the door. "Smithy!"

Eliza clasped my shoulder. "He said they wouldn't hurt us. He'll be back. Maybe we should quiet down."

"No. I don't like waiting for anyone, not for a man and definitely no rebel. "Smithy, you're not Cudjoe! Tell everyone to stop. Tell them Mrs. Dolly will see what can be done."

The chant "Long live King George" soared. Over eighty men and women worked Kensington Plantation. I didn't want Murray to hurt them. The governor's incompetence led to this.

More running and shouting.

Banging on the big oak door, I beat my palm against it until my skin scraped and bled.

Eliza took my hand and wrapped it in a handkerchief. "Gilbert will come for us. He'll stop this."

I loved my Eliza. She was always sweet and easy, but when would she notice that we weren't on the side of right?

The cellar was musty, but all this standing was too much for me. I sat and patted the ground for my scared rabbit. "Your Mr. Robertson isn't stupid. He'll see the fighting and the soldiers and turn back into town. He's not going to risk being gunned down."

"What about my boys? They might—"

I tugged her face, her baby-fat cheeks, into my bosom. "Let's not guess at trouble. The boys are in the city, that's the safest place to be."

"What if everyone forgets we are down here?"

"No one is going to forget."

"They won't forget about you, but me they will. Gilbert will have some new wife within a year."

"Eliza. Get a hold of your tongue. Don't be speaking death."

"He wanted a girl."

Her grief lingered over a decade. Lacing her fingers with mine, I hummed and breathed. "Your worth is not what you can or can't give. And you still have those round hips, girl. You see that Charlotte and Fullarton after all these years have two babies."

Eliza snorted. "You say Crissy is like you. Maybe old Charlotte is too."

"What? What are you talking about?"

"Seems mighty curious that she now has two babies when Fullarton travels so often."

My mouth dropped open. "What do you know, Eliza?"

"Nothing for sure, but your friend Thomas King has two other sons besides William, fine sons. They visit Demerara, too. Kinda curious that Charlotte named this last girl Sarah King Fullarton."

My head cleared, rang like a bell, and I tried to remember seeing any of the King boys with Charlotte. "Eliza, if I ever get trapped in a cellar during a rebellion, there's no other person I'd want to spend it with than you."

"Gilbert said the Hermitage will be sold by the courts soon."

Didn't know how to react except with shock and sadness. Cells had such pride in the plantation he built. "But he just sold it to his daughter."

"Something about too much speculation. It will be gone."

My heart hurt. All the things Cells had made were gone. All the lies amounted to nothing. Yet, if he'd been Mrs. Ben's grandson, he'd be enslaved. His long life would have been cut down by the sugar boilers of Montserrat or the slaughter of a rebellion.

I needed to tell him I understood, to write him that there was something worse than ghosts and death masks.

Regret.

Horses galloped outside. The belches of guns rocked the world.

Eliza sobbed.

This wasn't how things would end. My family still needed me. My legacy wasn't finished. "You're Eliza Thomas Robertson. You were conceived in love. That's who you are. When they say your name, you wear it with pride."

She curled into me and I held her. When she was born, I didn't have it in me to nurture her, but now I did. I prayed the violence would go away.

"Mama. It's quiet outside."

I sat up from my crouched position in the cellar of Kensington House. "I don't hear anything."

Hand in hand, Eliza and I stood together. "Get that scythe."

Eliza dragged it to me along with an old hammer. "I found this behind the barrel. Use it instead."

Not going to question why she just found it, I took it and struck the lock. I kept pounding until the metal cracked apart. "Bring the scythe as a weapon."

We climbed out. I swung my hammer. "Stay behind me, Eliza. This is our land! No one is going to take it! No one is going to intimidate us! You hear me! Mrs. Thomas, owner of Kensington Plantation, is here."

My shouts boomed. As we turned the corner . . . The fields, the sugarcane fields my son had cleared, were burned to the ground.

I ran to the hill. At the top, I could see the sea. It was blue and clear, but all of Josephy's coffee plantings were black as soot. Hundreds of pounds of damages.

Yet that wasn't the worst.

On the road, close to the house that Josephy built, I saw a stake in the ground.

A stake in the ground with a head on it.

A stake in the ground with the head of my cooper.

Smithy wasn't Cudjoe.

He just wanted to be free.

Eliza's screams filled the air, my lungs. This killing, like Nicholas's hanging of Cudjoe in Cells's tree—I knew it wasn't a sign to frighten the enslaved.

It was meant for me.

DEMERARA 1823: CONTENTION

Served sorrel punch and a nice bottle of Rosé de Saignée, Lieutenant Governor Murray feasted at my house on Robb Street. His advisers, Mr. Van Den Velden and Mr. Brown, came, too. The henchmen smelled of politics—old cigars and rum in black jackets.

Murray wore a uniform, a showy thing of garnet with gold braiding. It was nothing compared to the prince's, not as many medals, no sashes. As he drank my champagne, this fellow's flat chin lifted, offering a subtle sneer that showed command, not competence.

On my side of the table, I had the finest representatives of the Entertainment Society—Rebecca, my granddaughter Dorothea Coxall, and Elizabeth Ross. Each one well dressing in red, green, and blue, each proudly wearing a bonnet with trim and lace and flowers displaying our positions as freewomen, as businesswomen, as power.

Murray sat back in his chair, licking his fingers from the ginger biscuits. "Mrs. Thomas, no one does hospitality quite like you. You never disappoint. Still, I didn't see the tiger."

"It's a lion, and he only resides at my hotel. The ballroom at my hotel is for more formal gatherings. This is my residence. I wanted an honest conversation."

He huffed and adjusted his spectacles. "I suspected that was the case."

Mr. Van Den Velden leaned over his potbelly and refilled his glass. "Quite a house you have here. You've become very wealthy women. All of you ladies are very wealthy. Surprising."

Rebecca had that glimmer in her eyes. She'd been itching for a fight since her fellow broke things off with her. "It shouldn't surprise. We're enterprising women."

Murray wiped his thumbs on my starched white napkin. "Well,

I don't wish to take up more of your time. Let me begin with an apology. My soldiers were very heavy-handed. If I'd known they'd reached the Kensington, I would have stopped them."

Dorothea sipped her glass of punch. "I'm sure they knew. Everyone knows Dorothy Thomas's property."

The lieutenant governor had that nervous laugh, the pained mirth of being caught in a lie.

I smiled instead of poking. A man has to have room for his ego and to hang himself. "It was quite disturbing. Have you found who started the rumors that you disobeyed the king and refused to free the slaves?"

His eyes exploded, bulging behind his glass lenses. "That's a dangerous thing to say."

Fine. I poked a little. "Those are the rumors."

"Ma'am, a revolt of ten thousand slaves has to be dealt with."

"Ten thousand? Are you sure it was so high? There's barely that many slaves on the estates I know to be vandalized."

"Thirty-seven plantations were struck by those vicious slaves," Mr. Brown said. He had a curved nose like an iguana, like he'd been snooping on the roof and had fallen into a chair for my nuncheon fair.

Murray waved at Brown as if to settle him down. "We don't know how many would have joined the cause if the militia hadn't acted decisively."

"I own the most slaves in Demerara or very close to it. The numbers you are quoting are high. Mr. Brown, I don't think vicious is the right term, either. Angry or cheated is a better way to say it."

Murray shook his head. "The rebellion is done. It's put down. The numbers don't matter."

"Numbers are important, especially when you're exacting taxes. You've levied heavier taxes on huckstering and additional property taxes."

Mr. Van Den Velden set down his glass with a thud. "Those fees are needed. We have to rebuild. The slaves did damage." He leaned farther over the table. "Perhaps if you held a firmer hand on your chattel, rebellions wouldn't happen."

I leaned, too, and caught his small gaze. "If governing bodies were more fair, there would be less reason for rebellion. The governor's overseer, Lord Bathurst, sent you measures for amelioration. Your delay acting on his orders caused the rebellion. These brutal killings could sow the next one."

He sputtered, and I wasn't sure if that was because I knew about the amelioration plan or because I called Bathurst Murray's overseer.

Again Murray wiped his mouth. "The slaves burned government buildings, men were killed. Someone needs to pay for this."

Rebecca rolled the stem of her glass between her fingers. "You're making only the free colored women of Demerara pay," she said. "That's not fair."

"You ladies have it good," the governor said and slurped my champagne. "You have means and respect. We're just asking you to do a little more to help the colony."

"Everyone should be asked to do more, but you're targeting only us. That isn't fair. My property was damaged. Thousands of pounds of damage. Will you compensate me, Rebecca, or Dorothea for our losses because of the chaos of the militia?"

After mangling my linen napkin, Murray tossed it to the table, then stood. "Ladies, thank you for the hospitality. It is very much appreciated, but the council has voted. The taxes are in place."

"A new vote can repeal this tax." Dorothea's voice sounded even and patient.

I was never prouder of my granddaughter.

Murray pointed to the door, his companions hopping up like hounds. "Do you think your lifestyles escape notice? You've all grown rich from the kindness of the citizens of Demerara. Be grateful. Be patriotic. Pay your taxes. Good evening."

He and his smug associates exited my house.

I waited until I heard my outer doors close, then counted to ten.

Rebecca counted as well.

"Ladies," I said, "don't break anything. This is my house."

"The arrogance, Grandma," Dorothea hissed. "They clamor to buy our goods, eat our food, stay at our lodgings. It's no charity."

Leaning back in her chair, Rebecca looked up to the ceiling. "This is their opportunity to hurt us twice."

"They could hurt us more," my granddaughter said. "They could have the militia kill at will. That flamboyant minister John Smith is rotting in jail because he taught the enslaved the Bible. Smith is a white man. Papa used to tell my brothers to be careful, to not provoke the soldiers. He feared the consequences."

I rubbed my palms together. The smell of coconut calmed my spirit. "They can never win, and we won't sit around until they do."

"Let's at least give them a fight." Rebecca lifted her glass, but I set mine down.

Like my friend, I wanted to strike the council, but that was hard to do. They had the numbers and the guns. "What do you propose?"

"This is a job for the Entertainment Society. We'll get both Ostrehans—Ostrehans and Ostrehan Brett—Miss Ross, Miss Blackman, Miss Delphi, and we will come up with a solution."

"Let me get the good champagne." I motioned to a servant. "Bring up a few bottles of the best. I fear we'll need them."

"I fear you will, Dorothy." My friend gripped my hand. "You have the most connections to London. Prepare yourself. Part of any plan will involve you going to Lord Bathurst and convincing him to overturn these taxes."

"No, Rebecca."

"The route to fix this was through overseers. You know this, Dorothy. You must feel it."

Part of me did, but I also hoped for another path.

"Grandma, perhaps Prince William can help. He's your friend."

With Dorothea's hopeful eyes and Rebecca's begging ones, I shrugged and tacked on Mamaí's smooth smile. The last time I saw William, I spoke my mind and damned him for his wrong-headedness.

How could I turn to him now?

No, it would be Bathurst who'd fix things.

Yet how would I get him to listen when men felt not only entitled to the bodies of colored women, their dames de couleur, but our means too?

LONDON 1824: KENSINGTON HOUSE

A carriage arrives outside. It's stately and dead black, no shine or flashy crest. It was ever fitting for my *damfo* and her simple tastes. She came from nothing, but her steady nature has gained her everything.

I wait to hear the heavy soles of her slippers slapping the floorboards.

The parlor door opens.

Elizabeth Penner King, my dear friend, my niece, the woman I've been waiting for, has finally arrived.

I hug her. In her honest brown face, I grasp the painful truth. She's been unable to gain the meeting. "You don't know how glad I am to see you, Elizabeth. It's been three weeks."

"Making you wait is a sin, Aunty. I couldn't come unless I had tried everything. I have been to the War Office in Whitehall many times and have been turned away. I sought old friends of my father-in-law. No luck. Yesterday, I had my husband try. You'd think the secretary would want to know about the uprisings in Demerara."

"William King has been rebuffed too?"

Elizabeth nods, and I lock my arm with hers. "*Damfo*, we can't conduct business at the door."

I lead her to my tray of tea.

"Did you bring the candied ginger?"

My laughter returns and wells in my throat until it explodes. "I did. I left two jars with your husband. Guess they did not make it home."

Pacing, I sober. "I wish our visit was social, but I am in trouble. All the colored women are."

"Aunt, this is my fault. My husband and I have been active in the abolition movement. He's been cut off from access. With the exception of my in-laws and old family friends close to you, many King acquaintances blame me and our marriage as having corrupted William. People are resistant to change."

"People are people. They're resistant to losing."

"I'm sure if you can get an audience, Lord Bathurst will understand. I've seen him speak. He understands fairness." Elizabeth sinks into the chair, her plain shawl and ivory gown deflating like a closed fan. "I'm sorry I failed you."

The door flings open before I can offer comfort.

My Mary runs in with Miss Smith chasing. "Sorry, Mrs. Thomas. Mary! No running."

My granddaughter has a box that's wrapped in brown paper. She shuffles it between her palms and runs around the table then behind the chairs. "I want to do it. I want to give it to GaMa."

I give her the cross look. "Mary, stop running."

The little girl freezes. The box in her hand flies.

Elizabeth picks it up and Mary. She swings the child's wiggly body from side to side.

"Aunt, the package has your name on the note."

The note has squiggles, but those marks are familiar.

Miss Smith takes Mary and backs away. "Sorry for disturbing you, ma'am. The package just came. I had it taken out of its crate."

Before I settle, the flustered woman and Mary are out of the room.

Only my grandniece, this box, and me remain.

The note I rip away and give to Elizabeth. "Tell me what your *uncle* Cells says. I'll need you to send him a note of thanks."

"He's still in Barbados. Aunt, I had heard he'd quit Demerara for good."

My heart races. It's been months, almost a year since we last talked. "Does he mention anything? Is he in good health?"

"It says none of that, but to wear this for your meeting."

Even Cells thought me capable of gaining a meeting with Lord Bathurst, the secretary of war and the colonies.

"And he says, 'Good luck, my dear Dolly. Love always, Co-seveldt.'"

He sends me his heart though I dismissed his. "He used to bring back the nicest things from Europe."

I take my time, using this gift to delay the moment I have to accept my failure. I put the box into my lap and work my thumb under the ribbons until I get the lid free. When I dive in fighting tissue, I find a beautiful turban. It's white silk and cream satin, each worked together to form stripes. About the banding is an egret feather and pearls. It's the boldest and prettiest hat I've ever seen. It says, *Take notice of me.*

My sigh is long and hot on my fingers. "He has good taste."

Tears well, but I fight them. Lifting the hat out of the box, I place it on my head.

"It looks amazing, Aunt, like something for a queen."

"A queen, you say?"

Springing out of the chair, I twirl like Mary and dance to hymns of salvation in my head. "That old man has done it. He's given me a path, the strategy to get this meeting."

"What, Aunt?" Elizabeth stands and clasps my elbows. "Tell me so I can be joyous too."

"*Damfo*, I need to dress like a queen and go down to Whitehall and see if the secretary of the colonies wants to deal with royalty from the territories."

My niece's mouth hangs open. Her arms drop to her side. "You're going to barge in and get past all the men milling about? The clerks, the military officials?"

"That's what my granddaughter just did, and she accomplished her purpose. That's what I will do in this hat that says look at me. You and my godson can pay my fines at your magistrate if they intend to put an old woman into custody for speaking truth."

"Well, if you are going to do this, you should arrive in a Berlin carriage. The biggest that can be found with at least four or six horses charging straight to Bathurst's doorstep. That will gather everyone's attention."

"Do that, Elizabeth. I didn't come here to fail. It's time for me to stop waiting and go to war. To the War Department."

"If anyone can do this and not be arrested, it will be you, Aunty."

Picking up the hat box, she kisses my cheek and clutches my arm. "Let's get you ready for your meeting."

We head to my room. I've brought a number of gowns, and I have enough coins to procure talent from the school and local mantua-makers to make something special, something to match this regal hat.

With my *damfo*'s hand in mine, we get to it.

It's time to rebel with everything in my soul.

No giving up.

No yielding.

We colored girls, we island girls, have a fight to win.

Elizabeth heads into our carriage, a magnificent jet barouche pulled by six in hand—six equally sized gray horses. The carriage is open. Everyone can see us.

"This is bigger than a Berlin, Aunt. It will make the grand statement we want."

Two drivers on top wear scarlet coats. A lone footman in the rear matches the first two.

"We've done it, Aunt. We're a spectacle."

Elizabeth is blushing. Her tawny skin will soon be cashew cherry red as people along our path stop and stare.

I wore the cream hat Cells sent. It wasn't something you'd find in the warehouses of London's Cheapside. It was custom made from a milliner at Cheapside Street in Bridgetown, Barbados.

Elizabeth tugs her scarf about her as if that will hide her. She seizes a breath, then lifts her head. "I'm lucky to be with you on this adventure."

I clasp her arm to my bosom. The gold doubloons woven into my bodice jingle like medals.

"You look beautiful, Aunt. Bathurst won't be able to dismiss an island queen."

My Thomas used to call me that. I take him with me on this journey. I always will. I take Cells and Prince William, too. They each shaped and reshaped my heart with fire.

My children and Mamaí are with me. Kitty's here at my side, grinning at the ponies. Sally and my sister Ella, my *damfo*'s mother, too. Everyone who has added to my journey is in my soul.

I grip my grandniece's hand. "I don't know what I will say when I get the meeting."

Elizabeth looks at me. The gold pieces are reflecting in her eyes. I hope she notices I look confident from a life well lived, well loved.

Dark and lovely and not done trying, that's who I am.

The horses lead at a merry pace winding through the streets, then everything slows.

"The words will come," Elizabeth says and hugs me. We jingle like church bells.

"This is Whitehall, Aunt. That big building that looks like a castle is the War Department."

A footman jumps down and marches to the side. He flings open the door and leans inside. White glove, bright red sleeve, I clasp it with my smooth cotton glove and descend. I feel Elizabeth adjusting the train of my dress, yards and yards of silk with deep box pleats at the neckline. This farce might work.

Head high, I move forward. "Footman, I need you to open the door and announce Mrs. Dorothy Kirwan Thomas is here for Lord Bathurst. Make sure you say all the *s*'s. They are important."

Taking a few coins from my purse, I press them into his palm.

The man nods with vigor. I follow behind three steps as if he's a part of my regal court.

We enter a building made of limestone. The arches remind me of the temples, all the churches I'd visited, even the ones taken by the British. My chin rises a little more.

Up front, a clerk sits at a desk.

This could be Mr. Bates's office.

The footman clasps the lapel of his thick mantle. "Mrs. Dorothy Kirwan Thomas to see Lord Bathurst."

The fellow at the desk rises with eyes wide. "Let me go get his lordship."

Time ticks away.

People stare.

My footman returns to the carriage that spans the whole street.

A tall thin man with gray hair comes. His nose is long and sweeping. His tailcoat is ebony. Medals jangle from his pocket over his heart.

"Ma'am." He dips his head in a quick snap bow. "I'm Bathurst. It's my pleasure to welcome you to England. On behalf of the king, it is my honor to make your acquaintance."

"God save King George IV. I've come on pressing matters. I hope you have time to see me?"

"Of course, ma'am."

He leads me to his office. "It's not often foreign dignitaries show up at my office." To a clerk, he says, "Clear my schedule until this meeting is done."

The door to his office—a room the size of my parlor on Robb Street—closes. The curtains are open. My carriage, in all its glory, is still there.

"So Mrs. Kirwan."

"Mrs. Dorothy Kirwan Thomas."

"Yes. Have a seat, ma'am."

There's a simple rose-colored couch and two straight-legged chairs on either side of the low table. I ease onto the couch with my train draping beneath me.

Lord Bathurst goes to the opposite side and sits. "Where are you from? And what messages have you."

"I'm from the colony of Demerara."

"Demerara? That's not a foreign tribe from Africa."

"No, Demerara is not. It's a colony the British won from the Dutch and the French. I'm a survivor of the Rebellion of 1823. The government officials that report to you did not follow your instructions. They have made the plight of the enslaved untenable."

"Are you here for abolition? That's not something I can do. That requires Parliament and discussions."

"And reparations for the holders so they will willingly comply. Yes, yes. I know. That's not why I am here."

He pulls his wrists together and taps his fingertips. "Then tell me why?"

I dip in my reticule, slipping past my manumission documents, and pull out the papers with the arguments the Entertainment

Society prepared for me. Pushing them to Bathurst, I breathe a little easier because he can read them and then act.

The man sets the pages on top of his cluttered table that has books and rolled-up maps and checklists. "I can read these later. I want to hear from you. You obviously went to great effort and expense to be here."

He's right.

The life I've lived has led me to this point, but I'm tired. Words fail.

I sit in Lord Bathurst's office with my heart beating like a warrior's drum. It's thudding hard in my chest.

"Ma'am. Make it plain. I'm listening."

"I'm here to stop future rebellions. I think you created your Amelioration Laws to do that."

"I did. Rebellions are costly in lives and damage and resources. The navy is overburdened now. Amelioration can bring contentment to the slaves."

My gut burns at the notion of being satisfied as chattel, but I had to focus. Prince William's Parliament could end slavery, but Lord Bathurst can end this wrongful taxation.

Someone knocks on the door.

"Come in," Bathurst said.

A fellow brings a service of tea.

"Refreshment, Mrs. Kirwan Thomas?" Lord Bathurst points to the plain silver pot. Steam is rising.

My throat has dried from my tongue being too careful. "Please."

The clerk puts the heavy tray on top of my papers then stokes the fireplace.

Lord Bathurst tries to wiggle the pages free. Tea spills. Ink smears. My squiggles are blurry indigo waves.

"Sir, those are notices of the taxes. Women under attack. We've written all the reasons this is unfair."

He takes the wet papers and gives them to the clerk. "Johnson, see if these can be saved."

I stare at the man taking away the ruined pages, then to the street with my carriage with my *damfo*. My heart feels full and powerful. I remember I am here for her.

"Mrs. Kirwan Thomas, you know a great deal about this. Tell me the problem. You started eloquently. You can finish."

My pulse swooshes in my veins. The tea has scented the air with lemon, but the ash of the fireplace coals takes me to the moment I saw Josephy's burnt fields. My anger, my hurt, all the losses erupt from that bottomless well in my chest.

"I've come to talk about how to stop the killings, the next rebellion. One will come if nothing changes. It will be bloodier and more costly than the last."

He propped his hand under his chin and supported it with the other arm. "The unrest robs resources needed to govern the colonies. The rebellions in Grenada and Haiti cost so many lives. I'm listening, Mrs. Thomas."

"Lieutenant Governor Murray purposely withheld your orders. He did so to appease the planters who fear that the enslaved learning about the Bible would yearn for freedom. What the governor doesn't understand is that everyone yearns for freedom, everyone. When the enslaved believed King George had freed them and Murray was keeping them enslaved, they threw off their yokes, praising the king."

"Then it's a misunderstanding, ma'am."

"No. It's criminal. Everything being done builds a climate of mistrust. Can you blame anyone when your officials do not follow your orders?"

He sat back in his chair. "Murray may be the wrong man to lead Demerara."

"It's him and the council. They've placed taxes upon the free women of color to be punitive. They don't believe colored women should be free, or that we should have money and live in peace. The governor wants tyranny. That is why they behead or hang any enslaved person. They do that to choke off the hope of a people craving freedom, craving autonomy of their bodies."

"Murray's threatening free colored women, too? Are you leading insurrection, ma'am?"

"My being here is insurrection 'cause I'm not doing what those men want. Murray is using taxation to hurt us. The colonial council want us women alone to pay for damages to government buildings. As good colonists, we will do our share, but all citizens have need of those buildings. Shouldn't all people of means pay?"

He steepled his fingers and nodded. "That does sounds unfair, but how will this cause the next rebellion?"

"I was in Grenada. Many Catholic planters joined the Fédons because they felt the governor had treated them unfairly with taxes and confiscations. The council in Demerara will continue to abuse us by imposing harsh laws. Once men get away with something, they continue causing more trouble."

"That's a problem, Mrs. Thomas. Unrest and strife do enflame the populaces."

"If that means people will rise up, then yes. Many have been freed under the laws of England. If this council keeps making unjust laws, what will stop them from changing the manumission contracts? Nothing. Nothing will keep them from changing the terms of freedom. People will go to war over it."

He poured himself a cup of tea. "They'll never do that. You're overreacting."

"What's to stop this council of men? Decency? One of the enslaved was murdered by the militia for praising King George. He had no weapon. They cut his head off and put it on a stake in my yard. Does that sound like a reasonable action?"

The lord's eyes went wide, then he folded his arms. "What is it that you are asking me to do?"

"Abolish this tax on freewomen. Send notification to Demerara, Barbados, Dominica, Grenada, Montserrat, all the islands of the West Indies that the targeting of women will not be tolerated. Tell them that the tax code and the laws can't be used to erode the freedoms we've gained. Send that message. Make it loud."

"I'll take what you've said under consideration, Mrs. Thomas."

"Do more. Your inaction condones those old men weaponizing

laws to intimidate good citizens. Loyal citizens of the Crown. If you do not act, they will continue to inflict more pain. You will have another Grenada. Or Haiti. I hear those rebels won."

Bathurst swallowed and nodded. "You make good points."

A double knock pounds the door.

"Yes, come in," Bathurst says.

Johnson enters. "Here, sir. It's almost dry and mostly legible."

"Thank you."

As the clerk leaves, the overseer secretary takes the papers. By the window, he holds them up one by one.

He takes his time, and I stare out the window, wondering where my niece and I might journey next in our six-pair carriage. Around Kensington Palace? Gunther's for an ice? Shopping? Or back to her husband to plan my financial escape from Demerara?

I'm comforted.

I've done my best.

I can't think of anything more to say to sway Bathurst.

The man puts my papers on his desk then sits beside me on the sofa. "I see. I understand."

"Does that mean you will help?"

"That means I'll do more. I agree this tax must be abolished. I'll have orders written today. Do you want a copy sent or do you wish to wait for it?"

"If you don't mind, I'll sit here and enjoy this tea while I wait for your words. I'll take them back to Demerara. I'll let everyone know freewomen will be treated fairly under British laws."

"Yes, ma'am, Mrs. Dorothy Kirwan Thomas."

Savoring my warm cup, I enjoy the rhythm of all those *s*'s. His lordship called me by my proper name.

EPILOGUE

Holding Mary's hand, I stand on the rail of the sloop watching Demerara grow bigger and the water change from blue to green to brownish white.

The heat sticks to me. My short copper-colored sleeves are plastered to my arms.

As the weather has warmed, we've changed from our heavy clothes to simple muslin gowns. I love the dry heat on this side of the sea.

Though I have a copy of the decree, Lord Bathurst used his admiralty to send word directly to Lieutenant Governor Murray to abolish the tax. I hear the foul man was removed from office in April.

That's good, for I don't want to see him. I don't want to gloat. There's no need to test the fragility of an old man's ego.

Missing home presses my soul. For the first time in a long time I don't feel like everything will be taken away.

Lucy Van Den Velden struts up to my side. "Mrs. Thomas, thank you for helping me return to Demerara."

"You need to see your father. You need to get things settled right."

"Thank you, ma'am. Thank you."

I nod and turn back to Mary. She's staring at the water like Crissy always did. My youngest daughter says she and the major are in love, but they still haven't married. That won't end well.

"GaMa, I hear music."

My eyes shut. My pulse explodes. The transport of slaves on those frigates is supposed to be no more. I don't want to see men and women on decks forced to sing.

"GaMa, it's pretty." Mary's tugging my skirt hard. "GaMa."

With a mouthful of salty air, I let myself see. I look to the left.

No slave ships.

Then I let myself hear.

The rhythm is slow and sweet, cresting over the waves reaching me. It's singers on the dock. My Irish hymn has more rhythm. It has drums and bits of Twi in the refrain.

I take Mary, and we twirl and dance until the boat anchors.

When we climb onto the dock, my son Harry is there with his wife. He did marry that widow.

"Welcome home, Mama. Well done." He kisses my cheek, then picks up Mary and tosses her onto his shoulder and then gives her to the awaiting arms of her happy mother, my dear Charlotte.

"Why are they playing music, girl? What's the occasion?"

"It's for you, Mama." Charlotte hugs my neck. "You're the hero today."

I look out at the jubilant crowd. It's all my family and friends, cheering.

Rebecca Ritchie and her daughter are right up front.

My Eliza, Ann, Frances, and Mamaí and the scores of grands and great-grands are all here.

Mary Ostrehan comes up to me. "On behalf of the Entertainment Society, we would like to give you this silver plate to commemorate your leadership. You made change happen for us."

For the first time in a long time, I don't know what to say. I stand there ready to cry, ready to laugh and sing.

The plate shines. It's stars for my eyes. I hold it up and hope the sun catches it and gives dreams to everyone.

Polk is with the musicians. Good old Polk. That must mean he's back from Barbados with Cells.

Scanning the crowd again, I don't see Coseveldt.

Harry nudges me. "Come on, Mama. Say something."

My shoulders shrug. "I'm happy to help. Thank you all. Thank you for your friendship and love."

Walking and stopping for hugs and kisses, I hold this plate to my chest. It will go somewhere special. This silver is strong and unbreakable. That has to say something about this sisterhood of women.

I move a little deeper into the crowd, and I see Catharina. She's here, and she's clapping for me.

Hugging and kissing her, I wrinkle the black crepe of her dress. Another glance at the crowd, and I see no black hat.

My heart seizes.

I didn't get to tell him good-bye. I didn't tell Cells thank you. Or anything that matters.

Catharina clutches my arm. "Mama, what's wrong?"

"Are Simon and the children . . . Are they all well?" My voice is breaking.

"Yes. They're at Werk-en-Rust with Father. He's back from Barbados."

Coseveldt is alive. There's another chance?

Pulling her into a big embrace, I kiss her forehead. "Then why the black drape?"

"It's the finest thing I own, Mama. I wanted to look good for you."

I kiss her brow again. "You are beautiful, and you are loved."

When I release her, I offer my crying child a handkerchief from my reticule. The embroidered linen is right there next to my papers. I'll never leave the house without them, but I hope one day I might not dread being without them.

"Catharina, tell your father that I want him to come to supper and to bring his hat. Tell him I have a place to put it after all. I'm not afraid anymore."

The poor girl squints at me. She must think I'm crazed, but I'm happy. I have more time. "Tell him. He'll understand."

"Papa didn't come because he wanted you to have this moment. He needed it to be about you, and you alone. He said you'd know what that means."

I did, and it's wonderful.

"Supper tonight. Let him know."

My people surround me. We hum and sing of peace all the way home.

AUTHOR'S NOTE

Dorothy Kirwan Thomas

Dorothy "Dolly" Kirwan Thomas was born in Montserrat in 1756 and died in Demerara in 1846. Dorothy was a survivor of slave rebellions and experienced the wars that shaped the Atlantic world. She was a complex, conflicted woman who overcame every obstacle, even her vulnerabilities, to change history. Her story needed to be told. A single chapter centered on this woman's extraordinary ninety years is not sufficient to dispel the myths and misogyny that surround women of color, Black women, who endured colonialism and slavery. I am honored to be able to tell the world about her extraordinary life.

From legal transactions, newspaper articles, published anecdotal accounts, and legal records drafted at her direction, I have reconstructed her life. Mrs. Thomas was articulate, astute, and business-minded. She was a woman of passion who struggled with functional illiteracy, heart-wrenching losses, and betrayals. She was an original code-switcher who used simpler words with servants and family (like her favorite, *tarn*) and saved her polished parlor conversations for admirals, businessmen, and the gentry who sought her company. She was a passionate woman dealing with the issues of her time: racism, enslavement, incest, sexuality, marriage, entrepreneurialism, land ownership, taxation, and women's rights.

My author's note includes an extensive bibliography.

Women of Color: Who Tells the Story Matters

The first time I read *Pride and Prejudice* by Jane Austen, a contemporary author of the early 1800s, I fell in love with the time period. When reading her last work, *Sanditon*, I learned of Miss Lambe, a wealthy mulatto West Indian woman. This character of color is the wealthiest person in the book. Upper-crust suitors (white suitors) are scheming to marry her, which is counter to the prevailing narrative that Blacks (Blackamoors) were not desirable, had no access to money, had no ability to socialize in the upper classes, and had little agency as they were either slaves or lowly servants.

As a person of color, a Black woman, a Georgian and Regency history student, and a girl of Trinidad and Tobago heritage, I felt found discovering Miss Lambe, but now new questions arose. Was this character a creature derived from a progressive author's creativity or was this character based on persons of color that Austen learned about or saw or interacted with in her community?

If the answer was the former, it cemented my lifelong love of Austen. If the answer was the latter, then my ancestors had been victims of the whitewashing of history.

Whitewashing or the sanitization of the past occurs because the victors (those allowed to tell the story) more often than not cast history through the white gaze, a.k.a. the lens of white men. These narratives often describe rape of the enslaved by slave masters in terms of consent, even in cases of incest. You'll never imagine how many scientific papers and history books I've tossed against a wall as the author chose to call these violent unions *relationships*.

I'm not a fan of book burning, but nothing makes me long for the scent of kerosene and carbon more than reading paragraphs of how the wanton enslaved woman enticed her massa to satisfy dark cravings of her oversexualized body, a body that is often painted as not experiencing pain like others.

My quest to find *Miss Lambe* took me on a ten-year journey. Finding Dorothy Kirwan Thomas, the women of the Entertainment Society, and so many other Black women who had agency and access to all levels of power has restored my soul.

Now I possess two truths. One: Jane Austen was a progressive author. Two: The narratives of the eighteenth and nineteenth centuries whitewashed the roles of my people—the adventurers, leaders, and rule breakers—which were occupied by women of color.

Fictitious Characters vs. Real-Life People Depicted in Island Queen

Dorothy Kirwan Thomas left no diary. To discover her life, I had to rely on her legal documents, particularly the birth registries/birth order of her children and secondary accounts of people interacting with Dorothy.

The characters of Polk, Mr. and Mrs. Ben, Mr. Lionel, Overseer Teller, Mr. Johnson, Miss Smith, Mr. Runyan, and Mrs. Randolph are inspired characters or a mix of different true persons that I've found in my research of the times, traditions, and the inner workings of eighteenth- and nineteenth-century life.

Catherine "Kitty" Hunter (Lady Clarke) is an actual person who, as the wife of the governor of Jamaica, would be in both Prince William's circle of influence and within reach of Dorothy's business network. Her personality seemed a good mesh with Dorothy's and helped to fill in the gaps of the narrative.

Though some names have been changed to prevent confusion, all other thirty-nine-plus characters in *Island Queen* are true persons who lived during the time of Dorothy Kirwan Thomas's extraordinary life.

Dorothy Kirwan Thomas and Literacy

Secondary accounts describe Dorothy as illiterate. This could be wrong. The intricacy of her transactions and the anecdotal retelling of her having a scribe in her entourage contradicts her having this problem. I suspect Dorothy was functionally illiterate, or more literate than she would attest. Her drive to have her children and others of color educated also leads me to believe that she valued knowledge and learning. To explain this in *Island Queen*, I hinted at there being a problem reading, which would not be uncommon.

Dorothy Kirwan Thomas and William IV

My research tells me there were many Miss Lambes, each achieving unheralded accomplishments for their race and the plight of women. Upon finding a 1788 Gillray cartoon depicting Prince William's affair with a mulatto beauty, I discovered a newfound appreciation for the height of access these women achieved in Georgian/Regency society. The cartoon is remarkable in the fact that this woman of color is drawn to be beautiful and loving, not subservient or garish as Gillray had done to other women with dark skin.

Then I stumbled upon the story of Prince William dancing with a mulatto woman, Dolly Kirwan, at a mulatto ball in Roseau (the capital of Dominica), where the prince's frigates, the *Pegasus* and the *Andromeda*, would come to dock as he awaited orders. Firsthand accounts from people like Dr. Jonathan Troup of Prince William introducing him to his "handsome mulatto girl" recounted the prince's dedication to this woman. This interest and affection for his mulatto mistress was so great that he risked censure from his commanders to take her on board his ship and have her accompany him to England.

Rumors of Dorothy and William meeting again in 1810 spurred my belief of a longer, deeper association. William kept friendships with Black women he admired in the West Indies like Cubah Cornwallis of Jamaica. Henrietta, Dorothy's granddaughter, was friends with Lady Augusta FitzClarence, one of Prince William's daughters by Dorothea Jordan.

The depths of their relationship we will never know, as Dorothy kept no diary, and all of William's personal correspondence was destroyed upon his death.

Gillray cartoon of Prince William and his mulatto lover; first print of cartoon later redrawn and printed in 1788 *Rambler Magazine*

Prince William Henry, King William IV

Prince William Henry, the Sailor King, is a difficult person to assess. I wanted him to be Prince Harry in the historical record. At times, he was and seems very progressive with his friendships and socializations with peoples of color. At other times, particularly as he grew older and more attuned to the pressures of society and his position, he became a typical privileged white man of the eighteenth and nineteenth centuries.

Prince William as the commander of the *Pegasus* and *Andromeda* in the West Indies was young, full of life, and enjoyed the women of the islands as much as his duty. He often went against convention, riled up his superiors, and befriended women such as Cubah Cornwallis, the famed healer from Jamaica. When he and his fellow officers got so drunk that they vandalized a brothel in Jamaica, William felt so remorseful that he repaid the owner, a Black woman proprietor.

With his devotion to command, he impressed Lord Nelson, the revered admiral of the Royal Navy. Between patrols and occasional skirmishes, William was riotous. He went from pleasure to pleasure, woman to woman . . . until the island of Dominica. There, he met a beautiful mulatto woman who became his constant companion. In this relationship, we see more of the monogamous man that William became through the rest of his life. His association with his Irish mistress, Dorothea Jordan, lasted over twenty years (1791–1811). He was domestic with her, had ten illegitimate children with this union, and was reported as happy and faithful. When that affair finally ended and he married Princess Adelaide of Saxe-Meiningen (1818), William remained loyal to her until his death in 1837.

The less progressive side of William was exposed as he grew older. In 1799, ten years from his break with Dorothy Kirwan Thomas, Prince William, as the Royal Duke of Clarence, addressed Parliament to cast his voice against abolition outlined in the Slave Trade Limitation Bill. This legislation would have limited the transport of Africans being enslaved in British colonies. He gave a full-throated argument against the bill, which led to the bill's defeat.

In 1833, William, now as King William IV, signed the decree to abolish slavery throughout England's colonies. I'd like to think that he returned to his senses, but this was more his response to the mood of the nation. England wanted abolition.

Creole Determination of White

Because of the mixing of Black and white in the West Indies, definitions to define who was white, or colored, or Black became a topic of discussion and in a few of the colonies defined by law. In general, a person had to be three generations removed from Black blood to be counted as white. This was not uniformly employed. Definitions changed based on circumstances and relations and money.

John Coseveldt Cells was an interesting Creole man. Unlike other men I researched, his notations were always attached with the following descriptors—*he was very liberal, he was articulate* and *well-*

mannered, he spoke many languages well, he was well-liked. Well, well, well. While all these phrases sounded like compliments and were probably meant to be compliments, no other white man or white-acting man is described in such terms. It sounded to me like dog whistles, things one says when describing a man of color and are surprised by his upward mobility or success. Joseph Thomas, who possessed all the same attributes, is never described as such. Cells's characterizations in *Island Queen* are purely this author's assumptions based on my feelings. Thus, Cells became a tool to highlight this dichotomy of whiteness to Creole society and also to mirror who was expected to succeed based on skin color.

The Power of White Associations

The want of a white lover *to take you far* was true in the colonial West Indies. Whites, for the most part, had the economic power and autonomy over women of color as much as the Anglican religion held power over those of Catholic and Jewish faiths. These economics meant the ability to pay for manumission was often in the control of white hands.

Both sides, Black and white, understood this. When the governing council of Montserrat tried to raise the manumission fee, the price that had to be paid to free an enslaved person, the white planters of the island rose in protest, saying the fee needed to remain low to reward the *female slaves* for their *love and loyalty and service*. In the West Indies, more than any other territory, more women were freed than anywhere else. These men used the hope of manumissions to coerce a compliant mistress. Women who longed for freedom or even protection from abusive overseers and other plantation males complied. Please note the power dynamics and the inability to refuse make it impossible for slave-master relationships to be consensual.

In *Island Queen*, I wanted to dispel the assumption that Dorothy Kirwan Thomas pushed her daughters into relationships with white men to gain power or entered into such relationships to garner wealth. This is not true. Dorothy utilized white and Black allies to earn income, to protect it, and to grow it. Nonetheless, the network she built and maintained was because of her dedication, fortitude, and strength.

Like all mothers of the eighteenth and nineteenth centuries, she wanted her daughters to marry well. Mrs. Bennet's dilemma in *Pride and Prejudice* was a universal truth to all women of these times. Dorothy wanted her sons-in-law to have the means to protect her girls and to help grow the family mercantile network.

Charlotte's first husband, Jean-Joseph Fédon, Ann's John Gloster Garraway, and Catharina's D.P. Simons are not white Anglican/Catholic men. Frances never married, and Dorothy did not push her to do so. Eliza and Lizzy married white men whom they loved and stayed with until their deaths. Charlotte's second husband, John Fullarton, left her and went to Europe then remarried. Crissy's first choice was Robert Garraway, a mixed-race man. Her second was a wealthy Black Trinidadian plantation owner (Dorothy tried to play matchmaker). Her third choice was Major Gordon. However, all of these romances ended poorly. When Crissy lost a trial in court to prove the legitimacy of her marriage to Gordon, custody of her son, Huntly, was taken from her and given to Gordon. She returned to Demerara, where she married a merchant. Dorothy's sons-in-law took her money or depended on her means more than her daughters ever benefited.

Dorothy never seemed to be without a man. In the South, we'd say she was keeping time with a friend. With ten children, and several baby daddies, I was sure she enjoyed male company. Without a diary, I traced Dorothy's relationships through whose children she bore. She was very dedicated to getting their birth registries completed in the church parishes where she lived. Therefore, I can only document those relationships. But judging by her children's choices, I suspect she chose men by who had power and not by their race.

The Notions of Black Beauty and Power

A holdover of regressive, revisionist thought of the late Victorian era was that light skin was preferred and that African women were thought of as undesirable. During the eighteenth and early nineteenth century, there was more fluidity in the definition of beauty, with skin pigment and hair more centers of adoration.

Some people think that the terms *mulatto* and *mixed race* would refer to light-complexioned persons who then gain affinity because they are white adjacent. Dorothy was a beautiful woman who had dark skin. No personal portraits have been discovered, so I had to use secondhand accounts. How dark her skin was is lost, but her appeal was undeniable. She was a magnet to many men, even when she had no means. Her face and personality drew them first.

Dorothy, I believe, was undeniably beautiful by all standards. Her wit and charm sealed the deal and gained her access to the world of privilege. Dorothy learned their rules—their languages, their dances, their modes of dress, their ways of conducting business— and engaged on all levels. She earned her money and freed herself by her own gambits and built a legacy by utilizing the network she skillfully erected.

Later in life, she hosted a dinner for the governor of Barbados on behalf of the lieutenant governor of Demerara. She would not be given this honor and responsibility if she weren't a power broker.

Dorothy Kirwan Thomas as an Entrepreneur

Dorothy began selling goods in Montserrat and engaged in huckstering and housekeeping services in Dominica, Grenada, and Demerara. She and her daughters owned property and a store in Grenada. In Demerara, she constructed several hotels. Noted in

Island Queen were the one in Werk-en-Rust and her largest hotel in Cumingsburg.

Dorothy Kirwan Thomas as a Slave Owner

One of the hardest parts of Dorothy's story to wrap my arms around was her decision to own slaves. She hated enslavement. She worked tirelessly to get all her family freed. When news of an enslaved relative's whereabouts came to her attention, she immediately sought to get this person free, even engaging in lengthy, relentless negotiations to do so.

Therefore, I'm confident in her attitude about the topic in general and also confident in her fear of failure. Watching white planters punish those of different faiths and colored planters who did not conform to their systems and way of life was at the forefront of her mind. She saw from the beginning with the rebellions in Montserrat how leaders were targeted. She watched governments tighten rules on the Catholics in Montserrat and in Grenada. Grenada's council also terrorized free Blacks and coloreds who they felt weren't in league with them.

Fear of failing or being vulnerable had to be her top concern. I believe that this fear and her desire to protect her *fhortún* (fortune) and perhaps rescue persons from being purchased by harsher slavers led Dorothy to rationalize and accept the horrid position of becoming a slave owner.

Oral histories of Dorothy's enslaved persons show her to be a fair and liberal owner. As it took Dorothy sixteen years to earn the money for manumission, I can see how she could have put her enslaved on the same path to earn their freedom since she allowed them the same liberties she had in Montserrat: leisure time off, Sunday and Wednesday church service access, and the ability to hire out and huckster to earn their own money. The records are scant that show her freeing any enslaved person until emancipation (1833) when she freed them all. Before emancipation, Dorothy owned the most slaves in Demerara.

The Thomases' Legacy

The silver plate given by the Entertainment Society in October 1824 has vanished. The accounts of Dorothy Kirwan Thomas's life are left to snippets of paper: wills, newspaper clippings, business transactions, birth records, etc. With her death in 1846, she outlived many of her children, but the seeds of her boldness for life lived on through the generations. Charlotte continued to run Kensington Plantation. Though Dorothy Christina's gambit fails, she was the first Black woman to sue for legal recognition of her marriage in Scotland. Henrietta became a London stage sensation known as Madame Sala. Grandson Huntly Gordon advanced in the army to the rank of surgeon general. He continued in the sphere of interacting with nobility as he remained close to his half brother, the Baron of Drumearn. Harry Robertson (Eliza's son) studied in London to become a physician. Joseph Garraway (Ann's son) trained in law in Britain but then returned to Grenada where he was appointed a judge to the Court of Appeals.

Themes in Island Queen

Remarking on Dorothy's incredible life, I needed to assert and kill the superhuman myth. Dorothy was special, but she was not superhuman. Surviving incest and rape as well as witnessing the dehumanizing aspects of slavery and racism took a toll on my Dorothy's spirit. The lack of control over one's person, the inability to say no to sexual aggression, I believe deeply affected her. To become the person she dreamed to be, a well-respected woman of means, she had to control what she viewed and internalized.

To protect herself, Dorothy saw or invented good when there

may not have been any. She closed her mind and blocked out things meant to make her crumble. The birthing sadness was my tangible way to make all the things she'd survived resonate. I balanced it with the very real danger of dying in childbirth.

In the West Indies, the birth rate of the enslaved compared to other cultures as well as enslavement in the United States was lower. Was this a factor of the climate, the prevalence of yellow or bulam fever and other tropical diseases? Was the harsh nature of enslavement and debilitating effects on the mother's physical and mental health the culprit? What about the mother's unwillingness to bear a child of rape in captivity or the availability of herbs like the peacock flower, which can affect fertility? Could this have been the cause?

I don't have the answers, but these topics were addressed in my attempt to defeat the superwoman myth. Dorothy Kirwan Thomas was strong, beautiful, and determined, but not superhuman. She would look upon her life as lucky, *tarn* lucky.

ACKNOWLEDGMENTS

Thank you to my Heavenly Father; everything I possess or accomplish is by your Grace.

I met a lovely lady at the 2019 Historical Novel Society, Rachel Kahan, and I told her about my passion project, the amazing life of Dorothy Kirwan Thomas. She looked at me and said she wanted Dorothy's narrative. I'm not sure I heard much else that day, for my head was in a cloud. Thank you, Rachel, for believing in the power of story. Thank you for your nudges and polish and feedback. I am so proud to share *Island Queen* with you.

To my fabulous agent, Sarah Younger, I am grateful that you are my partner. You are my ride-or-die friend and sister.

To Gerald, Marc, and Chris—Love you bros.

To all of my family and my Alpha Kappa Alpha line sisters, NIA Fall 90, and my Destin Divas—Love you all so much.

To my assistants and teammates: Ellen, Emma, Alexis, and Lasheera—Thank you.

To Denny. Thank you for the contrary narratives, the gentle shoves, and every challenge. You've made *Island Queen* stronger.

To Chris Rathbone, one of Dorothy Kirwan Thomas's descendants, for your openness and encouragement. Dr. Albion Mends, for your beautiful Twi translations. Adjoa Andoh, for your care and dedication to *Island Queen*.

To those who inspire my pen: Beverly, Brenda, Farrah, Sarah, Julia, Kristan, Alyssa, Maya, Lenora, Sophia, Joanna, Grace, Laurie Alice, Julie, Cathy, Katharine, Carrie, Christina, Georgette,

Jane, Linda, Margie, Liz, Alexis R. and Alexis G., Rhonda, Vanessa, Kenyatta, and Jude—thank you.

To those who inspire my soul: Bishop Dale and Dr. Nina, Rev. Courtney, Piper, Eileen, Angela, and Pat—thank you.

And to my rocks: Frank and Ellen.

Love you all, so much.

Hey, Mama. We did this one, too.

Love you, always.

BIBLIOGRAPHY

Ashby, Timothy. "Fédon's Rebellion: Part Two (Continued)." *Journal of the Society for Army Historical Research* 63, no. 256 (1985): 220–35. Accessed August 25, 2020. http://www.jstor.org/stable/44229682.

Berry, Daina Ramey, and Leslie Maria Harris. *Sexuality and Slavery: Reclaiming Intimate Histories in the Americas.* Athens: University of Georgia Press, 2018.

Bradfield, Nancy. *Costume in Detail: 1730–1930.* New York: Costume & Fashion, 1999.

Browne, Randy M. *Surviving Slavery in the British Caribbean.* Philadelphia: University of Pennsylvania Press, 2020.

Brunias, Agostino. "Free Coloured Women of Dominica," 1780. Roseau, Dominica.

Brunias, Agostino. "Free Women of Color with Their Children and Servants in a Landscape." 1764. Dominica.

Brussell, David E. *Potions, Poisons, and Panaceas: An Ethnobotanical Study of Montserrat.* Carbondale: Southern Illinois University Press, 1997.

Buckridge, Steeve O. *The Language of Dress: Resistance and Accommodation in Jamaica, 1760–1890.* Mona, Kingston: University of the West Indies Press, 2004.

Candlin, K. *Last Caribbean Frontier 1795–1815.* New York: Palgrave Macmillan, 2014.

Candlin, Kit, and Cassandra Pybus. *Enterprising Women: Gender, Race, and Power in the Revolutionary Atlantic.* Athens: University of Georgia Press, 2018.

Casid, Jill H. *Sowing Empire: Landscape and Colonization.* Minneapolis: University of Minnesota Press, 2005.

Costa, Emilia Viotti da. *Crowns of Glory, Tears of Blood: The Demerara Slave Rebellion of 1823.* New York: Oxford University Press, 1997.

Duke of Clarence, William. "Substance of the Speech of His Royal

Highness the Duke of Clarence, in the House of Lords." *Speech to Parliament.* Address presented at the Speech to Parliament, July 5, 1799.

Equiano, Olaudah, and Werner Sollors. *The Interesting Narrative of the Life of Olaudah Equiano, or Gustavus Vassa, the African.* New York: Norton, 2001.

Essequibo and Demerary Royal Gazette. This is to Inform the Public, that the following Persons intend quitting this Colony: Dorothy Thomas, in 14 days or with the Ship Nereid, May 1, 1810.

Essequibo and Demerary Royal Gazette. A Memorial of Gratitude: Dorothy Thomas presented with a Silver Cup and Waiter valued at Fifty Guineas as a Lasting Testament of their (a few Coloured Ladies of Georgetown) Gratitude, October 9, 1824.

Essequibo and Demerary Royal Gazette. This is to Inform the Public, that the following persons intend Quitting the Colony: Dorothy Thomas, and Daughter, and two Servants, January 13, 1816.

Essequibo and Demerary Royal Gazette. Port of Demerary, Barque Indemnity, Sailed: Passengers Arrived Per Indemnity, Mrs. Thomas and servant; Messers. Fullarton and Robertson, Misses Fullarton and Garraway, December 31, 1831.

Essequibo and Demerary Royal Gazette. The Estate of Dorothy Thomas, born Kirwan, decd. who died in the city of Georgetown, co. of Demerary 5th August 1846, August 22, 1846.

Fuentes, Marisa J. *Dispossessed Lives: Enslaved Women, Violence, and the Archive.* Philadelphia: University of Pennsylvania Press, 2018.

Gardiner, Robert. *The Sailing Frigate: A History in Ship Models: Illustrated from the Collections of the National Maritime Museum.* Barnsley, South Yorkshire: Seaforth, 2016.

Gillray, James. "The Royal Captain," April 1788.

Hall, Herman G. *Belvidere Estate Fedon's House.* Brooklyn, NY: Herman Hall Communications, Inc., 2016.

Hay, John. *A Narrative of the Insurrection in the Island of Grenada . . . in 1795: With an Introduction by a Military Man, Resident for Nearly Thirty Years in the West Indies.* London, 1823.

Honychurch, Lennox. *The Dominica Story: A History of the Island*. Oxford: Macmillan Education, 1995.

Knight, Roger. *William IV: A King at Sea: 1830–1837*. London: Allen Lane, 2015.

Martin, Robert Montgomery. *History of the West Indies: Comprising British Guiana, Barbadoes, St. Vincents, St. Lucia, Dominica, Montserrat, Antigua, St. Christopher's &c. &c*. London: Whittaker and Co., 1837.

McDonald, Roderick A., and Richard B. Sheridan. *West Indies Accounts: Essays on the History of the British Caribbean and the Atlantic Economy in Honour of Richard Sheridan*. Kingston, Jamaica: University Press of the West Indies, 1996.

Murray, John. *Proclamation of Martial Law in Demerara: The Slave Revolt of 1823*, n.d.

Napier, Elma. *Black and White Sands: A Bohemian Life in the Colonial Caribbean*. London: Papillote Press, 2009.

Newman, Brooke N. *A Dark Inheritance: Blood, Race, and Sex in Colonial Jamaica*. New Haven: Yale University Press, 2018.

North, Susan. *18th-Century Fashion in Detail*. London: Thames and Hudson, 2018.

O'Garro, Dorine S. *Montserrat on My Mind: Tales of Montserrat*. Bloomington, IN: AuthorHouse, 2004.

Pocock, Tom. *Sailor King: A Biography of William IV*. London: Sinclair-Stevenson, 1991.

Prince, Mary. *The History of Mary Prince, a West Indian Slave: Related by Herself*. Chapel Hill: University of North Carolina at Chapel Hill Library, 2017.

Schiebinger, Londa. *Plants and Empire: Colonial Bioprospecting in the Atlantic World*. Cambridge, MA: Harvard University Press, 2007.

Troup, Jonathan. Journal of Dr. Jonathan Troup, 1788–1790.

Washington, George. *George Washington's Barbados Diary, 1751–52*. Charlottesville: University of Virginia Press, 2018.

ABOUT THE AUTHOR

VANESSA RILEY writes historical fiction and historical romance (Georgian, Regency, and Victorian) featuring hidden histories, dazzling multiculture communities, and strong sisterhoods.

This southern, Irish, Trini-descended girl holds a doctorate in mechanical engineering and an MS in industrial engineering and engineering management from Stanford University. She also earned a BS and an MS in mechanical engineering from Penn State University. Yet her love of history and lattes have overwhelmed her passion for math, leading to the publication of twenty-plus titles. She enjoys writing on her southern porch with proper caffeine.

Riley's novels have been reviewed by *Entertainment Weekly*, NPR, *Library Journal*, *Publishers Weekly*, the *Washington Post*, and the *New York Times*.

Stop by her website, VanessaRiley.com, and join her mailing list.